The Blue Nile Adventure

The
Blue Nile
Adventure

Linda Oxley Milligan

Library of Congress Control Number: 2017905074
Beak Star Books, Powell, OH

ISBN: 1-944724-00-1

Beak Star Books
Powell, Ohio 43065
www.beakstarbooks.com
Cover Design by Andy Bennett
www.B3NN3TT.com

Acknowledgements

Many thanks for my husband John Milligan's patience and expertise. His remarkable set of interests in travel, history, math, astronomy, computer science, and Egypt helped make this book possible. He was always there to read my drafts, check my use of astronomy and make further suggestions. A measure of his genuine support is in the many times he cleaned up the dinner dishes when I couldn't pull myself away from my writing. This novel was most definitely a joint adventure, as was our trip to Egypt, land of many mysteries.

Thanks too to Robert Bauval, Adrian Gilbert, Christopher Dunn, Robert Schoch, John Anthony West, authors and researchers who have further opened the doors of speculation into the mysterious civilization we know as Ancient Egypt.

To Marilyn and Margaret

The Course of the Nile

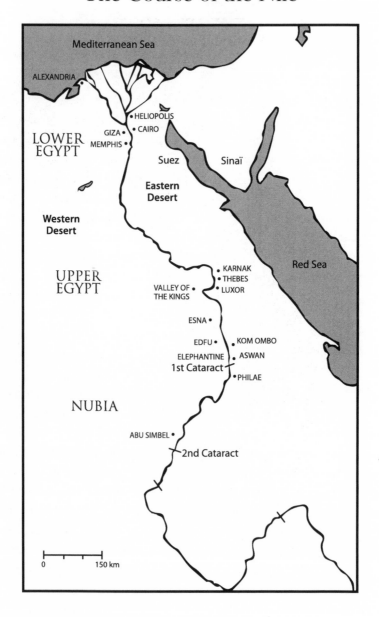

Prologue
EGYPT 1997

O ld man sun lifts his furrowed brow. Eyes blazing, he chases away the night goddess Nuit and her starry train. Haloed tips of three majestic pyramids materialize out of that darkness as silent reminders of human dreams. The sun climbs higher, casting a broad wave across the desert, revealing sand and stone that moments earlier had lain hidden. Then from behind the Great Pyramid's western face, an old German appears, dressed in the tan desert camouflage of the Egyptologist. He circles snakelike around its perimeter before arriving at its entrance. Hans Bueller has come to steal a statue hidden for thousands of years in the bowels of this mysterious wonder. The statue he seeks is worth far more than its gold or even the price it could bring on the black market.

He wastes no time unlocking the entrance, then slips inside, shutting himself in with a quick tug of the door. He takes a torch light from his pocket, shines it about as if to get his bearings, then makes his way through a narrow passage into the heart of the edifice and on to a second door behind which he descends into the dark underbelly of the colossal pyramidal mountain. Focusing his light, he methodically searches an area of wall, running his hand over now illuminated stones. When he finds nothing, he shifts the light to the adjoining section of wall, searches, and then moves to another and then another, before advancing further into the room. Eventually he reaches a crevice in the rear of the chamber into which his slim figure disappears. Twenty minutes later he reappears, his confidence waning for he knows it is well into morning now and outside the guards and visitors are beginning to arrive. He takes control of his emotions and begins to search again.

Midway between the stairway and the rear of the chamber on the opposite side of the room from where his search began, he discovers an alcove recessed into a sidewall. Excited, he sidles inside the narrow vault, his thin, white hand moving across its wall until it stops on a stone located near the floor. His finger traces an invisible line around it. Using a pick he pries it loose, yanks it out and shines his torch into the uncovered shaft. He pulls a retractable tool from his pocket, extends it and slips it deep into the opening. The sound of iron rubbing against rock echoes in the chamber as he extracts a small metal door buried within. Light pours forth. He reaches in, grabs a shining object and places it in a cloth sack that he tucks away in his jacket.

An unexpected noise grates into the room's silence. Alarmed, he looks in the direction of the crevice in the rear wall of the chamber as the sound becomes heavy and loud and causes the whole room to reverberate like a giant bell. He wonders what he could have missed when he so carefully inspected the crevice opening. He quickly pushes the metal cover back into the hole, places the heavy stone over the opening of the shaft, turns off his lamp and stands at the entrance of the alcove peering towards the rear of the chamber.

A lantern emerges through the narrow crevice. Bueller can make out a silhouette he assumes to be a guard who must have heard noise coming from the room when he removed the stone and iron door. The old man considers what would happen to him if he were caught and what could happen to the object he has just removed from its ancient hiding place. He would die in prison, and if the object fell into the wrong hands, Egypt's fate would be sealed, perhaps all of our fates. Doomed, we would be doomed, he thinks as he plans his escape. He knows he cannot leave the chamber as he had entered it without being apprehended, so just as the dimly lit intruder draws near the stairway that Bueller had earlier descended, the old man slips quietly into the crevice at the rear of the room and through a now opened iron door that had earlier been concealed with facing stone. Ingenious, he thinks, as he carefully pulls the door shut behind him.

Chapter One

Of the thousands of ancient burial crypts in Egypt, Imhotep's tomb is the most guarded. No curses fall upon those who would break its seal nor booby traps await those who would enter its corridors; rather, an unseen presence guards this tomb. I don't know what this mysterious presence is, but I do know it has intelligence because it enlisted my aid without my knowledge or consent.

When Dr. Hans Bueller pieced together the whereabouts of the artifact that had been concealed for millennia in an underground chamber at the root of the Great Pyramid, his fresh knowledge triggered actions neither he nor I could have anticipated. It's hard even now to wrap my mind around it, but it's as if once the location of that statue was discovered, its theft was a fait accompli that caused an unseen guardian to intervene.

It was mid-December, a week before the whole family would gather at my mother-in-law's house for our annual Christmas dinner. A blustery wind had picked up speed that early evening in the small town in Western Ohio where John and I had made the seventy-five mile trek from Columbus to dine with his mother, Madeleine, at the town's new Chinese restaurant.

"If you're going to drive back tonight, you'd better go now," Madeleine said after panes of glass in the storefront window began to rattle.

"This was really good Chinese," I said.

"They say the owner had been the head chef at the best Chinese restaurant in Columbus before opening this place. The food certainly tastes like it," Madeleine said as she ate the last bit of crispy shrimp with walnuts.

"You ate it all!" John said, noting that his mother, a light eater, usually leaves food on her plate.

"How could I resist? They say he had been wanting his own restaurant for years and thought it might be a good idea to open

3

someplace where there are not so many Chinese restaurants."

"He couldn't have picked a better place then," John said.

A woman in a black silk Chinese dress with gray piping and little silver stars embroidered in the fabric came to the table carrying the check on a small tray along with three fortune cookies. Her slicked back hair and red pouty lips gave her the expression of a disgruntled teenage girl, although she looked to be about forty. She removed Madeleine's plate—ours having been taken away some time ago—poured fresh tea into our cups and departed.

"That's the owner's wife," Madeleine whispered.

"She's very pretty," I said.

John glanced over at the woman and opened the wrapper around his fortune cookie. "She looks unhappy."

"This town may be a little lonely for her," Madeleine said. "She may be feeling like the proverbial duck out of water."

"Look at this." John passed his fortune over to me to read.

"You long to see the Great Pyramids of Egypt," I read out loud. "This is unbelievable!" I looked at Madeleine. "That's all he talks about," recounting how John had poured himself into Egyptology for the last year to escape the tedium of his computer database job.

"He has told me about some of those books he reads," she said.

"Books, if he only read books. Did you know that for more than a month he spent his entire evenings and weekends writing a computer program to test some astrological theories in those books?"

Surprised, Madeleine turned to her son, her eyes demanding an explanation.

"Astronomical not astrological," he sighed. "Although they're related."

"He needed a time machine so..."

"I wanted to see where the stars were located relative to the Great Pyramid at different historical times because that information is key to the argument that the earliest Egyptians had a star religion that later evolved into a solar religion. If that's true, it might also mean that the pyramids are far older than what most people think."

"You can write a computer program that can tell you that?" his mother asked.

4

"He can," I said, and turned to John. "But doesn't it have something to do with Leo the lion and the Sphinx having the body of a lion?"

"It's archaeoastronomy not astrology. You're confusing the astrological sign of Leo with the constellation." He turned to his mother. "Twelve thousand years ago the Sphinx pointed directly at the constellation Leo just as it was rising in the east. Some people believe this alignment marks the period when the Sphinx was built, which is an incredible idea if you think about it because that would mean that the Sphinx is twice as old as what is thought. It would also confirm the theory that an earlier star religion preceded the ancient Egyptian solar religion."

"So, he set out to prove it himself," I said.

"I wanted to test this argument, at least calculate the alignment. I wrote my own program and duplicated their findings."

"And it's true!" I said.

"Yes, it's true. Twelve thousand years ago the Sphinx, if it were already built, would have stared straight at its counterpart in the sky just as Leo was coming into view."

"Face to face!" I said.

"So, in that sense my program is a kind of time machine. Using it I was able to duplicate the night sky as it looked thousands of years ago."

"I've never seen a fortune like this," Madeleine said as she grabbed the thin strip of paper from my hand. "You would think if it were going to name an exotic place it would be in China."

I took back the slip of paper and read it again. "Yes, you would think it would say, you long to see the Great Wall of China or something like that."

"It really is a strange coincidence," John said as he snatched the fortune from my hand and looked at it again as if to check that we had read it correctly.

"It seems more than a coincidence," Madeleine said. "I would call it a synchronicity."

"What do you mean?" he asked.

"I'm not sure what I mean exactly. We've talked about synchronicities only a little in my Jungian group. Sometimes what appear to be coincidences are more than that. They're not as haphazard as coincidences seem but ordered in some way as if by someone."

"But by whom and why?" I asked

"Maybe by John himself. I don't know. I certainly haven't begun to master Jungian thought. But maybe the message comes from his own subconscious."

"But Mom, my subconscious didn't write this message and stuff it inside this fortune cookie."

"No, it didn't. I still think it's more than a coincidence." She looked down at her blue leather handbag, glanced again at the rattling panes of glass and back at her son. "Do you really long to see the Great Pyramid of Egypt?"

"Of course he does," I said.

"But I have no plans," he countered.

"The weather has been so bad," Madeleine said, "that I haven't gotten much Christmas shopping done. I'd been thinking even before tonight that in place of gifts I might offer to take us on a trip. My investments have been doing well. I've got the money. And I could use a vacation and don't want to travel alone. I don't know if the travel agent here would have much information about Egypt."

"I can check the internet," I said. "I can find a good deal."

A snowstorm coming out of the west nipped at our tires as we raced ahead of it to Columbus. We hardly noticed since we were lost in conversation about going to Egypt and about the fortunate fortune cookie that set the whole trip off. Hours later, my nighttime antennae came up and received a warning. What was I being warned of?

The sound of the storm's fury had momentarily diminished when I climbed out of bed and made my way downstairs to get a glass of water and look outside at what the storm had left. The moonlight was irregular, cutting in and out of fast moving clouds, landing here and there on the lawn, the trees, and the fence—the whole neighborhood looked like a snow-covered wonderland. Limbs and roofs, even the wire fence behind our house was weighted down with a heavy white coating. It was beautiful, but I worried it had come too soon and would turn to ice in the morning after the temperature rose. I remembered the devastation the ice had brought the year before when heavy coatings brought down tree limbs and electrical wires. Resigned that we may be in for the same, I went back to bed and fell into a dream.

Everything was white, I recall. It was not snow but sand. I was with John and Madeleine, and we were running from gunfire. We entered a dark place that felt very old. An ancient, ghostly figure beckoned us deeper into that place as we hid ourselves from some unknown frightening thing. Lines from Shelley's "Ode to the West Wind" echoed into my subconscious as I began to wake up:

O wild West Wind, thou breath of Autumn's being,
Thou, from whose unseen presence the leaves dead
Are driven, like ghosts from an enchanter fleeing....
Wild Spirit, which art moving everywhere;
Destroyer and preserver; hear, oh, hear!

"Hear what?" I shouted.

"What's wrong?" John said, my cry having startled him out of his sleep. "What's going on?"

"I thought I heard shots, but it must have been ice pellets slamming against the windows."

"It's winter," he said, and buried his head between two pillows.

"It's too early in the season for weather this bad," I said to no response. "I had a dream. It was frightening. I think it was supposed to be Egypt because we were surrounded by desert."

He lifted his pillow. "It was just a dream. Go back to sleep."

"Do you think we will be all right over there?"

"Of course. It was just a dream caused by the weather, not Egypt. We will be fine."

Chapter Two

I felt like an alien. Had I landed on Ray Bradbury's Mars? An ancient Egyptian face purported to be carved out of Martian rock leaped into my imagination, although I had seen it only once in a magazine story that claimed evidence of Martian habitation that was later discredited. Or was it? Get a grip, I thought, this is not Mars, and I'm not a space traveler. Egypt is only a very foreign country just a day's flight from home. And it is fantastic to be here.

Men clad in white gowns and turbans and women dressed in the black hijab mixed with others dressed in western style clothing in the terminal at the airport in Cairo. John craned his neck searching for a sign he could read. Although he had mastered several languages, Arabic was not one of them. Its characters, while beautiful with their arabesque curves, were disturbingly indecipherable even to him.

We were five. My sister-in-law Natalie had joined our travel party, along with our nephew Paul, who Madeleine believed would so benefit from the trip that she persuaded his parents to take him out of school for two weeks.

Placards bearing names of travel parties appeared once we crossed into the lobby, written in the familiar Latin alphabet. I looked for our name, eager to make contact and be assured we were welcome and expected. The trip had been surprisingly cheap. But alas, nothing is free, and even bargains have their price. Travel in Egypt was down for a reason. The U.S. State Department advisory warned that militant attacks directed at tourists remained a concern, particularly in the provinces south of Cairo and north of Luxor. This news threatened to throw a political wrench into our travel arrangement works, but in the end we found our courage and good travel insurance. Besides, we would not be in the area of Egypt south of Cairo and north of Luxor. We would fly over that dangerous place and arrive safely in Luxor before cruising further south on the Nile to Aswan.

John kept his arm tightly wrapped around his nephew Paul, feeling an enormous weight of responsibility. Paul tolerated John's arm, but he wasn't scared at all. He was too young at the age of ten to be scared of much of anything. He was tall for his age, and looked very slim in his neatly pressed slacks whose formality clashed with his baseball cap and the sizable pink bubbles that he blew and then popped. He said his mother packed plenty of gum to keep his ears from plugging in high altitudes.

A young man wearing black jeans and a white shirt held up a sign bearing our last name. "Welcome to Egypt," he said, directing his eyes towards John. "My name is Yusef. Come with me, and I will take you to your hotel so that you can rest after your long flight."

"What about the pyramids?" Paul asked, impatient with the thought of resting at the hotel after sitting in the plane for hours.

"I've saved the pyramids for your final day in Cairo before you fly south to Luxor," Yusef said.

"I'm not tired. I want to go now!"

"The rest of us are tired," Madeleine said in an effort to quiet him down.

"I tell you what Paul," Yusef said. "I'll drive through Giza on our way to the hotel, and you can see the pyramids from the van."

Our first glimpse of Cairo revealed a prosperous city with wide boulevards flanked by modern buildings that housed government offices, embassies and the university. As we traveled deeper into the city, its real character emerged. Under the blinding light of the white, hot sun the various shapes of men and women, cars and donkey carts seemed to dissolve into radiant facets of a rare gem at once old and new, individual and combined. Opulent and rustic merged, not awkwardly as one might expect, but effortlessly, naturally. Women draped in the black hijab and men in long robes passed other men and women dressed in contemporary European regalia with hardly a notice.

"The pyramids!" Paul shouted as he pointed out the window.

There they were, standing like great triangular towers that mocked any attempt at grandeur made by the large, new buildings that lined the boulevard from the airport. The sight of them made Egypt's long history apparent. The pyramids soar above everything with a history that stretches back to the beginning. There is old Cairo and new Cairo, cosmopolitan and rustic, and towering over it all is something very ancient. In spite of efforts made to fathom their meaning since Napoleon's incursion into Egypt, they still remain a mystery.

"They're huge!" Natalie said.

"Yeah!" Paul said. "And they didn't even have machines to make them."

"They had slaves to build them," Madeleine said.

"That theory has been pretty well discounted," John said.

"Well, then who built them?" Madeleine said.

"Some people believe they were built by extraterrestrial space travelers."

"They were?" Paul said.

John smiled and said, "No Paul, there's no evidence for the claim. I think those who say that just can't believe ancient people could have accomplished such a feat on their own."

Natalie laughed. "But they can believe in extraterrestrials?"

"Choose your belief," I laughed.

"It really is a mystery. That's for sure," John said. "I think the ancients have been underrated myself."

"How ancient are they?" Madeleine asked.

There was a brief moment of silence. I could tell by the look on John's face he was considering which answer to give. I had heard them all already and more than once. Would he give the short sweet orthodox answer, I wondered, or launch into the incomplete and very controversial answers arising from today's research?

Before John could say a word, Yusef proclaimed, "The Great Pyramid was built by the Pharaoh Khufu in 2560 BC to serve as his tomb. That would make it over forty-five hundred years old."

Not able to turn away from a good argument in which he believed he had the upper hand, John cleared his throat and began. "A couple of authors I've read, Robert Bauval and Adrian Gilbert to be precise, say to call them tombs is like calling the magnificent Palace of Versailles a house. Yes, King Louis Quatorze built it and lived there, but his palace was far more than a house."

"That may be true," Yusef said. "But such reasoning does not deny the fact that the palace served as the King's home, does it? So it is with the pyramids. They served first and foremost as tombs."

"Not everyone would agree with you, although I will acknowledge that's the conventional view."

The two men kept a truce for only a few minutes before Natalie broke the silence. "What's the unconventional view?"

"Oh, don't get him started," Madeleine said.

"Well, there's more than one. A pretty wild idea is that they served some technical purpose, somehow being able to geodetically create power."

"Geo...what?" Natalie said.

"Geodetics is the idea of looking at the earth as a source of energy and power. Imagine being able to harness the earth's magnetic field or the power of continents as they move, sliding over the lower strata of the earth."

"I should have listened to Mom," Natalie said.

Too excited to be perturbed, John reformulated his answer. "Imagine being able to harness the power of an earthquake."

"An earthquake!" Paul said. "How could the pyramids do that?"

"I don't know. It's just a wild idea."

"Can we do that?" Paul asked.

"Harness the power of an earthquake? No! We can't. But imagine how much energy we would have at our disposal if we could. There are all kinds of theories. The one I like best describes the pyramids as a monumental expression of a very ancient belief system. An expression of faith like the great cathedrals."

"You mean you think they're churches?" Madeleine asked incredulously.

"Not exactly. More like monuments to the stars in the constellation Orion."

"They were sun worshipers," Yusef said. "They worshiped Amun-Ra, the sun god."

"That was true later on, but the earliest religion had more to do with the stars. The three pyramids that form the Great Pyramid complex are an expression of this star religion."

"What's your evidence?" Yusef asked.

11

"Bauval and Gilbert present this hypothesis, and I think their evidence is compelling. You see it has to do with the shafts inside the Great Pyramid."

"Are you referring to the ventilation shafts?" Yusef asked.

"They take exception to the theory that the shafts were for ventilation and for good reason. Only one of the shafts actually exits the pyramid, the southern shaft found in the King's Chamber. The shafts in the Queen's Chamber never exit so how could they ventilate? Some Egyptologists argue that the pyramid builders just didn't finish them for some reason. I think that's just a convenient way to dismiss evidence that contradicts their hypothesis."

"Are there King and Queen mummies inside the King and Queen Chambers?" Paul asked.

"No, Paul, no mummies, only the King's sarcophagus," John said. Not easily distracted, he continued the argument. "Not only do they think the shafts were left unfinished, they think that the Queen's Chamber was abandoned for some reason. But that just doesn't make sense." He shook his head. "No, look at them! These pyramids were no trial and error project. The builders had complete mastery over massive building materials. Look at their precision. The fact that they have survived this long and in such good condition shows that their designers knew exactly what they were doing."

"I will agree with you there," Yusef said. "You've read quite a lot on the subject, haven't you?"

"You wouldn't believe how much," I said.

"So if they're more than tombs and not really churches, what are they?" Natalie asked.

John turned, looking out the rear window at the pyramids that now loomed in the distance. "No one knows for sure. But careful measurements of the angles of these shafts show they appear to be pointing out the meridian transit of Orion's Belt."

"Meridian what?" Paul said.

"Remember that time I pointed out the Belt of Orion?"

"Yeah, I remember. It was freezing cold!"

"Well, what did you expect? It was winter. I remember the stars were exceptionally bright that night. I can almost see them now. Well, the southern shaft of the King's Chamber, the shaft that opens out of the pyramid, points to the brightest star in Orion's Belt. Orion was associated with the god Osiris. The southern shaft of the Queen's Chamber points to Sirius, which the ancient Egyptians associated with the goddess Isis. Bauval and Gilbert show that these three pyramids replicate the position of these stars at the time when the pyramids were built."

"How could they even know that?" Paul said.

"It's mysterious isn't it," John laughed. "How did they know that? How did they know how to build pyramids? And how could they have built them so precisely? These are the questions that keep people guessing. Some people guess that because the shafts point to the star representations of the god Osiris and the goddess Isis the pyramids must have had religious significance. Some people even think religious ceremonies took place in the King's Chamber in which the soul of the dead pharaoh traveled to Osiris who resides in the constellation Orion."

"Like going to Heaven?" Paul asked.

"Something like that. Maybe the ancient Egyptians located Heaven in the Belt of Orion."

"Who was Osiris?" Natalie asked.

"The ancient Egyptians believed that in their earlier history he was the first divine pharaoh of all of Egypt."

"Earlier history! Earlier than what? Ancient Egypt is five thousand years old," Madeleine said.

"Yes, I know Mom, but ancient Egyptians thought their civilization was much older and recorded its early history in myths, just like the Greeks did. They believed that Osiris was the child of the sky goddess Nuit and the earth god Geb. So was his sister Isis. Osiris and Isis mated and produced Horus, who like his father became pharaoh and was believed to have been reincarnated in every pharaoh thereafter."

"Whoa! Brother and sister gods producing the pharaoh. That's complicated," Natalie said.

"Oh, it's more complicated than that. I gave you the simple version. Actually, Osiris was killed by his jealous brother Seth before Isis conceived Horus."

"This is beginning to sound familiar," Madeleine said. "Didn't

Cane slay his brother Abel out of jealousy?'

"That's right, Mom. These ancient stories share many similarities. It gets even better. Isis, using her magic, was able to resurrect Osiris long enough to produce their offspring Horus. After that, Osiris is said to have transformed into the constellation Orion where he rules over the heavenly kingdom of the dead."

"So Orion is Heaven!" Paul said. "How do you get to the King's Chamber?"

"Well, yes, at least many believe the ancient Egyptians thought so. You get there through one of the corridors inside the Khufu Pyramid called the Grand Gallery. It leads up to the King's Chamber. I sure hope we will be able to get inside that one."

"Why wouldn't we?" Madeleine asked.

"I've read that they rotate access to the pyramids to help preserve them."

"That's right," Yusef said.

"Do you know which one will be open when we visit?" Madeleine asked Yusef.

"Lately it's been one of the two smaller pyramids."

"I'll show you a map of the interior of the Khufu Pyramid and the King's Chamber so you will at least know what it looks like if we can't get in," John said to Paul.

"Oh, we have to get in!" cried Paul. "Wow, a shaft leading the way to Heaven. I've got to see that!"

Chapter Three

Armed guards stood at our hotel door, and they weren't smiling.

"Machine guns!" Paul shouted, pointing to their automatic weapons.

"Don't point," his grandmother said. She whisked him past the gendarmes and into the lobby.

John turned to Yusef. "What's this all about?"

"Nothing for you to be concerned with. There's probably an important official staying at the hotel. Whenever he goes, they go."

Madeleine yanked Paul away from the glass door he was peering through.

"Did you see that body armor?" he said.

"Paul, keep away," John said. "Those guards don't need you distracting them."

"I was just looking," he said.

This was the first sign that this vacation wasn't going to be entirely as we had planned. The second came when Yusef warned us not to leave the hotel until the morning when he would return to begin our tour. The third signal came when the hotel clerk suggested rather earnestly to John that we might want to rent two satellite phones.

"That's so cool!" Paul said to his uncle. "Can I have one?"

John looked at me, and I looked at Yusef and said, "Well, if we can't leave the hotel on our own, and if we must remain entirely under your supervision while we're in Cairo, I can't see the point of spending the extra money."

John concurred. "It won't be necessary," he said to the clerk.

"No, no," Yusef interceded. "The clerk is quite correct. As an extra precaution it would be wise to invest in at least two phones to make it easy to find you if by chance we should get separated, even though that's not likely to happen."

"Well, what do you think?" I asked John.

15

He bought the insurance. Paul was delighted when he was handed one of the phones to keep for himself, his grandmother and his aunt, whose room he would share. John kept the second for the two of us.

The hotel's atrium lobby was furnished with sumptuous Persian carpets and silk couches where two wealthy Sheiks sat conversing. I wondered if either one could be the important official that warranted hotel guards as I passed where they were seated on my way to the elevator. Our room likewise was spacious and beautifully furnished. As soon as John's head hit the pillow of our soft bed, he was asleep, which gave me the opportunity to do a little research without being noticed.

I searched through our guidebooks to see if I could find anything relating to our circumstances. There were no warnings to stay with your tour guide. There was nothing about armed hotel guards. Both books did suggest independent walking tour itineraries and a sojourn to Khan el-Khalile open-air market. Clearly, conditions had changed since these books were written, I thought. I reread a list of do's and don'ts, which were mostly the standard fare you'd expect. Drink only bottled water. Don't ask for ice in your drink. Eat only cooked food, preferably at hotels. Avoid fresh salads. Dress modestly. Always offer baksheesh for services rendered. "Baksheesh?" I read the passage more closely. *Baksheesh is not merely a tip. In Egypt it is a way of life and livelihood for thousands of its inhabitants for the many services they might render. Always offer baksheesh for services no matter how small.*

I'll have to remember that, I thought and left the room in search of a cool drink without ice and an English language newspaper. Paul greeted me when the elevator door opened.

"What floor Madame?"

"Oh! Hi Paul. Go with me down to the mezzanine. I'll buy you something to drink.

"Oui Madame." He pushed the designated button.

The hotel's mezzanine level was home to a number of international restaurants: Papa's Italiano, Pepe's Mexicano, Sapporo Japanese and over in the corner was a small juice bar with tables. We sat down and ordered Orangina.

Paul hadn't taken his eyes off a couple that sat a few tables away. "Quit staring," I said.

"They're talking on their phones," he said pointing at the couple.

I gently grabbed his finger and pulled it down and glanced over at the couple. "Yes, they're sitting together but talking to other people. That's not polite," I whispered.

"Maybe they're talking to each other," he said and pulled his phone out of his pocket.

"Who are you going to call?"

"You, I guess."

"I don't have the phone. It's up in the room."

"I'll call Uncle John."

"He's asleep. You don't want to wake him. Speaking of phones, have you called your parents to let them know you've arrived safely?" He began pressing the numbers of his parents phone in Ohio. "No, you can't use your cell phone for that. Put it away for now, and let's go down to the lobby."

We arrived in the lobby just in time to witness a staff person cleaning Paul's hand and nose prints off the glass doors where he had stood gawking at the guards. I considered offering the man baksheesh but thought better of it since he was a hotel employee. Instead I turned to the desk clerk and asked if he might have an English language newspaper.

The clerk raised his index finger to his mustache and twirled it as if he were making some sort of gesture I did not understand and said, "Madam, the *Cairo Tribune* will be delivered to your room in the morning."

"Do you have any of today's editions left?"

The clerk released his mustache, slicked back his hair. "Only the desk copy, but it must remain here for our reference."

"Well, can I see it? I could sit over there," I said, pointing to one of the silk couches.

He pulled it out from beneath the counter and held it up outside of my grasp.

I could see a very large picture of a man standing with the Vice President of the United States with a headline that read, "Meeting of Minds." The man's face was very full and very proud. He looked exceedingly dignified, more dignified than my own vice president.

17

"Who is that man?" I asked the clerk.

"Why, that is your vice president."

"No, the other one."

"Our president, of course." He looked at me intently, "A very great man."

"Yes, I'm sure he is," I said, although I had no idea whether he was or wasn't. The clerk quickly put the paper back under his desk and out of my sight. Reading the news was simply going to have to wait until tomorrow I concluded and thanked him. He responded with an abrupt bow.

Paul and I made our way back to our room to rouse John and phone Paul's parents. John was awake, however, sitting with his nose in his well worn edition of Robert Bauval and Adrian Gilbert's, *The Orion Mystery: Unlocking the Secrets of the Pyramids.*

"There you are," he said looking up from his book. "I wondered where you were off to."

"Paul, phone your parents on our room phone," I said, and turned to John. "I went down to the lobby and tried to get a newspaper. They were gone except for the desk copy that the clerk wouldn't let go of. I really couldn't read it, but I saw from a photo that our vice president is here."

"Hmm, I wonder if he could be the important guest?" John said.

"If he were here, I would think there would be even more security."

"You're probably right," John said just before his satellite phone started ringing. He looked up and there was Paul standing with his phone not ten feet away. "Come over here," John said into the phone. "I have something to show you."

John pointed to the page he had been reading. "Here, you can see the entrance to the pyramid, and down below the Queen's Chamber, and up here, see the Grand Gallery corridor that leads up to the King's Chamber."

"Cool!" Paul said and scurried out of our room.

We broke out laughing. "It's amazing how rapidly his attention shifts," I said. "In the van all he could think about were the pyramids and now it's his phone."

Chapter Four

"Hold on to your seats!" Samia said just before swerving past a double-parked car stalled behind a donkey cart.

"Woo," Paul said as he slid in his seat.

"I'm sorry," she said. "I didn't mean to scare you, but it's the only way to get through this mess."

Samia had arrived at our hotel promptly at 9:00 AM along with Yusef who introduced us to this youthful, dark eyed girl, who had stood before us smiling in her colorful headscarf and a fashionable black sweater. He apologized and said that pressing matters took him away from his duties and left.

"Is she old enough to drive?" Madeleine had whispered.

"She must be," John said, rather relieved. The fact that Yusef left Samia to guide us was further evidence, along with a thin and vacuous morning newspaper, that there was little danger in Cairo besides the traffic.

Samia was taking us to St. Sergious, a Christian church where, according to legend, the Holy Family took refuge when they escaped Herod two millennia ago. When we turned into the quarter, lanes became so narrow that we had to park the van and walk into the immediate area of the church. It was as old and dreary as the neighborhood where it sat; nothing I wanted to take a photo of until rattling along the cobblestones came a picturesque sight: two young boys driving a donkey cart loaded with metal milk containers. I aimed my camera and snapped. One of the boys wielding a wrench in the air snapped back in Arabic. His menacing face and movements clearly communicated his meaning. I was scared.

"You should not have taken his picture without his permission!" Samia scolded. She calmed the boys who went on their way. Shaken and embarrassed, I put my camera away and apologized.

Narrow lanes were made unnaturally dark by tight rows of shabby homes that lined them, which might have explained the pallor of a not very friendly face of a boy who stared at us from the front stoop where he sat cleaning his firearm.

"He has a rifle!" Paul blurted out.

"He's only cleaning it," Samia said, her movements hesitant as her eyes darted up and down the street. She quickly guided us to the cave Saint Sergious Church was built around. "This cave sat at the center of the ancient Roman fort of Babylon," she said.

I was too distracted by images of the rifle and thoughts of the hostile cart boy to care. The cave was dark and dank and located inside a very old, unkempt dwelling in this rundown and seemingly hostile Coptic area. We were ready to leave as soon as we had arrived, but before we could leave we had a very strange experience, another synchronicity, as Madeleine called it. We were approached by one of two men who had stood in the church together dressed in leather jackets and jeans. Neither looked pious nor Egyptian.

"Stuart!" Natalie said.

"Natalie? What are you doing here?"

"I'm here with my family on a trip. What are you doing here?"

"I'm here...I'm here buying jewels. Look, you shouldn't be here by yourselves."

"We aren't by ourselves. We're here with our guide. Samia, meet a friend of mine, Stuart. Stuart, our guide Samia."

He did not look reassured. "Where are you staying?" he asked.

"The Kingsley, but only for a few days. Then we fly to Luxor and board a Nile cruise ship."

"Which ship?"

"I don't know."

"It's called the Queen Nuit," John said. "Are you saying it isn't safe around here?"

Stuart ignored the question. "Look, get out of this district. I'll catch up with you either in Cairo or Luxor. Where are you going now?"

"Khan el-Khalile," Samia said, looking a bit puzzled, "the Alabaster Mosque, the Egyptian museum."

"Stay away from the market," Stuart said.

"Why? I wish to take them shopping."

"Do what I say. I'm warning you." He looked at Natalie. "Don't go there. It's not safe."

"Okay, I will take them to the boutiques instead," Samia said.

"So you'll get in touch?" Natalie asked.

"Get out of here now. I'll catch up with you later."

We walked briskly back towards the van.

"Who is Stuart?" John asked.

"I used to work with him at the General Accounting Office. He works for the State Department now."

"What's this about buying jewels?" I asked.

"I thought he only bought them in Brazil, but then I haven't talked to him lately, not since he transferred. He has an arrangement with some jewelers in Washington who tell him what they're looking for. He buys the stones and brings them back duty free. You know, we really ought to go to Brazil sometime. Stu says you can buy beautiful jewels there for far less than what they cost in the states."

"Oh, that Stuart!" Madeleine said. "I remember you telling me about him. Wasn't he the one you liked so much? Didn't you supervise a project with him?"

Natalie flushed. "I actually supervised him on that project."

Later that day, when Madeleine had John and me to herself, she confessed how worried she had been about their relationship. "She talked about him incessantly, and I didn't like what I heard. He's not the marrying kind, and he's always going off somewhere. He seemed so wild! I couldn't see what Natalie could possibly see in him."

"He's really good-looking," I said.

"I introduced her to Bob Schmidt's son," Madeleine continued. "He's an accountant now. John, you remember the Schmidts. They have a daughter your age. Natalie showed no interest whatsoever."

John did remember the Schmidts and their daughter. "Boring, boring, boring," he told me later that evening. He didn't blame Natalie a bit.

We loaded into the van quickly, not wanting to risk another encounter with angry boys. Samia pulled out into the cobbled lane then turned into slow moving traffic on an asphalt-paved street.

"I will take you to the mosque. It's much friendlier and far more beautiful," she said. "You will like it better."

She was right. The Mohammed Ali Mosque was named after an early 19th century Viceroy to the Ottoman Empire. It is widely referred to as the Alabaster Mosque because of the beautiful white stone it is made from. Like all mosques in Cairo, the Alabaster's many intricately carved minarets rise up into the sky like steeples. But unlike other mosques, this one is located in the Citadel, a fortified area with its own guards.

Our five pairs of sneakers and Samia's black boots mingled with the many other shoes belonging to worshipers who left them at the door before they entered. The floor was covered with spectacular Persian carpets, deep red hues being the dominant color. Globes of light suspended from metal rings and chains lit the massive room, giving the appearance of hundreds of chandeliers hanging from the huge intricately detailed domed ceiling. The walls were stone. Near one of them stood a golden stairway that shimmered in subdued light. There were no pews. Instead, the devout kneeled on small rugs. Their prayers echoed throughout the great stone building sounding like voices made into instruments of devotion.

Feeling like intruders into something very solemn and personal, Natalie, John and I quietly left the mosque and entered the grounds of the Citadel, which were very beautiful and more public. Perched above the city, we studied the ornate details of the minarets rising from Cairo's skyline for a few minutes before Natalie, confident that her mother was busy with Paul and Samia, brought up Stuart.

"He's a Gulf War veteran," she said. "Going out with him was quite fun at first. He had this game he would play, at least I thought it was a game. Reconnaissance he called it, to protect us from would-be Washington thieves. But after going through this more than a few times, I started feeling sad for him, and that's when our relationship, such as it was, fell apart. He didn't want my pity."

"What's wrong with him?" John asked.

"I don't know. It's probably post-traumatic stress disorder, but he won't talk about it. Washington isn't that dangerous. Not where we'd go, anyway."

"So you think he might have been exaggerating the danger of the neighborhood we were in and the danger of going to the market?"

22

"Could be. I don't know. He's prone to do that kind of thing is what I'm saying."

"So how close were you?" John asked.

"We were friends. Contrary to what Mom thinks, he was always a gentleman. I wanted more, but he never made romantic advances. Yet he is the most romantic man I have ever met. He definitely likes women, but I think something happened to him in the war. I think he was damaged, maybe psychologically. He just wouldn't talk about it. I've seen him very little since he went over to the State Department."

"You said earlier that you were his supervisor. Maybe that had something to do with it," John said.

"Only on one project. It was the last project we worked on before he transferred. It went okay I guess," she said hesitantly.

"Why only okay?" John asked.

"Stuart doesn't like to be supervised."

John, who began to get the picture, didn't ask any more questions.

Stuart is a very attractive man in a windswept sort of way: medium height, rugged build, longish blond hair and pale blue eyes. Yet I had always imagined Natalie with someone more like herself: a button-down guy in a suit, tie and sweater vest, not jeans and definitely not a black leather jacket.

Natalie's life, while not entirely conventional, is well ordered and pleasant. She has worked for the federal government as a contracts administrator since she graduated from college with a degree in English. Her career really took off after she earned her MBA. Washington has turned out to be a great place for her to live and work. She regularly attends lectures at the Smithsonian and takes the train to New York to see a play or two. She lives with her cat in a high-rise condominium in nearby Alexandria, Virginia and spends a good deal of time at the local pool or biking to Old Town. She has a nice life, so why mess it up. I wondered if Stuart ever really knew how she felt about him. Knowing Natalie as I do, I doubted it.

"Come on, we are going to the Cairo Museum," John said, pulling me up off the lawn and out of my reverie.

Gloom spread across Paul's face.

"Oh Paul, you will like the museum," Samia said. "I will show you the golden remains of Emperor Tutankhamen. He was pharaoh of all of Egypt when he wasn't much older than you."

"Any mummies?"

"Lots of mummies."

Napoleon's Egyptian Campaign (1798-1801) led to the discovery of the fabled Rosetta Stone, and although it fell into British hands after Napoleon's military defeat to the British, it was the French and the Egyptians who most felt its influence. Its discovery ushered in the modern era of Egyptology that forever linked the two nations. Napoleon's sarcophagus reflects the grandeur of the tombs of the ancient pharaohs. In 1989, as if to continue the relationship, the French completed the new entrance to the Louvre in the style of a magnificent glass pyramid. A two hundred and twenty-seven ton granite obelisk dating back to Ramses II sits in the Place de la Concorde in Paris, while Cairo's Egyptian Museum, built in French neoclassical style, has become the final resting place for Pharaonic bones, a French tomb if you will, in the heart of Cairo.

Samia hurried us past statues of pharaohs and princesses on our way to the museum's pride, the remains of the tomb of the boy emperor, Tutankhamen. They were beautiful, I thought, as we passed paintings of an ancient people who wore only the sheerest of fabrics. There was no prohibition against pictorial representations of their gods, I noted. Neither was there a prohibition against alcohol, as a display of devices used to make wine and beer suggested.

"He wasn't very big," Paul said as he studied Tutankhamen's golden coffin.

"He wasn't very old when he died," Samia pointed out. "And people then did not grow as tall."

"What happened to him?"

"We're not sure," Samia said. "He had a head injury. Maybe it was only an accident. If you look at all the things he was buried with, it looks like he was greatly loved."

"Yeah, look at all of this stuff."

Samia stepped back slightly and began her formal presentation. "The ancient Egyptians buried their dead with all the things they might need to reach heaven and, once there, make themselves comfortable.

Here is the boat and chariot King Tut would need for transportation. And there is his golden throne that he could sit upon. Look here," Samia said as she directed our attention across the aisle, "they even buried his mummified body with jewelry and food."

"How old was he?" Paul asked.

"He lived during the New Kingdom, three thousand years ago."

"I mean how many years old."

"He was only eighteen when he died. Look over here. This might help you better understand the ancient Egyptian view of the afterlife."

We followed Samia into another room that held the papyrus text of the Egyptian *Book of the Dead*. She directed our attention to the case that held the second depiction.

"The ancient Egyptians believed that the deceased were judged by Osiris to determine if they were worthy of an afterlife. Here you can see this very large set of scales. Notice a feather in one scale and a heart in the other. If one is pure, the heart will be as light as a feather."

"A feather doesn't weigh anything!" a visibly disturbed Paul said.

"You must be very, very good indeed," Samia said.

"Who are those men with dog heads?" he asked.

"Those are the Anubis, the servants of Osiris who are carrying out the task. See that baboon above the scales? That is a representation of the god Thoth, who records the judgment. Thoth is usually represented as a man with the head of an ibis, but here he is a baboon."

John said, "This reminds me of something else."

"The scales of justice," Madeleine said.

"That too, but it reminds me of a religious painting I saw in France. It showed the Archangel Michael holding a set of scales that looked very much like these, but instead of holding a feather and a heart, they held two men who were being weighed in judgment against each other. And instead of Anubis and baboons, a heavenly host of angels looked on."

"It makes you wonder just how old some of these ideas are," Madeleine said. "The Egyptians used the heart to represent our moral nature that long ago. And we still do, even though science tells us otherwise."

"Some ideas are extremely resilient," John said.

"Was Tutankhamen's heart light enough?" Paul asked Samia.

"I'm sure it was," she said to Paul reassuringly. "He was too young when he died to have done anything too bad. Come here, I will show you his family."

Samia led us back to Tutankhamen's funerary remains and over to a portrait of Akhenaton and his family.

"Akhenaton was Tutankhamen's father. Here is his beautiful wife the Princess Nefertiti."

"His mom?" Paul said.

"No, she wasn't. Archaeologists don't think she was anyway."

"Did his parents get a divorce?"

"No, Paul. Important men had many wives. Nefertiti was Akhenaton's most important wife but not Tutankhamen's mother."

"That's still true today among Muslim men, isn't it?" Madeleine asked.

"Only among the very wealthy who can support more than one wife."

"A harem!" Paul said.

"Yes, of sorts," Samia said. "It is a tradition with a long standing. But be aware that Tutankhamen's father was not a Muslim. Islam did not yet exist. For a man of his time he had great religious insight though. Like Muslims today, Akhenaton knew there was only one god. Before he ruled, ancient Egyptians believed in multiple gods as did the Greeks and the Romans."

"Wasn't the one god the sun god?" John asked.

"Yes, Aten, the sun god. After Akhenaton died and Tutankhamen became pharaoh, the priests made the young boy restore the Priesthood of Amun and the old religion."

"Look at this dog over here," Paul said.

"Another Anubis, a black jackal," Samia said. "He was there to guard Tutankhamen's tomb from grave robbers."

"I guess he didn't do a very good job," the boy adroitly remarked.

"Wasn't there supposed to have been a curse on his tomb, the pharaoh's curse?" John asked.

"Like in the mummy movie?" Paul said.

"Well, some claim that," Samia said, "but it is only a legend. According to British mystery writer Sir Arthur Conan Doyle, those who

26

unsealed the tomb would be cursed and die."

"Didn't one of them actually die?" John asked

"Lord Carnarvon died just two weeks after opening the tomb. But Howard Carter lived many, many years longer, and he was the one who had found it."

Her phone rang. She drew away for a few minutes while we pondered other golden objects removed from the young pharaoh's tomb.

"We've got to go now," Samia said with urgency and began to hurriedly push us along.

"We just got here!" John said.

"That was Yusef. He said it is time for us to drive out to the country for lunch. You don't want me to get into trouble with him, do you?"

"What about the other pharaohs' stuff?" Paul protested.

Making the best of a rapid turn of events, Samia said, "We've seen the best. The other pharaohs' tombs were robbed long before Howard Carter, so most of the gold was gone before Egyptologists discovered them. That is why Tutankhamen's tomb is so famous."

As Samia rushed us through the building and away from our abbreviated tour of the Cairo Museum, she fell back long enough to tell John and me why we were in such a hurry.

"Paul should not hear this," she said breathlessly. "There was an explosion at the market. Yusef said shots were fired. He thinks it best to leave the city for now."

"The market!" John said.

"Yes, the place your friend ordered me not to take you. He must have known something. Who is this Stuart?"

"We don't know him," John said. "My sister knows him because they used to work together in Washington. But she doesn't know what he's doing here."

"She hasn't even seen Stuart since he transferred to a different department of the government," I said.

Samia looked unconvinced, moved ahead and ushered Paul, Madeleine and Natalie out of the museum and into the van. She pressed the large vehicle through heavy traffic, hurriedly weaving around smaller cars and carts towards the city outskirts.

"Look over there," John whispered.

I bent forward to look out the window John sat next to. Several jeeps carrying armed men in uniform headed in the direction from where we had come. I expected a loud exclamation and finger pointing from Paul, but thankfully he was oblivious. His imagination had taken him elsewhere, probably back in the museum in front of Tutankhamen's golden throne still contemplating the boy pharaoh's fate. But how could he and the others not notice the blaring sirens that were going off, or were they only in my head? My mind was reeling.

"Who the hell is Stuart anyway?" I whispered to John.

We had no answers, which was the growing source of my frustration. I knew Samia hadn't believed John's and my protestations that we didn't know him, and that made me feel awkward. On the other hand, how could I blame her? Our meeting with him was a complete coincidence, I silently argued, a coincidence that never would have occurred if Natalie weren't with us. Without her, he would have gone unnoticed. But we did notice him, or I should say Natalie did. Maybe Samia didn't believe in these kinds of coincidences. For her there had to be meaning. Why would she think otherwise? Stuart, a U.S. State Department employee just happened to appear in the Coptic Christian area of Cairo on our first full day and warned us not to go near the market, the market that in only a few hours would suffer an explosion followed by gunfire. I could see why Samia was suspicious. Thinking about it made me suspicious, and I knew Natalie was above suspicion. But Stuart?

And yet maybe there is meaning to this coincidence of a very different order than Samia imagined. It was such a strange coincidence. It seemed more like one of Madeleine's synchronicities, the second that so far had marked this trip: the fortune cookie that had propelled us here and now this. It was as if our journey were being composed, but by whom? Us? We would have ignored the fortune cookie just as we had ignored countless other fortunes in other cookies had John not lately spent so much time studying Egyptology. Had his unconscious somehow constructed the events that were to follow, employing some kind of unknown causal mechanism? That still didn't explain the encounter with Stuart; that was Natalie's coincidence. Maybe because of where all of us were in our lives, for different reasons we were meant to take this trip. But why? Why any of it?

28

Chapter Five

Samia drove out into the desert rim at the edge of the fertile Nile Valley towards Sakkara, near the ancient capital Memphis.

"That's the Unas Pyramid," John said, pointing to what looked like a hill.

"It looks like a big pile of dirt," Paul said.

"It must be really old," Natalie added.

"Actually, it's Fifth Dynasty. It was built long after the Great Pyramid. They must have forgotten how to build them by then."

"How could they forget how to build them?" Natalie said incredulously.

"I don't know, but they did. Most of the grand pyramids were built in the Fourth Dynasty in a span of about one hundred years. By the Fifth Dynasty, the Egyptians seemed to have lost the technique."

"That seems a reversal of the natural course of technology," Natalie said.

"Yeah," said Paul. "They should have been able to build them bigger and better."

"Well, to me it's a case of a civilization losing knowledge. It wouldn't be the first time," John said. "Priests were famous for being secretive, and they held most of the deep knowledge. They must have carried it to their graves."

"You mean they didn't tell anybody—nobody?" Paul said.

"They told each other, but apparently that was too few. Unas looks to me like a bad imitation of the Great Pyramid. It looks like by then they had lost the knack."

"Look at this other one Paul," Samia said, directing our attention up ahead. "It's the oldest of all the pyramids, the Step Pyramid."

"It doesn't look like it's falling down."

"No, indeed," Samia said. "It was designed by Imhotep, the architect who invented the pyramid design."

"Was he a priest too?"

29

"He was the greatest of priests. In 2700 B.C., he was the High Priest of Heliopolis. And he was an astronomer and a physician too."

"They had doctors back then?"

"Sure" John said. "Medicine is another example of knowledge that got lost, temporarily at least. I've read that Imhotep made medicine from herbs, understood how our blood circulates and even performed surgery. That all had to be rediscovered two thousand years later by Hippocrates, the Greek father of modern medicine."

"Imhotep was so wise that people thought him a god," Samia said.

"Wasn't he associated with Thoth?" John asked.

"Yes, because Thoth is the god of wisdom and knowledge. And this is very important in measuring the esteem with which the ancient Egyptians held Imhotep. They did not usually recognize mortals as gods, but Imhotep brought so much knowledge to his people that he was said to be a god and a good man too."

"Can we climb up the steps?" Paul asked.

"No, it's much harder than it looks. Tomorrow you will go inside one of the pyramids at Giza."

"Imagine making someone a god because of their knowledge," I said. "When was the last time you heard about a scientist being made a saint?"

"The ancient Egyptians prized knowledge," Samia said. "That's how they were able to build a great civilization and accomplish great things. Did you know that the symbol for Lower Egypt is the Papyrus from which they made paper? This was a very important discovery because without papyrus all that would have been left is their tomb writings and paintings."

 "Where's Lower Egypt?" Paul asked.

"You are in it."

"Where's Upper Egypt?"

"It's to the south where you will fly in a few days. Ha, ha," she said. "Now you've learned that in Egypt north is down and south is up."

She pulled the van into the parking lot of a country restaurant that reminded me of a little oasis on the desert, a place where the desert dwellers might pitch their brightly colored tents. We sat under a bright blue, white and yellow canopy and ordered our lunch.

"That salad looks really good," I said, while peering at another diner's plate at a table next to ours.

"You know what the books say about uncooked food," Madeleine warned.

Samia looked at us as if we had hurled an insult. "It won't hurt you," she said. "This is a very clean place."

"I'm not going to risk it," John said

"I want lamb," Paul said.

"That sounds good," Natalie said. "Lamb kabobs would be fine with me."

"And me," Madeleine agreed.

After days of eating meat and cooked vegetables, the luscious tomatoes, crisp lettuce, olives and cheese became an irresistible temptation. Later that night I paid the price. The hotel sent up its standard remedy, a ten-ounce glass of squeezed lemon juice, not lemonade, just the pulp and juice of a lemon. It proved simple but effective.

"Rug making is an ancient craft in Egypt," Samia said on the way to the factory. "You will have a chance to make a purchase at a very good price."

"I'd be more interested in perfumes," Madeleine said. "I read that I can buy the pure extracts here."

"Yes, you can," Samia said. "I will take you to a perfumery when we return, but now we go to see rug making."

"This is shocking," Madeleine said to Samia's surprise, at the sight of a whole row of children weaving rugs. "They're only little girls!" she said. "Do they get an education?"

"Why yes," the proud factory owner said. "Look at their skill."

We watched their little fingers discolored with dye weave and knot the intricate patterns of their rugs from strands of wool.

"I mean, do they learn to read and write?"

"We do provide classes," he said, surprised at her indignation. "What they do here helps to provide for their families. That's very good."

The little girls didn't look miserable, I thought. They even smiled. I watched their delicate fingers weave and tie, weave and tie. I hoped he was telling the truth. "Where are the older girls?" I asked.

31

The owner looked confused by my question, so I rephrased it. "These girls are very young. What work do they do when they are older?"

"Oh," he said in comprehension. "They don't work here past sixteen. By then they are married."

What different cards fate deals us, I thought. I had no interest in making a purchase at the showroom, not wanting a reminder of whose tiny fingers wove the rug. When I was a child my mother would urge me not to let the food on my plate go to waste. She would say there are children in the world who go hungry. These little girls did not look hungry, but perhaps only because they spent their childhoods at work to prevent such a fate. I wished later that I had bought a rug.

Towards the close of what had been a busy and eventful day, we pulled up in front of Giza Giftery Perfumes near the pyramids. The perfumery was quite different from what my experience had been at American department stores, where well-groomed women stand behind glass cases filled with bottles of different sizes and descriptions and offer samples of fragrances from tester bottles that line the tops of those cases. Here we were greeted by sales manager Mr. Hassam, a tall, confident man whose poise and carriage suggested he was also the owner.

We walked up the stairs of the two-story building and entered the sales room, a sales room unlike any I had ever seen. The floors were covered in Persian carpets, and there were no counters or cases. Instead, sumptuous couches and cushions covered in beautiful, colorful silks in all shades of reds and roses and purples with golden tassels and trim filled the room. It was as if I had walked into a harem.

"Ladies and gentlemen, let me offer you some refreshment before we begin," Mr. Hassam said as he brought us to a little tearoom over to the side. "Tea or cola?" He left Samia to entertain Paul while he graciously escorted the four of us into his harem and invited us to lounge on his silk couches. As Madeleine, Natalie, John and I sank into the cushions, Mr. Hassam eyed all of four of us and then singled out John.

"You must be a Mohammed with many wives," he said to John and winked.

If I could have seen behind John's beard, I would surely have detected a blush.

"Oh no, this is my wife. And this is my mother and my sister," he said.

Mr. Hassam winked at John again and then began bringing little vials of scent for us to smell. "Try this, pure fragrance of jasmine. And here we have the rose and the lavender."

"Undiluted?" Madeleine asked.

"Pure and undiluted. Here are the fruit scents: lemon, orange and plum. Try them all."

The scents were brought to us in tiny glass bottles with gold tassels and caps. Their aromas filled the room. After we tested all the pure fragrances, and there were many, including frankincense and myrrh, Mr. Hassam suggested that we savor the prize of the house.

"We make our own blend. You must smell this." He looked at me and then at John, smiled and said, "You wear this and it will turn your man here into a horse." He looked at Natalie and said, "Wear this and you will have the man of your choice."

Embarrassed, we sniffed. It did smell good, really good. After about an hour of reclining on silk cushions and rating the scents, we made our purchases. We bought a lot. We took Mr. Hassam's card as he assured us that we could mail order further purchases later for Christmas perhaps.

Exhausted, we arrived back at our hotel. Samia walked us in as we nudged past the armed guards. "You stay here this evening," she said. "Enjoy one of the hotel restaurants. Yusef and I will be by tomorrow for your big trip to the pyramids." She pinched Paul on the cheek, we all said goodbye and Samia was gone.

"I wonder where she's off to," Madeleine said, her eyes following Samia through the door. "We know so little about her."

We had been in our room only a few minutes when Natalie called. "Meet us at the juice bar so that we can talk more about this?" John said. "You'd better not bring Paul." He hung up the phone, looking a little confused. "Stuart left a message at the hotel while we were out. He's left Cairo for Luxor just about an hour ago. You won't believe this. He's booked passage on the Queen Nuit. Natalie thinks it's pretty weird."

"Well, it is! Don't you think?"

"Unless he's trying to hook up with Natalie again and taking advantage of the opportunity. But that explosion in the market after he warned us to keep away makes me think there's something more going on here."

The juice bar was a poor substitute for a saloon, but you take what you can get. "Oranginas all around," I ordered.

"Don't you think the message from Stuart odd?" Natalie asked.

"Yes, I do," said John, not wanting to suggest the possibility that his motive could be romantic in case it wasn't. "If all he wanted to do is sail down the Nile, I'm sure there are many other cruises he could have booked."

"They must have had many extra rooms on ours," I said.

"Look Natalie, who is this Stuart guy anyway?" John asked.

"I've already told you everything I know about him. We used to date some, but I haven't seen him in months. I never felt comfortable asking him too much about himself when he was around, so I never did."

"I couldn't tell you earlier in front of Paul, but you know that phone call Samia got while we were at the museum?" John said.

"Yes, I was there when Yusef told her it was time to take us out into the country."

"Well, do you know the real reason why?" John asked.

"No, I mean, I just thought we were behind schedule, like she said."

About to burst, I said, "There was an explosion and gunshots at the market, the same market Stuart told Samia not to take us to."

Natalie looked stunned.

"We haven't had a chance to tell you before now," John said. "We didn't want to scare Paul and Mom."

"I had no idea. Do they know what it's about?"

"If they do, they didn't tell us," I said. "Samia said she doesn't believe it was a coincidence that Stuart told her not to take us to that market. I'm not even sure she thought our running into him in Cairo was a coincidence."

"Well, it was! How could it have been anything else?" Natalie said.

"Don't be upset," John said. "Samia hardly knows us so you can't blame her for thinking...."

"Thinking what?"

"Well, whatever."

"Maybe there will be something in tomorrow's newspaper that will explain it," she said.

"Don't count on it," I said. "This morning's paper was pretty slim on news."

"They can't ignore this. It happened in the biggest market in Cairo," John said.

"I've known Stuart for years," Natalie said, "worked with him, even dated him, and I have no idea what he's really about. We spent the entire day with Samia and she with us, and yet she believes we could be involved in some kind of conspiracy of secrecy with him. I have a headache. I think I'm going to get a quick taco at Pepe's Mexicano then go to bed."

"Good idea. I'll do the same but pass on the taco," I said, already feeling a bit queasy.

We awoke in the morning to the *Cairo Tribune* and the slimmest reporting possible on the events that had sent us scurrying out of the museum and the city. It reported that there had been an explosion at the market, likely caused by a vendor's faulty propane tank.

Chapter Six

Mystery number one when visiting Egypt are the Great Pyramids. Plenty of theories purport to explain them, but the supporting evidence is about as thin as the *Cairo Tribune*. Since our worldview suggests a linear historical progression from the Stone Age to the present, culminating in modern man at the apex of human development, our most accepted explanation supports that worldview. Slave laborers, we are told, built the pyramids by hauling gigantic stones on wooden ramps and piling them up somehow. This theory is full of holes, of course. In fact, when you look around Egypt linear historical progression is not evident. The rapid decline in pyramid engineering is just one example.

Mystery number two when visiting Egypt is modern Egypt. Yusef and Samia are part of a culture so different from our own that it is hard for us to comprehend. Training and employing children as rug weavers is seen as a social good when poverty is pervasive. And yet there is richness too. Wear this scent and you can have any man you want, Mr. Hassam had promised at his sumptuous perfumery. Then there are the politics of modern Egypt that to the tourist are opaque. Why did our hotel require armed guards to ensure the safety of its guests? And why did the article in the *Cairo Tribune* about the explosion at the market seem incomplete?

If we did not understand our hosts and their culture, they did not entirely understand us either. What was Samia imagining about us? Only one of us knew Stuart, and it was pure chance that she saw him yesterday. I had to acknowledge though that this Stuart guy is a bit of a mystery even for us. Why did he tell Samia not to take us to the very market that was likely bombed just a few hours later? And why did he book a reservation on our Nile cruise? Stuart is our common ground, I thought. None of us knows what he is up to. The very thought of him left me feeling exhausted.

I didn't ruminate long on these matters before the van arrived at the hotel. Paul, eager to go to the pyramids, pulled away from his grandmother, pushed through the doors, sped past the guards and leaped into the van. Madeleine ran behind in a vain effort to keep up. John scolded him but to little effect. Once we were seated, an intensely sweet odor filled the van and grew stronger the further we drove. I cracked the window open after I recognized it. It was unmistakable. It was Giza Giftery Perfumes Special Blend. And it was also unmistakable who was wearing it—Natalie. Fortunately, the drive from our hotel to Giza is short if the traffic is minimal, which it was.

"The Bedouin gather near the pyramids with their camels and offer rides to visitors like you for a small fee," Yusef said. "This is good; it helps them make a living."

"The Bedouin in Cairo?" I said.

"We're on the edge of the desert. They bring their camels in by day to make a living and return to their desert tents at night."

"Well, it sounds like fun," I said.

"Do they spit?" John asked.

"The Bedouin?" I said.

"No, the camels. I've heard that camels will spit at you."

A sly grin spread across Yusef's face. "Only if they like you. No, no, the camel driver will keep them from spitting on you. Although it is true that they spit sometimes."

"I don't want to ride a dumb camel. I want to go to the pyramids now!" Paul shouted full throttle.

"But Paul," Yusef said, "the camel driver will take you to the pyramids on a camel."

"That will take a long time. I want to go now!"

"I don't want to ride a camel either," Madeleine said.

"Well, I do," Natalie said.

"Yusef can drop Madeleine and Paul at the pyramids," Samia said. "I will stay with them. The rest of you can go out into the desert where the camel drivers are gathered. We can all meet at the pyramids when you ride in."

Giza, like most towns, has paved roads, shops, apartments and traffic. But all of that ends as one nears the pyramids. The Great Pyramid of Khufu is the most famous of the three. But almost as large

37

and standing next to it is the Pyramid of Chephren, and next to it, huge still but smaller than the other two, is the Pyramid of Mycerinos. The three stand together perfectly aligned on the flat, parched desert that surrounds them with the big Egyptian sky as their backdrop.

I expected large crowds but very few people were gathered. Then I considered that besides Stuart, I had not seen a single American since we arrived, not at the hotel, the museum and now the pyramids.

"You can get out here," Yusef said. Paul was the first to leap out of the van.

"Hold on Paul!" Madeleine ordered. Samia helped her out and the two of them ran to catch up with him.

"They will be all right," Yusef said. "Paul is just excited. I like to see visitors so excited."

Yusef stepped on the gas and drove past the pyramids and out into the desert where we approached a band of men in long traditional robes and turbans standing with their camels tied to makeshift posts. He made our arrangements for us and collected our fee, which he gave to the man in charge who brought out the first camel. Yusef explained that I would ride with John and Natalie would ride alone, but she wouldn't really be alone and neither would we. A camel driver would walk beside us, guide the camel to our destination and make sure it didn't spit, he said with a smile.

A handsome man in the prime of life came forward leading our camel. "Bon jour? Guten Tag? Good morning?"

"Good morning," John said.

"Ah, you English. My name is Moses."

"American not English," John said as he extended his hand. "I'm John."

The camel wore an elaborate saddle covered in a woven fabric of red, black, green and tan geometric designs, trimmed with long black tassels that hung well below the camel's belly. Brightly colored tassels adorned the base of the camel's neck, and a large red tassel sat on the top of his knobby head. He looked friendly enough.

The driver motioned the camel to kneel and then motioned John to climb up. John did so with a leap. Moses lifted me, raised the camel up on his hooves, and there we were, John holding the reins and me holding on to him for dear life. He asked for baksheesh. We were confused. We had just paid. The man in charge explained that we had paid for the use of the camel not our driver's services.

What could we do? We could never get off of this camel without Moses' help. So John asked how much, and he told us the recommended rate, which we happily paid. The men brought another camel forward for Natalie as we headed out into the desert. Everything in order and transactions complete, Yusef returned to his van to drive back to the pyramids where we would all meet.

You really do feel the hump you are sitting on when riding on a camel's back. It is hard to imagine galloping along on one of these beasts when you are clip clopping along in an ungraceful gait as we were. The desert in front of us was a vast, empty expanse, the pyramids off in the distance. To our rear was the group of Bedouin and Natalie, who with her driver had just begun her journey in our direction. After that long last look behind us, we paced onward towards the pyramids.

Moses was a very affable man with a command of English so we asked him many questions about life on the desert. His life and his preferences were like so many others who live outside the mainstream. This proud man would not give up his nomadic life for anything Cairo had to offer, he declared. His attachment to a culture that had survived on the barren desert for millennia was unassailable. What seemed a great hardship to us was no hardship for him. He was never without water or food, he said. He rejoiced in the camaraderie of his tribe and the pleasures and traditions of his culture.

As we rode along, chatted and laughed with this good-humored man we lost all sense of time. What is time on the desert anyway but sunsets and sunrises? We were alone in the midst of this great barren nothingness enjoying each other, the camel and the moment. As we drew nearer the pyramids, our comradeship was broken when another Bedouin appeared on horseback seemingly out of a blue sky. He smiled at Moses who warmly returned the greeting.

Moses looked at us and said, "He would like to take your picture on the camel." Surprised, John said that it didn't look like he had a camera. Moses pointed to the camera John was wearing around his neck.

"Oh! He will take our picture with my camera."

"Yes," Moses said.

John happily obliged, handing his camera to Moses who held it out to the man on horseback. The would-be photographer made a pass around Moses, grabbing the camera as he did. He then rode around us and began to snap pictures with the pyramids behind us. When he was done he sat motionless on his horse smiling, waiting. Moses seemed to be waiting too, but for what? Then we understood, baksheesh. What were we to do? He not only had the prized photos but our camera. And he had, after all, performed a service.

Our desert peace was short-lived after we realized that Natalie and her camel driver were nowhere in sight. We were close to the pyramids, and we could see nothing to our rear but empty desert, not even the camel station where our ride began. We asked Moses where Natalie and her camel driver might be.

He shrugged. "Do you want that I return you?"

We didn't know what to do. We might find Natalie and her driver if we headed back, but if we didn't, then what? Yusef had already driven the van back to the pyramids where we were to rendezvous. Besides, it would take a lot less time to get to the pyramids from where we were.

Buzzing erupted from John's person. He fumbled through the many pockets of his travelers vest before finding the heretofore-unused satellite phone. He clicked it on hoping to hear news of Natalie's whereabouts. "Hello, hello," he said, attempting to connect with a voice at the other end. There was only static until the phone clicked off. He punched in the numbers of Paul's phone. It rang, but again there was only static until the line disconnected.

"They must be trying to reach us about Natalie. Take us on to the pyramids quickly," John said.

"When I take camel back to herd," Moses said, "I fly like wind."

"Well, not that fast," I said knowing it wouldn't take much to topple me onto the ground.

We didn't fly, but we did pick up speed. John and I held on tight as we rocked to-and-fro perched upon our camel top saddle. Soon we could make out human figures, and as we got nearer, we could see they were waving at us. The phone rang again, but again there was only static until it disconnected. I counted the figures in the distance: one, two, three. If

Natalie were with them, there should be five: Samia, Yusef, Madeleine, Natalie and Paul. Natalie must be missing. But who was the other missing person?

"Maybe Natalie went back to the camel station and Yusef drove off to retrieve her," I said.

As we got closer the sizes of the members of this party became more evident. They were adults. Where was Paul? And if the calls we had received came from Paul's satellite phone, which they most certainly had, where was he calling from and why couldn't he connect?

Moses speeded up the camel as fast as was reasonable given that he had to walk beside it and we had to ride without falling off. Yet it felt like we were traveling across the desert at record-breaking slowness, as slow as time in a place that had none. At last we approached our destination to shouts piercing through the desert.

Moses lowered our camel to its knees, helped us off and thanked us for our company. As if to mock our riding ineptitude, he raised himself up on to the camel's back and rode like the wind, circling once and waving before he tore across the desert. He must be thinking how helpless these Americans are, I thought. And he was right. Out on the desert riding a camel we were helpless visitors from another world, foreigners who would not know how to survive in this harsh land without his aid and the help of our guides. I felt great admiration for this good-humored Bedouin. He had mastered the camel, the desert and the art of making a living from tourists like us.

Chapter Seven

"Quiet!" John said. "I can't make out what any of you are saying if you all talk at once. Mom, you go first."

"He ran off!" Madeleine said. "We arrived only to be told that we could not get into a pyramid until the afternoon, and today the Great Pyramid of Khufu will be closed. I bought afternoon tickets to visit the Chephren Pyramid. We went over there to that vendor," she pointed, "to get some bottled water, and when I looked up he was gone!"

"I think he was quite upset when he learned we would not be going into the Great Pyramid," Samia said. "He wanted to climb it, but I told him that is not permissible."

"This occurred before I returned," Yusef said. "I asked that the guards search the area for him. They agreed only to search Chephren since it is the only pyramid he could possibly have gotten into. They believe he is inside but have not yet located him."

"He must have tried to call me from his satellite phone, but all I heard was static," John said.

"All the more evidence that he's inside Chephren. Its massive stones would have disrupted the signal," Yusef said.

"Where's Natalie?" Madeleine asked, looking out at the desert in the direction from where we had just come.

"We don't know," I said. "When we left she was right behind us, but later when we looked for her she was gone. The desert was a blank."

"Maybe she was too uncomfortable on one of those beasts and asked to be taken back," Madeleine said.

"That's possible," Yusef said, looking worried.

"I thought that's what this dropped phone call was about," John said. "I hoped that Yusef had picked her up and brought her to you."

Yusef's expression turned to agitation. "John, you take charge of the search for Paul while I go look for her." He climbed into his van and waved goodbye before he shot across the hard, flat desert.

"Don't worry," Samia said to comfort us. "If anyone can bring

Natalie back, it's Yusef."

"What do you mean if anyone can bring Natalie back!" John said. "Why couldn't he?"

"Ninety percent of the time when this occurs it is only for robbery. They are left out on the desert until someone finds them. Yusef knows where to look," Samia said.

"What about the other ten percent?" he asked.

"She's attractive, unmarried and young. Someone might want her for a wife."

Madeleine began to sob. "What have I done?"

"Oh, Mom, it's not your fault," John said.

Madeleine had always wanted to go to exotic places. Her late husband had too many responsibilities to afford time for many family vacations, and Madeleine had four children to rear, which she had done admirably. But the most exotic experiences she could find near her hometown were her weekly visits to Dayton to meet with a Jungian dream group. So when this opportunity to go to Egypt arose, she was determined to take advantage of it. Besides, the message in the fortune cookie was a wonderful synchronicity that must be acted upon, and she was ready to see at least one of the ancient wonders of the world. But she never counted on her grandson running off or the disappearance of her daughter.

"You had better go with Samia over to the vendors and sit down," John said to his mom. He turned to Samia. "Could you make sure she gets more water? We're going to search for Paul."

"Well, what now?" I asked.

"Let me try phoning him again." John punched in the number. The phone seemed to connect, but quickly turned to static then click, disconnect. "Let's go over to the Chephren Pyramid and talk to the guards."

The guards were only letting so many people in at a time as others exited the pyramid, apparently not only to make the visit more enjoyable for the people inside but also to preserve the interior from too much exposure to human breath. We exhale carbon monoxide and moisture, which in too great a quantity can be damaging to walls whose remarkable preservation is due in large part to the dry, protected

43

conditions of their natural environment.

John approached a guard and explained that he was the uncle of the lost boy.

"He walked in; he must walk out," the guard said with an air of indifference. "It's only a matter of time."

Taken aback by the guard's nonchalance, John said, "Haven't you gone in to look for him?"

"He's hiding. He will come out when he's ready."

"How did he get in there in the first place without a ticket?" John asked.

"Because he's a child, he sneaked in unnoticed. He probably mixed in with a group."

"If he was able to sneak by you on his way in, wouldn't he be able to sneak past you on his way out?"

"We are looking for him now. We were not looking for him earlier."

"Could he have gotten into one of the other pyramids? I know he wanted inside Khufu."

"Not possible. This is the only pyramid he could have entered."

John did not feel reassured. In fact, he felt less confident these guards would find Paul than he had before he talked to this one.

"Why are you so agitated?" I said. "What the guard said makes sense. Paul has to come out sometime."

"If he's in there."

"Where else would he be?"

"I don't know, but their story makes little sense. There's no one for him to be hiding from. If he had gone in there, he would have come out by now."

"Well, if he isn't in there, where is he?"

"I know where he wanted to go, inside the Great Pyramid of Khufu."

"But he couldn't get in. It's closed."

"I know," John said as he looked around the area. "It looks like there's a dig going on way over there near the Sphinx. Maybe Paul got curious. Let's go over."

You really get to understand the size of these pyramids when you walk their outer rim. They are not just big they're massive.

"I can't believe they built these things five thousand years ago," I

44

said.

"Some people think they're older."

"Older! They are impossibly old already for their size and beauty," I said as I looked up at sharp angles leading to a sheared point. I was dumbfounded trying to imagine how with little or no technology they were built. "I don't know how they could have gotten enough men around these blocks of stone to lift them. And they couldn't just pile them up haphazardly and get these precise lines. Every huge stone had to be lifted and then put in place. What dedication, not only to build them but to figure out how to build them."

"They used to be covered in huge white granite casing stones," John said. "The stones weighed about fifteen tons each, and they were placed so close together that one could barely make out the seams. They must have shimmered in the sun when they were entirely intact. They practically do now."

"What happened to those casing stones?"

"They were stripped off of the pyramids to build 13th century mosques in Cairo. Evidence for the maxim that one age is built upon another."

"Yes, literally. Didn't you tell me once that the Romans invented concrete?"

"That's correct. I did."

"Well, the pyramids were built thousands of years before the Roman Empire so what's holding these stones together?"

"Nothing. They were cut and placed so precisely that they hold themselves in place."

I pictured the limestone fences along several country roads back home, stone fences nearly five thousand years newer than these pyramids. They too were built using no concrete, and most of them had already partially collapsed and looked decrepit.

"They really knew how to build them," I said. "Seriously John, I can tell you as a folklorist, a student of culture, that the society that built these pyramids was very old. Think of all the knowledge they had to acquire before these pyramids could have been designed and erected. These artifacts are ancient, but a far older culture must have preexisted them. To me they no longer look like the beginning or even the near beginning

45

of a civilization, rather more like its apex."

"Amen. You're preaching to the choir."

Once we were on the other side of the pyramid, we spied a man ahead of us looking as if he were listening to the heart of the earth with a stethoscope. He wore what you would expect an archaeologist engaged in desert digs to wear: khaki pants and shirt, even the traditional wide brim khaki hat. He looked up at us as we approached, smiled and returned to his work.

"I hate to interrupt," John said, "but it's important that I speak with you."

The distinguished looking gentleman who appeared to be around sixty looked up again and smiled patiently as if he were in no hurry and interruptions were quite tolerable. He held his hand out to John, "Dr. Barry Short," he said.

John shook his hand and replied as politely as he was addressed. "Dr. Short, I'm searching for my nephew, a ten year old...."

"I bet you mean Paul," Dr. Short interrupted. "Yes, we had a nice chat. He was here just an hour or so ago. He looks like you. Did you say he is your nephew?"

"Yes, he is. Do you know where he went?"

"Well, I can't say. He was here and then he was gone. I didn't actually see him leave."

"What did you talk about?" I asked, hoping there was a hint in their conversation of where he might have gone.

"There's only one thing to talk about when you stand here on the Giza Plateau."

"The pyramids," John said.

"Of course, that and my work."

"What are you doing out here?" John asked.

"Listening to the earth. If you listen closely, the sound creates a picture of what's below. That way you can avoid unnecessary digging."

"What are you digging for?"

"You see that dig site over there?" Dr. Short pointed towards the site we had observed nearer the Sphinx. "I have discovered the openings of what could be a series of tunnels leading in the direction of the pyramids, but before I excavate further, I am trying to map these tunnels using this

46

device." He pointed to his equipment.

I smiled in amusement, but I'm sure Dr. Short couldn't guess why. It was the irony of his name. He was such a tall man to be named Short. John's last name was just as ironic. I looked up its meaning once and learned that it meant short, bald man. Like Dr. Short, John is also tall and has exceptionally thick hair. These two men already share two things in common, I thought, their love of Egyptology and names that don't describe them.

Just then another piece of equipment activated. The satellite phone buzzed inside John's pocket. To his relief this time there was a voice, Paul's voice.

"Uncle John?"

"Where are you?"

"I got inside."

"Khufu?"

"Yes, the Great Pyramid. I tried to call you earlier but the phone wouldn't work."

"I know. It buzzed, but there was only static."

"I think the stone was stopping my signal from getting to the satellite."

"Where are you now?"

"I'm inside."

"Yes, I know Paul but where?"

"I don't know. Someplace. I've been looking for the opened shaft so my signal could reach the satellite. I must be at the right shaft now, the shaft of Orion because the phone works. The other ones didn't."

"You must have been in the Queen's Chamber before. Is there a sarcophagus nearby?"

"A what?"

"A big stone box."

"Yes."

"You found it! You're in the King's Chamber. Stay where you are, and I'll come get you."

"I'm cold!"

"Just hold on. Don't move from where you are. Do you hear me?"

"Yes, I hear you, but I'm cold. Are there mummies in here?"

47

"No, no mummies."

John, realizing just how frightened Paul had become, tried to give the boy something to focus his mind on while he awaited his rescue. "You found it Paul. You found the shaft, the path to Orion."

"Heaven?"

Feeling embarrassed to repeat such a naive interpretation in front of an obviously learned Egyptologist John nonetheless put his personal distress aside. "Yes, Paul, heaven."

Dr. Short smiled, "A young Egyptologist in the making. Aren't we all looking for heaven? Weren't they too, the ancient Egyptians?"

John blushed. "That's how he understood the explanation I gave him of the King's Chamber shaft pointing to Orion, you know, in *The Orion Mystery*.

"I know it well. Don't be embarrassed. I was serious when I said that Egyptologists are looking for heaven. Why else would we spend our lives trying to piece together this ancient civilization?" he said, with his arms outspread and his palms turned up. Then he put his fingers together making a pyramid with his hands, and with his eyes steady and piercing, he said, "We do it because the ancient Egyptians devoted themselves to the pursuit."

"How do you suppose Paul got into that pyramid?" John asked.

"Follow me." Dr. Short led us over to the dig site. "Well, well, my lantern is missing. We won't know for certain until we talk to the boy, but I suspect he made his way into one of these excavated tunnel openings and found a path. I will have to ask him which one. He might be able to help me with my charts. Such a young Egyptologist! Come with me, and I will have the officials unlock the entrance."

Chapter Eight

It only took a few words from Dr. Short to a certain someone and we were in.

"Perfect, they turned on a few lights. They're not much, but they're better than total darkness. Good thing the boy had the foresight to take my lantern."

The temperature plummeted as well as the light. It was hard to imagine Paul wandering around here alone in the dark with only a lantern. His determination to get inside must have trumped his natural fear.

"Watch your head," Dr. Short said. "If you think this passage is small, you should take a look at the original entrance. It was hidden away for eons and still isn't used. This one was slashed out much later by the Arabs."

We wandered down a narrow corridor until we arrived at a crossroads of intersecting tunnels.

"Look up there. That one leads to the original entrance," Dr. Short said.

Before us was an ascending tunnel that double backed in the direction we had just come from.

"Ouch," John said, putting his hand against his head in a reflex motion.

"Be careful," Dr. Short said. "That one's only three and half by four feet and leads to an entrance fifty-five feet above the ground."

"How in the world did they ever use it?" I asked. "Only a boy the size of Paul could get through, and even he would have to crawl."

"Just one of the mysteries we're trying to solve," Dr. Short said.

Instead of taking the tunnel that ascended to the original opening, we turned into a larger tunnel that descended until we came to a halt near an opened iron door that partially blocked an unlit passage that looked as if it sank into a dark hole.

"Hmm, that's interesting," Dr. Short said. "That leads to the

49

Subterranean Chamber. No one is allowed down there. Not even I am allowed to enter, and I'm licensed."

"Why not?" I asked.

"Too dangerous, they say."

"It doesn't look very inviting," I said. "I hope Paul isn't down there."

"I don't think so. Not now at least. But we'll check later if we don't find him."

"John, maybe you should give Paul another call to make sure he stayed put," I said.

"That probably won't do any good from where we are now," Dr. Short said. "It's your signal that would be blocked by these massive stones."

"You're right. My brain isn't working in here. Maybe there's not enough air."

"Onward and upward to the King's Chamber," Dr. Short said as he altered our direction and led us to a lighted passage that went further into the pyramid.

"This place is quite a maze," John said.

"It is particularly so for the uninitiated. Keep your head down."

We soon arrived at another fork and another decision.

"That corridor leads to the Queen's Chamber," Dr. Short pointed. "He's not in there because its shafts have no exits. Follow me through this other passage into the Grand Gallery."

"At last," John said, once we entered the Grand Gallery. He could finally straighten up. It opened into the King's Chamber from where we could see a flicker of what looked like lantern light. Covered in dirt and sand and leaning against one of the huge blocks of stones next to the southern shaft opening was the lost boy. He had not moved a hair, just as his uncle had ordered. Paul scrambled to his feet and rushed into John's arms.

"I told you we would be right here," John said. "You feel cold."

"I'm real cold. It took you a long time."

"We got here as fast as we could," John said and used his hands to rub some of his body heat into Paul's arms since none of us had anything to wrap him in.

"There, do you feel better?"

"Look here at the shaft of Orion!" Paul exclaimed.

John peered in but saw only darkness.

"They're quite long," Dr. Short said. "It's not like looking through a keyhole."

"Dr. Short!" Paul said, recognizing the man who had accompanied us. He looked nervously at the lantern he was holding and handed it over. "I borrowed this, thank you."

"I know. And it's a good thing you did too. You really could have gotten lost without it."

Overwhelmed with excitement and relieved that he wasn't in too much trouble, Paul pointed to a very large box on the opposite wall. "The sarcophagus," he said.

"Did you climb inside?" John asked.

"Are you kidding? There may be a mummy inside"

"No, there are no mummies in there. Look." John took Paul over and together they peered inside before he leaped up, climbed into the large stone box and stretched himself out. "See, it just fits." We all laughed.

"There are actually two shafts in here," Dr. Short said. "One points north and the other south. There's a northern and southern shaft in the Queen's Chamber too."

Climbing out of the sarcophagus, John asked whether Dr. Short knew anything about a hidden door in the Queen's Chamber. "Isn't someone building a small robot with a camera to get in behind it?"

"Oh, you're speaking of the work of Rudolf Gantenbrink. He discovered that door at the end of the shaft in the Queen's Chamber using the first robot he built, 'Upuaut.' He has determined there's some kind of hidden chamber behind it and has been trying to get permission to open it up to exploration using another one of his robots. Let's go down there, and I'll show you before we leave. Are you all right Paul?"

"Sure!"

We slowly descended the Grand Gallery, and at its foot made a turn into a corridor that led to the Queen's Chamber.

"This room is much smaller," I said.

"Yes, some people think it was abandoned in favor of the larger King's Chamber. Here's the shaft," Dr. Short said pointing to the

51

southern wall.

"Where's the door?" John asked.

"You can't see it from here. It's about two hundred feet in."

"That's peculiar," I said.

"Yes, and another peculiarity is that it's made of wrought iron. We didn't know they could make that metal when these things were built."

"What's behind it?" Paul asked

"That's another mystery."

"When do you think Gantenbrink will be able to explore it with his robot?" John asked.

"I doubt whether he will ever explore it. He's been denied permission, and the Egyptians have taken over the project."

"If he found the door in the first place, why did they stop him?" John asked.

"That's a bureaucratic mystery, but one more easily understood. Who has the right to explore? Who has the right to the discoveries? And in the final analysis, who has a right to the knowledge?"

"Who has the right to decide this?"

"Why the Egyptian government, of course. For years they had very few rights while the British and French came in and took what they wanted back to Europe."

"Like Napoleon," Paul said.

"Yes, like Napoleon. Thanks or no thanks to Napoleon, depending on how you look at it, one of the most important finds in Egypt, the Rosetta Stone sits in a museum in London instead of the museum in Cairo. So you can't really blame the Egyptian government, can you now."

"But the risks," John said, "the risks of holding knowledge too closely. They could repeat what happened that caused the secrets of the Great Pyramids to be lost."

"They could. We run the risk that the secrets of the great Imhotep himself will remain just that, secrets, if when they're uncovered, they are revealed to only a few. Right now I serve on a committee of Egyptian, American and European archaeologists trying to resolve certain issues involving the rights to research. I must tell you it's a thorny problem. We don't want the ancients to be exploited. We don't want valuable archaeological sites destroyed."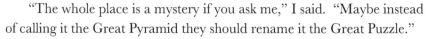

"The whole place is a mystery if you ask me," I said. "Maybe instead of calling it the Great Pyramid they should rename it the Great Puzzle."

"It's a puzzle to us," Dr. Short said. "But it must have made sense to ancient Egyptians. Our task is to get inside their minds and see it as they did. I'm not always sure that's possible. At other times I feel the opposite. I think the ancient and modern Egyptian minds aren't so different; both are equally protective of certain knowledge. Alas, my latter frame of mind leaves me no more optimistic than my former."

"You know what else strikes me," I said. "I saw photos of tombs at the Cairo Museum. Their common characteristics are the ornate decoration, detailed wall paintings and stylized hieroglyphics. The inside of this pyramid is plain. I would call it austere. Could they be products of very different times?"

"A good observation, but I'm afraid I have no answers. Only one thing has become certain to me about 'different times,' and that is that they might not be as different from our own in their fundamentals. All societies have their self-appointed guardians of knowledge. Even in our own time when we value a free exchange of information, we still guard or attempt to guard what we deem dangerous. We keep our weapons programs secret for as long as we can. To sell those secrets or give them away would be considered treasonous. And look how our politicians try to conceal anything that might reveal them as flawed human beings, which of course they all are as are all of us. But they believe that we demand from them human perfection, and maybe we do. So they must guard the secrets of their own fallibility."

"Could the mystery of the Great Pyramid be dangerous knowledge?" Paul asked.

"Yes, it's possible that this knowledge is truly dangerous. Or it's possible that its dissemination could have been believed dangerous to the priests for other reasons, political perhaps. And it's also possible that the current guardians of these pyramids find such knowledge potentially dangerous for entirely different reasons. So they, like their ancient ancestors, may want to control its acquisition and dissemination. But we should go now. They're probably wondering what happened to us."

So they were. As our eyes were adjusting to the bright desert sun,

John saw standing at the pyramid entrance the very guard he had questioned earlier at the Chephren Pyramid.

"You found the lost boy," the guard said.

"We did," John said.

"Dr. Short has a permit, but you do not. You must pay for three admissions."

"How much?" John pulled out his wallet without an argument, having gotten the best tour of the Great Pyramid of Khufu he could have ever wanted.

"Thank you. We will never forget it," John said, extending his hand to Barry Short.

"Or you!" I added

"Yeah, and thanks for the lantern," Paul said, "and coming to get me out."

"Wait!" Dr. Short said, "You're not leaving so soon, are you?"

"My mother's waiting for us over near the vendors. She's worried about Paul so we really ought to get over there."

"I can certainly understand why," Dr. Short said looking down at the boy. "But I have many questions for the young archaeologist. Do you mind if I tag along?"

"Of course not. But there's another thing I should mention before we get over there. My sister is missing too."

"Your sister!"

Chapter Nine

"If only Sam were here," Madeleine sobbed.

"Sam was your husband?" Samia asked.

"Yes, he would know what to do," she said as she twisted her hankie into knots.

"Don't worry. Yusef will find her," Samia said gently patting her arm. "Oh, look! Here comes Paul."

"You're back!" Madeleine said, opening her arms to the truant boy. "Where did you go off to? You nearly worried me to death."

"Oh, Grandma," Paul said with a hug.

"We found him inside the Great Pyramid," John said.

"How did he get in there?" Samia asked,

"That's a long story. Any news about Natalie?"

Samia sighed. "Yusef called about an hour and a half ago. He was not able to find her at the usual spots."

"Maybe this fellow left her elsewhere," John said.

"Yusef learned from the other men where their tribe is camped. He's driving further into the desert to try to locate them."

"Why would Natalie have been taken to their camp?" John asked.

Dr. Short butted in before Samia could answer. "Your sister has been kidnapped?"

"I wouldn't say kidnapped," John said. "She took a camel ride and hasn't come back."

"Is she married?" he asked.

"No."

"I thought not. You can't let a young, unmarried woman wander alone in the desert."

"We didn't let her wander alone in the desert," Madeleine insisted. "She is with us!"

"Oh, Mom, I forgot to introduce you. This is Dr. Barry Short. He helped us find Paul."

"It is very nice to meet you, and thank you for your help. I'm just so

55

upset."

"Why certainly you are. Who could blame you? I didn't mean to add to your worries," he said as he seated himself next to Madeleine. "I'm sure your daughter will be just fine. The camel driver may have thought he was doing her a favor."

"What do you mean?" John asked.

"Well, to these desert dwellers marriage is very important, more important than it is to us. He may have thought your sister was desirous of a husband. That's why they practice polygamy, you know, for the sake of the women."

"I can't believe it's for the sake of the women," Madeleine said.

"No, it is! If there are more women than men, which there often are, they believe it's a man's duty to see that all of them are protected."

Samia, a much more sophisticated Egyptian than the desert dwellers, concurred but added that it was also possible that Natalie had no money and the fellow is keeping her until we arrive and pay him for protecting her.

"Baksheesh?" I said.

Looking embarrassed, Samia nodded.

John turned his attention back to Dr. Short. "Why would this man think that Natalie wanted to be married?"

Now, I was embarrassed. I recalled the strong scent of Giza Giftery's Special Blend that morning when I sat next to Natalie in the van. And then I remembered what Mr. Hassam had said to her when he brought out the scent, "This will get you any man you want." I wondered if it could get you a man you didn't want. I blushed at the thought of it, but determined to keep this embarrassing detail to myself.

"Why did you run off like that?" Madeleine asked Paul.

"Because they weren't going to let us in the big pyramid, and I had to find that shaft of Orion. And I did Grandma, I found it!"

Madeleine shot a critical glance at John, as if to say, see what you've caused.

Dr. Short, still sitting next to Madeleine and apparently to good effect, told her how Paul happened upon him near his dig site as he was monitoring the earth in an effort to chart underground tunnels leading to the pyramid. "Paul is quite the young archaeologist. When I wasn't looking he took my lantern, crawled into one of the tunnel entrances we had only recently opened and charted the tunnel to the pyramid for us."

Enjoying the praise, Paul smiled.

Madeleine shot him a look. "You took Dr. Short's lantern without his permission!"

"I apologized!" he said.

"Yes he did," said the archaeologist. "Sometimes in this business you have to take a few risks." He winked at Paul. "Tell me now, what did you find? Describe the tunnel for me."

"When I first climbed down there were two. I crawled through one for a while, but it got real small. So I backed out."

"How small?"

"You wouldn't have been able to squeeze through it. I couldn't. So I crawled through the other, and the further I got, the bigger it got. Pretty soon I could stand up and walk."

"Could I have stood up and walked?"

"If you ducked your head you probably could."

"What was it made out of? Was it lined?"

"Big stones I think. It was dark. I just kept walking, and then there was this iron door that I had to push real hard to open. And then I was in a big, dark room I guessed inside the pyramid."

"How big?"

"Big! But there weren't any shafts. I looked! Then the door clanked shut behind me while I was looking around. I didn't know how it could do that, and when I tried to pull it open it wouldn't budge. I tried to call Uncle John right away, but the phone didn't work. I figured out that all the stone was causing interference with the satellite, and if I could get to the shaft of Orion my phone signal would probably work."

"Smart boy!"

"I saw some steps and an open door at the top. Uncle John had shown me a drawing of the pyramid, so I knew you had to climb up to get to the King's Chamber, so I walked up the stairs until I got to the door."

"Why Paul, I believe you found the secret entrance into the Great Pyramid! Hmm, maybe that's why the Subterranean Chamber has been kept off limits all these years."

57

"I thought I was in the Queen's Chamber, and if I walked up the path, I would be in the King's Chamber where the shaft of Orion is. That's the way the drawing looked. But when I went through the door there were three paths. One went down, so I knew that wasn't right. The other went up, but I thought I was already up enough, so I took the path that was flat that led into a chamber. I thought it was the King's Chamber. I even found shafts. I kept trying to call Uncle John, but the phone still didn't work. I tried lots of times."

"Were you scared?" I asked.

"A little. So I took the other path that went down, but then it started going up. It got real small. I had to get down on my hands and knees again. So I decided to back out."

"You took the path to the original entrance," Dr. Short said. "If you had kept going, you would have come out fifty-five feet above the base of the pyramid. An iron grate would have stopped you from crawling out of it, and if you had yelled, I don't think you would have been heard."

"But he could have used his phone," John said.

"Yes, yes to be sure. Then what did you do?"

"I took the other path leading up. It was big."

"The Grand Gallery," Dr. Short said.

"Then I got to the other chamber, the real King's Chamber. I found shafts there too, and when I tried the phone, it worked. So I found Uncle John and the shaft of Orion."

"What did you do while you waited for us?" John said.

"I just sat and thought about things. What it would be like to be shut up there forever. I thought that if it were night, I could see Orion through the shaft. I wondered if Orion lights the chamber at night, but I hoped I wouldn't still be in there to find out. I wondered what heaven looks like—things like that."

"You looked really happy to see your Uncle John," I said.

"I was!"

We all sat silently for a few moments, all of us imagining what it would be like to be lost and shut up in the Great Pyramid. I was thankful that we had rented the satellite phones. Then the sound of Samia's satellite phone broke our silence.

"You've got her!" she said into her phone and then looked at us.

"Yusef's got Natalie. He will return with her soon."

"Thank Heavens!" Madeleine said.

"I can't wait to hear her story," I said.

Dr. Short turned to Paul as we awaited Natalie's arrival. "When you are a few years older, I hope you come back. You can help me with my work."

"Please don't give him any more ideas," Madeleine said.

"Now, Madeleine, it would be very good for him," Dr. Short said. "You will realize this later on. In a few years Paul will be quite an accomplished young man. I guarantee it."

"That's them," I said, detecting a fast approaching spot out on the desert.

John adjusted his glasses. "You've got sharp eyes."

Minutes later Yusef pulled up. Natalie looked okay. In fact, she looked pretty good, not frightened or frazzled at all. "Hi," was all she said. I was puzzled by her nonchalance.

"What happened to you?"

"Oh, nothing, nothing, Amr just took me for a little ride out into the desert to meet his family."

"Nothing! I've been worried sick," Madeleine said.

Natalie curtly apologized and fell silent. I know Natalie's moods, and I could see she wasn't going to tell us anything until she was good and ready to.

Yusef waved John and me away from the reunion. "I'm sorry to ask, but I had to pay one hundred American dollars for Natalie."

"Baksheesh?" I said.

"No, robbery," John growled.

"Baksheesh," Yusef said. "This was a most unusual situation. The camel driver showed Natalie great hospitality. His mother and sisters cooked for her. They welcomed her into their tent."

"This Amr fellow wasn't intending on making her one of his many wives, was he?" John asked.

"I think he and his family hoped she might become his only wife; a fellow like that can only afford one. She had no idea. She seemed fine when I got there, happy to see me, but fine. So, I took Amr aside, and it took some negotiation on my part."

59

"Well, wouldn't that have told her something, I mean, if he made a pass at her," I said, finding it inconceivable that Natalie didn't have a clue.

"You don't understand these people. His family was courting her. She did not understand the way a woman of his tribe would have understood, and he and his family did not understand that she did not understand. Her gracious acceptance of their meal, from their point of view, indicated an interest in an offer that, fortunately, had not yet been formally made before I arrived. It's a good thing too. It saved her much embarrassment."

"It sure is a good thing you got there," John said, pulling his wallet out of one of his inside vest pockets. "No, I mean it. I really appreciate the rescue. Is a travelers check okay?"

The others had already made plans to have dinner that evening with Barry Short by the time we rejoined them.

"What about the Sphinx?" John asked the group.

"Yeah," Paul chimed in. "I want to go to the Sphinx."

"Thanks to you I'm exhausted," Madeleine said. "I've got to get some rest before this evening."

"If you will be back in Cairo after your Nile cruise, I would be happy to give you the grand tour of the Sphinx," Dr. Short said.

"They will have a final day here," Yusef said, "in about a week when they return."

"So, dinner at eight and the Sphinx in a week," John said.

We piled into the van minus Dr. Short. Samia whispered to Yusef who nodded in agreement. She turned around to us and said, "There's a shop I would like to take you to before we return to the hotel. I think you'll like it."

"What kind of shop?" I asked.

"A jewelry maker," she said. She showed us her necklace, a long gold chain with a golden oblong piece hanging from it containing beautiful carved images. "This is a cartouche."

"What are those carvings?" I asked.

"My name written in hieroglyphs." She looked at Natalie. "It will protect you. The ancient Egyptians carved the names of the most important people into stone and encircled them like this." She pointed to the elongated circle of gold that surrounded the beautiful hieroglyphs. "Your name is protected in this manner as is your person."

A cartouche, I thought, an Egyptian charm, more evidence that ancient Egypt continues to live on in modern Egypt. They share its identity, even its magic.

Yusef made a quick turn into a street full of people, outdoor markets, shops, donkey carts and cars squeezed into spaces that weren't designed for them, which is where we parked before entering a shop called The Golden Bazaar.

Two very polite young men greeted us to ascertain our interest. Natalie and I were the sole takers, apparently the only two of our group who believed we might need a little protection. Or perhaps we were the only two who were superstitious enough to think that our names carved in golden hieroglyphs and enclosed in an elongated circle would provide it. One showed me several sizes of cartouche I could choose from and different lengths of matching twenty-four caret gold chains.

"Write your name here for me," the designer said. "Please print."

I wrote out the letters of my name.

"That is a very good name," he said.

"It is?"

"Yes, it is," he said, stealing a glimpse into my eyes. "You are your name. This is a good one."

"How so?"

"The first letter 'L' is the lion. The golden lion is Ra, who represents courage and protection of others. It stands on the second letter 'I,' which means feather, a very important hieroglyph."

"Doesn't your heart have to be light as a feather to be admitted into heaven?"

"Yes, the feather is truth, justice, morality. If you have all of these, you will be admitted. It is a good base upon which the lion stands. And the feather rests on 'N,' the hieroglyph for water, which is the source of life and wisdom. And below, that is the hieroglyph representing your letter 'D,' the helping hand, an expression of greatest wisdom. And the last letter here, 'A' represents the eagle, who is the protector, the goddess of all nature." He looked up at me. "The goddess nature is the wellspring from which emerges her highest self, charity. It is from charity all wisdom comes. Her greatest gift of charity, which she has given to humans, is our capacity for truth and justice, which Ra, the golden lion protects."

"My name says all of that?"

"It is a beautiful name."

I had always thought of my name as rather plain and never really considered it to have any kind of moral dimension. Now, I felt I had a lot to live up to, and I didn't feel up to the task. After all, I came here to get protection not to learn that I must be protection.

The transactions were quickly completed. Our cartouches would be made that night, and Yusef would pick them up in the morning.

Chapter Ten

John finally broke several minutes of silence as the three of us quietly sipped Oranginas at the hotel juice bar. "Well, what happened?" he asked.

"I'm not sure how to explain it," Natalie replied.

"Well, try. I am all ears."

"It's simple really. The camel driver and I got to talking and the next thing I knew I looked around and didn't see you guys. I told Amr—that's his name—I said to him, I couldn't see you. He said you were just up ahead, that the sun obscures one's vision out on the desert or something like that."

"What were you talking about?" I asked.

"He told me about himself and about how they live on the desert."

"Our driver talked a lot about that too," I said. "It was interesting. I almost felt like we had become friends."

"I felt the same way. He even asked me questions about myself."

"You didn't tell him you weren't married, did you?" John asked.

"Well, that did come up eventually, but not like that. I told him I was originally from Ohio, but I moved to the Washington D.C. area for work, and I live alone with my cat."

"Oh, lord Natalie. He probably felt sorry for you."

"I told him that he needn't, that I love my job, enjoy my life and just haven't met the right guy. Then he told me about his family. His father died several years ago so he supports his mother and sister. He said they were camped nearby and asked if I would like to meet them and see for myself how the Bedouin live. He said it wouldn't take long."

"So you agreed to go," John said.

"Yes, he didn't kidnap me, if that's what you thought. I assumed it would be only a few minutes out of our way. I couldn't really tell how far away we had gotten until Yusef drove me back."

"Well, what happened while you were out there?" I asked.

"Nothing much. The camp is an amazing sight. All those tents gathered on the desert. I was surprised at how attractive and comfortable they are. He introduced me to his mother and sister who are very nice. They offered me food and drink. I didn't want to be rude so I accepted. I thought it would only be a snack and he would take me right back. I didn't realize they meant to cook a whole meal. At that point I didn't know what to do. After accepting their offer, how could I say I've changed my mind, I want to go back now? They were so gracious. How could I say that?"

"What did they serve?" I asked.

"There was lamb. And there were these little spicy pancakes. I don't know what they're called, but they're delicious. They told me they'd teach me how to make them. And there was fruit. I don't know where they get it on the desert, but they had a lot of it."

John, barely able to contain his temper, said, "They would teach you how to make them! When were they going to do that?"

"I know, I know, it got a bit awkward. I didn't know what to say. They were very kind people, and I didn't want to insult them. Then Yusef came."

"You were lucky for that," John said, his mood slightly assuaged. "So what happened then?"

"Well, he asked to speak to Amr privately. When they returned, Yusef asked me to go with him. Amr's mother and sister looked quite upset. I don't know why. I was going to leave eventually anyway. Amr looked sad too when he helped me up and led me to Yusef. It was a very awkward parting."

"Did Yusef explain to you what had happened?" John asked.

"Not really. He told me desert people are a very old people, with very old traditions that are far different from his own or mine, and that I should forgive them. I told him I had nothing to forgive them for. They were very kind and polite. He didn't say any more about it. We talked mostly about Paul's disappearance."

"He didn't tell you that you were being courted?" I asked.

"Being courted! No, he didn't say anything like that."

"He told us that you were being courted," John said, "not only by Amr but by his whole family. Your acceptance of their hospitality from their point of view indicated your interest."

64

Natalie flushed. "How embarrassing. It began to feel awkward, but...."

"Think about it," John said. "Why would they offer to teach you how to make little spicy pancakes if they hadn't thought you'd be around for a while?"

"I see what you mean. But why would Amr think I would marry him?"

"Dr. Short says in their tradition women don't stay unmarried for long," I said. "How old is Amr's sister?"

"I don't know, about thirteen or fourteen. Still a baby I guess."

"And you're thirty!" I said. "Amr probably thought you're desperate to get married."

"Oh, I feel like an idiot. I had no idea. I wonder what Yusef thinks of me now. He probably thinks I'm an idiot."

"No he doesn't," I said. "That's what he was trying to tell you about different traditions. He knows you didn't understand what was happening, and neither did Amr and his family for that matter. It was all a cultural misunderstanding."

John, not so inclined as I to dismiss the incident so lightly, particularly since he had to pay out one hundred dollars to get Natalie out of this mess said, "Well, it's a good thing that Yusef found you when he did or you probably would have married Amr in your eagerness to be gracious, and we would have all ended up in Bedouin divorce court."

"John!" I said, giving him a look that would quiet an angry bear. "Natalie, just chalk it up as a very interesting experience. No harm done. But if I were you, I would be more careful when and around whom I wear Mr. Hassam's Private Blend." She blushed again.

We rested in our hotel room for several hours without incident. There were no abductions, no lost child, no mysterious messages from Stuart and no explosions in the market. All was peaceful in the Cairo Kingsley during this late afternoon. Paul knocked on our door at about seven to make sure we were up and ready for dinner. He had been riding the elevators and surveying the hotel's restaurants for the last hour or so. He was scrubbed cleaner than I had ever seen him.

"Looks like your grandmother did a job on you," I said.

"Yeah. Can we go to the Japanese restaurant tonight? They have

65

sushi."

"We will all decide when we meet in the lobby. Now, don't get into any more trouble," I said, as I shooed him out of our room.

John shook his head. "Now he wants sushi."

By eight we were all gathered in the lobby to meet Barry Short who had arrived promptly. Dr. Short had obviously made a real impression on Paul in part because he recognized this ten year old was special, and the ten year old knew it. Thus, a mutual admiration society was formed. The subject rapidly shifted to which of the hotel restaurants we would choose. Paul lobbied hard for the Japanese.

"Why eat Japanese when you're in Egypt? I'll take you to one of the nicest little restaurants I know," Dr. Short said, "the Blue Nile."

"Yusef said we shouldn't leave the hotel without him," the ever-cautious Madeleine said.

Barry assured her and the rest of us that we would be perfectly safe with him. Paul easily relented on the Japanese restaurant, so that was that. We were off to a place called the Blue Nile.

Dr. Short gave the hotel guards baksheesh for watching his jeep. Or maybe baksheesh was necessary payment for parking in an unlawful spot. We didn't know, and we didn't care. We were in good hands, and we knew it. Yet I detected a certain reckless glint in Barry Short's eyes, a kind of rebelliousness that I sometimes see in Paul's face when he is about to do something naughty. In Dr. Short's much older face, however, the expression didn't suggest a transitory state of rambunctiousness but a more permanent condition, which made me wonder about him just a little. This man is an adventurer, I thought, but a competent one.

"I'm sorry, you're going to have to pile in. It's not often that I carry six in this thing. It's good for running back and forth across the desert, but that's about all. Madeleine, you get in the front with me."

Paul sat on John's lap to make enough room for the rest of us to squeeze into the back seat. We peeled along Cairo streets, the wind in our now mussed hair as the stars rose into the clear night sky. Soon we were back in Giza. We turned down a little strip, slowed, and there we were just outside the Blue Nile, written in Arabic on a neon sign. Next to the letters were three wavy blue lines one on top of another like the hieroglyphic symbol for water I had seen earlier at the jewelers. The enthusiasm with which Dr. Short was greeted when we walked in made it obvious he was a welcome and regular patron of this establishment.

After greetings and handshakes, we were escorted to a very nice table in the rear. The restaurant's name was appropriate, I noted, as we walked past a row of tables that were flooded with low, watery blue light that seemed to rise up from the floor and poured forth from wall sconces. Over to the right was a little stage with white lights where a small group of men played and sang in traditional Egyptian style. Horned instruments made high-pitched sounds that seemed to mimic the undulating curves of the written language while the singer's chant vocalized emotion in its sounds.

"Better than Japanese," Dr. Short said and winked at Paul.

We were seated around a large round table. The waiter began handing us all menus, but Dr. Short stopped him telling him we would only need one.

"The menu is in Arabic," he said. "Unless one of you surprises me and tells me you know the language, I will order for us all."

"That would be wonderful," Madeleine said. "Please do."

"I'll order a feast we can all share. Take what you like. Don't take the other. That sort of thing. Is that okay?"

"Sounds great," Natalie said.

The waiter returned and the order began. "We will have a large maza with zabadi bil toon, hummus, babaghannuug and Ta'miya. Then we'll have fuul midammis, semaan mahshi and kebab on tarek. Do you have samak bolti tonight?"

The waiter nodded yes.

"Very good. Samak bolti, rice, lubiya and bassila for sides."

The waiter bowed his head and left our table.

"I got the rice, but what was that other stuff?" Paul asked.

"You will see when it comes. I just ordered appetizers, and as main courses lamb kabobs, fava beans, quail and tilapia fish along with some sides."

"This sounds like an adventure," Madeleine said.

"You mean another adventure," the adventure-worn Natalie said.

"It's a feast," Dr. Short said. "Enjoy yourselves."

"Should we toast?" Madeleine asked.

"Certainly. Waiter, please bring us some San Pellegrino and six glasses. We will toast Egypt."

"And adventure!" Paul said.

"And being here together on the evening of our first meeting," Dr. Short added.

As we waited for the food to arrive and listened to the musicians playing in the background, Natalie brought up a dream she had while resting this afternoon.

"An afternoon dream, that's interesting," Madeleine said.

"I was out on the desert again, but this time I was alone. A car appeared, but no one was in it. Suddenly I found a key in my pocket and knew it belonged to this car. I got in and began to drive, but the steering wheel didn't work, and I was going all over the place. The brakes wouldn't work either, and then I woke up."

"Well, I think this dream reflects your feelings about what happened to you earlier today," Madeleine said.

"But today a van appeared and Yusef was driving it," Natalie said.

"The car in your dream is more than a car. It represents you. You had the key, but you couldn't control the vehicle. You feel out of control."

"That's good Mom. I think you're right," Natalie said. "Amr drove the camel I was riding and Yusef the van. I was out of control."

"In more ways than one," her brother said smiling.

"Yes, you must be feeling it very deeply," Madeleine said.

"You're interested in dreams?" Dr. Short asked.

"A little," she said modestly.

"A little!" said her less modest son. "Mom has been studying Jungian dream analysis for years. She goes to these meetings in Dayton."

"It's just a study group."

"That's fascinating Madeleine," Dr. Short said. "Dreams and visions of various kinds figure large in Egypt. Right now there are people from the Edgar Cayce Foundation doing research here based on visions he had. The importance of dreams is as old as the Bible in this part of the world. Remember the story of the Hebrew Joseph who was sold into slavery to the Egyptians?"

"Oh yes" Madeleine said. "Didn't he correctly interpret the

pharaoh's dream, and wasn't he made a rich man and the pharaoh's most important advisor as a result?"

"Yes," Dr. Short said and recited the story for the rest of us. "The pharaoh had a dream in which there were seven fat cows and seven lean cows. The lean cows ate the fat cows. Disturbed by the dream, the pharaoh called all of his most important advisors but none could interpret it. He was advised that a Hebrew slave might be able to. Joseph rightly interpreted the dream. It was fated, Joseph said, that there would be seven plentiful years and seven lean years. To protect his kingdom the pharaoh should build warehouses and store food grown in the plentiful years to prevent famine in the seven years of drought. So dreams and their interpretations can be very serious business, a matter of life and death."

A small, elderly gentleman approached our table. He looked gaunt and nearly bleached. He spoke to Dr. Short in English with a heavy German accent. Dr. Short, looking slightly uncomfortable, interrupted the man and turned to us to make introductions. "This is Herr Doktor Hans Bueller. These are my new friends from America."

Bueller gave a perfunctory nod and smile before resuming his complaint about the difficulty he was having with certain Egyptian archaeologists. Dr. Short cut him off, shifting the conversation to our misadventures earlier in the day.

"Are you in Cairo for long?" Bueller asked.

"No, we fly to Luxor tomorrow morning. Then we board a cruise ship," Madeleine said.

He took a few seconds to look intently at Madeleine and said, "Which cruise ship, may I ask?"

She looked uncomfortable coming under his stare and looked over at her son.

"The Queen Nuit," John said.

"Oh, z'at is a very fine ship," he said, looking back at Madeleine.

"You've been on her?" Madeleine asked.

"Oh, yes, several times. It is very coincidental z'at you are going to Luxor tomorrow. I have z'is little package to send z'ere. It would be ever so much faster if you could take it with you. If you could do me z'is kind favor, I could have someone pick it up at your ship before you debark on your cruise."

Dr. Short tried to butt in but before he could get the words out Madeleine said smiling, "Oh, that would be fine. I would be happy to do you the favor."

"I just happen to have it with me." Bueller pulled a small package out his pocket, wrapped in brown paper and tied in string. "You will not lose it, will you? Oh, of course you won't," he said as he handed it over. "Take good care of it. Someone, I'm not certain who just yet, will come to your ship to request it." He offered his apologies for disrupting our little party and took his leave.

"Madeleine! Why did you? Oh, I suppose you were just being gracious," a visibly disturbed Dr. Short said.

"What's wrong?" she asked.

"Oh, nothing, nothing," grumbled Dr. Short. "There's just something about that man I don't like."

"What can you tell us about him?" John asked.

"He is a noted archaeologist. He should be. He's been involved in Egyptology for what seems like a hundred years."

"A hundred years!" Paul said.

"It only seems like a hundred years. I think he has been working here on and off since he was a young man in the early 1940s or late 1930s."

"That's almost a hundred years," Paul said.

"I could tell by his accent he's German," John said.

"Yes, but I think he maintains a residence in Austria."

Madeleine reached into her pocket and touched the small package. "What have I done?"

"It will be all right Madeleine," Dr. Short said. "Just steer clear of the person he sends to pick it up once you've handed it over. Stay with your tour guide. That's something I meant to bring up with all of you before you leave to go south. Your trouble today came about when you separated. Young Paul here broke free from his grandmother, and Natalie unwisely agreed to be taken off by her camel driver."

"Well, I didn't think he was taking me off," Natalie said.

"I know you didn't. But there's a lesson to be learned here. Stick close to each other. As long as the five of you stay together, no harm will come to any of you. But trouble could come to any one of you if you wander off. Egypt is no different from any other place. It has its dangers. But those dangers are greater for all of you because you don't know the culture or the people. So will you take my advice?"

We all agreed to be more cautious, but I wondered if the advice came too late. I worried about that little package in Madeleine's pocket. She was being gracious just as Natalie had graciously accepted Amr and his family's hospitality without understanding their intent. And then it was such a weird coincidence that we should happen to be going to where Dr. Bueller wanted to send this little package that he just happened to have in his pocket. Am I being paranoid? I wondered. Or was our meeting with Bueller yet another synchronicity in a trip whose inception grew out of a synchronicity and had been marked by synchronicities ever since? Could all of this be fated somehow like the pharaoh's dream of impending famine? Was our grain stored away for safe keeping, metaphorically speaking?

Thoughts of famine rapidly disappeared as two waiters came to the table with our appetizers.

"Hmm, this looks good," said a delighted Paul smiling at an equally delighted Dr. Short.

"It is my boy, it is! Let me dish it out on your plates."

To satisfy Paul's eagerness Dr. Short began by serving him. He scooped out a portion of a whitish looking substance swimming in olive oil and garlic.

"I hope you don't mind ladies. I would usually serve you first, but I can see this young man needs to eat."

"That's fine," Madeleine said.

"You will be next," Dr. Short said to Madeleine with a wink.

Paul, who had begun to feel like a guinea pig or maybe the court food taster, asked what the substance was.

"It's Egyptian yogurt cheese. It's delicious. You will love it."

I knew Paul probably would. He did not have the palate of a ten year old but rather like his Uncle John, of a man who loves good food. Dr. Short added falafel to his plate, hummus in lemon juice, roasted eggplant with lemon, tahini, garlic and olive oil.

"I always say, savor the appetizers. They are so delightful," Dr.

Short said.

Soon all of our plates were full, and we enjoyed them immensely. The olive oil and lemon tasted of the Egyptian sun.

The waiters came and gathered up our appetizer plates as we finished, brought fresh plates, and then brought out the entrees and sides, fitting them into the center of our large, round table.

"I think we can serve ourselves," Dr. Short said. "Chinese restaurant style. Is that all right?"

"Sure," said Paul the eager epicurean, "but tell us what it is first."

"These are fava beans, simmered with garlic, onion, olive oil, tomatoes and spices."

"I love fava beans," Natalie said.

"This is baked stuffed Quail."

"At least it's not pigeon," Paul said.

"These are leg of lamb kabobs. This is tilapia, a fish found in the Nile. They bake it here with garlic and add cilantro and tomato sauce."

"This is the first fish I've had since we arrived," a grateful Madeleine said.

"Of course there's rice. I ordered two different vegetables, black-eyed peas in tomato sauce and sweet peas in tomato sauce. Waiter, could we have another bottle of water? Make that two."

We supped slowly on the best prepared, most well seasoned and exquisite Egyptian food of the entire trip in the blue light of the Blue Nile restaurant as the musicians played their exotic flutes. At midnight we returned to our hotel in Dr. Short's convertible jeep under the brilliant stars of the Egyptian sky. This would be a night to remember. We all knew that.

"Will I see you when you get back?" our splendid host said.

"Of course," Madeleine said. "We will phone you from the airport just before our return."

"I will be there to greet you all."

Chapter Eleven

When I get the flying jitters, I remind myself what Percy Bysshe Shelley would have given to glimpse snowy landscapes above dense white clouds. But I think the most intriguing views are the panoramic landscapes, visible when the sky opens to the whole spectacle of the land, revealing a larger, truer picture than can be seen from the ground.

Our plane followed the course of the Nile, which from high up appears a thin bluish line curving its way south. On either side of the river are swaths of emerald green where Egypt's agricultural products are grown and where most of its people live. The fertile valley is formed by a combination of seasonal flooding and irrigation. The river bottom soil flows up from the Blue and White Nile, spills over the Nile's banks, inundating the land with its richness. The rest of the year irrigation ditches carry the river's treasure outward into cultivated fields. The valley looks to be only five or ten miles wide. Beyond it, Egypt is baked earth and sand. Harsh and unending in its vistas and nearly uninhabitable, apart from this blue and emerald river valley spiraling down its middle, Egypt with its great, ancient monuments seems the beginning of it all. Was the beginning like this? Humanity huddled together in a fertile enclave on the edge of oblivion?

I fingered the cartouche hanging around my neck. Samia and Yusef had delivered little jewelry bags to Natalie and me before taking us to the airport. Samia personally fastened Natalie's cartouche around her neck and told her not to take it off, but I wanted to look at mine before I wore it. It was such a beautiful little piece of gold. The oval cartouche was attached with a fastener to a long chain. It had a polished gold rim. The gold inside the rim was brushed to diminish its sheen and to set off glistening hieroglyphs, the symbols for my name, lined up one above the other over the length of the cartouche. A sideways view of the lion, sitting with his paws outstretched was the first symbol, followed by a representation of a feather, three lines for water and the helping hand.

73

The last symbol was the profile of an eagle standing ready. It looked as if the lion and the eagle at either end stood guard over truth, justice, charity and the essence of life, water. The landscape below revealed why ancient Egypt had such protective symbols. The lion stood guard on one side of the Nile Valley and the Eagle on the other, protecting life itself from the ravages of the desert. What a harsh and beautiful land, I thought.

Over time personal relationships trump cultural differences and suspicion and misunderstanding ends. I saw that most particularly when Samia placed the cartouche around Natalie's neck. She knew Natalie had nothing to do with whatever Stuart is up to, that the encounter at the Coptic church was a coincidence, perhaps a dangerous one. This was obvious in Samia's injunction that Natalie should buy and wear a cartouche for protection against being led into another mishap. She and Yusef had urged us not to separate just as Dr. Short had done. They reminded Paul that he no longer had a satellite phone, and that if he should get lost again, he might not be so easily found. I wished Yusef and Samia could have traveled with us south.

We most particularly missed them once we arrived at the airport in Luxor and realized how very different our tour of Upper Egypt would become. In Cairo we had our travel guides and van to ourselves, but in Luxor we were met by a young man who woodenly recited a prepared speech after loading us into a bus with a dozen or so other travelers to take to our ship, the Queen Nuit.

"Welcome to Luxor." He paused a moment and smiled as he looked at us. "My name is Ahmed, and I will be your guide. We will go directly to the ship where you can take your bags onboard. You will have the rest of the day to yourselves until dinner when we will all meet in the ship's dining room. After dinner we will go to a fabulous sound and light show in Luxor. Tomorrow morning we will re-board the bus and go to the Valley of the Kings. In the afternoon we will tour Luxor. The following morning our ship will depart."

"This sounds like camp," I said, "regimented."

"We could all probably use a little regimentation and a nap," Madeleine said, with one eye on Paul. She grabbed him by the shoulder and walked ahead towards a troop of stewards ready to take our bags and us to our assigned compartments.

John and I read each other's looks. We had just arrived in Luxor, formerly known as Thebes, the ancient capital of Egypt's Middle and New Kingdoms. No nap for us. We spotted a driver with a horse drawn buggy parked at the side of the pier. Ahmed ignored him expecting us to do the same as he herded everyone aboard the ship. "Go to the upper deck and relax in the sun before dinner," he said. We would have none of it and discretely tipped a steward, asking him to take only our bags to our cabin. The steward was more than happy to oblige, and we quietly backed away from the herd, telling no one where we were going, and approached the buggy driver.

"How much for a tour?" John asked.

"Twenty-five pounds," the driver said. We hopped into the shiny black buggy with red wheels and brilliant blue interior pulled by a tired looking chestnut horse.

"My name is John, and you?

"Mustafa," he said. "Where would you like to go?"

"Wherever you would like to take us."

That began our very different tour of Luxor. This was not yet apparent to us at the beginning when we passed the University of Chicago's Archaeological Institute, a large and beautiful building with palm filled courtyards. Nor had we noticed when we passed a far less beautiful public school building. Our attention was elsewhere. We were struck by how few automobiles we saw. Cairo balanced the old and the new with its mix of many cars alongside fewer donkey carts. Here the balance took a decided shift backwards in time, with many fewer cars, more carts and most people on foot.

Mustafa was not a college trained tour guide. He wore the long traditional robe of the male Egyptian and a long scarf around his neck, which would become his turban when the sun was higher. Deep lines etched into tan face made it hard to judge his age, but he looked to be in his late thirties or early forties. He was married with children to feed, he said, and eked out a living from tourists, apparently not unlike the Bedouin camel drivers at the pyramids.

He avoided the ancient sites and drove us instead into narrow streets where Egyptians like himself live and work. Merchants seeking shade

75

leaned their chairs against the walls of buildings. Makeshift outdoor markets lined the sidewalks with woven goods piled high and baskets filled with grains, beans and bread, all sheltered from the sun by sheets of white muslin strung up on poles. Mustafa informed us he had five children as we passed a bevy of live chickens ready for sale.

"Chickens like these. I would need at least two to feed my family. I cannot afford such luxury."

I sensed his bitterness. He made a living driving what he perceived to be rich tourists around while he struggled to put food on the table. As I looked about at all the people that looked like him, I felt surrounded by bitterness, even hostility. Were we safe? I wondered. Had we made a mistake in taking this ride? Are we the unwitting enemy in a drama we don't understand?

Mustafa invited us to look around a little shop owned by friends. He would be back to fetch us in a few minutes. We climbed out of our carriage and entered a shop filled with beautiful Egyptian goods unlike the tacky tourist trinkets we had seen elsewhere. I saw an exquisite Bedouin dress, but there was no price tag. If we wanted the dress, we were going to have to bargain for it, which neither John nor I was prepared to do. How much was too much and how much was too little? We had no idea.

One of the store's owners, a woman, named a price that we inexperienced bargainers guessed must be too high. We walked away and began looking at other things, and the woman shot back with a lower price. Having no idea if the offer was high or low, John and I thought it better not to buy anything under the circumstances and headed towards the door, thinking we would wait outside for Mustafa to return.

"See this workmanship," the woman said. "All beads hand sewn. This a wedding dress."

The beadwork was incredible. It looked authentic and lovingly made. She lowered the price, and we bought the dress, proud of our accomplishment. We had bargained ourselves into a very good price without having to name one. But as the woman handed John our change, I detected pain in her polite smile that communicated we had paid much less for the dress than its true value, and I felt ashamed.

Mustafa returned and brought us back to the Queen Nuit. His tour and our experience in the shop gave me insight into the situation for many Egyptians. They depend on tourists for their livelihood. We offered Mustafa baksheesh, another twenty-five pounds over the twenty-five he had requested. We were not his enemy; we were his hope to put chickens on the table. And he was our teacher who offered a different course of study from what the college trained Samia and Yusef had to teach. Mustafa taught us charity. Of course, I considered that his tour was designed with that outcome in mind, to increase his pay without him having to bargain for it. It was a good lesson. What you offer to pay is measured not only in the value of the goods or services rendered but in the need of the recipient and in the depth of your own charity.

When we arrived back at the boat we were met by a rant of frustration.

"How were you able to go anywhere?" Natalie asked. "Our vice president is here so they've placed us under guard. They wouldn't let me off the boat!"

"We never got on," John said. "We gave our luggage to one of the ship's stewards and hopped a ride in a carriage parked at the pier and took a tour."

"Well, I'm glad you enjoyed yourself while I spent the day worrying about you. They've even postponed the sound and light show until tomorrow night. You're lucky they waited for you to come back because they're going to move the ship for our protection. Did you get into any trouble?"

"Almost," John said.

"Before we left Cairo weren't we told not to separate?" Natalie said.

"We didn't go off by ourselves. We went with each other," John protested.

"That's a technicality."

I knew she was right. For the rest of the trip we must all be together all the time.

"What's the vice president doing here anyway?" I asked.

"I don't know," Natalie said. "You will have to ask Ahmed."

At that moment Ahmed appeared, loudly clapping his hands as he delivered orders. "Prepare yourselves for dinner. We will move the ship a few miles up the river, and then dinner will be served."

"Girl Scout Camp," I said. "Hey, Ahmed. What's my vice president doing here?"

"He is here for a private tour of the temple ruins with my president, a very great man."

"Yes, I've heard that."

The ship began moving away from the pier. John turned to Natalie. "Has anyone come to collect Bueller's package?"

"No, not yet. Mom took Paul to the cabin to take a nap. I've been out here waiting for you the whole time."

"I'm sorry. We should have said something before we took off." He looked out at the receding pier. "I wonder if this person will be able to find us now?"

"Even if he does, will he be able to board the ship if it's under guard?" Natalie said.

Our cabin was paneled in dark wood with arabesque detailing that lightened its heavy appearance. The same wood and arabesque style was used throughout the common areas of the ship. We lay down in our respective twin beds to rest before dinner and unexpectedly dosed off. Thirty minutes later Natalie, Madeleine and Paul rapped at our cabin door, all dressed in their best clothes.

"Sorry," John said. "The boat must have rocked us to sleep. If you don't mind our appearance, we're ready."

"You look fine," Natalie said.

I quickly brushed my hair, and we were off.

"Who are you with?" the waiter said. "Which is your guide?"

"Oh, Ahmed," Madeleine said.

"Follow me." The amused waiter looked at John and asked, "And are these all of your women?"

"Let me introduce you to my mother, my sister and my wife. And this is my nephew Paul."

"Ah, I see. You are not only a good husband, but a good son and a good brother."

"And uncle," Paul said.

The waiter's words, meant as a compliment, further reminded John of his responsibilities and weighed him down.

Three long tables were reserved for Ahmed's group, each only large enough to hold eight. There were three times as many tables in the dining room filled with French speaking people. Apparently, the numbers of English speaking tourists had dwindled to the point that we were just an add-on. Even with the addition of our numbers, the ship's dining room looked nearly half empty. Tourism was clearly down.

"We must be on a French cruise," I said to John and Natalie. The waiter overhearing agreed.

Our group of five took up most of a table. Only reporter Michael Sargent joined us.

"Did you see those guards standing outside our ship?" Natalie said. "We didn't realize it was this dangerous here."

"I don't think most people did," Michael said. "My paper was invited to send me over here for next to nothing. We decided I should go and determine first hand whether travel in Egypt is safe enough to recommend just now. I've already talked to most of the Americans onboard. Half of them are travel agents or relatives of travel agents cashing in on these really low prices. Few are as aware as I of what's been going on here. Egypt's working very hard to get their tourists back by offering these huge discounts. That's for sure."

"How dangerous is it?" John asked.

"That's what I'm here to find out. It looks to me like the authorities have locked things down. I stayed on shore last night and could make out guards with semiautomatic weapons all along the docks in front of the ships and even on the decks of ships that are not in use."

"Do you think that's because the vice president is here?" I asked.

"Partly, but he wasn't here last night. They've beefed up security even more since then. That's why they moved us. The government here has locked up many rebels. There hasn't been a major incident in almost a year except for that explosion in Cairo, and I still don't know what that was about."

"We were in Cairo for that," John said. "The newspaper said it was a vendor's propane tank that accidentally exploded."

"I'm not so sure of that. There was a military response to the incident, which I doubt would have been the case if it were only the vendor accident they reported. I think we will be all right though or I wouldn't be here. But there are some Egyptians who sure don't like us."

"Why not?" Madeleine asked. "What do we have to do with them?"

"They don't like their government, and they blame us for its ability to survive. We give them lots of money."

"Well, what's wrong with that?" Madeleine said. "It looks to me like they can use lots of money."

"They can, and they have. That's the point. Egypt has been doing relatively well. As long as that's the situation it's not ripe for revolution, which is a disappointment to some. Anything that stands in their way is the enemy. That includes tourism because it brings in major cash. So tourists no matter where they come from have become targets."

Madeleine shuddered. "If I had known, I would not have come, and I never would have brought my grandson."

"I didn't mean to frighten you. Look, we'll be just fine. Just stay close to Ahmed."

John and I looked at each other and thought how foolish we were to have wandered off on our own. It turned out okay, but if we had met up with the wrong person, who knows what could have happened. We vowed once again not to separate, and then it was our table's turn to line up at the buffet.

It wasn't the Blue Nile restaurant, but the food was good. We passed on the salads and had a wonderful lamb dish that was like a stew. We added rice, cooked vegetables and flat bread to our plate and poured hot tea. Just as we were finishing our rice pudding, I saw Madeleine nearly leap out of her chair. Behind her stood a small, very elderly man with a pasty white complexion, who had just patted her on the shoulder.

"Dr. Bueller!" she said.

"I did not mean to frighten you dear lady. I could find no one on such short notice to pick up my package, so I z'ought I would come and pick it up personally. I need a little vacation anyway, and z'ere were plenty of cabins still available."

"You're coming on our cruise?" she asked, hardly believing what she had just heard.

"Ja, I hope you don't mind. I z'ought I would relax and do a little drawing."

I remembered that Dr. Short had said to stay away from whomever Bueller sent to claim the package. What he hadn't imagined is that

Bueller would send himself. What were we to do now? How were we to stay away from him in such close quarters without seeming very rude?

Madeleine got up from the table. "I will be just a minute. I'm going to my stateroom to get your package."

"I will go with you Mom," Natalie said.

Bueller smiled and sat down, and Michael, true to his profession, began asking him questions. In short order Bueller told his story, or at least the version he wanted us to hear.

Dr. Bueller had been involved in Egyptology since 1939. The Nazis had been very interested in it, and he got involved under their auspices.

"A Nazi! You're a Nazi?" Paul said.

"Oh, my boy, we Germans were all Nazis back z'en. You had to be. I wasn't a higher up, SS, or anything."

"What would happen if you quit?" Paul asked.

"You could not quit. Not until Germany was defeated," Bueller said in a hushed tone, as if he still feared being overheard by informers.

"Who do you work for now?" Michael asked.

"A private foundation supports my work. I no longer dig but consult. Egypt has become my second home. I spend most of z'e winter and early spring here. I spend z'e summer in Austria."

"What were the Nazis looking for in Egypt?" Paul asked.

"Evidence of z'eir own greatness, I z'ink. Why did Napoleon come to Egypt? And Lord Nelson?"

Paul was silenced by this answer that neither he nor the rest of us could fully comprehend. Madeleine and Natalie soon arrived, handed Bueller his little package, and we all made our excuses and retired for the night.

"I'm glad that's done," Madeleine said.

"I wish he wasn't on our ship," Natalie said, echoing all of our sentiments.

"Hey, where's Stuart?" John asked.

"I don't know. Maybe he changed his mind," she answered.

"Too bad. This is turning into quite a party."

Chapter Twelve

"Quick, be seated," Ahmed said to his charges as we climbed the steps into the waiting vehicle. "Our bus will take us to the Valley of the Kings. You may purchase a basic ticket that will allow you to visit the tombs of the Ramses and other pharaohs. For an additional fee, you may visit the tomb of Tutankhamen. Afterwards, we will go see Queen Hatshepsut's Mortuary Temple before we return to our ship for lunch."

"Wow! Tutankhamen's Tomb!" Paul said.

"I don't think I want to visit any tombs," Madeleine said as she waited in line to board. "I don't like being herded around like this."

"I don't either," John said. "But after what that newspaperman told us last night, I begin to appreciate Ahmed's situation."

We seated ourselves near the front of the bus since we were the last to board. Fortunately, Bueller was sitting in the rear. He made a little wave of his hand when I boarded. I waved back but was pleased to turn away in my window seat as Ahmed began his lecture.

"The sunrise in the east, marking a new day was associated with life," he said. "While the sunset in the west was associated with death. The ancient Egyptians, keeping with this understanding, located the city of the living, Thebes, which we now call Luxor, on the east side of the Nile while locating their burial grounds for kings and queens on the side of the setting sun."

His voice faded into a quiet drone as my imagination focused on the sights outside my window. Farmers using primitive implements and donkeys worked the irrigated fields that hugged the Nile. The scene could have predated the European settlement of America, I thought. Yet that long ago past is still present here. Soon, the green, lush cropland gave way to desert. Sand and rock devoid of anything living triggered a memory of a dream I had awakened to that morning. I had answered a ringing phone. My mother spoke to me. I could hear her voice plainly. "How did you know I was here?" I asked. "Your brother told me. I want you to know I am here with you," she said. I looked out at the air made dirty by blowing sand and hoped that her resting place is a far better place than this one.

"Put on your face masks to protect yourself from fine grains of sand you would otherwise breathe in," Ahmed ordered. The urgency of his tone brought his voice back into my foreground.

"I'll wait for you on the bus," Madeleine said, ignoring his command.

"You're not going?" Natalie said.

"I don't think so."

"I'll stay with you then."

Madeleine and Natalie were not the only two who decided to stay behind. A few other women had made the same decision. I looked out of the bus window at the dry patch of desert that ran between craggy hills with jutting cliffs, inside of which tombs had been carved out of rock. Not too inviting, I thought. I couldn't blame them.

"The tombs you are about to see were built during the Middle and New Kingdoms," Ahmed began. "The pharaohs of this period built their tombs in these mountains to be inconspicuous to grave robbers who had ravished pyramids built to house Pharaonic remains during the Early Kingdom."

"That explanation is too simplistic," John whispered.

"Why? It makes sense."

"Do you really think the Valley of the Kings is inconspicuous? Don't you think grave robbers would have learned about this place? The fact is that they did and most of these graves were robbed. Remember what we saw in Lower Egypt? They forgot how to build quality pyramids by the Fifth Dynasty."

"Yes, I remember. When were these tombs made?"

"These were built in the Eighteenth Dynasty. The knowledge was completely lost by then."

John, Paul and I bought our passes along with the extra pass for Tutankhamen's tomb, placed the masks over our mouths and noses and followed Ahmed.

Passages carved out of rock led to burial chambers vibrant in color and design, preserved by darkness and a dry climate. Paintings of gods

83

and goddesses, some with the head of an animal or a bird, covered the walls. Cartouches both carved and painted preserved the names of the dead. The long, sinewy body of Nuit, the sky goddess, draped across the ceiling in the tomb of Ramses VI, her long arms stretched above her head, her body seeming to contain all the stars in the universe. And there was the Ankh, the Scarab and the Eye of Horus, whose horrific gaze served as a warning to any who would violate what Horus protects.

"That looks like a dollar," Paul said pointing to the Eye of Horus.

"Yes, it does look like the eye in the pyramid on the dollar," I said. "Ahmed, can you explain this?"

"The Eye of Horus was believed to protect health and bring prosperity," he said.

"Why would the eye be in these tombs then? These people are dead," I said.

"You forget that everything in these tombs is here for the purpose of the afterlife. The Eye of Horus would help the mummy to regenerate and live again. Look around you at all the paintings of boats necessary to make the immortal crossing and the representation of troops and provisions to make that crossing in safety and comfort."

"Are there mummies in here coming back to life?" Paul said.

"Oh, no Paul," I said, trying to calm him. "They've all been taken to the museum in Cairo."

"Remember where you are!" Ahmed said. "You're inside the tombs. Many mummies remain here still."

Paul eyed the tunnel high and low. "I saw the movie *The Mummy*."

"When I was a kid about your age I saw the original *The Mummy* on TV when I would stay up and watch late night horror movies."

"They showed it on 'The Cool Ghoul Scream-in' out of Cincinnati when I was a kid," John said.

"They show it on the oldies movie cable channel where I live," Paul said.

"You've seen the original?" I said, surprised since I thought kids today only watch movies filmed in color with computer generated special effects.

"Yeah, the one with Boris Karloff. It looks like here."

"Yes, they did a really good job of replicating this place. Ahmed,

84

what's that dog?"

"That's a jackal, an Anubis; it guards the tomb."

"It doesn't look too friendly," I said. Just then I felt a draft of dusty air pass over my flesh, and something lightly grazed my shoulder from behind. Startled, I jumped involuntarily before I turned around and gazed upon a very old man dressed in Egyptian garb fanning me with palm leaves. He smiled. I understood. I offered him baksheesh for services rendered.

"Who was that?" I asked Ahmed after the man had left.

"One of the locals."

I was beginning to better understand the system here in Egypt. Access was a reward. Someone had given this man the opportunity to perform a service for those who could afford to pay. That was the deal.

When we stepped out of the last tomb of the major part of the tour, I spotted Bueller perched on a sunny cliff drawing with his pad and ink. He looks like an unwrapped mummy, I thought. I shuddered both at my uncharitable thoughts and his general creepiness. While the others walked back towards the bus, Ahmed directed John, Paul and me to the entrance of Tutankhamen's tomb.

"Why aren't they coming?" John asked.

"They don't seem too interested in tombs," Ahmed said. "That's not always so, but it is with this group. You will be all right on your own, won't you? I should attend to them."

"Sure," John said.

"Be quick. You don't want to keep them waiting long."

We walked down the long corridor leading to an antechamber when we were met with a voice coming from behind us.

"Z'ese are all fakes," Bueller said. "Z'e original artifacts are in z'e Cairo Museum."

"Yes, we've been there and seen them," John said.

"Let me take you to z'e real treasure." We followed Bueller as he led us into another chamber. "Z'is is z'e burial chamber."

Before us was an incredible golden sarcophagus. "Is this a fake too?" I asked.

"No, z'is is real. Z'is is z'e mummy of Tutankhamen."

"His real mummy?" Paul said.

85

"Ja," Bueller said with a smile of delight as he looked down at the trembling boy. "His body had been so disturbed z'at z'ey dare not move him."

"How did he die?" Paul asked.

"Some z'ink he was murdered," Bueller said in a low withering voice.

Sadistic old man, I thought. "Tell me Dr. Bueller, why didn't you go into the other tombs with our group?"

"I've seen z'em all many times."

"Yes, of course you have, including this one."

"I think we had better get back to the bus," John said. "I've seen enough of the Valley of the Kings." He gave me a little push towards the exit. This time I didn't mind being herded. I was sure that the only reason Bueller had followed us into Tutankhamen's tomb was to frighten Paul.

"Take your original seats," Ahmed said as we stood looking about.

"Where are my mother and sister?" John asked in alarm.

"I sent someone out to look for them," Ahmed said. "The driver said they left the bus along with two other women some time ago."

"What on earth were they thinking?"

"Your mom seemed in one of her rebellious moods this morning," I said as I took my seat. "She hates having people tell her what to do."

Two women boarded, followed by a man who briefly spoke to Ahmed.

"Your mother and sister were not found with these two women," Ahmed said. "We must leave now if we are to arrive at Queen Hatshepsut's Temple in time."

"You can't leave without my mother and sister!"

"Someone will find them and bring them back later," Ahmed asserted.

"Oh, no you don't. We can't leave here without them."

I looked out through the window at this barren, dead place just as a gust of wind sent blistering sand against the rocks. How horrible to be abandoned here, I thought. Besides the few people who work here—who were closing down as they prepared to leave—there was no one, nothing, except the mummy of Tutankhamen, if he still counts as someone.

Ahmed took a quick vote. Fortunately, the majority of the group agreed to wait.

"Hi, I'm Beverly," whispered one of the two errant women. "They were right behind us not long ago. They'll be comin' along here soon."

"Why did you leave the bus?" John asked.

"We got a little bored, that's all," she said.

"We got tired of sittin' around waitin' for y'all," the other errant woman added.

After about twenty very long minutes, Madeleine and Natalie appeared accompanied by Ahmed who had personally gone to search for them. He smiled when the three boarded. They, on the other hand, looked visibly disturbed and a little annoyed as they were rushed towards their seats. The impatient driver put the bus into gear before they were seated, causing them to collapse into place.

"Why the heck did you leave the bus?" John asked.

"We just thought we'd look around a little bit," Natalie said. "This nice man offered to show us a few things, and we let him."

"No, you let him." Madeleine said. "I stood guard. I didn't want both of us disappearing this time."

"You've got to be kidding!" John said.

"No, I'm not!" Madeleine said. "After showing us around a few tombs, this nice man, as Natalie puts it, wanted to lead us up a mountain path and behind some rocks. I was suspicious and wouldn't go. I waited down below so that if Natalie should get lost again, I could quickly get someone to search for her. That's when Ahmed showed up." Looking quite pleased with herself, she added, "I believe I foiled his plan."

"Mom, it wasn't like that," Natalie said. She looked over at John. "He just wanted to show me a better view from on top of that hill."

"Grandma, you held up the whole bus," Paul scolded from across the aisle.

"Paul stop it," John said. Turning back to his mother and sister he said, "I thought we decided to stay together to avoid situations like this. The two of you could have been lost. Ahmed was going to leave you behind. If these good people hadn't voted at my urging to wait, he would have too."

"We needed some fresh air, although you could hardly call the air here fresh," Madeleine said with a slight cough.

"How did you get separated from the other women?"

"We wanted to go in one of the tombs, and they wanted to shop for trinkets," Natalie said. "This man approached us and said he could get us inside without tickets."

"If you wanted to go inside a tomb, why didn't you come with us?" They were silent, there being no reasonable answer to John's question. "Please don't do anything like this again," he said. "I know Ahmed can be tedious, but he has a job to do."

Silence continued among those in our group as the bus made its way on the dusty road leading to Hatshepsut's Temple. Then Ahmed stood up in front and began his lecture.

"We will be arriving at Hatshepsut's Mortuary Temple in just a few minutes," he said. "This temple is another one of the great Eighteenth Dynasty masterpieces. Although it was built to be a mortuary temple, her body was never placed there. Hatshepsut's lover, the architect Senmut, built the temple. She was married to her brother, a common practice then, but no children were born from that marriage. Some believe it may never have been consummated. Hatshepsut outlived her brothers and became Queen and then King of Egypt."

"How could Hatshi be a king if she was a queen?" Paul asked.

"Good observation," Ahmed smiled. "That's pretty funny isn't it? The easiest way for you to say her name is to repeat the words, 'hot chicken soup.'"

"Hot chicken soup," Paul said and laughed.

"Now, say it faster."

"Hotchicksoup," Paul said.

Ahmed laughed. "We can tell from renderings of her that Hatshepsut was a very beautiful woman, but when she declared herself king, she began to dress like a man. She even put on the false beard of the pharaohs. You will see this on the statuary in the temple. We're almost there now."

From the parking area we could see a beautiful temple with huge tiered columns piled up three stories. It looked like it was cut from the high rocky ridge that was its backdrop. It also looked deserted. Ahmed asked us to stay seated as he hopped off the bus and headed towards the temple's entrance. We watched as he spoke to someone at a ticket office, and we watched as he skipped back to the bus and spoke to the driver before speaking to us.

"We're too late," he said. "The Temple closed a few minutes ago. It won't reopen until tomorrow morning, and by then our cruise will have departed. Since we have a little bit of time, I've adjusted our itinerary and directed the driver to take us to Ramesseum so that you might see the Colossus of Ramses the Second."

"So I can't see Hotchicksoup?" Paul whimpered.

There was a deep, heavy growl from other perturbed travelers before the bus fell back into silence. It was as if the very Eye of Horus itself burned through Madeleine, Natalie and the other two women who had held the bus up. After about a mile or two the bus pulled up in front of a partially standing temple ruin.

Ahmed insisted that we all get out of the bus so that he might properly explain its significance. This time no one dared to object. "Here before you is the Mortuary Temple of Ramses the Second, known as Ramses the Great because he was ruler for a very long time, sixty-seven years during the New Kingdom period, three thousand two hundred years ago. His reign was long and prosperous, which allowed him to build many of the great temples that still exist in Egypt today, most notably Abu Simbel, which some of you will visit in Nubia."

"Did this one fall down?" Paul asked.

"No," Ahmed said. "It was destroyed by Christian monks."

"They came all the way down here?" I said.

"They tried to establish a Christian church here, but all they accomplished was the destruction of this temple. There is some talk of rebuilding it." Ahmed pointed to four large statues of headless figures standing guard over the temple. "These are Osiris statues without their heads. But over here is what I brought you to see. How many of you know the English poet Percy Bysshe Shelley?"

I raised my hand.

"Then you know the poem 'Ozymandias,'" Ahmed said. "Did you know the poem was written about Ramses the Second?"

"No, I didn't."

"I will show you." He pointed to pieces of what had been a very huge statue: the head severed from the torso, the torso severed from the

89

legs. "Here lies Ramses the Second. Look at this." He pointed to what looked like a large cartouche carved into the statue's severed arm. "The translation of the hieroglyphic means, 'king of kings.'"

The full line reverberated in my head. "My name is Ozymandias, king of kings; Look on my works, ye Mighty, and despair!" The irony cuts two ways, I thought. The first is clear enough and as Shelly and perhaps Ahmed intended. But the other?

There is mystery and grandeur in ruins that speak of an irretrievable past as nothing else can. Perhaps that is why artists who Napoleon dispatched to Luxor made drawings of this temple ruin, which in turn inspired Shelly to write one of his most famous poems. If the goal of those antique monks had been to diminish Ramses, they achieved the opposite. The poetry of this ruin has brought greater recognition to his name than if the temple with its giant colossus had been left intact. Ramses' revenge perhaps?

Chapter Thirteen

Is that Barry Short standing by the gangplank? I thought as the bus pulled up at our ship. The combination of window frame, glass and sun made me wonder if he weren't an apparition, such was the surprise and the tenor of our day. But he was real enough.

"There you are. I'm so happy to see you safe," he said before any of us could speak or ask the obvious questions.

"Why wouldn't we be safe?" Madeleine asked. "And what are you doing here?" He looked a little stunned and slightly disappointed by the reception. Seeing his changed expression Madeleine said, "It's not that we're not happy to see you. I'm very happy to see you. I'm just a little surprised."

"Well, of course you are. I hope you don't mind, but I booked passage on your cruise."

"You're going with us?" Paul said

"If you don't mind."

"Oh we don't mind. That's wonderful," John said, relieved after the day's events to have help monitoring his unruly mother and sister.

Dr. Bueller got off the bus and locked eyes with Dr. Short. "Barry, what a surprise. I didn't realize z'at you were joining your little troop of Americans."

"Yes, I'm sure you didn't. I must say that I am more surprised to find you here."

"Well, yes. My decision to make z'e trip was unplanned. You see, I could find no one to pick up z'e package your Madeleine so graciously carried for me, so I had no choice but to make z'e trip so z'at I might pick up z'e package and deliver it myself."

"Which you've no doubt done by now."

"Oh! I don't think he would have had the time," Madeleine said. "Dr. Bueller has been with the tour since I gave it back."

Dr. Short gave Madeleine a look that would silence a choir. Bueller smiled and took the opportunity to move ahead of us. He turned and bowed his head before boarding the ship.

"What's going on here?" John asked, looking Dr. Short close in the face.

"I'm not sure. Maybe smuggling. I just don't want any of you hurt." He looked at Madeleine, his face visibly softening. "This time I am the one who had a dream, or maybe I should describe it as a nightmare. I woke up very early this morning feeling rather shaken, called the Institute to see if they had a plane available that I could use, and well, here I am."

"You know how to fly a plane?" Paul asked.

Dr. Short smiled. "Well, of course I do."

"Natalie," Madeleine said, "could you take Paul on board and get him ready for lunch?"

"Sure Mom."

"Now, tell us Barry, tell us about this dream," Madeleine said.

"I dreamed you were all at the Blue Nile just as we were. The restaurant transformed into a ship that seemed to set sail on its own blue light. The musicians were playing their flutes on stage when the flutes abruptly turned into automatic rifles. It appeared as if all of you were being held hostage and you might be shot. Bueller appeared. He looked a fright, and it was that particular vision that woke me up. Not taking such dreams lightly, I determined to get here as quickly as I could. And what do you know, Bueller is here."

"I'm glad you came," Madeleine said.

"I sense danger too," John said. "But what can we do about it?"

"We do nothing, for now. We just observe Bueller, keep our distance but not so far that we can't keep an eye on him. And we stay together and wait. Right now we should go have lunch."

After readying ourselves, our party entered the ship's dining room to be seated. We had grown from a group of five to six, so the waiter escorted us to the only table where we could all be seated. We joined the two ostracized women who had left the bus with Natalie and Madeleine at the Valley of the Kings.

The two plump women sat smiling, wearing something resembling floral patterned shapeless sacks. Their short hair frizzed out around round faces. "Hi, how y'all doing," said one of the women. "I'm Beverly. My friend here is Gabby."

We greeted the two women and exchanged preliminaries about who we were, where we were from and why we were there. Gabby lived up to her name, and Beverly did all right too. They talked nonstop and did tell some pretty humorous stories. They were both in their fifties, from Tennessee, where they had left their hardworking husbands behind as they globe-trotted together just about everywhere.

"Our men are workaholics. We're shopaholics," Beverly giggled. "We made some wonderful finds in Istanbul. Just bought some beautiful things. Had to have them shipped back. Can't wait to go into Luxor. Nothing much at the Valley of Kings."

"Except dead people," Gabby said and broke out in a fit of laughter.

"You were in Turkey. I've always wanted to go there," John said.

"The bazaars are fabulous," Gabby said.

"I heard there's political unrest there right now," John said, trying to lead the conversation out of the shopping mall and into the political arena, an area he found far more interesting.

"Oh, that. Who cares about that," Gabby said. "Hardly noticed a thing."

"We were in Peru during the Shinin' Path uprisin'," Beverly said.

"You were!" an incredulous John said.

"Sure we were. I love tellin' people 'bout that. They're always so surprised."

Gabby turned to Beverly. "We bought some lovely things in Peru. Remember that handmade knitted sweater with the matchin' hat and gloves I bought for my niece? She just loved that."

What fun, I thought as these women rattled on. I have heard of people who go into war zones hoping to get the photo opportunity of a lifetime or people who need to be on the edge to feel alive, but I've never before heard of adventure shoppers, particularly not two faded southern belles like these. The conversation continued in the same vain throughout lunch, or should I say the entertainment continued until it grew tiresome. I began to imagine their workaholic husbands' pleasure in the quiet of the golf course, their only spousal duty to sign for the heaps of packages sent home by their wives.

Lunch over, we returned to our cabins to ready ourselves to go into Luxor, vowing next time to be more careful about where we let the waiter seat us. A few minutes later we were marching off the boat and

93

onto the waiting bus for a short ride to Karnak Temple where Ahmed began his lecture.

"Karnak Temple to your left was the focal point of Thebes when it was the capital of the New Kingdom. The temple complex was begun in the Middle Kingdom, with the majority of the site being constructed between 1570 B.C. and 1100 B.C. Notice these particular sphinxes," he said as he directed our attention to rows of large sphinxes that lined each side of the walkway leading to the temple. "The body is a lion, the head a ram, the ram representing the god Amun-Ra, one of the most venerated gods in the Egyptian pantheon and to whom this temple was dedicated."

"I'm awestruck," I said to John.

"Yeah, I had no idea anything like this was here," John said echoing my thoughts as I gazed at the long rows of giant lions perched on pedestals, the great horns of their rams heads dominant. Each held a statue of the god Amun between its front paws.

"I have never seen anything quite so mystical," Madeleine said to Natalie.

"Yes, these sphinxes seem to stare right into your soul," she replied.

"Most impressive," Dr. Short said.

Paul's youthful gaze saw other possibilities. "Can I climb up and ride one of these lions Uncle John?"

"No, Paul, you can't. This is like being in a church, a very ancient church, so you must behave like you would in your church at home." Paul's expression abruptly transformed into something very solemn and respectful.

"We are approaching the main entrance into the first pylon," Ahmed said. "The temple has numerous pylons but the first and the second are the most significant. Notice how they lean into each other." We followed Ahmed into an open area. He continued, "The temple or I should say temple complex, since it is made up of numerous smaller temples, was built over a period spanning more than a thousand years. Where we stand now is the newest addition. As we walk back the structures become older. Notice the pillars that surround this courtyard. They are called Osiris pillars. In ancient times we would not have been permitted to enter the Temple of Amun-Ra as we do now. Only the priests and pharaohs had that privilege. The walkway we are following was the pathway their religious processionals followed into the magnificent Hypostyle Hall that we are about to enter. It leads all the way back to the Sacred Lake."

The Osiris Pillars looked like a cross between pillar and statue. I tried to imagine the grand processionals of priests and pharaohs walking on the path we now followed on their way to mysterious religious ceremonies where congregations were not allowed. Secret then, their ceremonies are just as obscure now, even to my imagination. Before me was yet another pylon marking another entrance, but what caught my attention were two great statues about fifty feet tall flanking each side of the pylon, one intact and the other in ruins.

"Who is that?" I asked Ahmed.

"That is a statue of Ramses the Second."

"And the other?"

"That was another statue of Ramses the Second, but it was destroyed."

"By whom?"

"We don't know, but if you look around these ruins you will see much of the destruction was intentional. It wasn't just Christian monks who destroyed things. Ancient Egyptians afflicted with jealousy sometimes tried to wipe out the memory and accomplishments of their predecessor. Look over there. See that cartouche with all of its hieroglyphs destroyed? That was an effort to erase from memory the person whose name it contained."

"Oh, kind of like the way history is recorded," Natalie said. "What do they say? History is written by the victors."

"The victors for the moment," Ahmed said. "This history tells us that winning is transitory. The ancient Egyptians tried to make their history permanent by recording it pictorially. Memory was preserved in statues, cartouches and relief carvings that depicted great events. But an enemy might attack your memory by defacing your statue or destroying your cartouche. Another interesting effort to diminish a legacy lies ahead. A great obelisk was built to the Pharaoh Hatshepsut that towered ninety-seven feet. In an attempt to diminish her and it, one of her detractors built a great wall to enclose the lower part of the obelisk to

95

lessen its appearance and thereby lessen Hatshepsut's legacy."

"Hot chicken soup," Paul repeated.

Ahmed led us past a group of artisans busy with restoration, past the remaining statue of Ramses the Second and through the second pylon into a great hall, a huge hall with gigantic pillars.

"Here is the Hypostyle Hall. It was begun by Ramses I, completed by Seti I and his son Ramses II and dedicated to the god Amun. Larger than a football field, it contains approximately fifty-four thousand square feet. There are one hundred and thirty-four columns in this hall, the tallest being sixty-nine feet and the smallest forty-two feet. They are each eleven and half feet in diameter. These pillars are known as an artificial forest. Notice the paint remaining at the top of that one over there. The bas-relief that decorates all of these columns was once painted in vibrant colors such as those."

I couldn't listen any longer. I didn't want to look at Ahmed or hear him. I just wanted to be in this place, to feel this place, to experience its spirit. As I wandered through this forest of stone trees that took the form of colossal pillars with huge bas-relief carvings depicting all manner of scenes, and gods and cartouches filled with hieroglyphs, I believed I was in a land of giants. These pillars dwarfed the human frame as if this temple were built for beings much larger, much greater than we. And perhaps it was. Perhaps that is why only priests and pharaohs were permitted to enter because this great temple was not built for ordinary men and women. Was our presence here violating this sacred place? I found the answer in the poem Ahmed had mentioned that very morning, Shelley's "Ozymandias."

I met a traveler from an antique land
Who said: Two vast and trunkless legs of stone
Stand in the desert . . . Near them, on the sand,
Half sunk, a shattered visage lies, whose frown,
And wrinkled lip, and sneer of cold command
Tell that its sculptor well those passions read
Which yet survive, stamped on these lifeless things,
The hand that mocked them, and the heart that fed:
And on the pedestal these words appear:

96

'My name is Ozymandias, king of kings:
Look on my works, ye Mighty, and despair!'
Nothing beside remains. Round the decay
Of that colossal wreck, boundless and bare
The lone and level sands stretch far away.

The sun lowered in the west as we continued our trek through this mammoth temple on our way to the Sacred Lake in the rear where the sound and light show would soon begin. We passed through more pylons and temples, saw Hatshepsut's great obelisk reach towards the sky as well as the obelisk of her father, Tuthmosis. We saw two square heraldic pillars that represented the joining of two empires, Upper and Lower Egypt. The papyrus, symbol of where we had been, was carved into relief on the north pillar while the lotus, symbol of where we were now, was carved into relief on the south pillar. Together they represent a unification that has lasted to this day. But Egypt has changed so much from what it was that its past is as inscrutable to its inhabitants today as it was to us, visitors from a far off land. "The lone and level sands stretch far away," kept repeating in my mind.

Ahmed's timing was impeccable for we arrived at the Sacred Lake just as the sun was setting. Lights came on, flooding the temple in amber set against a darkening sky. The light seemed to be coming up through the ground and diffusing itself through nooks and crannies creating an effect much like the lighting at the Blue Nile restaurant. But this backdrop was beyond comparison. A narrator recited the history of this great temple, or at least as much as is known. I watched as the reflection of the lights danced upon the Sacred Lake and scattered to the stars.

"Look up there, Orion," John pointed.

Paul and I followed the direction of his hand to the three stars that compose the constellation's belt. They were bigger and brighter than I had ever before seen them.

"Al Nitak, Al Nilam and Mintaka," John said as he named each star.

"Heaven," Paul said.

"Heaven," I repeated, wondering if those pharaohs and priests whose temples we had just trespassed were looking down on us mere mortals with compassion or contempt.

Chapter Fourteen

The slow rhythm of the ship gliding down the Nile soothed my dreams until they fast dissolved into flickering stars and vague thoughts of gods after a loud tapping at the cabin door broke both my reverie and John's sleep. He lay in the other twin bed, his head buried between two pillows to block the sunlight streaming through the cabin window. He mumbled an incoherent protest that was answered with "Are you up?" It was Natalie. I shook John and went to the door to let her in. She looked flushed.

"Are you sick?" I asked.

"No, I'm fine."

"What time is it?" John asked.

"It's almost eight," Natalie said.

John buried his head this time in protest.

"I need to talk. I couldn't sleep. Do you mind?"

This was very unusual behavior for Natalie. She rarely needs to talk and generally keeps her feelings to herself. John uncovered his head and fumbled for his glasses in surprise.

"What's wrong?" he asked.

"Stuart is here. He pulled me aside last night just as I was going to the cabin. Mom and Paul had already gone to bed."

"Well, what's wrong with that? He said he'd be here."

"It's not that he's here that bothers me. It's how he's here."

"What do you mean?"

"He's incognito. He's in his cabin now, but he says when he arrives at breakfast we should act like we don't know him. So I had to tell you early before you go to the dining room. He says he will introduce himself and work himself into our group soon enough, but we should act like we've never met."

"What the heck is this about?" John said.

"He wouldn't tell me why. I have no idea what he is up to, but after what happened in Cairo..." She began to cry.

"Did you tell Mom?"

"Yes," she sobbed. "I've told her. She thinks it sounds strange too, and Mom says she isn't in the mood to get in the middle of another intrigue after what happened with that Dr. Bueller. She said it would suit her just fine not to know him."

"Calm down," John said.

"What about Dr. Short?" I asked.

"He doesn't know a thing, and Stu wants it to stay that way. That made Mom feel very uncomfortable and me too for that matter. What should I do?"

"I don't think you have much choice," John said. "For now at least you should do what Stuart asks until we can figure out what's going on. Natalie, do you have any idea what he could be doing here? Who he works for?"

"The State Department, but I don't know who he works for in the State Department. We both worked in contracts at the GAO until he transferred. So I assume he works in contracts over there. I've hardly seen him since he transferred so I don't really know. But I can tell you this much. Our contracts work at the GAO sometimes requires travel, but never outside of the United States and never under a false name."

"Didn't you say he used to buy jewels in Brazil and take them back to the States to sell?" I asked. "And didn't he say he was doing the same thing here?"

"Well, yes, but that didn't have anything to do with his work at the GAO. It's a little side business. Selling the jewels paid for his trips. I always thought it was nifty the way he worked that out."

"Maybe he's doing the same thing here," John said. "Still that doesn't explain the alias unless he's in some kind of trouble over it. We will try to figure this thing out, but for now we'll go along with his request. Give us a few minutes and we'll go up to breakfast with you," he said as he escorted Natalie out into the hall.

"Mystery cruise," I said. "That would be a better name. It's not enough that Dr. Bueller and Dr. Short showed up, but now Stuart. Oh, I forgot. I'm not supposed to know his name."

We dressed in a flash, joined Natalie in the hall and went to the dining room. Madeleine, Paul and Dr. Short were sitting together at a

99

table with newspaper travel writer, Michael Sargent and two African American women whose acquaintance I had not yet made. There were only two open seats left at their table. Bueller, along with several other people including Gabby and Beverly sat at another table so we bypassed that one. That left only the third table where Stuart sat with two attractive women, a redhead and a brunette, dressed in brightly colored casual wear that one might expect to see at a Florida beach resort. We seated ourselves.

Stuart looked quite different from the fellow I had seen in the shadows of the Coptic church in Cairo wearing jeans and a black leather jacket. Here he was dressed in casual khakis and a navy polo shirt. He was still very good-looking, blond with regular features, but in the full light of day at the breakfast table on the Queen Nuit, he did not look as mysterious as I had remembered, although the mystery around him certainly had increased. The two women he sat talking to introduced themselves as Barbara and Joyce, travel agents from Indianapolis, Indiana.

"We take several trips a year," Joyce said. "We work for the biggest agency in Indianapolis and serve a very elite clientele. People like that expect you to know what you're talking about, so the agency sends us on a few of these specially priced trips every year so we can make knowledgeable recommendations to our clients."

"It's one of the perks of our profession," Barbara said. "Usually they send us to Las Vegas or Disney World so we can keep up with the latest attractions and the newest hotels. We stayed at the Luxor Hotel in Las Vegas last fall. Isn't that fun? Sometimes they send us to new hotels in Jamaica or Cancun. The agency couldn't pass up the rock bottom deal for this trip, so here we are."

"Three years ago they sent us on a ten day tour of London, Paris and Rome," Joyce said.

"Last year it was the Disney cruise," Barbara said. "They're fine if you like kids, but I prefer the Carrousel cruises myself."

"A Nile cruise must seem really exotic after that," I said.

"Well, yes it is," Barbara said. "But this ship is nothing like a Carrousel Cruise ship. Why, they have their own shopping mall right on board and a bar. I can't get used to not having cocktails."

Stuart spoke up, "They have a bar here."

"They do?" John said. He had painfully adjusted to dinner without wine since we had been in Egypt but was fully prepared to readjust.

"Yes, they do. But it's only open while we're cruising so as not to offend the locals. Egypt even has some of its own small wine producers."

"I couldn't find any wine in Cairo," John said.

"You have to know where to look," Stuart said.

"I suppose you do," Natalie said.

It would have helped if we knew what to call Stuart, but he went silent, unwilling, it seemed, to introduce himself. After an awkward few minutes Joyce made the introductions.

"I guess you haven't met Walter yet. How could you after all? He just came on board last night. Walter, this is—what did you say your names are?"

"John. Glad to meet you." He put out his hand.

"Natalie. And what did you say you do Walter?"

"I didn't."

"Walter's a writer," Joyce said. "Isn't that exciting? He writes books."

"What are you writing about?" Natalie asked.

"I'm planning a book on Egypt. I'm doing research."

"Egypt! That's a big subject. Are you writing about the antiquities, the politics or what?"

Stuart shot eye darts at Natalie before blurting out, "Egyptian wine. I'm researching Egyptian wine production."

"Well, that narrows your topic to something pretty slim in a country where ninety-five percent of the population doesn't touch the stuff," Natalie said, goading Stuart into further lies.

"I will be looking more broadly at Egyptian agricultural techniques as well."

"From what I could see of Egyptian farming you may have to concentrate on mule power," she quipped.

"Maybe the Amish would be interested in your book," I interrupted, hoping to diffuse the sarcasm.

"Most Amish don't drink wine," John said.

Stuart abruptly rose from his seat. Joyce, sensing her travel agent charm was not going to smooth this one over, rose as well. Barbara followed.

"We will see you guys later," Joyce said. She took hold of Stuart's arm and led him towards the upper deck.

"Whew," I said. "What's his problem?"

"I don't know," Natalie said. "I'm going to my room for a little while if you don't mind." She left the dining room just as abruptly as Stuart had.

"What do you think is going on?" I said to John.

"I don't know, but I don't like it."

"I think Natalie must really still like him," I said. John looked at me quizzically. "She's jealous," I said. "That Joyce woman has taken possession of the goods."

"Mom's right. That guy is up to no good. I don't like him."

"But Natalie does. He was really angry with her too. Did you see that?"

"I saw it. I saw enough to wish he was off of this boat and away from my sister."

"Well, we can't get him off the boat, but I bet Joyce will do her best to keep him away from your sister."

Madeleine, Paul and Dr. Short arrived at our table just as our conversation was winding down. "Where's Natalie?" Madeleine asked.

"She went to your cabin." John said.

"Oh, I was just wondering if she and the two of you would like to join us on the upper deck. I thought we could relax and enjoy the scenery until we arrive at—Barry, where did you say we are going?"

"Esna."

"That sounds fine Mom. We'll go get Natalie and meet you up there."

It became apparent that the stairway to the upper deck had become a well-worn path. No one was left in the dining room besides ourselves and the waiters who were busing breakfast dishes into the ship's kitchen. That is except Dr. Bueller.

"How are my American friends?" Bueller asked. "Did you enjoy Karnak yesterday?

"Yes, we did," John said. "Didn't see you there."

102

"Well, of course I have been z'ere many times before, and I had some rather pressing business to attend to."

John stepped backwards trying to disengage, but Bueller stepped forwards and continued the conversation.

"It is too bad z'at your tour guide didn't take you to z'e Luxor Temple, a very esoteric place, yes, very esoteric, Pythagorean in fact. Some call it a temple of man. I did a great deal of work z'ere in my youth."

"What is Pythagorean?" I asked.

"You've heard the theorem, the square of the hypotenuse of a right triangle is equal to the sum of the square of its sides," John said.

"Yes, I think in geometry class or some such place."

"It was Pythagoras who figured that out. It's called the Pythagorean theorem."

Bueller looked at the two of us with a smile that only partially concealed contempt. He raised his voice in indignation, and said, "Pythagoras was much more z'an a mathematician. He was a mystic. He knew z'at number was z'e essence of all reality as reflected in z'e perfection of proportion, which is manifest in z'e Luxor Temple. You can practically hear z'e music arise from its harmonic proportions."

John looked puzzled. "I think I may have missed something here. I'm aware that the Pythagoreans believed there was a connection between mathematics and music, but are you claiming that the Luxor Temple..."

"Claiming!" Bueller said. "It is a fact! Z'e music of z'e spheres—haven't you heard of z'at?"

"I'm not disagreeing with you about the relationship between math and music. After all, where would we be without Kepler?"

"Precisely," Bueller said.

"Who is Kepler?" I asked.

Bueller stared at me with a look of disgust.

"I majored in English," I said in my own defense.

"Johannes Kepler discovered the laws of planetary motion," John said. "He was inspired by his belief in the Pythagorean idea of the harmony of the spheres to look beyond Tycho Brahe's empirical observations and as a result, discovered that the planets move in a perfect geometrical form, not the circle, which he first believed, but the ellipse, with one of the two foci of the ellipse being the sun. Without Kepler and Pythagoras, our science could not have advanced. You've heard of Sir Isaac Newton haven't you?"

"Yes, of course," I answered. "He discovered the laws of gravity."

"He formulated the theory of universal gravitation," John said. "And theories of light and laws of motion. Our science would be nowhere without Newton, and Newton's discoveries are unthinkable without Kepler's discovery of the laws of planetary motion."

Bueller looked at John with a new respect. "You are quite right," he said.

"But Pythagoras was Greek, wasn't he? What does this have to do with Luxor?" John asked.

"Yes, he was. And Kepler was German." Bueller's voice began to quiver. "Pythagoras learned from z'e Egyptians, from z'e ancient priests of Heliopolis when he traveled to Egypt as a young man. Z'eir priests selected others of merit like Pythagoras to carry z'is wisdom elsewhere. Z'e Greeks may have taught us about harmony, proportion and even irrational numbers, but it was z'e Egyptians who first knew of z'ese things. Z'e highest wisdom of what we call modern science originated in Egypt!"

John steadied his own voice in marked contrast to the growing passion of Bueller's. "This is very interesting," he said. "Perhaps we can talk more about it later, but we are meeting my mother and Dr. Short on the upper deck right now, and I must go get my sister."

"I hope she is all right," Bueller said calmly now that the subject had shifted. "I saw her leave z'e dining room rather suddenly."

"She's fine." We turned towards the stairs going down to the cabin area, leaving Bueller alone in the dining room.

"I didn't hear any music when our bus drove by the Luxor Temple, did you?" I asked once we were outside of Bueller's earshot.

"Maybe a few strains of Wagner," John quipped.

"Natalie," John said as he rapped on her cabin door. "Don't let this guy spoil your trip."

Natalie opened the door. Her eyes were bloodshot. "Oh, Stuart," she said. "That's just how he is. It doesn't bother me. I just came back here to get a jacket."

"Good," John said. "Mom wants us to come up to the upper deck and join them."

At the rear of the upper deck was a small swimming pool and deck chairs. Many of the French had gathered around the pool in their bikinis, tanning themselves in spite of the moderate temperature. I looked self-consciously at my long sleeves. Everything I had brought with me had long sleeves as recommended by my culturally sensitive travel book. Looking at the French women I began to think I had overdone it. Joyce and Barbara were at their own table. Stuart had freed himself from their company and was sitting poolside with the French while speaking to the two black women Madeleine, Paul and Dr. Short had breakfast with. Gabby and Beverly were talking Michael Sargent's ear off. Madeleine, Dr. Short and Paul sat in the patio area at the opposite end of the deck under a large awning. It appeared that they had been served drinks. Sitting alone at a table near them was Dr. Bueller.

"Bueller is determined to keep close today," John said.

"He gives me the willies."

John nodded in agreement.

We seated ourselves in white wicker deck chairs with our little group. "It's a little early in the day for wine, isn't it?" John said to his mother.

"Not when you haven't had any for a week," she said.

"This wine is very light, very low in alcohol content," Dr. Short assured John. "They serve it chilled. It's just the right thing to drink when you sit out on a sunny day. I will order you a glass."

Bueller was rapidly drawing on his sketchpad. I followed his eyes to see his subject matter. It was most beautiful to look at. Two white robed farmers stood near a donkey in a verdant green rural landscape dotted with giant palms. Not far from them was a third farmer cutting into the soil with his donkey driven plow. Near the shoreline, a small rowboat carrying grains and produce made its way up the Nile, probably heading to the very market in Luxor that Mustafa had driven John and me through.

This scene could have been a thousand years old. Here we were intruders from another time sailing through their world as they carried on their daily lives just as their ancestors had done eons before. I looked at the scantily clad sunbathers in their black and pink bikinis, and I looked again at the long sleeves of my white shirt. I had not overdone it. And then I looked again at what Bueller drew and wondered if my judgment of this man, sensitive enough to render such a sight, had been too harsh.

"Who are those women over there by the pool, the two who sat at your table at breakfast?" John asked his mother as he eyed the two women Stuart was talking to.

"Oh, Shauna and Pearl. They're very nice. They're here to learn about their roots."

"They're Egyptian?" I asked.

"Well, it's hard to speak with precision on these matters," Dr. Short said. "A lack of records and distance in time makes that impossible. But they could be. If they are descended from the inhabitants of Upper Egypt or Sudan—well, it was all known as Nubia in the past—then ancient Egypt very well may be a part of their heritage. It's a very controversial subject these days."

"What's the controversy?"

"Race is always controversial," he answered. "Some claim ancient Egyptians were black Africans; others argue they were white. If you ask me, they were both."

"It looks that way," I said, observing the ship's stewards quietly waiting on the passengers and envisioning Ahmed, who thankfully was not on deck lecturing at the moment.

"We're speaking of ancient Egypt, not today. But your observation is quite correct. Why would it have been any different? They were a cosmopolitan people, still are. They traded or fought with the Phoenicians, Libyans, Assyrians, Persians, Nubians. Some historians argue they educated the Greeks long before Alexander the Great's conquest of Egypt. Heck, we know Nubian kings ruled Egypt for seventy-five years during the 25th Dynasty, and some speculate earlier pharaohs were black. Why, if you look closely at the features in representations of ancient pharaohs and their queens, you'll see many Nubian features. That's not always true, of course. Did you know Cleopatra was Greek?"

"She was?" I said only half believing.

"Yes, she was!" Dr. Short said emphatically. "She was the last in the line of the Ptolemaic Dynasty who ruled Egypt as pharaohs for nearly three hundred years following Alexander the Great's conquest. Unfortunately, they ushered in Egypt's demise. The last of them, Cleopatra, sealed the deal. I shouldn't say that. She certainly didn't mean to. She fought for Egypt and loved it well. Unlike her forebears, she even learned their language. Sadly, she just wasn't strong enough to withstand Rome."

"She married Mark Anthony, didn't she? He was most certainly a Roman," I said.

"Before that she was Julius Caesar's lover," Dr. Short said. "I think it was all a political calculation on her part to ward off a Roman occupation. But it wasn't enough I'm afraid, *Alea iacta est.*"

"I hadn't really thought of her as political, more romantic than political. Maybe my imagination has been contaminated by Elizabeth Taylor starring in the role."

"Cleopatra was a romantic, that's for sure. I do believe she passed herself off as a goddess. But even that wasn't enough; *the die had already been cast.* The Egyptian empire died at the hands of both the Greeks and the Romans. The Greeks neglected it, making it easy for the Romans to later subjugate the land. The temple ruin we'll see in Esna today is a product of both occupations. It was begun by the Greeks and finished by the Romans as ancient Egypt moved from one sphere of influence to the other before it vanished."

"But we're standing in Egypt now," I said.

"We're standing in modern Egypt. That's a different kettle of fish."

"The way you describe it, Egypt sounds almost multicultural," I said.

"Yes, it was and is along with the countries that conquered it. Conquests, occupations, expanding empires have that effect on vanquishers and the vanquished alike."

"What do you mean?" John asked.

"In the center of Saint Peter's Square at the Vatican stands an ancient Egyptian obelisk," Dr. Short said.

"I've seen it," John said.

"It's more than a piece of art," Dr. Short said. "It represents a set of cultural ideas, and at a deeper level its movement from Egypt to Rome marked the transfer of those ideas."

"I've even wondered," John said, excited by the direction of the conversation, "if the pope's miter, his bishop's headdress, is Egyptian in origin. It looks so similar to the pharaoh's double crown. And the pope's staff is reminiscent of the crook carried by Osiris. I've wondered if in the ancient past Osiris was considered a good shepherd too."

"I've never thought about it before, but that's a really fine observation," Dr. Short said.

"So much speculation going on here," Bueller said having put down his pen and pad and pulled his chair over to our table. "So you z'ink z'e Roman Catholic Church absorbed z'e knowledge of z'e ancient Egyptians," he said looking at John and Dr. Short.

"We were having that discussion. You are welcome to join us," Dr. Short said, highlighting the fact that Bueller had already joined them without an invitation or an apology.

"Much ancient Egyptian knowledge was lost by z'e time z'e Romans arrived in Egypt," Bueller said. "Not z'at z'e Romans did not learn things. But z'e earliest knowledge, z'e knowledge z'at built z'e Great Pyramids had disappeared from Egypt long before z'en."

"Certainly it had," Dr. Short agreed.

"But it had not disappeared altogether," Bueller said. "It went north."

Dr. Short raised his eyebrows and sighed.

"It went north, carried by z'e inheritors of z'at pure wisdom."

"I know, I know, the Aryans," Dr. Short said, sounding doubtful.

"Precisely," Bueller said.

"Where is the evidence? I haven't heard any German archaeological digs turning up replicas of the Great Pyramid in the homeland," Dr. Short snarled sarcastically.

"Z'ey would be further north, under z'e ice. That's where z'e Aryans resided in z'ose times."

Listening, we could tell that these two men were repeating an argument they had fought many times, a bitter argument, one for which there would be no agreement.

"I'm sorry," Dr. Short said to us. "I should have told you before that Herr Doktor Bueller has spent his entire adult life—what are you now?

Eighty-five? He's spent over sixty years looking for this purported evidence, the evidence that the Aryan race were the inheritors of the ancient knowledge, that they in fact were the inheritors of the priestly knowledge of the first temples in Egypt."

We said nothing, but Paul, not quite as genteel at his young age, offered an observation. "I know about that kind of Nazi stuff. I've watched all the Indiana Jones movies."

"You were a Nazi?" Natalie asked.

"Well, no. I mean, yes. I was only in z'e Luftwaffe, z'e German Air Force. I had a good post. I was an artist because my uncle, who was a higher up, used his influence. Eventually I was assigned as an artist to z'e archaeological expeditions. I never was involved myself in all of z'at Nazi business, of course not. But I have continued my archaeological work ever since z'e war's end."

"Funded by people who continue to seek to prove what Hitler never could," Dr. Short said.

"It is my life's work."

"Your Hyperborean theories are an embarrassment to the profession," Dr. Short snapped.

My feelings were torn between revulsion and pity. What horror the myth of the master race brought upon the earth. Yet I could not but feel some pity for a man as old as Bueller who had devoted himself so singularly, so unwaveringly, so unsuccessfully to the pursuit of the phantasm of his own superiority.

Our silence was broken by the soft-spoken tones of our Nubian stewards, who without pretense or guile humbly called the foreign vacationers to lunch. Unlike Bueller's heart, their hearts are as light as feathers, I thought as I looked down at the symbol of divine truth on my cartouche. They are the inheritors of that ancient wisdom, that pure wisdom. They are its embodiment.

Chapter Fifteen

Our peaceful lunch was interrupted by the harsh sounds of loud clapping hands and the voice whose commands we had sadly become accustomed to. "We will be leaving in five minutes. Hurry up!"

I gobbled down the rest of my lunch before I rushed off to our cabin to prepare. We arrived at the gangplank seven minutes later. The entire group, minus Bueller, was ready to leave in fifteen minutes, ten minutes later than Ahmed had announced.

"You are late!" Ahmed scolded. "Now, I want us to stay together this time," he said glancing at Natalie and Madeleine. "We will walk to the Temple of Khnum. Do not stop to shop. You will have time to shop after we make our visit."

"Girl Scout camp," I complained as we were led off the ship like school children being taken on a field trip. My complaints ceased when I saw two military police armed with automatic weapons standing on the pier at the end of the gangplank.

"What are they here for?" I asked John.

"I don't know," he said quietly.

Three was the maximum number that could walk side by side through the gauntlet of merchants who met us on the road that led from our ship to the temple. John grabbed Paul's shoulder pulling him between us. Natalie, Madeleine and Dr. Short trailed behind. Stuart was just ahead with Joyce and Barbara on each side; their arms locked into his as if he were being taken prisoner. A new threesome had formed that I hadn't noticed before. It was Ahmed, an older woman and a pretty teenage girl with full, bushy hair and long thick eyelashes. The looks that passed between Ahmed and the girl suggested a budding affair. Love boat, I thought. I could tell by the way the other woman kept her eyes on them that she must be the girl's mother. Good for her mother, I thought, remembering myself at that age.

Ahmed must have seemed exotic to this young girl and quite knowledgeable. He was a handsome young man of twenty-three or so.

Dark eyes and neatly styled hair, he showed off an athletic build in European fitted shirts and pants. He looked the height of sophistication in his polished Italian leather shoes. The boys in her life until then had probably been the typical American suburban variety, all sports, Reeboks and beer.

Like good school children we marched undeterred past merchants eagerly hawking their wares. It must have been absolutely painful for Gabby and Beverly, I imagined, as we passed yards and yards of fabric, baskets and all kinds of trinkets being shoved at us. At last we arrived at our destination.

"Khnum was one of the last Egyptian temples to be built," Ahmed said. "All that remains is the hypostyle hall, which as you can see stands well below ground level. The ruins of the rest of the original temple remain buried under the surrounding buildings of the town. Columns form the facade. In all, twenty-four columns support the building. The capitals often take the form of a flower. Here," he said pointing upwards, "is an example of the lotus flower design you saw at the Temple of Karnak in Luxor."

Karnak had spoiled me. It was magnificent beyond comparison and dwarfed this temple in its grandeur. Nothing here captured my imagination until a statue of a sultry woman with a lion's head and a full mane of hair caught my eye.

"Who's that?" I asked.

"Moneyed," Ahmed said, "the lion-headed goddess who was to be Khnum's consort."

Consort! I thought. I looked at the young girl with the bushy hair standing next to him and was relieved to see her mother.

"This temple was dedicated to the god Khnum," Ahmed said. "He is said to have fashioned humankind on his potter's wheel from the mud of the Nile. The rear wall in front of you is the oldest part of the temple and was once the facade of a Greek temple. The Romans built the rest of the building, including the newer columned facade. Over here is an example of Roman influence." He pointed to a scene carved on one of the temple's pillars. "Here is the lion goddess Menheyet, and here is the Roman Emperor Trajan dancing before her."

I couldn't help but find this scene amusing. Who was the butt of the joke, I wondered, the Roman emperor engaged in the dance or the Egyptian goddess who believed his flattery sincere?

John pointed to the magnificent ceiling. "Look, the signs of the zodiac up there."

"Those are Roman," Ahmed said. "Look at the northern half of the ceiling. These carvings represent Egyptian astronomical figures. The Roman zodiac is in the south; the Egyptian is in the north. And there is evidence that this temple was built on the site of an even earlier temple that dates back to Pharaoh Tuthmosis the Third."

"This is a good example of the layering of history," John told Paul and me, "a civilization quite literally built on top of an earlier civilization. Khnum temple compared to modern Esna sits in a pit, but that was ground level at the time it was built. Further below that pit lie the few remains of an even earlier Egyptian temple."

Ahmed led us into the courtyard. "See those blocks over there. Those are all that remain of an early Christian church."

"Is this multicultural or what?" I said.

"Multicultural isn't the right word," John said. "Egypt was under siege. The Greeks, the Romans, the Christians were all vying for power here while the Egyptians were trying to retain their influence. Some compromises were made, half the ceiling, for example, and the Emperor Trajan dancing before Menheyet. But it must have been a struggle."

"And all that is left of that struggle is a ruin in a sleepy Egyptian town no longer influential enough for anyone to fight to control. What a waste," I said, which made me think again of Hans Bueller.

Bueller had attached himself to a vision of the superiority of his lineage and spent his whole life trying to find evidence to prove it. He never would find such evidence, of course, not if he lived to be one hundred and ten. Why was the German defeat in World War II and the revelations of the unspeakable atrocities committed by the Nazis not enough to convince him of this folly when he was still young enough to remake his life?

I reminded myself that not all visions are so empty. Some can be quite constructive even if only temporary. Ancient Egypt must have embodied a powerful vision that gave to its people the imagination, intellect and will to build the monumental Pyramids of Giza and the magnificent Temple of Karnak in Luxor. What else could explain the existence of these masterworks? I could understand why Bueller wanted to wed his lineage to ancient Egypt. He wanted its power and the legitimacy such a lineage would bestow, the right to say that my people are the inheritors of a great tradition, that we are the descendants of a priestly caste. This was all hubris, of course.

This temple is a reminder that such proclamations are in vain. Power, empty of the vision that inspired it, quickly dissipates. Before it runs out though it turns to brute force and destruction, and like this temple eventually disintegrates into rubble, nothing more. That is what was so melancholy about this place. Its ruins tell the story of ancient Egypt's decline. In the hands of the Romans, Egypt's vision was reduced to a joke: goddess Menheyet, consort of the god Khnum, is seduced by Roman Emperor Trajan who dances like a court jester before an unwitting queen.

My somber mood was short-lived, transformed by the riotous mayhem of the market once we returned to the street vendors and were free to shop. Gabby and Beverly looked nearly ravished as merchants sensing the two women's shopping lust gathered round them prepared to satisfy. Natalie, Madeleine and Dr. Short were standing in front of a market stall, fingering various brightly colored cotton fabrics. Michael Sargent snapped pictures of the market madness with his very expensive camera. Stuart leaned against a building, having freed himself from Joyce and Barbara who had become enamored with billowing yards of cloth. Ahmed and the young girl were likewise free, the girl's mother being engaged in bargaining with a merchant for his fine cotton goods. They snuggled close. They kissed briefly as if they were alone, which for all practical purposes they were since everyone's attention was elsewhere except for my prying eyes.

John, Paul and I approached a vendor who was selling the long white traditional robes we had seen worn by so many men in this part of Egypt.

"What do you call these?" John asked the vendor.

The vendor pointed to his wares with such reticence that we guessed they were intended for the townspeople rather than the tourists. John nodded. The vendor pulled one out, a long robe that he held up to John. John nodded again and pointed to Paul. The vendor found a smaller one and held it up to Paul. "Galabayya" the vendor said as if he had understood John's question.

I pointed to a stack of long white cotton scarves, the ones used to make the turbans the men wore, and held up three fingers. Thus we made our purchases and learned the name of the robes we had seen repeatedly since we had come south. "Galabayya," I repeated out loud, but my voice was drowned out by the sudden shrieks of automatic gunfire.

The shots seemed to come from the direction of our boat so running towards it was not an option. Like deer stunned by headlights, we froze not knowing who was firing the weapons or where we should run.

Stuart appeared, grabbed hold of Paul, John and me and said, "This way." We moved along between stalls and down a narrow path between two buildings. Waiting for us were Natalie, Madeleine and Dr. Short, who Stuart had already retrieved.

"No time to talk now, keep moving," he said

"Where are we going?" Natalie asked.

"Back to the ruin."

Stuart went before us, looked out ahead, then returned to take us further on a route through what amounts to the back alleys of Esna, twisting, turning and pausing along the way as he led us safely back to the temple.

"Now get down in there," he said, pointing into the pit where the temple sat. "Get behind those pillars, and stay out of sight until I come back for you."

"What's going on Stu?" Natalie asked.

"No time now. I will tell you when I come for you. Just go inside and stay quiet."

"I thought that young man's name is Walter," Dr. Short said.

"It's a long story," Madeleine said. "Natalie will tell you all about it later."

Minutes passed slowly as we sat silent and huddled together behind the pillars at the rear of the temple near the original Greek facade. All we heard in that great silence was weapons fire. We did not talk or try to explain to each other what had brought us there or who Stuart was. We were focused on one thing, our survival. I gazed up at the Roman zodiac carved into the temple's ceiling and wondered if our future could be calculated through some ancient form of divination. Gradually the weapons fire diminished. At first it sounded as if it were moving away from us, and then the sounds of firing grew more sporadic. Eventually we heard nothing, nothing until the sound of rustling grew near. We froze again, knowing something or someone was approaching but not knowing who or what it was.

Dr. Short caught a glimpse of blonde hair behind a column as a shadowy figure moved towards the rear of the temple. "It's Walter," he said to us. In a loud whisper he called out, "We're over here."

Stuart's figure fully emerged in what was now dim light that filtered into the temple as the sun lowered in the west. Natalie was beside herself in tears as Stuart put his arms around her to comfort her.

"It's over," Stuart said. "I'll take you back to the boat now. We're pulling this ship out of here and docking for the night further up the river where they've got better security."

"Is everyone else all right?" Natalie asked.

"Only the guards were seriously wounded. That newspaper reporter was hit, but he'll be all right. It's only a scratch. He must have gotten some great photos."

"What was this all about?" John asked.

"There's a power struggle going on in this country. We were just in the wrong place at the wrong time."

"But why our boat?" I said. "Why do we have to be guarded? What do we have to do with anything here?"

"Your dollars keep the peace. There are political forces that don't want peace. The weaker the economy in towns like this one, the greater the discontent, and the easier it would be to overthrow the government."

"Why don't they just vote the government out of office if they don't like it?" Paul asked.

"If it were only that simple." He roughed up Paul's hair.

Stuart, who worried that there could be a sniper hiding along the main road waiting for another opportunity to maim or kill, took us back just as he brought us, through the twists and turns of Esna's byways. We came out into the market area that had earlier been the scene of lively commerce but now was its own kind of ruin, with broken market stalls

115

smashed against pavement. A great flood light beamed from our boat, illuminating both the gangplank and the roadway leading to our ship. We lumbered aboard exhausted from the ordeal.

"Hurry up, hurry up," Ahmed said. "You are the last to board. We want to leave now."

Once onboard, Ahmed directed us to our cabins to relax. "Dinner will be a little late tonight, or if you like, it could be brought to your rooms. We will eat like the French," he said and broke into a smile, "Dinner at ten."

We were happy with the prospect of rest, a shower and dinner in our rooms, but most of all we were happy to be leaving Esna.

"Remember, I'm Walter. None of us have met before this cruise. I'm a writer. I just helped you out a little. Got it?"

Chapter Sixteen

Discussion at breakfast grew quite animated as stories flew back and forth across the three tables occupied by the Americans. No one wanted to leave the cruise. No one demanded more armed guards. Instead, everyone reveled in telling their story of where they were when the shooting broke out. True, no one onboard had been hurt or harmed except for travel reporter Michael Sargent who wore his wound like a badge of honor. He was only grazed, he told us, as he happily accepted his new stature as the man on the scene, the reporter on the spot.

"I was standing close to the ship so that I could take comprehensive photos of Esna's bazaar when a shot came from my right and then a second from behind. I turned just in time to see the ship's guards firing in the direction of the shooters who had taken cover at the far end of the pier. I could make out figures ducking behind barrels and boxes before they fired back. It looked to me like the guards were their targets so I stood my ground and took photographs. Well, as you all know, bedlam broke out in the market. I got some excellent pictures of that too. Then I saw the gunmen pop out from where they were hiding, move away from the pier and cut a path between two nearby buildings. I thought they were hightailing it out of there, but I was mistaken in that. Before I knew it I was right between them and the ship's guards as they approached the boat from the direction of the market. One of the guards went down, then the other. Then I was shot. I dropped to the ground thinking it was all over when three trucks carrying gendarmes arrived on the road just beyond the market and began firing. I stayed on the ground until the firing stopped, and man did I pray. I raised my head up just enough to get a great photo of troops on foot chasing those armed rebels out of there. Well, you heard the rest." He sighed a long sigh.

"Yes, we did," Beverly said. "We heard all that gunfire for at least an hour. Why, Gabby and I were scared to death. It was so nice of those good townspeople to take us into their shop. Where did the rest of y'all hide?"

Nearly everyone reported a similar experience. Not wanting to lose paying customers, the merchants hid them in their shops. And they were handsomely rewarded in generous purchases by these grateful tourists, particularly Gabby and Beverly who proceeded to ask Ahmed if there was a post office at the next port where they might mail all their loot bought in the heat of battle.

Then Gabby's eyes turned upon us. "Where were y'all?" she asked our little group who until then had remained silent.

"We hid in the ruin," Madeleine said.

"The ruin! How'd y'all get all the way back there?"

Dr. Short spoke up, "Walter took us."

Gabby's eyes turned to Stuart as if she were seeing him for the first time. Barbara and Joyce shot daggers at him. "You could have taken us to the ruin too, Walter. I'm sure we would have been a lot safer." Their gaze fell on Natalie, and if looks could kill....

Stuart said nothing. The rest of us said little, thinking the less said the better. Finally, the silence was broken by Ahmed's claps. He was determined to keep the cruise on track regardless of events that threatened to derail it.

"Attention everyone! Today we will stay on board. You can swim or sunbathe on the upper deck if you like. Tomorrow we will arrive at Aswan. But tonight we will have a special treat, a talent competition. I need three men to volunteer for a play."

Paul stepped forward.

"Men not boys," Ahmed said.

Stuart ducked up the stairs to the upper deck. Michael pointed to his arm in a sling and was excused. John, Bueller and Dr. Short were ordered to come with Ahmed to learn their parts and try on their costumes while the rest of us were directed upstairs.

I lay in a lounge chair next to Natalie on the upper deck fiddling with my cartouche while looking out at the bucolic scene and wondering what danger lurked behind the wild grasses along the shoreline or the large palms scattered in the fields of crops. I knew nothing of Egyptian politics. I only knew what I had observed. Life in Egypt is fragile and depends on what can be produced on a band of fertile soil running alongside the Nile in an otherwise barren land. Egypt has little oil unlike some nearby countries. But what it lacks in oil it makes up for in the remnants of a rich civilization, perhaps the richest in the Middle East. War-torn Sudan lies to its south, Libya to its west, the Mediterranean to its north. The Red Sea lies directly to its east with Saudi Arabia situated on that sea's other shoreline. Touching its northeast corner is Israel. Perhaps it is this northeast corner that brought the Vice President of the United States here, I thought. I did not want Egypt pulled into others' strife but kept outside, protected from its destructive impulses. I wanted Egypt to survive: beautiful, tranquil, the home of one of the greatest civilizations to have ever existed, a civilization that spoke of the greater aspects of human nature. I wanted that to survive. I was jealous for it to survive and not succumb to the great undoing, as I thought of it, the great undoing that was tearing apart humanity's finest endeavors.

"Thanks for keeping my cover," Stuart said to Natalie, waking her up and breaking my reverie. "I would never ask you to do this for me if it wasn't very important, believe me."

Natalie replied without emotion. "That's okay," she said and yawned. "You need not apologize."

"I didn't come over here just to apologize. I thought we might talk."

She was unmoved, but why, I thought. She's crazy about this guy, and she won't give him the time of day. I tried to fill in the awkwardness of the moment.

"I want to thank you for what you did for us yesterday. I don't know what would have happened if you hadn't pulled us out of harm's way."

Stuart looked at me and then at Natalie. "I was happy to help. It was a very dangerous situation we were in. I don't think people realize how dangerous it was. We're lucky none of us was hurt."

Natalie took a sudden turn towards Stuart and heatedly said, "What's this all about? What are you not telling me?"

"I wish you wouldn't ask. I can't tell you."

"Well, here you are," blurted Joyce in her loud, brassy voice.

Stuart sighed. Natalie turned her gaze away from him and back towards the river. Barbara caught up with Joyce and looked venomously at the back of Natalie's head as Joyce, in what sounded like mock sweetness, urged Stuart to go with them over to the pool as he had promised.

119

"Where are your trunks Walter?" she asked. "You were supposed to change into your trunks and meet us back here. Well, that's all right. You go change now, and we'll be waiting for you at the pool."

Natalie looked sick after hearing these women order Stuart about. He looked at her and then at them, raised himself out of his chair and made his way down the stairs apparently towards his cabin as commanded. The two women pulled off their tropical flowered wraps and sauntered towards the poolside lounge dressed in only their bikinis. I noted that Stuart didn't return for almost an hour. When he did, he challenged Paul to a little diving competition that the two heartily enjoyed. I heard Stuart laugh for the first time. Joyce and Barbara, reclining in their lounge chairs under the full Egyptian sun, were left to watch Stuart from a distance and entertain each other.

"Why did you rebuff Stuart?" I asked Natalie.

"I didn't rebuff Stu."

"Yes you did."

"How?"

"Well, he clearly wanted to talk, and you cut him off."

"No I didn't."

"Yes you did! You acted angry. And he had just, well, he could have saved our lives yesterday."

"I know." She looked off into the distance. A moment later she said, "Do you think he felt rebuffed? I didn't mean to...."

"Yes, I think he did. Why are you upset with him anyway? Because he hasn't told us what he's doing here?"

"Yes, that and—he used to do that to me before, when we dated. There were things that were going on in his life that he kept from me. And there were many Joyces and Barbaras."

"So that's it. If you would think about it for two seconds, you would realize that it was you and your family he thought to save from gunfire, not Joyce and not Barbara. Why did you and Stuart stop seeing each other anyway?"

"I told you that already. He was transferred. Our dates had been informal after work events, but when he was transferred, well, I just didn't see him any longer."

"Did he call you?"

"He did a few times, but I made excuses…"

"Not to formalize those dates," I said, finishing her sentence.

"It seemed pointless. I thought he's been transferred. I can make a clean break from him."

"But why? He's a great looking guy. He seems intelligent, and he has courage."

"And many women."

"But he really cares for you. That's obvious. You're the first woman that I've known to reject the advances of a good-looking guy because he's good-looking. I wonder if he even knows your feelings. Did you ever tell him?"

"Of course not."

"He doesn't know then." Natalie looked at me as if she were surprised by my revelation. "He doesn't know!" I repeated. "You keep it in. You keep everything in. Maybe you're afraid to risk opening up. Believe me Natalie, he doesn't know. If you don't want to lose him to the likes of Joyce or Barbara, you will tell him."

Joyce's loud voice boomed across the deck. "Walter, you're going to wear that boy out. Why don't you come over here with us?" She proceeded to pat the seat of an empty lounge chair as if to entice a lap dog.

"Stuart rescued us yesterday. You should return the favor."

"You're right," Natalie said. "Let's go over there."

We joined Madeleine who was rubbing a beaming Paul down with a towel.

"Thanks for entertaining Paul," Madeleine said to Stuart.

"My pleasure." He gave Paul a high five.

"My pleasure too," Paul said, smacking the flat of his hand hard against Stuart's.

The ship's stewards ascended the stairway to the upper deck carrying trays laden with sandwiches and cold drinks. The ship's horn blew and the boat turned slightly as if it were heading into a town that lay in front of us.

"I didn't think we were stopping today after what happened yesterday," Madeleine said.

"Neither did I," Natalie said.

121

"Neither did I," a slightly worried Stuart repeated.

A steward offered us our choice of sandwiches: sliced cold lamb, cheese, or hummus spread on flat bread. He said that the boat was making a brief stop at the request of one of the passengers who desired a post office. To expedite the request, lunch was being served informally today.

"May we all go on shore?" Madeleine asked.

"If you are brief," he answered. "We are not to be here long."

Stuart and Natalie stood awkwardly together, not knowing quite what to say to each other. I broke the silence. "Do you want to go with us? We may need your protection."

Stuart smiled, "I will go change into something dry."

"I'll see you at the gangplank," Natalie said.

Joyce and Barbara were still sunbathing, as we were about to leave. Their eyes fixed on Natalie as if to say, you won this round. I returned their glance, my eyes saying, it's all over ladies. She won the war.

"It doesn't look friendly," I said to Natalie as I looked out from the upper deck at the gendarmes that lined the town's pier. "Let's go put on something modest."

Natalie and I went to my cabin so that I could get two of the long, white scarves I had bought in Esna the day before. "Put this over your head and shoulders," I said as I covered my own head. "Maybe these will help us fit in just a little."

John walked into the cabin free at last from his drama practice. "What's up?" he asked.

"We're going in," I said.

"No, what's up with the headgear?"

"We wanted to look inconspicuous."

"I thought we weren't stopping anywhere until we get to Aswan."

"We thought so too, but apparently Gabby and Beverly needed a post office before then. Did you get a sandwich?"

"Yes, Ahmed got me one. Hey, look at this." He laid a long blue robe with gaudy gold satin trim on the bed.

"Your costume?" Natalie laughed.

"What's the play about?" I asked.

"It's a surprise. You will have to wait until tonight to see."

Chapter Seventeen

Gabby and Beverly paraded down the gangplank, accompanied by two porters weighed down with packages wrapped, tied and ready to mail. Eager to break the tedium of confinement on the ship, several other passengers followed behind.

"Do you ever lose any of that stuff?" Stuart asked the two women. They looked surprised, startled in fact, as if they did not comprehend his meaning. "Sending it from places like this," he said. "Does it all arrive or is some of it lost or stolen?"

"Oh, oh," Beverly said. "It almost always arrives. We've lost very little even usin' these rural post offices."

Gabby joined in. "Mailin' things ahead is the way to go. If we had to carry all of this with us, well, they wouldn't let us on the plane when we fly home."

"We'd be overweight!" Beverly chuckled, unable to resist making a good joke.

At the bottom of the gangplank stood a horde of children hawking an assortment of items for sale or simply asking for money. The two women marched through the throng undeterred.

Natalie, looking down at the mayhem from the ship's deck said, "Wait for me. I have to go back to my cabin and get something."

We waited and watched while others left the ship. Barbara and Joyce walked passed us in a huff. Ahmed, looking very important, gestured the young girl and her mother to follow him for a private, unofficial tour. Even Bueller who had avoided most of the previous sightseeing, nodded to us before he trotted down the gangplank.

"I read about this in my guide book," Natalie said when she returned and handed out boxes to each of us, each box containing twelve pens. "You're supposed to give children pens instead of money when they beg. That way, you won't encourage them to ask for money, and the pens will be useful for them in school."

"I'd rather get money," Paul said.

The rest of us thanked Natalie for the pens and complimented her for so thoroughly preparing for the trip. We made our way down the gangplank, the last of the passengers to disembark. Chaos followed as beggar children to whom we happily distributed the pens overran us. Unlike Paul, these children were delighted with their new acquisitions. The gendarmes weren't so delighted as they tried to hold the children back, fearing any kind of disorder, even the disorder of happy children. After they cleared a path for us leading into the market area, I was confronted by an old man who stared at me with unfriendly eyes. He pointed to my headscarf and spoke in a language I could not understand but with nuances I could. It was as if he said, "You had better wear that scarf."

"I don't know if this was such a good idea," I said to John.

"We'll be all right. We won't be here long."

Ahmed had arranged a buggy ride for his pretty young friend and her mother. The driver looked at the girl approvingly and winked at Ahmed before they rode off. We milled around with nothing to do but shop, but shopping in this environment was anything but leisurely. It was bedlam. Children arrived in front of us with their hands held out with every turn we made. By then all the pens were gone. The gendarmes proved more forceful as they pushed and shoved the little horde, a security issue they claimed. We agreed that we would be better off going back on board sooner rather than later.

"You go on board. I have something I must do," Stuart said. He turned and disappeared into the crowd.

Natalie looked perplexed, but along with the rest of us eagerly removed herself from the unpredictable chaos of the town to the familiar environs of our boat. The three of us stayed on the bridge to wait for Stuart while Dr. Short, Madeleine and Paul moved to the quiet of the ship's interior. We stood alongside a group of French passengers who had the good sense not to disembark but rather to watch the confusion our unexpected docking met with from the ship's rail.

"These people's whole livelihood must depend on tourism," I said.

A French woman overheard me and said in halting English, "Oui, no tourists, no money, no food."

A Frenchman joined in. "Few tourists now."

A young boy broke through the barricade of gendarmes and pushed towards our boat holding a statue of a small bird in his outstretched hand. "You want?" he shouted. One of the gendarmes moved towards him. The boy scrambled up a huge stack of boxes piled high on the pier, bringing him to the height of the deck. I thought that any boy who would risk defying these armed police to make this sale must be desperate. His eyes met mine, "You want?" he repeated.

I went to the rail and yelled, "How much?"

"Fifty pounds," he said.

I assented and took a fifty-pound Egyptian note from my bag. He moved toward the edge of the boxes while I reached as far as I could, which was not far enough. John grabbed the bird, took my bank note and stretched out his arm to the boy. The exchange was made. The boy slid down the boxes and rejoined his friends in celebration before they ran off, evading the guards who were chasing them.

I held the prized bird in my hands. The body and tail of the statue had delicate carvings of stylized feathers etched in gray lines on black stone. Twin metal legs held it up. A regal neck, graceful head and very long beak were its glory. It was worth every cent of the fifty pounds I paid for it.

"It's an ibis," a French woman said. "You could have gotten it at any market for ten pounds."

"I don't care," I said. "This bird is that boy's triumph."

Gabby, Beverly, Joyce, Barbara, Bueller and Stuart were still not accounted for when the sound of gunshots echoed from a short distance.

"Not again!" I said, looking out over the pier.

John strained to see something, anything that might tell him what was going on while a silent panic spread throughout the crowd of shipboard spectators who made a rapid retreat into the boat's interior. Only three of us remained on the bridge along with Ahmed, who had just returned from his buggy ride. A few minutes later Gabby and Beverly and their two porters climbed up the gangplank huffing and puffing.

"They tried to rob us!" Gabby said.

"Who tried to rob you?" John shouted over the din rising up from the frightened townspeople below.

"Some man," Gabby replied. "Walter tried to stop him."

Forgetting herself, Natalie involuntarily said, "Stuart!"

"Stuart who?" Gabby asked.

"There's no more time for talking now," Ahmed said. "The gendarmes say we must leave this port. Are we all here?"

"No!" Natalie said with some urgency. "Walter hasn't returned."

"Neither has Dr. Bueller," I added, "or Joyce and Barbara."

"There's Bueller now," John said.

Dr. Bueller sauntered up the gangplank, passed me as he made his way to his cabin and out of the corner of his eye caught sight of my bird. "An ibis," he said. "How nice." Minutes later Stuart arrived to a waiting Natalie, followed by Joyce and Barbara. The boat immediately prepared to leave.

"What happened out there?" Natalie asked.

"I will tell you about it later," Stuart said. "I want to talk to the three of you to see if you can help me put this thing together, but let's get out of here now."

The four of us climbed the stairs to the safety of the upper deck and looked out over the town, as our ship pulled into the middle of the Nile ready to continue its voyage. Activity on the other side of the deck quickly captured my ear. Gabby and Beverly had attracted the attention of a small group of French passengers who watched and laughed as the two women reached over the rail and shouted downwards into the river. I walked over to get a better look and saw two men prancing about in a small rowboat, holding up long gaudy robes. "Oh my god!" I shouted in disbelief, as the crowd of onlookers grew larger.

A deal was quickly struck as the four negotiated a price and a method of exchange. One of the boatmen wrapped the two robes together in a tight ball and hurled them up and onto the upper deck. Gabby and Beverly grabbed the robes, inspected them and displayed them for all to see.

An Egyptian woman wouldn't have been caught dead in either one of these gowns, covered as they were with painted jewels and headdresses, painted golden wings and scenes of camels, palm trees and pyramids skirting the hems. A Frenchman looked at Gabby, Beverly, these robes and then at me, and the two of us broke out laughing together at the absurdity of the whole scene.

The shoppers still had to figure out how to toss their payment down so it would land in the rowboat instead of the river, and fast. Our ship was approaching concrete locks that the rowboat could not enter without risk of serious injury to the men it carried, which created a good deal of drama for the French bystanders who rooted for a successful outcome.

Beverly made a failed test attempt with scraps of paper that blew off course before rapidly going underwater. Together they determined to keep it steady, they needed to weight the money, but there were no stones or anything else on hand to weight it with. Plus, if it were too weighted, it would sink. A hush fell over the crowd as the cruise ship neared the locks. With little time to spare, Gabby wrapped their payment in a plastic bag and tied the bag into a ball and dropped it down. The package floated to the cheers of the onlookers, and the rowers paddled to retrieve it. When it was opened the boatmen shouted in joy for their effort had been amply rewarded, far above the value of the gaudy robes or the price they had asked. Amidst all the cheers and shouts and smiles, Ahmed clapped his hands and ordered us downstairs to the buffet.

Our group had officially become seven with the addition of Stuart, so we nearly filled a table with only one available space. Bueller emerged from the cabin area and made his way to that single space at the end of our table, which happened to be right next to me. He said he was drawn to my prized ibis that I had placed on the table next to my plate. I told him the story of how I acquired it.

"Very interesting," he said. "Z'en it is already very precious to you."

"Yes, it is."

"Do you know who z'e ibis is, what it represents?"

"No, I don't other than what it represents to me: that boy's spirit to survive against all odds."

"Ja, and more. It represents z'e god Thoth, god of all wisdom and knowledge."

"Oh, I remember something about Thoth. When we were in Lower Egypt we learned about Imhotep, the renowned priest who designed the Step Pyramid."

"Some z'ink Imhotep was a god, a manifestation of Thoth." Bueller paused for a few minutes composing exactly what he wanted to say.

"Thoth created our reality, all knowledge, including z'e mystical arts."

"Mystical arts?"

"Magic," Bueller said. "Some would say z'at our reality is a kind of grand magic trick, a conjured up reality z'at can be manipulated. I find it interesting how z'e ibis came to you. I z'ink z'ere may be deep import in z'at. Did you say you are a teacher?"

"Yes, I am a university English teacher."

"You teach writing," he said with something peculiar in his smile. "Thoth taught us to write along with the goddess Seshat who invented z'e art. So perhaps z'e ibis was drawn to you because you practice z'at art."

"Which art?" I said, "Magic or writing?"

"Writing, if done properly, can be a form of magic. It can shape a new reality as Imhotep's designs did. He ushered in a new age. Sadly, much has been lost."

"Yes, we learned about that in Lower Egypt as well. How the knowledge of pyramid building was held by the high priests but soon was lost. And how all subsequent attempts to build pyramids failed in comparison to those designed by their inventor, Imhotep."

He whispered, "Can you come to my cabin for just a moment? I have something to show you."

"I think the others would wonder..."

"It's very important z'at you see. Meet me z'ere in ten minutes."

Bueller left the table. I chatted with the others for a few minutes and then excused myself to go to the powder room. I made my way to his cabin expecting I didn't know what, but I was unable to resist the temptation of seeing whatever he had to show me. His door opened immediately at my first knock.

"I'm glad you are here. Please be seated."

I watched as he rummaged through his bag and took out a package. It was the same package he had given to Madeleine to take with her to Luxor. He carefully untied the string, cut open the tape that secured it, unwrapped the paper and pulled out a box which he opened as he walked towards me so that I might see its contents.

Lying in the box on a pillow of white cotton was a small golden statue. It had the body of a man with the head of an ibis. Bueller

128

reached into the box and lovingly lifted the statue out. It glimmered in the moonlight that flooded his cabin.

"Thoth," he said.

"It's beautiful. Where did you get it?"

"It is part of Imhotep's funerary artifacts."

"It must be very valuable."

"Ja, it is. I have spent z'e better part of my life trying to acquire z'is object, but not for z'e value of its gold or its antiquity."

"I'm surprised you gave it to Madeleine to bring to Luxor."

"I'm a good judge of character after all z'ese years. I knew she would carry it to Luxor safely. And I knew z'at none of z'e antiquities inspectors at z'e airport would think to search her or her luggage. She doesn't look z'e part."

"Madeleine certainly is the last person one would suspect as a thief," I agreed.

"You must think me a common thief," he said sounding aggrieved. "I'm nothing of z'e kind!" He raised his voice. "It is not z'e monetary value of z'is object z'at I am interested in. Z'ere is a power z'at lives in z'is object. Thoth's spirit, z'e same spirit z'at animated Imhotep, is captured inside it. It wants to come out. Don't you see?" he nearly shouted. "He brought writing to mankind, and you, a teacher of writing, drew the ibis to you. Thoth shares your spirit. Thoth is trying to speak. Don't you see? He wants to remake z'e world. He wants to speak through you!"

I didn't like Bueller's references to me. "What will you do with it?" I asked in an effort to redirect his attention.

"I will offer myself to it. I will let it work through me. We had dreams once of remaking z'e world. Humanity had been reduced to weak, niggling beings. We were going to cleanse and perfect ourselves and start anew. Z'at dream has not ended. Not as long as I'm alive!"

How pathetic and frightening, I thought. The old Nazi dream is standing with me here right in this room. How little Bueller had learned in his eighty-five years. I recalled the image of the Osiris scale at the Cairo Museum depicting the worthy heart as light as a feather, a belief from which Bueller could truly benefit. My immediate problem, however, was how to retreat from his cabin now that he had told me his secret.

"It's Ahmed," a voice said, following a few raps on the door. "Dr. Bueller, are you in there? We must get ready for our play. Are you there?"

Bueller cleared his throat. "I'm here. I will be upstairs in just a few minutes."

"Good. Hurry up."

"Does Ahmed ever get tired of bossing us around?" I asked.

"Ja, z'ere is much of z'at on z'ese tours."

"Well, I'd better get upstairs so you can get ready," I said. "I can't wait to see the play."

Bueller looked at me with a steady gaze. "You will be discrete, won't you?"

I shook my head yes, but I hated to make a promise I wasn't sure I would keep.

"You have a role to play in this drama. I'm sure of z'at."

Chapter Eighteen

The dining room was transformed into a theater in the round, tables having been removed and chairs rearranged in circular rows. Egyptian musicians had come on board and begun to play lively instrumental music. The audience took their seats as Ahmed read his brief introduction to the play. The lights were lowered.

Out from the stairwell marched John and Dr. Short leading a processional in their satin robes, contrasting vests and mitered crowns. They walked side by side with their arms crossed over their chests Osiris-like, but the solemnity of their appearance was made slightly ludicrous by Dr. Short's sunglasses worn to complement John's necessary but historically inappropriate eyeglasses. Two weeping women followed behind them, their heads, faces and bodies covered as if they were in mourning. They moved a wheeled cart upon which a body lay under a white sheet.

John in the role of High Priest of the Temple of Karnak stood over the body with his arms outstretched and proclaimed, "Oh Amun-Ra, god of the pharaohs and Karnak, hear our prayer. Hear us as we pray over our recently deceased Pharaoh Tutankh Bueller. Tutankh Bueller was a GREAT pharaoh, but he is dead meat now!" He paused. The audience howled with laughter. "Following in the ancient traditions that have been passed down through the priesthood we shall MUMMIFY him! We shall remove his entrails and store them in canopic jars where one day they will be discovered by French archaeologists." The French broke out in loud applause.

Dr. Short wielded a butter knife he had been carrying and pretended to make an incision into Bueller's body. John began pulling out entrails.

"Mon dieu! C'est incroyable!" John said, as be pulled out a bottle of wine. "Voila!" he said, pulling out a cigar. The audience laughed, and the weeping women wailed.

Having finished their mummification ritual, the two priests ceremoniously walked off center stage. The women continued to weep while standing over the covered body of the dead Tutankh Bueller. The lights dimmed; the tempo of the music picked up and the lights brightened. One of the weeping women doffed her coverings, revealing herself a belly dancer gyrating to the rhythms of the Egyptian flutes in her gold embroidered skirt and halter. Black tassels fell from her breasts, sensuously swaying over her bare midriff and belly. Up popped Tutankh Bueller, who abruptly raised himself on his stretcher to the excitement of the women and the amazement of the priests. The audience screamed with laughter and applause. The very ancient Dr. Bueller, who almost looked like a mummy in actuality, hopped off his bed, smiled lustily and began gyrating with the exotic dancer. The lights dimmed once more until they were off.

"Assassin! Assassin!" the belly dancer screamed.

The audience thinking this was part of the play began to laugh and applaud. Stuart leaped from his chair and went for the light switch. Once the lights were back on, a sickly Bueller stood before the audience pale as a ghost, his hand holding his wounded arm that still had a knife stuck in it. Blood trickled from his sleeve onto the floor.

"No one move!" Stuart ordered.

Several of the ship's stewards disregarded him and went to assist Bueller who by then had dropped to his knees in stunned silence. I walked over to join John and Dr. Short and whispered, "This can't be real. It's like an Agatha Christie novel." They shook their heads in agreement as Stuart, realizing that no one had any reason to follow his orders, began to explain himself.

"This is a crime scene," he said. "We won't be able to bring the Egyptian police on board until we dock. We're pulling into a port soon. Are we not Ahmed?"

"Yes, I have ordered the crew to bring the ship into Kom Ombo. As we speak, they are radioing the police there who will board at once. No one may leave the ship unless or until the police give their permission."

"For now," Stuart said more calmly, "we should stay where we are to expedite the investigation. If anyone saw anything, anything unusual at all, he or she should gather their thoughts now."

"Can we remove this man to his room?" asked one of the two stewards who were cradling Bueller. "He should be made more comfortable."

Stuart shook his head approvingly and then looked over at Ahmed and asked that he go with Bueller and not let him out of his sight.

"Of course," Ahmed said. "I have radioed ahead for a surgeon. He will come on board when we reach port."

"Good," Stuart said. "Keep a close eye on him because the attacker is still among us."

I don't know why it took Stuart's remark to make us aware of the obvious. The attacker was still here. We began to look at the others uncomfortably. No one had been missing from the performance except for a few of the crew whose job was to operate the ship. Even the stewards had joined us.

The boat pulled into the pier about thirty minutes later and was boarded by the police and the surgeon. It did not take much longer than that for my Agatha Christie fantasy to evaporate. The doctor tended the patient, and the police took a report. That was all. The wound was not mortal, the police said, and no one present could identify the assailant, they pointed out. No brilliant detective used the powers of deductive reasoning to narrow the possibilities down until, there you have it, the assailant had been identified. Instead, the police recommended that we continue on to our ship's destination, Aswan, which was not far off, and that we should keep Bueller under lock and key so that the assailant, whoever he is, would not get a second opportunity. From Aswan Bueller could be flown back to Cairo, they argued. This plan, I believe they referred to as "preventive." Within an hour of our arrival our boat was back in the middle of the Nile inching its way to its final port of call.

Our group huddled. Stuart had promised to reveal what he was doing to Natalie, John and me, but this new turn of events meant that the discussion would include all five us. We squeezed into John's and my cabin for a powwow.

"Okay, what can any of you tell me about this Bueller fellow?" Stuart asked.

"Oh, no Stuart," Natalie interjected. "First, you tell us about yourself. What are you doing here?"

Stuart looked down at the ring he was wearing, a jade ring set in eighteen-caret gold, turned it from side to side on his finger, as he seemed to be thinking about how he would respond.

"I'm surprised it isn't a diamond," I said. Stuart looked at me as if he didn't understand my reference. "Your ring," I said. "I'm surprised it's not a diamond ring. You do trade in diamonds, don't you?"

"Oh, yes, I see," he said. "I do trade in diamonds, but I never wear them. Never."

"Why not?" I asked.

"Many are tainted currency."

"Are they fakes?" Dr. Short asked.

"No, they're real enough. But many are tainted with innocent blood." He looked at us and realized we had no idea what he was talking about. "They're the standard currency of terrorists these days. They were traded for the guns and bullets we encountered in Esna, the bombs and artillery elsewhere, even the lives of those who willingly sacrifice themselves as they murder others."

"And you think Hans Bueller is involved in that?" Madeleine asked.

"I don't know what Bueller is involved in. I was hoping one of you could enlighten me." Stuart looked at us very seriously. "I've told you a lot already, more than I should have perhaps for your own well being. I will tell you the rest if you promise to keep it to yourselves."

This was the second time that day I was asked to keep a secret, but this one I believed would be easier to keep. Madeleine asked if she should send Paul over to her cabin, but Stuart thought Paul knew so much already it wouldn't make enough difference to remove him now.

"You're a spy!" Paul said, beaming with admiration. "I knew it! I knew it a long time ago. I watched you. You said you were a writer, but you never write. You nose around a lot. And you knew how to rescue us and dodge all those bullets. I thought maybe you might be a Navy Seal because you sure can swim and dive."

"Paul!" Madeleine softly reprimanded.

"He's all right," Dr. Short said, patting Paul on the arm. "He's a smart boy, very observant. He tunneled his way into the Great Pyramid at Giza before I had detected the route."

Stuart's smile returned as much admiration for Paul as Paul had for him.

"He may be smart," John said, "but he almost got himself into a lot of trouble at those pyramids, running off like he did. Paul, do you promise to keep everything you hear to yourself?"

"Yeah, sure Uncle John."

"And you won't try to be a spy yourself?"

He agreed, if reluctantly.

"I am not a spy, I'm an investigator," Stuart said.

Natalie's facial expression rapidly changed from astonishment to understanding. She sighed.

"For several years now I've been part of an ongoing investigation into illegal diamond smuggling. We know who the terrorists are that are engaged in this trade. But we don't know exactly who's assisting them, who is, so to speak, laundering these diamonds." Stuart surveyed us closely and went on. "Look, it works like this. Some of these groups are connected with African diamond mines that use what amounts to slave labor to supply these gems. At first they were able to directly trade the jewels for weapons, but that didn't last long because we made disposing of those diamonds very, very difficult for the weapons suppliers."

"How'd you do that?" Paul asked.

"Because these weapons suppliers operate in the open as legitimate businesses."

"You call selling weapons to terrorists legitimate?" John asked.

"I don't call what they do legitimate, but they operate in the open. The terrorists use middlemen so the sales look legitimate. We've employed every means possible to seek out illegalities in their operations and shut them down. Swapping weapons for diamonds offered us that opportunity in several instances because these arms dealers were not licensed to legally dispose of the diamonds. To protect themselves the arms dealers began to demand cash and refused the gems."

"Oh, so the terrorists had to find another method to sell their diamonds," Natalie said.

"Exactly. Now they've got to sell the jewels to raise the cash they need to get their weapons. That's what we are trying to shut down. If the terrorists can't sell their diamonds, their money will dry up and their weapons buying will cease. Reduce their capacity to buy weapons, and you diminish their ability to foment war. It's that simple." Stuart looked at Natalie and continued, "I've been working undercover as an investigator for the last year. I had been following a lead on this cruise

135

when Bueller presented himself."

"When he was stabbed," John said.

"Before that. I observed him engaged in odd activity in Edfu before he was stabbed. I am hoping you could tell me something about him."

"Who else do you suspect?" Natalie asked.

"I can't tell you that now. I've probably told you too much already."

"Hans Bueller is a German Egyptologist who has been professionally engaged in this line of work since 1938 or 1939," Dr. Short said. "He has preposterous and sometimes repugnant ideas about a relationship between the very secretive ancient Egyptian priesthood and what he imagines to have been some ancient tribe of Aryans who sat at the feet of the great Imhotep. In short, Bueller is an old crank, but he's harmless. He is an embarrassment to my profession, but I've never known him to engage in crime, except for occasionally smuggling ancient artifacts out of the country."

"Who supports his work?" Stuart asked.

"I believe his work is supported by a group of former Nazis now living in Austria. Bueller began his work with the Nazis, and after they were defeated this group provided the means for his work to continue."

"Since 1945?" Stuart asked.

"Yes, that is a long time," Dr. Short acknowledged. "That would be for over fifty years now, wouldn't it?"

"Who is this group?" Stuart asked.

"I don't know," Dr. Short said. "I just know they are supposed to be some kind of Austrian foundation."

"I will do some checking. Follow the money. That's my motto. It often leads to answers or sometimes only to the right questions, but without those questions, investigations go nowhere. Anything else anyone can tell me?" Stuart asked, looking around the small compartment.

My face flushed. What can I do? I thought. I said I would be discreet, but I can't under these circumstances. What if Bueller were to be murdered because I had not revealed his secret? "I have a little to add," I said. Everyone's eyes were upon me. I quickly explained the mythology surrounding my newly acquired ibis and how it led to my strange meeting with Bueller in his cabin just before the performance.

"I thought you went to the powder room?" John said.

"I'm sorry I lied. But I only did it because I promised him I would be discrete. And well, I was afraid after what he showed me, if I wasn't, I feared I might be in some kind of danger."

"What did he show you?" Stuart asked.

"He showed me the contents of that box he had given Madeleine at the Blue Nile restaurant in Giza just before we left."

Eyes lit in rapt attention, particularly Madeleine's.

"Well, what was in it?" Dr. Short asked.

"It was a small golden statue of a man with the head of an ibis. Dr. Bueller talked about it as if it were Imhotep or connected in some way to Imhotep. He said something about it containing Imhotep's spirit. He thinks Imhotep is trying to speak to him from the land of the dead. And he has this crazy idea that the ibis I bought from the boy—I guess because of the great effort on the boy's and my part to make the transaction—is a sign that Imhotep may be attempting to speak to me as well, although I am not aware of any such attempt." I grinned, but no one else was grinning. Instead, their eyes focused on Dr. Short who looked anything but amused.

"Could it be?" he said.

"Could it be what?" Stuart asked.

"There is a legend that the great priest Imhotep was buried not only with a golden treasure large enough to rival any pharaoh's, but that his treasure had magical qualities and that it contains the essence of his whole wealth of knowledge, which was considerable."

"And lost," John said.

"And lost," Dr. Short repeated. "Imhotep's tomb has never been found, at least not to my knowledge. But if this statue you describe is a genuine artifact and if Bueller believes it is a link to Imhotep, well, that could only mean that the tomb has been discovered. That would be a huge find, the biggest discovery ever made in Egypt, bigger than Howard Carter's discovery of Tutankhamen's tomb."

"Dangerous knowledge?" Paul asked, remembering an earlier conversation with Dr. Short who explained that secret knowledge was often kept secret because it was deemed dangerous.

"Perhaps," Dr. Short said.

137

"What does this have to do with your investigation?" Natalie asked Stuart.

"I don't know. Maybe nothing. Bueller was in the vicinity of what I believe was a diamond smuggling transaction, which is why I started watching him. Remember those shots that were fired in the town while you were on board the ship?"

"I remember them," Natalie said. "I thought the two ladies, Gabby and Beverly—I thought someone was trying to rob them and you came to their rescue."

"That's what they thought, but it was a little unclear. Bueller was there as well, but I couldn't tell what he was doing. I thought maybe he was tailing them, but I couldn't be sure. The ladies had stopped to look at jewelry. They were negotiating the price with the merchant when the shots were fired. Bueller stood nearby looking at a stall full of fake antiques, old books, ink drawings, not the kind of thing you would expect an antiquities expert to have much interest in. Shots came from behind the stall towards him, flew above him when he dropped to the ground and onwards towards the ladies. They assumed they were the targets, but had Bueller not collapsed as he did, he very well could have been killed. I shoved the ladies out of the way of the bullets and went after the assailant myself. I chased him down a narrow walkway between two buildings before he disappeared into the crowd at the poultry market. There was no point in attempting to follow him further. He blended in with the crowd, and I was not able to get a good enough look at him to have picked him out. So I returned just as the ladies and their porters were returning from the post office and escorted them the rest of the way back to the boat. Bueller evidently followed right behind us. This episode nearly spoiled my whole operation and raised my suspicions about him. Dr. Short, you say Bueller has engaged in smuggling antiquities. Maybe he's smuggling more than that these days. Could that be how he's financed?"

"I would hardly think so," Dr. Short said.

"But then there was the second attempt on his life during the performance," Natalie said.

"Yes, it does begin to look suspicious," Dr. Short said.

"To think I carried his package for him from Cairo to Luxor,"

Madeleine said.

"You put yourself at risk, that's for sure," Natalie said. "Maybe all of us, Mom."

"Well, what do we do now?" John asked. "We're in the middle of this thing. I don't think we have much choice but to see it through."

Stuart looked over at me, his eyes now intense. "You say that Bueller has taken you into his confidence. Well, you must remain there if I am to figure out what's going on."

"You mean I have to go along with his crazy ideas? Seriously? You expect me to do this?"

Stuart gave me a steady gaze. "You don't have to do anything tonight. Bueller is recovering from the knife wound. But tomorrow you must go see him before we disembark in Aswan. You should arrange that you and he stay close."

"I had hoped we could all take the optional excursion to Abu Simbel before flying back to Cairo," Dr. Short said.

"And I thought the police recommended that Bueller be put on a plane and sent back to Cairo right away as a preventive measure," John added.

"They did. They have no interest in finding the culprit. But I do. More lives than Bueller's may depend on it. We know that whoever is responsible for this attack is among us. It will be a whole lot easier to flush the culprit out in Aswan than to try to do it in Cairo. Believe me! There will be another attempt on Bueller's life. Two attempts already indicate determination."

We all surrendered to Stuart's plan pretty easily, beginning with Dr. Short. "Well, if we're going to stay somewhere for a while, I can't think of a nicer place than Aswan. I will try to get us rooms at the Old Cataract first thing in the morning."

"The Old Cataract?" Madeleine said.

"It's a fine old hotel Madeleine. You will love it."

"I guess that's that," John said. "But how do we know Bueller won't return to Cairo as the police recommended?"

"Because of your wife here," Stuart said. "If he thinks she can be of use to him, he will stay near."

"Oh," I said, wondering how I ever got myself into this.

Stuart looked at me reassuringly. "You will be all right. I will be watching you at all times. Just get some rest now, and tomorrow begin where you left off with Bueller before the performance."

Paul looked at me with an astonished expression on his face. "Gee, you're gonna play spy. Grandma played smuggler!"

Madeleine, wishing now she had put Paul to bed earlier, grabbed him by the shoulders and turned him in the direction of the cabin. "I didn't play smuggler, and your aunt is not playing spy. This is a very serious matter, too serious to be thought of as play anything, and certainly too serious for a ten year old boy to think about. It's time we all go to bed."

Flickering lights from our ship reflected dimly on the Nile as we glided like a sleepwalker towards Aswan. Only the night sky looked truly awake. Nuit draped herself over her namesake ship much as she had over the tomb of the pharaoh in the Valley of the Kings. Her radiance, woven into her dark robes, was evidence in the shadows that now enveloped the shoreline that life persists, even in darkness.

A subtle transformation had taken place, imperceptible when it happened but apparent in its aftermath. It was far more delicate than the stark differences we experienced when arriving in Cairo from America, more like the change we observed after leaving Cairo for Luxor, where we felt ourselves slip back in time. Now it was not our place in time that seemed altered but the rate of time itself, like the earth had slowed on its axis. The Nile too ran slower. The breeze that embraced John and me as we stood on the deck together had become sultry, the smells more sensuous, with scents of musk, amber and palm canceling out the harsh, dry, sandy odors of the desert. We had crossed some invisible demarcation between Northern Africa and the Southern continent. Our senses full, sleep came easily.

Chapter Nineteen

"Who's there?" John asked.

"It's me, Uncle John. You've got to see this place. Sailboats are everywhere!"

"What time is it?" I asked.

"It's ten already."

"So late!" I opened my eyes and saw the ibis standing duty from its perch on the dresser across the room.

"We'll throw on some clothes and be up in a few minutes," John said. "Make sure they save some coffee and pastry for us."

"And tea for me."

"Will do," Paul said, and scurried off to get our breakfast before the morning buffet was taken away.

It was a good thing too. By the time we showered and got to the dining room it was nearly empty except for a few porters who were clearing the last of the dishes and edible remains from the large buffet table. Paul sat waiting for us with a basket of pastries, orange juice, and tea for me and coffee for John.

"Good boy," John said. His hungry eyes surveyed our cheerful breakfast.

"Why so much service?" I asked.

"Dr. Bueller has been in his room all morning," Paul said. "The porter said he's still recovering, but the porter thinks he's okay, just scared. The porter said he expects him to come to the dinner tonight because it's our last night on board."

"That's a good report. But you know you're not to get involved with spying," John said.

"I'm not spying. I'm investigating. Wait till you see all the sailboats! We can go on a sailboat ride today to a Nubian village if we want, or else we can go see the Aswan Dam."

"I bet I can guess what you want to do," I said.

After breakfast we went up on deck and admired the view. The Nile at Aswan opens wide into an area surrounded by green tropical plants, palm trees and small pastel buildings that harmonize with the distant desert landscape. But the most spectacular sight is the feluccas whose long, graceful sails give them the appearance of sailboats. They lined the shores, white sails hoisted against the blue sky.

The trip to the Nubian village was arranged impromptu at the urging of a few of our companions on the tour who wanted to see something more of Nubian life, something authentic. A little authenticity was fine with John and me who were happy to see more of Egyptian everyday life. That's real travel, we agreed. The others had decided to visit the Aswan Dam and Philae Temple so it was quite a relief to Paul that we had chosen otherwise. He wanted to ride in a sailboat. Our small group would be accompanied by the cruise ship's head steward who like most of our crew was Nubian and lived here in Aswan when he was not shipboard. We would sail about the Nile before visiting an authentic Nubian village on one of the islands. Ahmed would take the others to the Aswan Dam, an engineering marvel of the 1960s designed to hold water to allow year-round irrigation of the Nile Valley. Its construction meant the destruction of many ancient ruins, so UNESCO funded the relocation of one of the greatest of these ruins, the Philae Temple, which they would also visit. Stuart had never seen the dam and Dr. Short had sailed in many feluccas so these two men and their ladies chose the alternative outing.

"Will Paul be all right with you?" Madeleine asked.

"Of course he will," John said, wrapping an arm around Paul's shoulders in lieu of a harness.

"I see that Shauna and Pearl will be with you. I think this is the place they wanted to come to all along. It was their idea, you know," she said.

"No, I didn't. Ahmed mentioned that someone on the tour had wanted to see something more authentic but didn't say who. I think it's a great idea myself."

Barry Short looked out from the railing of the ship's deck. "If they've come here to discover their roots, this is the place, but time has so altered the human landscape, I think they may be disappointed."

"Not to change the subject, but have you visited Dr. Bueller this morning?" Stuart asked.

142

"No, not yet," I said. "I thought I would wait until I was sure which hotel we will be staying at."

"Oh, didn't Paul tell you?" Madeleine said, "The Old Cataract."

"I had no trouble getting reservations," Dr. Short said. "I remember when you had to book months in advance to get into that hotel. They're not expecting us until after dinner tonight. I didn't want to disrupt our last grand dinner buffet."

The last supper, I thought. As I no longer had an excuse to postpone my morning visit to Bueller, I felt a tinge of irrational resentment towards Stuart. After all, if it were not for him.... "Not to change the subject," I said to Stuart and Natalie, "but it looks like you will be enjoying the company of Joyce and Barbara while visiting the Aswan Dam." Stuart looked uncomfortable at this turn in the conversation and walked over to the bar. Natalie and I looked over at the two women, dressed in coral and orange, who stood as far away from us as they could get.

"Do you suppose Stuart suspects the travel agents? If you think about it, that might explain why he bothered to become acquainted with them. It's the only reason I can think of," I said, as I watched the two women saunter over to the bar towards Stuart

"I don't know. He won't tell me who he suspects," Natalie said. She stared at the three of them seated together with their backs towards us. They were engaged in a conversation we could not overhear, Barbara and Joyce having muted their voices. "But you could be right. That would explain it."

I took a kind of delight in thinking they were about to be nabbed by the man they had been chasing after throughout the cruise. I imagined Stuart escorting the women off the ship, this time in handcuffs, their flashiness transformed into the stony faced visages of harden criminals caught by the man they had pursued. That would be justice, I mused. Then I checked myself, realizing just how petty I had become.

"It could be them," I said. "But it could be anyone. No one really looks the part." I looked about at an assortment of travel agents, shoppers, heritage seekers, a teenager, a newspaperman and our tour guide. "If it had not been Bueller who was stabbed, I would be convinced it was him."

One of the ship's stewards hand delivered an envelope. I opened it quickly and read who it was from before scanning its contents. Bueller's name was signed in a rather fine hand. I moved away from the group as I read the brief note.

I very much enjoyed our talk last evening before my little accident. Please come by my cabin before you leave on your outing today so that we might make future arrangements.

> *Yours Truly,*
> *Hans Bueller*

"Take a look at this."

"Well, good," John said, "an invitation to do exactly what Stuart asked you to do. You can only visit for a few minutes though. You don't want to miss our felucca."

"Oh, don't worry about that," I said, and walked towards the stairway leading down into the cabin area. I didn't want to burden John with my feelings, but I dreaded taking up with Bueller. The situation was just too weird. Yet fate had brought me to this position, and how would I feel if I turned my back on her and something dreadful happened as a consequence? But how will I feel if something dreadful happens anyway? Well, I thought, at least I would have tried. And then it struck me. This is another synchronicity. That boy whose determination to sell me my ibis prompted him to risk arrest, set in motion another round of actions just as that fateful fortune cookie had in what now seemed ages ago. I knocked softly on Bueller's door hoping that perhaps he had fallen back to sleep and wouldn't answer.

"Is z'at you dear?"

Dear, I thought. When did I become dear? "It's me Dr. Bueller. I got your note."

"Yes, I would let you in dear, but z'e door is locked for my protection, and I'm just too weak right now to get up and open it."

I sighed with relief knowing that for now the door would stand between us as we spoke. "That's all right. You wrote something about making future arrangements."

"Yes, z'ey wanted me to fly back to Cairo, but I'm not sure I want to do z'at. Where will you be going dear?"

"Dr. Short has made arrangements for us to transfer to the Old Cataract Hotel after dinner tonight."

"Oh, z'e Old Cataract, a fine hotel. I've always enjoyed my stays in Aswan."

"It certainly is beautiful here."

"It is one of z'e most beautiful places on earth. Now, don't tell our little secret. I must rest now."

"Okay, have a good rest. I will see you at dinner tonight."

"Till tonight."

I returned to the upper deck before anyone but John had noticed I was missing. "That was quick," he said.

"I know. Bueller couldn't let me in his room because the door was locked to prevent a would-be assailant from entering. He just wanted to know where we would be going next and said he would see me at dinner tonight. He called me dear."

"He likes you."

"I feel like such a crud. I don't like to be so duplicitous."

"You lied to me last night when you said you were going to powder your nose."

"That was just a little white lie. This requires an ongoing deception. And what if he goes to jail for smuggling or something?"

"He won't. He's too old. Think of it this way. What you are doing could save his life."

"Oh, yeah, yeah. I told you when we came south to Luxor our tour had turned into Girl Scout Camp. Now you're telling me I've got to do my duty."

The loud clap of Ahmed's hands abruptly called us to attention. "Everyone, please gather around," he said. "In just a few moments we will divide up and begin our final tours of the cruise. I want to thank you all for coming. I hope we have made you welcome. Now that I have you all together I want to remind you that it is customary for you to give a tip to the stewards and porters for all the attention they have given you during your cruise. Please be as generous as you can. I will provide you each with two envelopes, one for the ship and crew and one for me. Thank you very much. Once you've deposited your envelopes over here at the bar, please join your group for the final scheduled tour. Those of

145

you who are going to the Aswan Dam with me, please gather to the right. Those of you who are going to the Nubian Village, please move over to the left."

"More baksheesh," John grumbled.

"No, just a regular tip," I said. "You always tip on a cruise. Could you combine ours?"

Shauna, Pearl, the pretty girl and her mother joined the three of us, along with our ship's steward who would be our guide. I was surprised the pretty young girl was not going with Ahmed on the last day of our tour. It suggested the affair had ended. I had been so caught up in my own drama I was nearly oblivious to this shipboard romance, I realized. I wondered how many other scenes had played out I hadn't observed. I thought of all the French on board and wondered how much of their theater I had missed. Later, sitting alone in the felucca with our steward guide while choosing from the array of beaded necklaces he had for sale, I learned from him there was yet another drama playing out among our ship's crew.

Many of our porters and stewards were struggling to make ends meet at a time when the source of their livelihoods, tourists, had dwindled. They were lucky to have work, he told me. Otherwise, they would be forced to risk arrest like the young boy who sold me my ibis, or risk a boat accident like the men who nearly rammed into the river locks while trying to retrieve payment for the robes they sold to Gabby and Beverly. He was not telling me this to elicit pity or baksheesh. He told me because he knew I was genuinely interested. I knew this because he was without guile, soft-spoken, humble, gentle in his ways and kind in his manner. He and his workmates were some of the finest examples of humanity I had ever met. I began to understand why it is said that the meek will inherit the earth. While others are off making and fighting wars and creating all kinds of intrigue as a means to line their pockets, these simple folk quietly exist out of the way of all the bullets and strife. They, who go unnoticed as they busy themselves waiting upon others, will continue to stand when all else has fallen. They are the human seed, those who will be here to engender the earth when little else remains.

As he talked I studied his beads. They came in an array of rich colors: various shades of red, deep purple, turquoise and sea blue. He even had some lovely creamy-white necklaces made of small shells.

"Are these white shells from the Nile?"

He softly answered, "They come from the Red Sea."

"They are lovely. So are the colored beads. I think all of my friends back home would love them."

He smiled, and we struck a deal.

Chapter Twenty

At a distance feluccas look like graceful sailboats, but close up they take on the appearance of large, flat-bottomed rowboats whose interior ring is lined with built-in benches. We sat together on the boat's freshly painted white, curved seats listening to our Nubian boatmen's serenade. Their song was quiet and melodic, even as the musicians clapped hands and kept the rhythm with a handheld drum. Soft harmonies blended into Aswan's subtle breezes, curled about its fluttering palms and yielded to the gentle lapping of the river as we glided down the Nile towards the authentic Nubian village.

Sunglasses protected our eyes from the intense light, but for added protection we wore the long white scarves I bought in Esna. John looked as if he had gone native, the fringed scarf wrapped about his head and draped down near his waist, his bright yellow sun visor resting on top of his dark sunglasses. Paul sat quietly, his white scarf held in place by his Cleveland Indians baseball cap. The pretty young girl looked pensive, almost melancholy as she stared off towards the shore. Her mother, looking equally pensive, stared in the opposite direction. Shauna and Pearl studied their Nubian counterparts as if from them they hoped to learn their own history.

A small, red wooden boat, no bigger than a large washtub, approached us carrying a single passenger, a very small boy who used his arms and hands as paddles. As he neared he smiled and began to sing in a high-pitched child's voice:

> I come from Alabama
> With a banjo on my knee
> I'm going to Louisiana,
> My true love for to see
> Oh, Susanna,
> Oh don't you cry for me
> I come from Alabama
> With a banjo on my knee

We laughed in delight. To see and hear this small boy entertain us with a song that most of us hadn't heard since we were school children was an exceptional experience when sailing down the Nile at the southern edge of North Africa. The little boy in a tiny red boat was amply rewarded with baksheesh.

We were to meet the village elder when we arrived at the small, rough pier at the village. Instead, we were greeted by a horde of children who paraded alongside us as our guide led us through the tiny mud brick town. Antennas rose up out of the low roofs, and Nubian women, momentarily distracted from their TVs, watched us from the small windows of their houses.

A young girl, one of eight daughters and two wives of the village elder, greeted us at his home before introducing us to her father, a slight man, wearing a traditional white robe and turban and a less traditional large mustache. Prosperous by village standards, he kept two houses, the sidewall of each residence providing partial closure for a large courtyard that was the common area shared by his two families. Painted murals decorated the walls of the courtyard with brightly colored scenes of the Nile, the desert, feluccas and camels, all done with felt-tip pens. He greeted us politely as welcomed guests, seated us comfortably on the courtyard's long, white benches and offered us tea or Cokes. Formalities complete, his eyes were drawn to Shauna and Pearl, who he seemed particularly charmed by. "You are Nubian like me," he said, pleased to be introduced to the two attractive Americans.

He led them into a few minutes of conversational flirtation, complimenting them on their looks and items of their dress until at last they dropped their reserve and began asking the questions that had brought them to Egypt. Could he tell them the unwritten history of the region, its people and their people? He answered with stories of his own past, this village and his people. No matter how they framed their questions, he took them as an invitation to provide ever more detail about how he rose to prominence in what for these New York City women was a very tiny village. His confident smile, his carefully placed self-deprecating remarks made to elicit polite praise, made it clear he mistakenly interpreted their interest in their heritage as an interest in him. Talk between them ceased after he slyly suggested he would like to

149

add two more wives to the two he already had.

Conversation having exhausted itself, our host left and returned with a large rack of colorful beaded necklaces. Since he had offered his hospitality and we had accepted it, we all bought necklaces before our guide escorted us back to the felucca. The women who had peered at us from their windows as we entered the village were waiting outside with their own handmade beaded necklaces as we left. We hurried past them, trying to ignore their dejected faces before boarding our felucca where no sweet child in a little red boat would serenade us as we sailed away.

"That was awkward," John said.

"It wasn't what I expected," I said. "Maybe we should have gone to the Aswan Dam with the others."

"What did you expect?" he asked.

"I don't know. Maybe no one trying to sell us beads."

"If you think about it, why else would they take the time to talk to us?" he said. "They're just trying to earn a living, that's all, just like Ahmed."

"I guess so. It was those women with their anxious faces. Everyone had bought all the beads they were going to buy."

"They sure were at the bottom of the pecking order," he agreed. "Maybe we should have bought more."

What we had missed by not going to the Aswan Dam was official tourism, with its paid, educated, middle class guides like Ahmed, Yusef and Samia, who speak fluent English, dress in western garb and are well versed in official explanations of ancient and modern sites. What we gained by visiting the Nubian village was not an escape from tourism but further contact with unofficial tourism. As awkward as that can be sometimes, it offers the most insight into the heart and soul of Egypt's vast population. Villagers like those we had just met, greet their guests with a song, offer them a Coke, invite them into their homes whose walls are decorated like picture postcard drawings and then try to sell them their wares. The boy with the ibis for sale and the men who sold robes shipside from their rowboat had not even a song or a Coke to offer, just determination. Our buggy tour in Luxor had afforded us a view of Egypt we might otherwise have missed had we not heard Mustafa explain the real price of chicken and had he not taken us to the kind of shop where I learned that bargaining is as much an ethical enterprise as a business transaction. From the Bedouin we learned the desire to share was a deep value. The camel drivers at the pyramids cooperated with each other to divide the services rendered and thus the income produced among several men as a way to share the little wealth they earned. The further we reflected on our experiences, the greater our awareness that in Egypt the weight of one's heart still matters. We had been to an authentic Nubian village, and what we learned there is the need is greater than the resources to share, tourists' dollars being the primary resource.

Shauna and Pearl were disappointed for different reasons. Like many Americans who search into their genealogies, they found that time and place had so removed them from their historical roots that the gap between the culture of their ancestors and the culture of their birth is all but insurmountable, that the occupants of their present day ancestral home are nearly as removed from those forebears as they. Yet the evidence of a link is undeniable in traces of their own likeness in paintings and carvings of pharaohs and queens that adorn wondrous ruins from a time so remote that to bridge past with present requires an act of the imagination. The past must be allowed to speak through its vivid remains. The present, on the other hand, is inescapable and sometimes burdensome.

Paul said, "When I come back to Egypt I'm going to bring lots of coloring pens. Aunt Natalie's ink pens are okay, but coloring pens are better. They can color pictures on their walls even in their bedrooms, and make them really nice."

The pretty girl seemed even more distracted than she had been earlier. She looked impatient to get back to our ship, her eyes searching in its direction for a sign that we were nearing. What did she want to do when she returned? I wondered. I knew who she wanted to see. Her distraught mother was not reticent to tell me about her daughter's situation.

Soon we were back at the Queen Nuit now docked at Aswan. We offered what little cash we had left to the crew of the felucca. The ship's steward invited us to go to the upper deck, relax and wait for a light lunch that would be served soon. We were happy to comply but unhappy that the others were not yet back. The French had gone on an excursion too, leaving only our small group, which deprived us of the kind of privacy one finds in a public place when large numbers of people are present.

"When will they be back?" the pretty girl asked one of the stewards.

"Later. They will be having lunch elsewhere while they are out."

Deeply agitated, she shouted to her mother, "I am going to Abu Simbel!"

"But we agreed to go back to Cairo tomorrow," her mother said.

"You agreed," the girl began to cry. "I don't care. I'm going to Abu Simbel." She ran off down the stairs followed by her overwrought mother.

"What's that all about?" John asked

"Oh, love," I said. "You know, Romeo and Juliet style love."

"No, I don't know."

"Since Paul isn't around I will tell you. Where is he anyway?"

"He went down to his cabin to change into his bathing trunks."

"Okay, I'll be quick. The mother told me that her daughter is in puppy love with Ahmed, but the two of them agreed not to see each other anymore because neither wants to consider moving to the other's country. Of course, that was the mother's version. It looks like there's more to it than that."

"What's that got to do with Abu Simbel?"

"Well, I would guess the reason the girl insists she is going is that Ahmed is accompanying the excursion group. That girl looked miserable today. My guess is the only reason they chose the Nubian village option is the mother is trying to keep her daughter away from Ahmed when she can."

"Why? He seems like a nice enough guy, a little controlling maybe, but a pretty decent guy. Let the girl have some fun."

"You obviously didn't observe her today. She's not having fun; she's in love, at least she thinks she is. Maybe she is. I don't know. At any rate, girls like that don't want to have fun; they want to get married. And I'm sure the mother doesn't approve of the idea of her daughter moving to Egypt. My guess is Ahmed's parents wouldn't approve of him moving to the U.S. either."

"Romeo and Juliet. I see what you mean."

152

"I've seen 'Romeo and Juliet,'" Paul announced. "Oh Romeo, Romeo!"

"Where did you come from?" I said.

Taken aback by my tone, he said, "I came from my cabin."

Embarrassed, I apologized for being so rude.

"Dr. Bueller's gone," Paul said.

"He's what!" I said.

"He's gone. The porter said he left today while we were off the ship."

"Where did he go?" John asked.

"The porter said that he thinks he flew back to Cairo like the police said he should because they were afraid someone would try to kill him again. That's why he left when everyone was gone, so the killer couldn't follow him."

"But he told me he would see me at the grand buffet tonight," I said.

"I guess he lied," Paul said.

"To me?" I began to question whether I ever really had Bueller's confidence. "By the way Paul, didn't we tell you not to play spy?"

John pointed out that if Paul hadn't thought to ask a few questions, we might not have known that Bueller had left until the buffet this evening.

"You're right. I'm sorry again. Well, what do we do now?"

"Nothing," John said. "There's nothing we can do except tell Stuart when he gets back."

"It's probably for the best. I didn't really want to do this anyway." Although to my surprise, I felt let down that my adventure had prematurely ended.

The stewards brought up a tray of sandwiches and cookies and another tray with tea and fruit juice. The pretty girl and her mother did not return for lunch. The few of us who were left gathered around the table where the food was laid out.

"When they said light lunch, they meant light," John said.

Shauna agreed, "What I would love to have right now is a big juicy hamburger, cooked out on the grill with everything on it."

Pearl said, "Cheese, bacon, lettuce, tomato, pickles, mustard, catsup."

"And French fries," Shauna said.

"And some shakes," Pearl said.

Instead, we had to content ourselves with little cold lamb sandwiches on buttered bread, thin white cookies and hot tea and orange juice.

"When are you two returning home?" I asked.

"Tomorrow," Shauna said. "We fly to Cairo tomorrow and from there back to New York."

"Did you find what you were looking for?"

They looked at me like I was a little crazy, replied only that they had had a wonderful trip.

*****

"Wake up! They're back!" Paul said.

"Did I fall asleep?" I said.

"You both did."

Still blurry eyed, John and I looked at each other, which easily confirmed Paul's pronouncement. John was drawn down in his lounge chair where he had managed to curl up. He straightened himself out, surveyed the deck but didn't see anyone.

"They're back?" he asked.

"They just got here, the French too," Paul said. "They will be up here in a minute."

People started emerging on deck from the stairway below, but no one from our party appeared.

"Maybe they'll go to their cabins first," Paul said after a few minutes.

The three of us spilled down the stairs squeezing past people trying to make their way up on deck. Natalie and Madeleine were about to enter their rooms when we came upon them.

"Did you have a good time?" John asked, taking a moment to be polite.

"It was very nice," Madeleine said. She looked fresher than one would expect after a long day of tourism.

"Yes, wonderful!" Natalie said. "I want to go to Abu Simbel. It's supposed to be even more spectacular than Philae."

"There seems to be a good deal of sentiment for going there," I said thinking about the conversation between the pretty girl and her mother.

"Do you know where Stuart is?" John asked Natalie.

154

"He went to his cabin to change clothes and rest a bit, pack, that sort of thing. We had quite a tour today."

"I'll talk to you about it later," John said. "We've got to get down there and talk to him before he falls asleep."

"Why, what happened?" Madeleine asked.

"Bueller left while we were all off the ship."

"Oooh!" Madeleine said in the long drawn out tone that indicates she is thinking more than she is willing to say.

The three of us turned and headed towards Stuart's cabin when Madeleine called Paul back to help organize his things for packing. John looked at Paul and then at his mom, "Good idea," he said.

The two of us arrived at Stuart's cabin just as he was unlocking his door. The glass of wine Stuart was holding explained his delay. He looked tired and not too happy to see us.

"Sorry to intrude," John said. "But we thought you would want to know that Paul learned from one of the porters that Bueller left today for Cairo while we were all out."

"How did porter know where he was going?"

"I don't know. The porter told Paul that Bueller was following police recommendations. I didn't talk to him myself."

"Didn't Bueller ask you where you were going to be?" Stuart asked.

"Yes, he did. I told him Dr. Short had arranged for rooms at the Old Cataract. And he said he would see me tonight."

"At the grand buffet dinner."

"Well, that's what I thought he meant, but thinking back, he said only that he would see me tonight."

Stuart looked down at his feet for a few minutes.

"So what do we do?" John asked. "Cancel our reservations and fly back to Cairo?"

"No." After a few more minutes of awkward silence, he said, "I don't think Bueller went to Cairo. I don't think he would have made a point of finding out where you were going if he were planning on leaving. We should check into the Old Cataract. If Bueller doesn't contact you in a few days, we will leave. Meanwhile, I will ask my contacts in Cairo to keep an eye out for him."

"Good enough," John said.

"Well, what about Abu Simbel?" I said. "Natalie wants to go."

"I need to go down there too," Stuart said. "Barry is checking to see if he can get us on the plane tomorrow. It only takes about a half hour to fly there."

"Why not take a boat?" John said. "That felucca was great. I wouldn't mind doing it again."

"We would have to cross a cataract that could pull a felucca under. People go by bus sometimes, but I don't think we could find a driver willing to risk the one hundred and seventy mile road trip with all the shooting going on. The road runs through some rebellious territory down there near Sudan. So, that leaves the plane. If you don't mind, I need to get a little rest before dinner."

"Oh, sorry," John said. "Didn't mean to keep you up."

"That's okay. Thanks for keeping me informed."

We entered our own cabin to begin packing. "Shooting," I said. "I wonder why Stuart is so eager to go to Abu Simbel?"

"Bueller isn't the only person on Stuart's mind."

"Right, I nearly forgot about that. I wonder how long we will be down here? We've already added on days at the Old Cataract and now Abu Simbel."

"I think when you fly down there you come back the same day, but I don't know how long we'll be in Aswan. It's up to Stuart. I'm ready to burn out though. I'm tired."

"It has been eventful hasn't it," I said.

"You say that in the past tense. It's not over yet."

A few hours later Paul appeared at our door to call us to dinner.

"You're a regular alarm clock," John said.

"I saw Romeo and Juliet kissing."

"What?" I said.

"They were in the hall in a corner kissing."

"Ahmed and that girl?" John asked.

"Yep!" Paul said with an impish smile.

The last supper more than made up for the skimpy lunch. An array of Egyptian delicacies was spread out before us, which we all ate with relish. Ahmed, sitting at the head of one of the other tables, presided over his ducklings. All the talk was about tomorrow's supplemental excursion to Abu Simbel, which apparently most of our fellow travelers had reserved in advance. The young girl sat at Ahmed's side and her mother next to her. Michael Sargent sat at Ahmed's other side, taking copious notes, as he was finishing up the story he was preparing for his newspaper back home.

Ahmed stood up and walked over to our table and said, "I'm so pleased you changed your minds and decided to take the excursion."

John turned to Dr. Short, "Were you able to book all of us?"

Barry wore the smile of a confident man who knew how to pull the right strings at the right time. "No trouble at all."

Not everyone looked happy about this news. Gabby and Beverly and Joyce and Barbara shot daggers in our direction.

"Did you see that?" I directed John's attention towards them.

"Yes, I did. I wonder what we missed today on the tour of the Aswan Dam?"

"More than engineering, that's for sure."

Chapter Twenty-One

Ahmed and the other Americans transferred from the ship to a new hotel, equipped with swimming pool, nightclub and air-conditioned rooms. Barry Short preferred the Old Cataract with its gardens and verandas rising out of the Nile.

"It's a landmark. It dates back to Howard Carter and the Czar of Russia. Wait till you see the view from the terrace. Let's check into our rooms and go have after-dinner drinks out there."

"They have drinks here?" Madeleine said.

"We're in Aswan!"

Natalie pointed up at the rooms overlooking the Nile. "Do we get one of those?"

"Sorry dear, too pricey. We have the garden view, but we've still got the terrace."

Dr. Short checked us in and had our bags sent up to our rooms before giving us a short tour of the hotel's public areas and taking us out on the veranda.

"Agatha Christie wrote *Death on the Nile* here," he said.

"In Aswan?" I asked.

"Right here in this very hotel. Her husband was an archaeologist, you know."

"No, I didn't."

"Yes, he was. This is where they would stay while he was down here working."

It wasn't hard to imagine Agatha Christie ensconced quite comfortably here while her husband was off on his digs. Old-fashioned British elegance made the lobby an attractive place to spend one's time. Guests relaxed in large, comfy chairs as waiters dressed in starched white jackets attended to their needs. Barry led us out to the veranda that was surrounded by gardens and had a breathtaking view of the Nile. There we shared a bottle of champagne while Paul sipped his specially prepared cherry cordial. John took advantage of the opportunity to ask about their excursion to the dam.

"It really is an engineering marvel," Stuart said. "The structure looks as monumental as anything the pharaohs ever built."

"But not nearly as beautiful," Natalie said.

"A monument of another age perhaps," Dr. Short said. "The Russians had a lot to do with the construction. And it shows. To me it has that post-Stalinist utilitarian look."

"It is utilitarian," Stuart said. "It's a dam, after all, not a monument."

"I agree that its function is utilitarian," Dr. Short said. "But one could argue that the pyramids were utilitarian in function too, at least at the time they were built. Yet they are awe inspiring."

"I think the Aswan Dam is likewise awe inspiring," Stuart retorted. "And it revolutionized Egyptian agriculture."

"Not all for the good," Dr. Short said. "Some think the agricultural land was better served by the natural flooding of the Nile."

"I was disturbed when Ahmed pointed out the dam's construction swallowed up many antiquities," Madeleine said. "I'm happy they thought to preserve the Philae Temple rather than let it be submerged, but what about everything else?"

"What was the Philae Temple like?" I asked.

"It's beautiful!" Natalie said.

"Yes, it is," Madeleine said. "Imhotep was there. Ramses and Imhotep I believe are the most remembered names in Egypt. You hear about them everywhere."

Dr. Short, in a mildly argumentative mood, now came to the dam's defense. "Actually Madeleine, if it had not been for the construction of the new dam, Philae might have been lost forever. The old dam caused massive water erosion at Philae, which was rectified with the construction of the new dam."

"Oh, I didn't know that," Madeleine said.

"While there were other losses that resulted from the building of the new dam," Dr. Short continued, "nothing as monumental as what was saved: Philae and Abu Simbel. I might add that the Philae Temple is dedicated to Isis, whose name I believe is more widely known and venerated than Imhotep. Although you are correct, there is a Temple of Imhotep at the Philae Temple complex."

Madeleine looked slightly mortified as she acknowledged Dr. Short's expertise. The truth is that I had never seen him quite so, well, I guess one could say aggressive in asserting that expertise, at lease not with Madeleine. It was clear that something more had happened while they were on their expedition than simple sightseeing.

Shifting the conversation to the more social aspects of the excursion I said, "Did the others enjoy the outing?"

"I don't think Barbara and Joyce did," Natalie said.

"Oh really! I'm surprised to hear that after your descriptions."

"And that Gabby and her friend," Madeleine said. "They really embarrassed themselves today."

"Now, now Madeleine, they were not that bad," Dr. Short said.

"You might be an expert in Egyptology, but you're no expert in women," Madeleine pronounced, refusing to give up ground where she knew she had the greater knowledge.

"What happened?" I asked.

"They wouldn't leave us alone. They walked everywhere we walked as if we were together," Madeleine said.

Natalie added, "They're so embarrassing. All they wanted to know about everything they saw was its price. For them shopping has become a disease. They kept bugging Dr. Short about the price of this and the price of that, where replicas might be bought, how they might be crated and sent home."

"Crated!" I said. "What were they trying to buy?"

"They would have walked away with the very columns that hold the temple up if they could have," Madeleine said.

"Now ladies," Dr. Short said, "you're being too harsh." Looking past Madeleine and Natalie and over to me he said, "They were interested in stone and marble replicas of the various decorative columns, some tablets and a few carvings available at the temple complex museum. They were asking me to assess the relative value of these replicas because they're quite expensive."

"But Barry," Madeleine said. "Why didn't they ask Ahmed? He's their guide, not you!"

"Maybe they prefer Barry's charms over Ahmed's," Natalie said. "I think Ahmed is probably pretty sick of them by now anyway. They're so loud."

"Speaking of loud! Did you hear Joyce practically command Stuart to walk with her and that other woman?" Madeleine said.

Looking disturbed at the direction the conversation was taking, Stuart begged to be excused to phone his contact in Cairo to see if by chance Bueller had been spotted there.

Dr. Short followed Stuart with his eyes as he walked away from the table. "He's a handsome man. You can hardly blame those women for being attracted to him."

Natalie's blood rushed to her face. She wasn't so much angry as she was embarrassed, embarrassed that she had allowed herself to once again become involved with a man whose good looks could only bring her grief. She replied coolly, "It's always been that way with Stuart." Then she heated up. "He attracts aggressive women. This is not the first time something like this has happened in my presence."

"Just because he attracts women like that doesn't mean he is attracted to them," Madeleine said.

"I agree with your mother," Dr. Short said. "If ever I saw a man give two women the cold shoulder, it was him today."

"And their reaction was to get louder. They were louder than that Gabby and Beverly, if that's possible," Madeleine said.

With that remark there was a pause in the conversation, which offered me a good opportunity to excuse myself. I looked over at John who was stretched back in his chair gazing out towards the Nile about as far removed from the conversation as he could be. By now he was probably entirely concentrated on mentally mapping the stars, I thought, so rather than disturb him I excused myself and said I would go search out our room and be back before John returned to planet Earth.

It felt good to be away from all that gossip and on my own for the few minutes it took me to climb a flight of stairs to our second floor room until I began to sense foreign eyes upon me. I'm only imagining things, I thought. I'm in a strange place and not quite sure where I'm going, and I may be a little spooked by ghosts of Agatha Christie and the Czar of Russia. I was relieved when I found our room and could anticipate getting out of the open hallway. Just as I unlocked the door I heard my name spoken in a whisper as if from another world.

"Dr. Bueller!" I said startled, when I turned towards the voice.

161

Peering through the opening in the door of the room directly across the hall stood a thin, ghostly figure that looked even whiter than he had before he was stabbed. He came towards me and smiled almost sweetly. I felt a cool pat on my hand.

"Could you come in and talk with me a bit?"

"The others are waiting for me downstairs. I told them I would be gone only a few minutes."

"It will only take a few minutes."

I realized as I stood in his room that we were just above the others who sat below us on the veranda, but I couldn't have felt farther away.

"Have you had any communication?" he asked.

"Communication?"

"Has Imhotep made himself known to you?" he said, his sweetness turning to impatience.

"Oh, no," I said half afraid to say anything else. But I continued by reporting Madeleine's observation that there is a Temple of Imhotep at the Philae Temple complex. Seeing this didn't please him, I explained that we had been very busy, that John and I had gone to the Nubian village and that we were to go to Abu Simbel tomorrow.

"Tomorrow you go to Abu Simbel! Z'is is Providence at work. Did you know that Abu Simbel is dedicated to z'e great sun god Amun?"

"Well, no," I said, feeling woefully ignorant for someone Imhotep was supposed to be trying to commune with.

"Only twice a year, one day in October and tomorrow, February 22, z'e sun shines into z'e most sacred area in z'e temple and casts its light on z'e great statues of Amun-Ra and Ramses. It is said z'at on z'ese two days the sun opens the door between heaven and earth. Don't you see z'at it is providential z'at you should be z'ere on z'is very day?"

I didn't see. I only felt puzzled.

"Imhotep wants you z'ere so z'at he might speak.... Wait, just another minute. I've got something for you z'at you must take."

Bueller rifled through his bag and pulled out the little package that he had first given Madeleine at the Blue Nile. I knew that it was the golden statue of the man with the head of the ibis, Thoth.

"Take z'is with you," he said as he shoved the package towards me. "Go to z'e Great Temple and meditate with z'is in your hands. It has

162

magical properties. It will make it easier for you to understand. And z'en return it to me here along with z'e message you receive. Take pen and paper and write it down."

"Do you really want to entrust this to me? I know how much you value it," I said, wanting to hand the package back to this scary little man and be done with the whole thing.

"I value z'e knowledge it could bring me more z'an its gold. I want to be put on z'e path. Will you do as I ask?"

"Wouldn't it be better if you went yourself so that Imhotep can speak to you directly?"

"Z'at had been my plan when I came to Luxor, but z'en you appeared with z'e ibis. I knew z'at it was a sign. And here I am now unable to go," he said bringing his wounded arm forward. "And you are going to z'at very place I intended to go myself, and on z'is most important day. It is providential, I tell you."

I had to agree that Bueller did not look well enough to make the trip. The wound was only beginning to heal.

"Will you do as I ask?"

"Yes," I said since no other answer was possible.

"Hide z'is in your room z'en, and go back to your friends. Z'ey are waiting for you. You would be wise not to tell anyone you have it. If z'e wrong person should find out, z'at could put you in mortal danger."

"I will bring it back to you tomorrow."

Fumbling in the dark, I switched on the light half expecting to see a ghost, but when the light came on I saw only a lovely room decorated in steel blue and gold and outfitted with French furnishings. Over to the side stacked neatly upon a rack was our luggage. I hid the little package in a place I was sure no one would look, deep in the bottom of our dirty laundry bag, which was by now quite full. Turning off the lights and locking the door behind me, I walked quickly down the hall, down the stairs and out to the veranda to the people who awaited me. The champagne must have done its work. They were calm, I noted, at least everyone except John.

"Where have you been?" he asked.

"I went to our room."

"Well, I know that. The others told me. But why so long? I was just

163

about to go look for you."

"You won't believe this when I tell you. I ran into Bueller. He has taken the room right across the hall from ours. Just as I got to our room, he opened his door and called me over."

"Oh, I believe it," Madeleine said.

I thought back to earlier in the day when we told Madeleine that Bueller left the ship. She gave that vague reply of hers that over the years I've learned means she is thinking something she doesn't want to say just yet, but whatever it is, it usually turns out to be right.

"Why do you say that?" I asked.

"I didn't believe he had really left," she said. "He might have left the ship, but I didn't think he had gone far."

"Been having any dreams lately Mom?" John said.

"Well, yes I have now that you ask. Dr. Bueller was in my dreams just last night. I can't remember the details, but he was very present, very intense about something. I knew he wouldn't have left us so soon, not until his business is finished."

"That's what Stuart thought too." John turned back to me. "What did he say?"

"He wondered if I had any communication with Imhotep."

Dr. Short snorted, "I never liked the man, but I didn't think he was completely mad until now."

"I told him no. But when I mentioned we are going to Abu Simbel tomorrow he got quite excited. He thinks it is providential. Something about tomorrow being February 22. He made me promise I would sit in the Great Temple before the statues of Amun-Ra and Ramses and meditate. He is convinced Imhotep will deliver a message for him through me. I am to write it down."

"Oh, I had quite forgotten," Dr. Short said. "Yes, on February 22 and sometime in October, the sun shines into the temple just as it rises. This happens just twice a year only on these two days. Amun-Ra, of course, is the great sun deity, so these days were particularly important to his worship."

"At sunrise!" I said. "Bueller didn't tell me that."

"That was a major oversight on his part," Dr. Short said. "But it doesn't matter anyway. It's all poppycock."

164

"Dr. Bueller said that when the sun shines into the temple it opens a door between the worlds of the living and the dead, so he thinks it is providential that I will be there. But if I can't be there at sunrise, then perhaps he won't think it so providential, and I can forget the whole thing."

"Don't worry, you will be there," Dr. Short said. "Our flight leaves at a quarter till six. It takes about forty minutes. Sunrise occurs around seven this time of year. So if you don't dillydally around, you will have plenty of time. The airport is right there."

"A quarter till six!" Madeleine said. "You didn't tell me that."

"Oh, I didn't? I'm sorry. I'm quite looking forward to it. Sunrise at Abu Simbel is beautiful, although I prefer to experience it outside the temple."

"We're going to have to get to bed!" Madeleine said. She looked over at Paul who was already curled up asleep in one of the lounge chairs.

"Wait a minute," Natalie said. "Didn't Ahmed mention today that they moved Abu Simbel when they built the Aswan Dam? Wouldn't that have changed the way the sun hits it, the direction and everything?"

Gathering himself, Dr. Short explained how carefully the relocation of Abu Simbel was done, right down to situating the temple just as it was in relationship to the sun so that it would gather its rays just as it had for the more than two thousand years before it was relocated.

"That's amazing!" Natalie said. She looked at me. "Are you going to do it?'

"Well, I guess I have to. Stuart said I should go along with Dr. Bueller while he tries to figure out what's going on. And since we will be there at sunrise and all."

Dr. Short reassured me that the whole story of a door opening between the world of the living and the departed was nothing more than legend, that I could make something up to satisfy Bueller, but that I didn't have to worry that Imhotep would speak to me.

"Oooh, we shall see," Madeleine said under her breath as she gathered Paul up and the two of them made their way to their room.

I knew that Madeleine was thinking a lot more than she was willing to say, which had the effect of canceling any reassurance Dr. Short offered.

"I will be up soon Mom," Natalie said. She shifted the conversation to another tidbit of news. "Stuart just found out something very interesting." She looked over at Stuart.

"This is no surprise to you now. My contact in Cairo reported that Bueller did not return there."

"Yes, but what about the money," Natalie said.

"Bueller isn't getting his money from a foundation in Austria. It's defunct. It has been defunct for at least fifteen years. My contact was able to look at Bueller's bank records, which show deposits of large sums. But he has not yet been able to identify the source of that money."

"That old liar!" Dr. Short said. He roused himself from the table to make his way to his room and sleep.

"We'd better go to bed too," John said. "We're going to have to get up by five if we're going to make that flight."

Before I rose out of my chair I asked Stuart what he thought this means.

"It means that Dr. Short is right. Bueller is a liar. But I'm not sure what else. He could be smuggling stolen artifacts out of the country for a handsome profit. Or there could be more to it. He will be staying here at the hotel tonight and tomorrow, you say?"

"That's what he told me, and I believe him. He's still recovering from his wound, and I don't think he will go anywhere until I return with the message he's expecting."

"That's good then. I don't have to keep an eye on him tomorrow, at least not until we're back and you've talked to him."

When John and I arrived at our room we found a note under our door. I recognized Bueller's handwriting right away.

Dear, I failed to tell you that you must be in the Great Temple just before sunrise. I checked with the airport and learned that your flight should get you there in plenty of time. Am looking forward to your safe return.

Yours Truly, Hans

Chapter Twenty-Two

T he sound of water splashing against tile walls alerted me that John was up and in the shower. Time to get out of bed and move that statue out of the dirty laundry before he comes out, I thought. Instinctively I snuggled deeper into the sheets before I forced myself out of bed and made the transfer to my purse.

"We sure could use a washer and dryer," John said as he stuffed wadded up shorts, T-shirt and socks into the overflowing laundry bag. He flung it over his shoulder. "I'm going to take this down to the lobby and see if the hotel can have it washed while we're out."

"Good idea," I said, relieved that a personal catastrophe had just been avoided. What would he think of me? This was the second time that I had kept him from the truth. I leaned against the marble vanity, stared into the bathroom mirror and began a silent conversation with myself about the wisdom of my concealment. Am I being duplicitous by not telling him? Or would I be duplicitous if I did, and a coward too, putting John and everyone else at risk? I retrieved the ibis sandwiched between two soft shirts in my luggage and placed it on the vanity wishing it could speak. The sight of it reminded me of the bravery of the boy who sold it to me. I calmed down, showered, dressed and prepared to go down to the lobby for a light breakfast with John, who by then had returned to our room *sans* dirty laundry.

Ahmed had phoned Barry earlier to say his group was running late and couldn't pick us up in their bus. We were staying at the wrong hotel, he declared, and we should make our own arrangements. Barry went into overdrive locating us transportation to the airport. Most of the hotel staff had not yet arrived so Barry had his work cut out for him, but he soon was able to secure the hotel limo and its driver. Paul looked an object of pity, teetering half asleep next to his grandmother who kept her eye approvingly on the man in charge.

When the vintage Rolls Royce limousine was brought around, we all agreed that Ahmed was absolutely wrong. We were staying at the right hotel. The car's glistening brown paint and chrome were polished to perfection. Its hood ornament sparkled under hotel lights. The interior was soft brown leather, with contrasting tan leather door panels. I felt like royalty. The sleepy driver whisked us off to the airport where we arrived long before Ahmed and the rest of the tour group.

"They want us to board now," Dr. Short said.

"Where are the others?" Madeleine asked.

"They're running late," he said, looking about as if he expected them to make an appearance any minute. "They'll be along soon."

We climbed into the waiting prop plane, seated ourselves and listened to the engines warm up. John's watch showed that it was exactly a quarter till six, the time our flight was scheduled to leave.

"I have to be in the Great Temple at sunrise," I said impatiently.

"I wouldn't worry if you don't make it," John said. "Just tell Bueller you were there on time."

Three minutes later the door leading out from the airport terminal flew open and Ahmed and his group rushed out towards the boarding ramp. Hair blowing and hands covering their eyes to protect them from the dust the propellers kicked up, they climbed aboard. One steward seated them haphazardly while another steward closed and locked the plane's door.

I slid my hand inside my handbag to feel its contents, squeezed the little package containing the golden treasure, feeling quite ready for my adventure however it turned out. A hand touched my shoulder from behind. Startled, I turned around and met Stuart's face stretched forward over the back of my seat.

"Did you see Gabby and Beverly board?"

"Come to think of it no," I said. "But we couldn't see much of what was going on in the front of the plane, so they may have boarded without my seeing them."

Stuart leaped out of his seat, banging his knees into the backs of John's and my chairs, climbed over Natalie and moved up the aisle to the consternation of the two cabin stewards who had already prepared for takeoff. He spoke briefly to Ahmed, then rushed to the boarding door, which he tried to push open. In seconds, the stewards were on top of him. He appeared to be trying to negotiate when they forced him into a seat and buckled him in. We were in the air.

Natalie reached her head around the aisle. "Did you see that?"

"I sure did!" John said. "Gabby and Beverly! Could they be...?"

"That's unbelievable," she said.

Stuart was permitted to return to his seat after the plane had reached altitude. It was hard for us to hear Natalie and Stuart over the din of the engines so John, unable to contain his curiosity any longer, craned his neck around the rear of his seat and joined in. Natalie and Stuart confirmed what we had already surmised. Gabby and Beverly were suspected of buying and smuggling diamonds in a terrorist financing operation. Ahmed had just told him that he and the others arrived late to the airport because he waited longer than he should have for Gabby and Beverly, who to Ahmed's surprise, were not in their room when he phoned to hurry them up. That was enough to convince Stuart the two women had begun to suspect him. He believed they were taking advantage of his absence in Aswan to meet their contact there before fleeing to Cairo where they could more easily disappear.

"Can't Stuart fly back to Aswan shortly after we land?" I asked John.

"He's going to see what he can do, but he says that Abu Simbel is pretty desolate. The only people who go there are tourists, and that's us. And our plane isn't scheduled to return until after lunch at two."

"Tourists aren't the only people who go there," I said thinking of Agatha Christie's husband. "It's an active site for archaeological digs, so archaeologists must go there too. And they don't fly on tourist excursion planes."

"Good thinking!" John said, before reaching around to tell Natalie.

Stuart again hovered above the rear of our chairs. "Look, if I try to get up again, those guys are going to chain me to a seat. John, could you head for the toilet and stop on the way and talk to Barry to see if your idea is viable?"

John made his way down the aisle, stopping briefly next to Dr. Short, who got up and followed him to the rear of the plane. They returned looking animated, like two men on a mission. John plunged back into his seat. "Dr. Short's going to call the Institute when we arrive at the airport and see if anyone is down there who could get us back to Aswan pronto."

"But I've got a mission too," I protested.

"Don't worry," John said. "You can go to the temple while Dr.

169

Short makes some calls."

At last we landed. Dr. Short left in search of a telephone, followed by Stuart.

"I think I should go with them," John said.

"You're not going with me?"

"You'll be all right. I'll come get you after we've figured this thing out."

Ahmed herded the rest of us to a bus waiting to take us to the temple. Fortunately, the trip was quick, but by the time we arrived coral light was already breaking through the eastern horizon and shopkeepers had begun to open their stalls. I was having some difficulty adjusting to the new reality I had been presented with on the plane and half expected to see Gabby and Beverly chattering away at the vendors. They seemed so goofy, I thought, and yet they had outmaneuvered Stuart. Clearly, there was a lot more to these women than meets the eye, but you'd never know it in a hundred years, the perfection of their disguise being the greatest mark of their intelligence.

The others followed Ahmed to Lake Nasser to watch the sun rise over Abu Simbel from the shoreline. He thought that the most beautiful vista and told us that the next time we visit Egypt we should arrange for a Lake Nasser cruise. I was left standing alone in the dawn light with no idea how to get where I needed to go. Just at the moment I felt the most abandoned, an Egyptian approached me and offered his services as a guide.

He was not dressed in traditional Egyptian garb. Neither was he dressed stylishly like Ahmed. He wore simple white cotton pants and a white open collar linen shirt. Instead of a turban, he wore a white baseball cap with its rim pulled low on his forehead, which emphasized his stern, dark eyes. The only peculiar aspect of his wardrobe was the very large walking stick he carried. He introduced himself as Ibrahim.

"Do you need a guide? I take you all around Abu Simbel for five pounds."

"I don't want to go all around, but I do want to go to the Great Temple."

"For the sunrise?"

"Yes, I want to see the sun shine on the statues of Amun-Ra and the

Great Ramses. I really need to get there on time. I will be happy to pay you."

He winked as if he understood. I handed him a five-pound note, and he turned and walked briskly as I skipped along in the near dark. On the way he recited a rather peculiar lecture.

To understand how odd his lecture was, you must first realize that Abu Simbel is considered so great a monument that huge sums of money were spent to disassemble its mammoth stones and move them six hundred feet to the west and two hundred feet above their original site to save them from being submerged when the New Aswan Dam was built in the 1960s. People travel thousands of miles to see this temple built by and dedicated to Ramses. Ibrahim in fact earns his living by providing his services to these tourists once they arrive. But he was not much enamored with the Great Ramses and made no bones about it.

"He thought himself a god," Ibrahim said. "He was no god. He had too much pride to be a god. A god does not build a temple to himself."

As we walked down the rock and sand path leading to the temple's entrance, he greeted other guides by raising his walking stick high into the air over his head. He did not raise it as you would expect, holding the handle and raising its pointed tip upwards; instead, he grabbed hold of its tip and raised its curved handle. Perhaps he thought the gesture less threatening when done in this manner, I thought. It did not take me much longer to realize I could wonder in vain. Ibrahim would remain an enigma.

"You look at Amun when the sun rises," he said. "When the sun and Amun unite, that is God. Ramses built this grand temple, but it is Amun-Ra who keeps it standing."

I could see little detail of the temple as we approached it, but I could detect the mammoth size of carved forms that made up its exterior.

"These are all statues of himself," Ibrahim said, pointing his walking stick into the darkness. "They are colossal."

He guided me into the entrance carved in the rock flanked on either side by two huge statues of Ramses that he said were sixty-seven feet tall while seated on their thrones.

"If the statues could stand up, how tall might they be?" I asked.

"Too tall to be a god." He led me deep into the sanctuary. "You are

171

lucky. It won't be crowded since they won't let the caravans through. Last year on this day it was so crowded you couldn't fit inside."

I looked around and saw only a handful of people. Puzzled, I asked for an explanation.

"Most people come by caravan. Much cheaper than flying," he explained.

A picture formed in my imagination of a large group of camels carrying their load across the desert. In this case, loads of tourists. I could hardly imagine this so I pursued him further on the subject. "Tourists come by camel?" I asked.

Amused by my naiveté, Ibrahim, who had not smiled until then, grinned broadly. "Oh, you think I mean a desert caravan. Bedouin. No, that is not what I mean. A caravan of motor coaches."

"Tour buses?" I said.

"Yes, tour buses."

"Why a caravan of buses?" I asked.

"For security. Soldiers guard the buses for protection."

At that point I realized that what he meant was a convoy. Tour buses travel here in large convoys protected by the soldiers.

"Why are they not coming now?"

"Too dangerous."

Ibrahim pointed to the statue of Amun-Ra that stood next to a statue of Ramses and several other large statues. "Look at Amun when the sun comes," he ordered. He left eager to present his singular perspective on the monument and its builder to other tourists who may have traveled thousands of miles to see it.

I seated myself next to a wall in the rear of the sacred area. I felt for the little package in my handbag, pulled it out and unwrapped Thoth from the paper and string that bound him and placed him on my lap as I pulled out my pen and sheets of hotel stationery. Prepared, I sat in the darkness thinking about today's revelations concerning Gabby and Beverly, wondering if Dr. Short's phone call had resulted in anything, imagining the state of Stuart's ego after having been outwitted by two southern belles. I wondered what John was doing that was so important he couldn't come to the temple with me. I imagined Natalie, Madeleine and Paul standing with Ahmed on the shore of Lake Nasser listening to him lecture. He meant well, I knew. He just didn't understand that to experience Egypt for the first time requires some periods of silence to take in the enormity of what one sees. I doubted the pretty girl found fault in him though. She probably thinks he's brilliant. My mind wandered about like this until the rising sun began to present itself inside the temple.

Light looked ghostly in this place that was made for darkness as it inched its way inside. At last it reached one of the great statues, then another and finally touched Amun-Ra, on whose likeness I focused all of my attention as Ibrahim had ordered. My hands clasped hard around the golden statue of Thoth as I meditated. At last my mind was at rest until I nearly leaped out of my waking slumber when I saw my lap ablaze. The sunlight had touched Thoth, emitting a flash of white light. It was electric! My hand took on a life of its own. I was the typewriter and not the source. It picked up the pen without my mind commanding it and began to write with no thought in my head directing it. What my hand wrote upon the hotel stationery was in a language I had no comprehension of.

There were a row of symbols I recognized as hieroglyphics, although I didn't know their meaning: a vulture, an owl, a foot, a mouth, an arm, a basket and a vulture again. My hand moved down the page to another line and began to draw symbols horizontally across it. The first looked like a twisted rope, then a baby bird, the owl again and the feather and lion that I recognized from my cartouche. My hand drew a kind of lump of something and ended this line with two feathers. Carriage return. My hand drew a mouth again and a vulture, a lion followed by another vulture and then some kind of cord and a vulture once again. Carriage return. The line began with a box with lines in it, followed by a mouth, another feather, a hand and I ended with a final vulture. My hand dropped down to the bottom of the page and drew a much larger feather than what I had drawn before and next to it an Ankh. And then my hand stopped.

Chapter Twenty-Three

"Wake up!"

"Huh?"

"Wake up! You're asleep."

"What time is it?"

"It's a quarter after eight. The sun's been up for an hour." John looked down at my lap. "What's that?"

I took the man bird into my hand. "It's Thoth," I said. "I must have passed out. It's a good thing no one tried to steal him." I took out the paper and string stashed in my handbag and began wrapping him up.

"That looks like the package Bueller gave Mom," John said

"It is. Bueller asked me not to tell anyone when he gave it to me to bring down here because he thought it might put me in danger."

"Great! You listen to a guy like that instead of trusting me. If I had known, I would have stayed with you. Anyone could have taken it right out of your lap or worse, stuck a knife in you too."

"I know. I should have told you." I stuffed the now wrapped statue back into my bag. "I was afraid word might spread to the wrong person."

"See, you don't trust me!"

"No, that's not what I'm saying. I felt like if I told you, I would have to tell everyone else. And after what happened to Bueller on the ship, I knew having this thing is dangerous. I tried really hard not to take it from him, but he insisted. So I thought it was safer for the rest of you and me if you didn't know anything about it."

"You've got to tell them now. You know, you were really lucky. Anyone could have seen it on your lap."

I looked down at the piece of paper lying next to me with the hieroglyphics. "I had this incredible experience I want to tell you..."

"Tell me later. We've got to go back to the airport pronto. I came here to tell you to stay with Mom and Natalie, but I think you had better fly back with us."

"Did Dr. Short find a plane?"

"Yes, but it's only a four-seater. His Institute got some British archaeological group down here to lend it to him. The others are going to come back with Ahmed. I thought you could come back with him too, but not now."

"That's probably a good idea. I feel pretty wobbly."

"Are you scared?"

"I feel really uneasy. I want to hand this back to Bueller as soon as I can."

It took us less than fifteen minutes to get to the airport taking the public shuttle that runs between the airport, the temple and a few scattered hotels. I could tell by the look on Stuart's face he wasn't expecting to see me and didn't approve.

"Is our plan okay with the others?" he asked, implying that it had not been okay with me. "Do they have any problem staying here with Ahmed?" he said, suggesting that I did.

John replied as tactfully and unapologetically as he could. "No, they had no problem at all. In fact, I would say they're delighted to stay on."

"I have to go back with you now," I said. "I had a very unusual experience at the temple that may have put me in danger, and I have a feeling that something is going very wrong in Aswan."

"You can tell us all about it once we're in the air," Stuart said. Looking at John, he said, "Barry told me to bring you out on the runway as soon as you arrive."

"Well, let's go then."

Stuart led us through a side door near the runway where a small white plane sat ready for flight. Dr. Short was already sitting in the pilot's seat. The plane had large letters painted on it, which meant little to airplane novices like John and me.

"Do you know what kind of plane this is?" John asked. "It looks vintage."

"It is," Stuart said. "Barry says it's a Cessna, built way back in 1959. He's pretty psyched to be flying it."

John boosted me up into the seat. "I've heard of Cessna. They're supposed to be good planes, aren't they?"

"Well, hello," Dr. Short said just before he revved up the engine. "I thought you might want to come back with us."

175

"Let me tell you what happened!" I said. Before I could say anymore the engine noise had drown out my voice.

"It'll have to wait until later!" John shouted. I acquiesced.

If it were not for the engine noise, it would have seemed we were in a glider. The wind was exceptionally calm. We flew low at the plane's top speed, which was only ninety-five miles an hour. I looked down at the landscape trying to discern the danger that prevented the convoys of tourist buses from traveling between Abu Simbel and Aswan. I could see nothing except an inhospitable desert. There were no towns, no people, no camels, nothing at all until we reached Aswan, which looked like an exotic oasis in the middle of a vast desert.

"There's our hotel," I shouted over the din of the engine.

The Old Cataract looked half garden and half building perched against the Nile. I could see the terrace where we had sat and talked the night before sipping our bottle of champagne. Was that last night? I thought. My sense of time was lost. So much had happened it seemed like days had squeezed into hours. I'm just tired, I thought, and I knew I was hungry. Our last meal had been the grand buffet the night before on the Queen Nuit. Why did it seem so long ago?

Dr. Short radioed the airport and we landed. Once he arranged the return of the plane to the Institute personnel, he was ready to eat. Stuart's panic overrode his appetite. He took off in a taxi while the rest of us trotted back to the hotel in a horse drawn carriage. Once there, we headed straight for the veranda.

"For a British hotel this menu is very French," John said noting it featured a prix fixe luncheon with crème brulee for dessert.

"Well, the French own it now," Dr. Short said. "The British haven't been in this part of the world for a long time."

After the waiter served our dessert, John looked at me and said, "You'd better show it to him now."

I was sure Dr. Short recognized the little package as I opened it. His eyes grew twice their size when I pulled the golden statue of Thoth out of its wrappings.

"Let me see it more closely," he said and pulled the statue nearer to scrutinize. A few minutes later he handed it back. "Wrap it up and put it out of sight. It looks authentic. Of course, tests are needed to authenticate it, but the workmanship, style and materials definitely place it in the Old Kingdom or even the Predynastic period. Did Bueller give this to you?"

I explained why he had, when he had and why I hadn't told anyone, then asked him about what he had said the first time the subject of this statue came up. "You said that it could be funerary treasure from Imhotep's tomb, and that the treasure there was supposed to have magical properties."

"Yes, I did say that. That's the legend. But I don't know for certain it came from his tomb. You see, Imhotep's tomb has not yet been discovered—at least I thought it hadn't. And even if it had, the legend is only folklore." The expression on Dr. Short's face contradicted his assurances. He looked worried, very worried.

"How much do you think it's worth?" John asked.

"It depends. Its gold has a great deal of value, but if it really came from Imhotep's tomb, its value is incalculable. Knowledge of the tomb's whereabouts is even more valuable."

"It's hard to imagine somebody would kill for it," I said.

"Don't be naive," he replied.

"Bueller thinks it is magic." I explained what happened at the Great Temple at Abu Simbel when the light entered. "It was electrical. My hand began to write or draw, whatever you want to call it, as if it were taking dictation from someone else's mind. And then, I don't know, I passed out or fell asleep."

"What you describe is automatic writing," Dr. Short said. "Let me see what you wrote."

I pulled the sheet of hotel stationery out of my handbag and handed it to him.

"These are hieroglyphs! Do you know what they say?"

"No, I thought maybe you would."

"I would need a translator. Hieroglyphics isn't my specialty. Arabic yes, hieroglyphics no. A blind spot I have."

"I think we should get up to Bueller's room right away," I said and rose from the table.

"Put the bill on my tab," Dr. Short said to the waiter.

We marched off into the lobby and up the stairway to Bueller's second floor room. Dr. Short rapped at the door. We waited. No response. He did this several more times.

"Our room is right across the hall," John said. "We can call the desk to make sure Bueller didn't check out."

John unlocked the door and carefully entered as if he half expected to find an uninvited guest, but the room was quite empty. He called the desk. Bueller had not checked out, and to their knowledge had not left the hotel. They hadn't heard from him since breakfast, which was delivered to his room at about 9 o'clock.

"Had they picked up the tray?" Dr. Short asked.

"Yes, an hour later."

"Well then, we know Hans was alive and well just a few hours ago."

"I shouldn't have wasted time eating lunch," I said.

"Don't scold yourself. We had to eat something soon." He directed John to ask the desk to ring Bueller's room to rouse him if he happened to be asleep.

Seconds later we heard ringing coming from across the hall. There was no response. Dr. Short grabbed the phone from John. "We think we may have an emergency. Can you get someone up here right away to unlock Dr. Bueller's door? Yes, I'll be waiting right there."

The hotel manager appeared in the hall minutes later and hammered his fist against Bueller's door. Getting no answer, he unlocked it. Sunlight blazed so brightly through the balcony doors that shapes and forms in the interior of the room dissolved into whiteness until our eyes adjusted. Bueller's room had been totally ransacked.

"I will get the police," the hotel manager said.

When John walked across the room to close the drapes he saw Bueller looking as white as a ghost lying on the floor on the far side of the bed with blood running down his cheek. "Better get the hotel doctor first. I'm not sure he's alive."

Dr. Short bent over his old nemesis to check his vital signs. "He's alive. Please get a doctor at once," he said to the stunned manager.

"He's not on duty today. He had business to attend to in Luxor."

"Well, find someone else then! And get'em here in a hurry."

We lifted Bueller up onto the bed although he was so light it hardly took the three us.

"I wonder what the intruder was looking for?" John asked.

"My guess is he was looking for our little package here," Dr. Short said. "Look, the police will be here shortly. I suggest that none of us say anything about the statue just yet, not until Stuart gets back and we see what he thinks. As for me, I think the story is so astounding they might not believe us anyway, but if they would and the news gets out, well, a story like that could turn priests into tomb robbers. In fact, tell no one until Stuart and I figure out the safest thing to do, not even Madeleine and Natalie."

Dr. Short wetted down a towel and daubed Bueller's wounds. I watched him gently cleanse the head and cheek of the man he had earlier said he intensely disliked. That animosity was probably directed more at Bueller's beliefs than the man, I thought. That Nazi superiority thing is pretty nasty stuff and had horrendous consequences. But as I looked at the pale wisp of a man lying unconscious, he looked as much a victim of that worldview as anything else. The Nazis exploited his love of archaeology. They instructed him in their supremacist beliefs when he was young and impressionable. Here he is now, an old man left alone in a world where no one any longer shares that mythology, hanging on by a thread to outmoded beliefs that had proven themselves false half a century ago. And then I wondered just what those hieroglyphics I so mysteriously wrote down meant.

"The wound doesn't look too serious," Dr. Short said. "Hans is probably suffering more from shock and his age than anything else."

Chapter Twenty-Four

"Is anything of value missing?" the detective asked while looking haphazardly around the room.

"I really don't know," Barry said. He looked down at Bueller who lay in a fitful sleep. "He hasn't spoken to us yet. We're waiting for the doctor."

"When he recovers have him come to my office and file a report. There is nothing I can do except return what is missing if it should turn up, but I need to know what I am looking for."

"What about the person who broke into his room?" I asked. "He could have killed him!"

"But he didn't. Hotel robberies like this are common. The only uncommon element here is the victim was in his room. The robber must have expected the room to be empty and was probably as surprised by this man's presence as this victim was by his. In a panic he struck him and searched for what he could find of value. We rarely capture these thieves but sometimes the goods show up on the black market, particularly jewels. But if all he took was money, it's lost."

After the detective left, we looked at each other thinking, why had we bothered.

"It's a good thing we didn't tell him about the statue," John said. "He might have confiscated it and still have been of no help."

"That's right," Dr. Short said. "It's not under his purview anyway. It wasn't in the room at the time of the robbery, and we only suspect the thief was after it. Let's hope Stuart has more success."

Minutes after the detective left there was a rap at the door. I thought perhaps it was the detective returning with more questions, but when I opened the door there stood a very young man in a white linen suit carrying what looked like a doctor's medical bag.

"You are the doctor?" I asked, embarrassed that my question may have betrayed my astonishment that a man so young could be a doctor.

"Yes," he answered politely. "I am Doctor Shabaka. The hotel reached me and said you have a wounded man."

"Over here," I said and I directed him to the bed.

Dr. Short, John and I stood back while studiously inspecting the young M.D. as he reached down and touched the wound on Bueller's head. He felt his pulse and checked his heart, and then he carefully examined the patient from head to toe. His eyes look older, more experienced than his face or physique, I thought after studying him. When he looked up at us, they even looked gentle.

"What happened to this man?" he asked.

"We don't know for certain," Dr. Short said. He directed the doctor's attention around the room. "Apparently there was a robbery. He didn't answer his door or his phone. No one at the hotel had seen him leave, so we had the hotel manager unlock the door for us. We found him lying by the side of the bed here unconscious. The police detective was just here and concluded that the robber expected to find the room empty and panicked when he saw Bueller and struck him."

"You are his friends?" the doctor said.

"Yes," Dr. Short reluctantly said.

Doctor Shabaka opened up his case and took out a mortar and pestle. Then he pulled out several vials. He poured the contents of one into the bowl. It looked like some kind of oil. Then he added an amber powder that he mixed with the oil creating a very yellow, gooey material.

"What's that?" I asked.

"Turmeric. It is good for healing. I am making a poultice for his wound."

He then poured a golden sticky substance with a sweet odor from another vial into the oily yellow stuff.

"Is that honey?" Dr. Short asked.

"Yes, it will prevent infection."

In a not so subtle effort to check the doctor's credentials, Dr. Short shifted the discussion to the personal. "Are you originally from this area?"

"Near here. I am originally from Luxor. I studied medicine in Cairo," he said as if he understood what Dr. Short really wanted to know.

"At the doctors training hospital?"

"Yes, I studied there. I also learned a great deal about the traditional

181

healing arts from my father. I find them invaluable."

"Your father is a doctor too?"

"Yes," answered the man who was now administering a poultice to the wound on Bueller's head. "My father, my father's father. I come from a family of doctors all the way back."

Dr. Short relaxed a little. "What will the poultice do?"

"It will heal and disinfect the wound. But I think there is something more that afflicts this man. Can you tell me something about his life that might be causing the imbalance in his system?"

"He's a German archaeologist," Dr. Short said. "He's not married, never has been to my knowledge. No children, no living family at all."

At this point I couldn't remain quiet any longer, harboring knowledge, I suspected, that this very unusual doctor might be able to use to effect a cure. I felt confident in him. He was as caring as the police detective was uncaring, and I believed he deserved the truth or as much of it as I could give him without mentioning the golden statue. I began by recounting what I knew of Bueller's background until I arrived at the present.

"He's on a kind of quest, or at least he thinks he is. He thinks Imhotep is trying to communicate with him to bring him the ancient secrets he believes are the true heritage of the Aryan race, whose lineage he believes traces back to the ancient Egyptian high priests."

"'Aryan,' I am familiar with that word," the doctor said. "The Nazis thought they were descendants of the true Aryans, didn't they and slaughtered countless innocents believing they were of an inferior race?"

"Fortunately, Bueller didn't participate in that," I said in his defense. "He wants secret knowledge like all seekers do, but he thinks he's special and more likely to find it. I think that's how this Aryan thing figures into his thinking. It has made him believe that he will find what has escaped everyone else who has rooted through ancient tombs and monuments, searching for I don't know what, I guess some kind of deeper truth, a source of power."

"Hmm," the doctor said. "The disease is well established and widespread throughout his system."

"Then he got this crazy idea. He saw me with a statue of an ibis that I bought from a boy who risked life and limb to sell it to me. In his mind that purchase along with the fact that I teach writing meant something. He became convinced that Imhotep was going to use me to convey this secret knowledge to him. He asked me to help him. I agreed to do it only because Stuart...."

Doctor Shabaka looked up at John as if he thought he was looking at Stuart.

"No, not him," I said. "Stuart's not here right now. He's out trying to find some smugglers."

"He is with the police?"

"No, I'm not sure exactly who he is with. He is some kind of investigator who had been following some smugglers and then got interested in Dr. Bueller and asked me to go along with his scheme while he continued to investigate."

"You are a spy?"

"No, I'm not a spy," I said feeling very embarrassed about what I had been doing. "I am an English professor on a tour of Egypt. I never intended any of this. I've even gotten to like Dr. Bueller."

Doctor Shabaka nodded his head, communicating that he accepted my description of my role in this affair.

"Yesterday, when Dr. Bueller learned I was going with the others to Abu Simbel he got very excited and wanted me to be inside the Grand Temple when the light of the rising sun entered it. I agreed, expecting nothing to happen, when something did happen for which I have no explanation."

Dr. Short said, "You experienced automatic writing."

The young doctor's face opened up. His kind, wise eyes focused on me.

"My hand started drawing hieroglyphs," I said. "I have no idea what they mean. I wasn't thinking anything at all, so I can't see how they could have come from me."

"Might I see them?"

I pulled the piece of hotel stationery with the hieroglyphs from my handbag. Doctor Shabaka studied the piece of paper. Dr. Short moved behind him so that he might study it too.

"This first word," the doctor said pointing to the long row of hieroglyphics my hand drew on the first line, "means to, how shall I say

183

it, hug, embrace. It means to embrace."

I was surprised that all of those symbols only translated into one word.

"This second word means charity, embrace charity," he said.

He pointed to the third line of hieroglyphs, "This third word means to let go. And the last word below means pride. Embrace charity, let go of pride."

He looked down at the large feather and the Ankh at the bottom of the page. "These are meant to be interpreted symbolically, I believe. The Ankh is the ancient Egyptian symbol for eternal life. And the feather has to do with the heart."

"The heart as light as a feather," I said.

"Yes," he said. "You understand. Maybe I can help this man's malady."

He asked me to start a hot bath for the patient and gave me a little vial of some kind of fragrant herbs to add to it. He poured a glass of water and added some lemon juice he carried with him and another little vial whose contents I did not recognize. He asked the men to help him rouse Bueller and sit him up. Before Bueller could speak, he made him drink the medicine he mixed. Bueller drank it down then began to collapse again into sleep.

"No, no," said the doctor in a gentle voice. "You've had enough sleep. It's time you wake up."

The men helped the doctor get Bueller over to the bath, and then Doctor Shabaka told us that we could leave while he bathed and massaged this very old man. By then we all had the greatest confidence in this young doctor and took our leave.

It was a bit of a relief to get out of the sick room, but our sense of relief was short lived as our minds returned to other concerns. We wondered where Stuart was and whether Madeleine, Natalie and Paul had returned safely from Abu Simbel.

"What time is it?" I asked, my natural sense of time having been lost hours ago.

"It's five," John said.

"Madeleine, Natalie and the boy should have returned hours ago," Dr. Short said. "Their plane was to leave Abu Simbel at two, making its

184

arrival here at three. I wonder if they are here at the hotel or if they've gone off somewhere in the town?"

"Maybe they ran into Stuart," I said.

"I wonder where he went off to?" John said.

The phone began ringing in our room while we stood outside in the hall. John rushed in to answer it expecting more trouble.

"It's Natalie," he said.

I became nervous as I watched John quietly listening to what she was taking a very long time to say. I don't know exactly what I was nervous about. I guess I was just on edge, having found Bueller unconscious in his ransacked room and having flown all the way to Abu Simbel only to turn around and fly right back. And then I had had such a strange experience that morning in the temple.

"We will expect to see you tomorrow then. If there is another delay, call me," John said into the phone.

"Why tomorrow?" Dr. Short asked before the phone hit the receiver.

"Natalie says their flight was delayed, at least until tomorrow. They weren't given any explanation. She says there was a bit of a scene at the airport. The tour group was supposed to fly back to Cairo tomorrow morning and leave Cairo the following day for New York. Some of them are really angry and threatening to sue if they miss their flight."

Dr. Short walked over to the window. "The weather looks fine. No wind to speak of. I can't imagine that they could be having a sand storm down there without our getting some sign of it here."

"She said the weather is okay. She said nothing appears to be wrong with the plane. Ahmed apparently doesn't know what the problem is either although she told me some in the group are taking it out on him. Mom found a room for the three of them at the Nubian Desert Hotel, which is where they are now."

"Well, I'm sure they will be all right," Dr. Short said hesitantly. "There's probably something wrong with the plane and the airport officials are just not telling them."

"Paul was in the background yelling something into the phone. He kept saying Juliet was bawling."

"Oh, god!" I said. "It's that young girl who has the big crush on

185

Ahmed."

"Isabelle?" Dr. Short said.

"Is that her name? The pretty girl who is here with her mother, the travel agent?'

"Practically all of them are travel agents, but yes, her name isn't Juliet, it's Isabelle."

"Paul calls them Romeo and Juliet because their parents, at least Isabelle's mother, doesn't approve of the relationship."

"Which means if Juliet is bawling..." John said.

"There must be some kind of big mess going on down there between Isabelle and Ahmed."

"And her mother," John added.

A very tired Dr. Short said, "Well, at least no one has been robbed or hit over the head. I think I should take a short nap before dinner. How about you?"

"That sounds good. Maybe Stuart will be back by then." John closed our door, and the two of us dropped onto the bed fully clothed and were asleep within minutes.

Chapter Twenty-Five

The sun was still streaming into our room when loud knocking awakened us.

"You forgot to close the drapes," John complained.

"We both did. Could you get the door? I want to go back to sleep."

Curled up under the bedspread halfway between sleeping and waking, I heard Dr. Short's muffled voice and then John say, "What? Twelve hours! We must have been dead tired."

"I am sorry to disturb you," Dr. Short said as he walked into our room. "I started to worry, particularly in light of what has happened."

"That's all right," I said as I climbed fully dressed out of the bed. "I'm glad somebody is worried about us. So, what's happened now? Nothing new, I hope."

"I'm afraid so. Not directly to any of us," he added quickly. "But it might explain why your family is grounded in Abu Simbel. He took coffees, buttery croissants and a newspaper from his bag that he put down on a small table by the large picture window. "I thought you could use this since you missed dinner."

I ate my croissant and slowly sipped the bitter coffee, wondering whether this French hotel might serve hot chocolate. Dr. Short opened the English language paper and read the story from the front page.

Attack at Temple

Luxor: Tourists were attacked yesterday morning at the famous funerary temple of Queen Hatshepsut. Survivors of the attack reported seeing a group of masked men carrying automatic weapons appear suddenly out of a van parked next to several tour buses. The men fired randomly on tourists who were in line to buy tickets to the attraction. Government officials have undertaken a dragnet to capture the guilty men. Officials have issued the following warning: 'To any who would participate in such evil deeds. Such attacks defile both Egypt and God and will be subject to the harshest of punishments.' The number and country of origin of the dead and wounded is unknown at this time.

"Hatshepsut's Temple!" I said. "We were there, weren't we? I can't picture it."

"That's because we didn't get inside," John said. "That's the stop we missed because Mom and Natalie got lost in the Valley of the Kings and held us up. Remember?"

"Oh, now I remember. It was closed."

"I don't recall that," Dr. Short said.

"You hadn't joined us yet," John said. "You came right after the incident. Mom was probably too embarrassed to tell you about it, and out of courtesy to her and Natalie, the rest of us haven't brought it up."

"I'm glad now we didn't get in," I said. "It would have made this story all the more real to me than it already is. It could have been anyone. It could have been us!"

"What does this have to do with Mom, Natalie and Paul?" John asked. "How does it explain their airplane trouble?"

"I don't believe it was airplane trouble that grounded them," Dr. Short said. "No planes are flying. I had dinner with Stu last night, and he told me all the planes in Aswan are grounded too. This story explains why, although there has been no official statement. I suspect most planes are grounded all over Egypt. They're not taking any chances."

"On more attacks?" John said.

"A plane wasn't attacked yesterday," I said.

"My guess is that wherever tourists might be is heavily fortified right now: planes, boats, hotels, monuments. The paper said they've issued a dragnet. That's an extreme measure for Egypt to take. I suspect they want to make sure no more innocents are killed, and they also want to make it hard for the guilty to leave the country."

"Have you been outside the hotel today?" John asked.

"No, I haven't. But I bet guards are posted at the door."

"Like in Cairo," John said.

"Sad to say, like in Cairo."

"Our Cairo tour guides told us not to leave the hotel without them," I said.

"You took a chance with me then when I took you out to the Blue Nile," Dr. Short said grinning from ear to ear.

"There wasn't much risk in doing that," I said, "except for your

188

driving."

"I'm an excellent driver."

"Maybe it wasn't your driving," I allowed, "as much as it was the Jeep you squeezed us all into."

"It was a tight fit," he conceded. "I'm not accustomed to driving five people around Cairo."

"You said you talked to Stuart last night. What did he say?" John asked.

"As much as we've all been through together you would think that he wouldn't be so closed mouthed."

"It's a habit," I said.

"I suppose so. What I gathered is that he is committed to following those two women in the hope of learning who their contacts are. He said they were back in their hotel room when he got over there, and they stayed there all day. When he learned that the planes in Aswan are grounded, he felt safe coming back here and having a meal and getting some sleep."

"Did you tell him about Mom being stranded in Abu Simbel?" John asked.

"Yes, I did. He wasn't too concerned. In fact, he thought that might be a good place for them right now, far out of the reach of trouble."

"He's just thinking about his own trouble," I said, "those two women. I would feel a lot better if we were all together."

"So would I," Dr. Short said.

"Will planes be allowed to fly today?" John asked.

"I have no idea. When I asked Stuart last night, neither did he."

"We'll have to see what we can find out," John said. "Look, give us a half hour to shower and dress, and meet us down in the lobby."

"I'll poke around a little and see if I can learn anything more before you come down," Dr. Short said before leaving the room.

John was first in the shower, determined he could get downstairs in a hurry and figure out what was going on with the flights while I showered and dressed. But a phone call from Natalie answered the question about air travel, at least for that day, before his shower was done.

"Mom arranged another night here at the hotel," she spoke into her phone. "No one is telling us anything. Have you heard anything up

189

there?"

"Yes, we have," I said. "Dr. Short was just here. Apparently, there was some kind of attack on tourists near Luxor yesterday, and he believes they've grounded planes all over Egypt to try to keep those responsible from getting out of the country. And get this! He thinks there could be another attack planned and the Egyptian government is beefing up security just in case."

"It must have been serious," Natalie said.

"The article in the paper said details of the number of dead and wounded have not been made public yet, so, yes, it sounds bad."

"Well, that explains the other part of this," Natalie said. "They're asking us to stay in the hotel. Not that there is anywhere to go here once you've seen the temples. But that made me nervous along with the fact that they've given no explanation for why our flight didn't leave yesterday and won't leave today."

"Well, you've got one now."

"Small comfort."

"I'm sorry I didn't have better news. Hey, I just heard the shower turn off. Do you want to talk to John?"

"No, this is expensive. Call us here if you learn more."

"Will do. And let us know as soon as you learn anything about your return flight."

I reported my phone conversation with Natalie through the closed bathroom door. A few minutes later John appeared fully dressed and ready to go. "I don't like this at all," he said. "I think we need to do something."

"But what?"

"I'm not sure, but hurry and get dressed and come downstairs. I'll go find Dr. Short and see if Stuart's around."

I showered and dressed in record time, eager to learn what John and the others had decided to do about the situation, but when I arrived in the lobby I could not find John, Dr. Short or Stuart. I went out on the veranda expecting to see them gathered around a table, but they weren't there either. I consoled myself with a poached egg, croissant and hot chocolate. The chocolate was served French style, not like the pale chocolate premixed cocoa of my childhood. The waiter brought a steaming teapot of hot, creamy milk and a covered bowl of shaved bittersweet chocolate. I poured the hot milk into my teacup and spooned in as much chocolate as I liked, making a dark, rich brew and waited while slowly eating my egg and croissant and drinking the hot chocolate as I leisurely looked out upon the Nile. John appeared quite abruptly and stood over me at the table.

"Stuart picked up a van. We're driving down there now."

"To Abu Simbel? I thought the road is closed?"

"Officially it is. But Stuart learned that Gabby and Beverly checked out of their hotel early, and according to the desk clerk, offered quite a lot of money to any taxi driver willing to risk the trip. Stuart arranged to follow them. I told him Natalie called this morning and reported they are trapped in their hotel, and he agreed that under the circumstances it would be better to bring them back here by car. So, I just came in to let you know I'm leaving. We should be back by evening."

"You were planning to leave me here?"

"It'll be a whole lot safer for you."

"No way! There is no way in the world that you are going to leave me alone here while you go off. I'm going too!"

"It's okay with me, but I don't think Stuart's going to like it."

"That's too bad for Stuart. He didn't mind putting me in a potentially dangerous situation earlier when he wanted me to spy on Bueller. But now that I don't serve his purpose, he would rather I get out of the way. I don't think he likes women much."

"He's very worried about Natalie."

"I know he is, I know," I said, regretting the charge against Stuart I had just made.

"Well, come on then if you want to go. To tell you the truth, I couldn't quite imagine you would stay behind. But I thought I would give it a shot for your own safety."

"What was the last thing Samia and Yusef said to us when we left Cairo? Stay together," I said, and sipped the last remaining chocolate from my cup before getting up from the table.

John and I walked past the guards that now stood at the door of the hotel and climbed into the black van that awaited us. Dark tinted windows concealed Stuart's look of disapproval until I was seated inside.

I didn't care. I expected it. Dr. Short greeted me warmly enough. "I knew you would come along. You're a real trooper."

"No more than the rest of you," I said.

Stuart pulled away from the hotel and up to a small gas station before we left Aswan. He topped off the nearly full tank and pulled a very large gas can from the back of the van, filled it and placed it back inside. "Just in case," he said, before whipping the van out of the station towards the highway to Abu Simbel.

"In case of what?" I asked.

"There aren't likely to be any gas stations between here and Abu Simbel," Dr. Short explained.

I recalled how desolate it looked when we flew over the desert. I remembered that I couldn't imagine where a staging point for an attack might be since from the air everything looked flat and barren. The black tinted glass I stared through created the illusion of our van as a cocoon, its darkened windows a veil I could hide behind if we ran into trouble. A hushed cocoon, I thought, as the silence in the van seemed to replicate the desolation of my recollection.

To break the silence as much as anything, I said, "Has anyone notified Madeleine and Natalie that we're coming?"

"No, it's probably best that they don't know," Dr. Short said.

"Why not?"

"I don't trust the phones," Stuart said.

"Technically this road is off limits," Dr. Short said. " It's closed and probably for good reason. We don't want to alert anyone that we are on it if we can help it."

"Oh." I began for the first time to feel afraid.

The distance between Aswan and Abu Simbel is about one hundred and seventy miles. Stuart expected we would get there in less than three hours if all went well. Within minutes after we drove out of Aswan I saw Egyptian farmers with their mules tending fields, which lay between where we drove and the great, ancient river. The sight reminded me of Stuart's cover while we were on the cruise boat. He was researching Egyptian wine production and agricultural methods for his next bestseller, he had said. I smiled, which momentarily lessened my apprehension about what might lie ahead on the prohibited highway.

We turned onto another road, a wider road, which looked newly paved. It took us further from the Nile, although it continued to follow the river's path. Gone were the farm fields as the fertile, irrigated land gave way to the desert. We cruised for a short time. Then Stuart threw the van into high gear and barreled along between seventy and eighty miles an hour, whipping up sand as we flew down the highway. Breaking through the silence that had overtaken us all was the sound of little stone pebbles crashing against the van's fenders and windshield.

Chapter Twenty-Six

The landscape looked as empty from the ground as it had from the air save for the occasional sand and rock hill. Yet experiencing the desert from two different vantage points offered competing pictures. From the air the landscape shone with intense golden light as we glided over it. The van's tinted glass, however, stole that gold from the sand and rock formations, leaving only grayish, shapeless forms that sped past my sight, almost like the end of a reel of black and white film spinning out on a projector. I resented the darkened glass for stealing the sun, but I also found comfort in its seeming protection. I felt safe, hidden away, much like I did as a child when I would peer out of my second story bedroom window surveying the neighborhood out of sight of those below. Whose sight I was concealed from now I did not know for there seemed to be no one out here on the desert.

"Seems peaceful enough," Dr. Short said.

"Maybe all the action is up north in Luxor," John said.

"Yes, that must be why we haven't seen any police patrolling this road."

"How far have we gone?" I asked.

"We're about half way," Stuart said.

"Good."

"Are you nervous?" John asked.

"A little."

"It seems futile to close a road and have no one around to enforce the closing," Dr. Short said.

"It appears that the road closing order has a built in enforcement," I said, looking out of my veiled window at the empty landscape. "It's incredible. There's absolutely no one around. You'd think more people than us would try to get through by car."

We ceased talking about the eeriness of the place, but that didn't alleviate my anxiety. Perhaps the locals knew something I didn't know, I thought. Perhaps a government order to close the road is to them what a tornado warning is to me. When I hear one I go to the basement.

Stuart continued to drive at freeway speeds. It would have been hard to do otherwise for the road was wide and well paved and belonged entirely to us and to the dust that whipped past us and the pebbles that gently pelted the sides of the van and occasionally its windows. Suddenly the size of the pebbles increased and crashed loudly against the sides of the van near the darkened windows.

"Get down!" Stuart shouted as he raced the van to top speed.

Instead we looked out of the windows trying to understand what was happening.

"Get down!" he shouted again. "We're under attack!"

The loud crashing sounds began to make sense. These were not rocks but bullets. We ducked down to the floorboards. Soon, the racket moved to the rear of the van. It sounded like someone had launched a pile of rocks at high velocity in our direction from behind. One bullet shot through the rear window and flew out of the front, and then there was silence.

Stuart continued to drive fast while the rest of us clung to the floor until he finally told us it was safe to take our seats. Dr. Short dusted himself off, although nothing had entered the van save the one bullet, which had missed us. Under normal circumstances I would have objected to ripping along the highway at one hundred miles an hour, but not this time, not after that.

"Where did they come from?" I asked. "I didn't see anything."

"Neither did I," Stuart said. "They must have been lying low in depressions that formed behind the sand. Or maybe they have some kind of underground bunkers to hide in. The good thing is they apparently aren't mobile. They're not following us."

"Who are they?" John asked.

"I don't know. They could be disgruntled Egyptians or rebels who came up from Sudan. They recognize no borders. Could you keep a lookout for any abandoned vehicles?"

"Yes, of course. How much farther?"

"At this rate of speed I would say we're only thirty minutes away."

"I think it is unreasonable to consider a return trip now that we know what would await us," Dr. Short said. "We can't possibly expose

195

Natalie, Madeleine and the boy to this danger." He looked at me. "You should have stayed back in Aswan."

I didn't say anything. What could I say besides maybe we were all foolish to attempt this trip? We were reckless. We ignored the danger signals around us as if we thought we were immune.

"I think we should fly back no matter how long we have to wait for the planes to fly again," John said. "We still have seat reservations."

Our thoughts were now in Abu Simbel where we imagined our reunion with the others, our wait for the plane and our safe return to Aswan. We would be sensible and safe and avoid putting ourselves in such a dangerous situation again. But we were not yet in Abu Simbel. We had perhaps fifteen more miles when the van started to lose speed and the engine died out.

"We're out of gas," Stuart said.

He opened the door and slid out of the front seat, standing entirely exposed outside of the van. I looked along the side of the road for evidence of places where someone might be hiding in wait. I could see none, but I couldn't see any before so that wasn't much comfort. He hopped back inside. I felt relieved.

"There is a slight rupture in the tank," he said. "It doesn't look large. Come take a look."

We hesitantly hopped out of the van in full of view of anything or anyone who could be watching. Stuart pointed to a trickle of gas that extended from the van back down the road for as far as we could see.

"One of the bullets must have grazed it," he said. "It could have been a lot worse than this if it had been a direct hit."

"Is your extra can of gas undamaged?" Dr. Short asked.

"Yes, but what are we going to patch this hole with? We've got enough gas in the can to make it to Abu Simbel but not if it all runs out of the tank again."

I reached in into my bag and felt around the bottom. "Look what I've got," I said, holding up two pieces of Paul's bubble gum.

"That's an idea," Stuart conceded. "But I don't know if bubble gum will hold."

"Maybe if we added some sand," Dr. Short said. "It would give it more body, make it into a kind of cement. There's nothing to do but try."

Dr. Short took the bubble gum, unwrapped both pieces, popped them into his mouth and began chewing and chewing, trying to get the gum to the right texture. He didn't want to chew it too long because it might get stringy and hard. He wanted it chewed just to where it is soft and malleable. It was clear by his understanding of the various stages that bubble gum undergoes that at sometime in his life he had been an avid chewer. That was hard to imagine now. He looked so dignified, so professorial. In fact, the juxtaposition of his appearance and the chewing were comical, but I was too scared to laugh. Once he got the gum where he wanted it, he mixed it with some fine sand, "Not too much," he said, and handed the pasty slab to Stuart who crawled under the van and inserted the substance ever so carefully into the tiny hole and spread the remainder out around the metal tank to secure it.

Stuart climbed out from underneath the van. "It looks good. John, can you help me pour gas into the tank? You two get back inside and be prepared to blast out of here when we're done."

Dr. Short and I climbed into the van and watched John and Stuart lift the heavy can and carefully pour its contents into the tank, avoiding spilling any for there was little to spare. They threw the empty can into the rear of the van, hopped inside and Stuart tore down the road to Abu Simbel.

We sat silent once again. My anxiety shifted from snipers to that little piece of bubble gum that Stuart used to plug the hole. I strained to see if we were leaving a telltale trail of gas behind us, but we were moving so fast I couldn't make much out through the gray glass.

Three and a half hours after leaving Aswan we arrived at Abu Simbel, although it felt like we had been on the road much longer. It was now mid-afternoon. Stuart thought it would be best to leave the van at the airport since there was little public parking except where the buses load and unload tourists going to and from the temples. We parked the van in an inconspicuous location at the rear of the airport building. It was a good thing too since the sight of it might have caused a panic. We must have been too distracted or too frightened when we stopped to patch and refill the gas tank to notice. The van looked like it had been through a war.

"At least they were using mostly low caliber ammunition," Stuart said as he walked around the van looking at its pockmarked body.

"How do you know?" John asked.

"Anything else and the thing wouldn't be covered with dents but shot full of holes. That's probably what saved our lives."

We stood there for a few minutes looking at the van, grateful that it had taken the bullets intended for us and grateful that we had arrived safely.

"What's going to happen to it?" I asked.

"It will probably be junked. Or maybe some local will want it. Who knows," Stuart said. "It's somebody else's problem now. Let's head over towards the temple. I've got an appointment to keep with two ladies."

"Not the same two ladies we're meeting," Dr. Short said in jest.

"You're right about that. At least not until after work."

"How can you be sure they arrived?" I said. "They could have been attacked along the road too, only worse!"

"That's right, they could have been. But if it were worse there would have been traces left behind, an abandoned vehicle, something."

I shuddered in both horror and relief, horror at what could have happened and relief that it had not. Finally, I felt what the French call the *joie de vivre*, which comes on strongly following the successful outcome of a harrowing experience.

"It's holiday time around here," Stuart joked as he looked around the closed airport and the empty parked buses. "When tourism ends, employee vacations begin."

Stuart was more talkative than he had ever been, I thought, as we walked down the road towards the temples, shops and hotels. We discussed better and cheaper transportation than buses that could carry tourists the short distance we were walking. Donkey driven carriages would have been pleasant, we all agreed. It was a relief to see him behave like a real person, like one of us. He's probably feeling good that we made it here in one piece, I considered, and he's probably also feeling excited to have his quarry cornered and be about to make the catch. At the sight of the Nubian Desert Hotel we parted. Stuart headed towards the public area to learn the whereabouts of Gabby and Beverly while the rest of us walked towards the hotel.

The hotel's architecture lacked distinction, but to its credit it appeared to have a nice garden and landscaping. We stood for a few moments inside the sliding glass doors leading out to the patio and pool and noted by the numbers of people that the hotel was crowded. Having the planes grounded had been good for business at this location at least. Paul bounced on the low diving board and plunged into the water, arms straight, hands folded one on top of the other. He was the first to see us as he pulled himself up and out of the water. His face lit up. He made a dash towards us, which Madeleine, who sat with Natalie further back under a large umbrella, followed with her eyes until they met ours. Paul led the three of us across the patio to where they sat.

"How did you get here?" Natalie asked. "I thought the planes are grounded."

"And so they are," Barry said. "We came in a van."

We pulled additional chairs around the table and recounted all that had happened when we returned to Aswan: how Bueller's room had been entered and ransacked, how we found him lying unconscious on the floor, how Stuart went looking for Gabby and Beverly, how he thought they were in their hotel room unable to leave because the planes couldn't fly and how he learned early this morning that they had left by taxi for Abu Simbel. We told them how Stuart, with the help of his contacts, was able to get a van to follow them down here, and how we decided to come along so that we could all return together.

"Where is Stuart?" Natalie asked, looking around as if she expected him to appear any moment.

"We left him near the temple," John said. "He'll show up eventually, but he wanted to locate Gabby and Beverly first."

Dr. Short looked about the pool as if he half expected to see them. "Have you seen them today?"

"I still can't believe those two women are smugglers," Madeleine said. "No, I haven't seen them since we left the cruise ship. Of course, we've been here all day. You knew we were asked not to leave the hotel, didn't you?" Then looking at John she said, "Speaking of which, Natalie told me there was an attack on a group of tourists near Luxor. Have you heard any more?"

"No. I suppose Natalie told you that Dr. Short and Stuart believe that's why the planes are grounded."

"Yes, she did. I'm so glad you've come for us. I really would like to leave here now."

"I'm sorry to tell you this Madeleine," Barry said. "We won't be driving back in the van. We're all stranded here until the planes fly."

He told her of our harrowing drive to Abu Simbel, about the utter desolation of the desert and about the ambush. In contrast to the pleasure she had expressed only minutes before about our having driven down to get them, Madeleine now chastised him for violating the order to stay off of the road.

"I must say Madeleine," Dr. Short said, "no one was more regretful of our reckless behavior than I. We are all thankful to be here and alive."

"I wish I had been there," a wide-eyed Paul pronounced.

"If it hadn't been for your bubble gum Paul, we'd still be out on the desert right now," John said.

Paul looked up, eyes even bigger. "My bubble gum?"

John described how we ran out of gas because the tank had been punctured by one of the bullets, how Stuart had had enough foresight to have extra gas in the back of the van, but how we didn't know how we were going to patch the van's tank.

"Then I remembered your bubble gum in my handbag," I said. "Dr. Short here, an obvious expert in bubble gum as well as Egyptology, chewed it to a perfect consistency and added a little sand making an excellent patch for the tank." We all laughed uproariously.

"Where's the van? I want to see it!" Paul shouted over our laughter.

"It's way back at the airport," John said. "You don't want to see it. It would frighten you."

"Yes I do!"

"It looks pretty bad, son. I can assure you of that," Dr. Short said. "Can we get some lunch? I'm famished."

"We've already had lunch," Madeleine said. "The hotel had a luncheon buffet earlier, but maybe you could get a sandwich."

Dr. Short looked more closely at the hotel. "It reminds me of the New Aswan Dam, very functional. I'll just go inside and inquire about food. I should also check on a room for the night. Does anyone want to come with me?"

John and I joined Dr. Short. Paul decided to come along just in case we had another adventure on the way. We passed Joyce and Barbara sitting at a table looking quite bored. I wondered if they would be recommending this trip to any of their clients. At a table near them sat Isabelle and her mother. On the other side of the pool were Ahmed and Michael Sargent looking as if they were deeply engrossed in conversation.

I calculated that we should check into the hotel before we asked them to make us sandwiches, which turned out to be a good decision since there were only two rooms left. Then Dr. Short reminded me that it wasn't likely that hordes of new tourists would be arriving anytime soon to take them. He was right. This new reality hadn't quite sunk in.

The hotel clerk ordered the cook to make us cold lamb sandwiches to hold us over until the dinner buffet. The waiter would bring them out to the patio in fifteen minutes along with some soda, he said. Meanwhile, we could take our luggage to our rooms.

"I never thought to bring any luggage," I said. "I sure hope the planes fly soon."

"They can't keep them grounded much longer," Dr. Short said. "The whole economy depends on travel."

"I hope you're right. I think I'll go to our room anyway so I can at least wash my face and hands."

"I'll come with you," John said.

"Are you afraid I'll get lost?"

"That too," John said. "But I need to wash up as well."

Looking at Paul with a sly smile on his face, Dr. Short said, "These two aren't tough enough for a real archaeological expedition. Why, I've spent days in the desert without a shower or clean clothes."

"Yeah!" Paul said.

"We will see you two later out on the patio."

"We'll only be a few minutes," John said.

Our room wasn't far from the lobby, so we had no difficulty finding it. In fact, it seemed too close to the lobby and too close to the housekeeper's closet, which was the only room between it and the lobby.

"This is like getting the last table in a crowded restaurant, you know, the one that they don't use unless they have to, the one with the view of the washroom door," I complained.

John unlocked the door and opened it wide. Inside were two very small twin beds squeezed into a room that could barely hold them and to the side a small bathroom.

"It sure isn't the Old Cataract," John said.

"It sure isn't."

We looked at each other and laughed, realizing why everyone at the hotel was out on the patio. They wouldn't want to spend much time in these rooms. We quickly returned to the others and to our lunch, a rather tasty cold lamb sandwich on flat bread. The sun while lowering was still brilliant. The sky was intensely blue. We were happy and grateful to be together and alive.

Chapter Twenty-Seven

Ahmed hurried to our table just after the waiter removed our luncheon plates. "All flights will resume tomorrow morning," he said breathlessly. "I should know our departure time by dinner. Will you be joining us for dinner here at the hotel?"

"Why yes, of course," Dr. Short said.

"I only ask because I presume you spent last night at a different hotel."

"Why, yes, that's true." He paused to clear his throat. "That is very true indeed, but tonight we will be staying here if you don't mind."

"Why would I mind?" Ahmed said quizzically. "I am asking the airline that we be put on the first flight in the morning since the others need to fly to Cairo immediately to catch their return flight to New York. And you? Will you be returning to Cairo?"

"Yes, we will all be going to Cairo. But I think we'd prefer to stay in Aswan at least one more day if you can arrange that for us. Is that agreeable with all of you?" he said turning to the rest of us.

"That would be very nice," Madeleine said, "to have one more day."

Looking at Ahmed, Dr. Short went on, "I will be staying in Cairo, and I hope the others will be my guests there for a few more days before returning to the States."

"Our return flight to the States is going to have to be rearranged anyway since we added on Abu Simbel at the last minute," John said. "I can't see how adding a few more additional days will make a difference."

"The airlines are very understanding of your situation," Ahmed said.

"Can you do me a favor then and notify Yusef and Samia of our arrival time once you've arranged our flight back to Cairo, and ask them if they could look into flights back to the U.S.?"

Ahmed was most eager to offer his services, and we all agreed that he had been a wonderful guide even if his lectures had at times been tedious and his style a little regimented.

"Okay Paul, now what was it you were shouting into the phone, something about Juliet?"

Paul brightened up. "She was bawling and bawling at the airport because she thought those two ladies over there were going to hurt Romeo." He rather tactlessly pointed to the table where Joyce and Barbara sat.

"Romeo and Juliet?" Natalie said.

"Ahmed and Isabelle," I explained.

"Oh, definitely. That's an excellent description."

"What exactly happened?" I asked her.

"Well, Joyce and Barbara threw a fit when Ahmed told us our flight was grounded. When he couldn't give them any reason for it, they went ballistic. They said if this had happened on a Carrousel Cruise, heads would roll. They threatened to have him fired for incompetence."

"Oh, really! That doesn't sound fair."

"Well, yes, that and for fraternizing too freely with one of his clients."

"They meant Isabelle?" I said.

"Obviously. He explained that the flight cancellation was out of his control, but they wouldn't hear of it. There was quite a scene at the airport."

"And it got worse!" Madeleine said. "They made a phone call to someone, and Isabelle became quite upset. She called them—Well, I won't repeat what she called them. She confided in us that Ahmed was very worried that if he lost his job it would be difficult to find another."

"So what happened?" I said.

"Not too much that I could see," Madeleine said. "I've noticed that Ahmed and Isabelle have kept their distance since we've come to this hotel."

"Probably to protect his job," Natalie said. "At dinner last night I told everyone about the attack in Luxor. I told them about all the planes that have been grounded in Aswan and probably all over Egypt. Our very professional travel agents sitting over there never offered an apology, even after all of that."

"It sounds like that expletive Isabelle called them is accurate," I said. "But I don't think Ahmed's company would fire him. They know what happened."

"Just the same," Madeleine said. "I think we should write a letter to our tour company and praise Ahmed and Samia and Yusef as well. I'll draft a letter that we can all sign."

I looked across the patio at Joyce and Barbara who stared back as if they knew we were talking about them. And I looked over at Isabelle and her mother huddled together in conversation, oblivious to us and everything else going on around them. I wondered what would become of this shipboard romance. Then I thought about Stuart. It was getting late, and he didn't know we would be leaving tomorrow.

"Do you think it would be all right if we go out for a little while," I said to the others. "The emergency appears to be over. I think we should try to find Stuart and tell him the flight leaves in the morning."

"It should be safe enough," Dr. Short said. "But for caution's sake, I will go look for him myself. The rest of you can stay here."

"Oh no! Not this time," Madeleine said.

"Yeah, I want to come," Paul said.

Natalie's eyes said what words didn't need to. So with that, we all got up from our table and left our fellow travelers at their respective tables to sort out their affairs while we sorted out ours.

We were not sure where to look for Stuart, but Abu Simbel was small enough that we didn't think finding him would be too difficult. There was only the airport, the temples and the bazaar near the temples, a few hotels and some small houses where the people who staffed the tourist site live.

"Let's begin where we left him," Dr. Short said.

The shops were all closed for business. Very few people had ventured out, and those who did were obviously the staff. When we approached the temple we saw a small group of guides talking boisterously among themselves, hardly noticing us, as their attention seemed riveted on a game of backgammon. Paul ran over to get a closer look, and as he did, one of the men looked over our way.

"Ibrahim!" I said. He recognized me instantly and offered one of his rare smiles.

"Did you do as I said?" he asked. "Did you look at the sun shine upon itself?"

I knew exactly what he meant although the others looked a little perplexed. "Yes, I did. I looked at Amun-Ra as you told me to."

"Did you learn what you came here for?"

205

I blushed and told him that I had and thanked him for his help. Then I introduced him to the others, and he asked if they too would like to be taken into the temple.

Dr. Short spoke up. "We're looking for someone. Maybe you can help us. A young man of about thirty-five. He is about so tall." He raised his hand up to show Stuart's height. "He is muscular."

"Light hair, blue eyes?" Ibrahim said.

"Yes, that's him."

He told us that he saw such a man earlier and asked if we would like him to guide us to that location. We agreed and offered him thirty Egyptian pounds, which he happily accepted. We marched behind him towards Lake Nasser.

"This man asked about ships arriving and departing," Ibrahim said, brandishing his cane in the air as if to add emphasis to his speech. "We have not had many these last few days, one maybe two. He asked if I saw two women."

Ibrahim stopped dead in his tracks. We stopped as well, like cars braking to avoid a collision. He turned around and pointed his cane at Madeleine and Natalie and studied them for a minute or two. "No, you are too slim," he said, and turned around and resumed his march to the lake. He took us to a small boarded-up ticket office. "This is where we talked. It's closed now." He squinted his eyes and looked westward away from the lake and towards the temples and the setting sun. He circled around looking north and finally east towards the lake's shore. He pointed the crook of his cane. "Over there in the field of reeds."

Barely discernible in the distance was the figure of a man, his form blending with the shimmering water as the sun cast its last light of day upon his back. It was Stuart. He stood looking out over the lake, arms down to his sides as if he were poised to meditate on whatever he was watching. Ibrahim took us towards him on a little path that cut through the bulrushes growing along the lake's soggy shore.

Sensing that something was very wrong, Dr. Short stopped us before our arrival. "I should go alone. Wait for me here."

We watched Barry continue to cut through the reeds. We watched as Stuart turned around and acknowledged him and waved at us. We watched as the two men spoke. And we watched as Dr. Short returned to us alone.

"Stuart will be along later," he said when he arrived back to our little band of travelers. "We should get back to the hotel before it's completely dark," signaling in his tone if not in his words that further discussion of Stuart would have to wait.

I had arrived in Abu Simbel a few days before in the early morning darkness. And Ibrahim, lifting his cane with its rounded almost snakelike handle into the air, had led me to the temple and to the sun god Amun just as the first light of the morning was arriving. And now, I thought, it is fitting that this man, brandishing the same cane, should lead us back to the safety of our hotel as the last rays of light descend upon Abu Simbel. We were very quiet on that walk back. As we stood outside the gate leading into the hotel grounds Ibrahim wished us a safe voyage home.

"How did you know we would be returning home soon?" I asked.

"You said that you had learned what you came here to discover," he answered as if our whole trip were only for that purpose.

I thought better of inquiring further. Besides, his guess was correct. We would be returning home in only a few more days. I thanked him for all of his help. Madeleine pulled another five-pound note from her handbag and handed it to him, which he gratefully accepted. We did not stop to talk much once inside the well lit lobby but instead agreed to meet back there after we had a chance to go to our rooms and wash before dinner.

John and I were the first to return to the lobby. Dr. Short arrived only a few minutes later. We joked together that appetite was the controlling factor in the time it takes to get ready for dinner. Quite unexpectedly Stuart emerged through the hotel door looking a bit lost, like a desert wanderer who had found his way back to civilization but is not so sure he wants to return. We greeted him and he us. Dr. Short gave him the key to his room, which he kindly offered to share with Stuart that night and told him we would wait for him to go wash up for dinner. Stuart nodded his head and continued through the lobby, into the hallway and out of our sight.

"I suppose I should tell you now," Dr. Short said. "They got away."

"Where? How?" John asked.

"To Sudan. They left on a ferry earlier in the day."

"Is he going to follow them?" I asked

"I don't know what he's going to do. You'll have to ask him."

"That might be a bit awkward," I said. "I don't want to say anything that might make him feel worse. He looks distressed already."

"We will make him feel worse if he knows we are avoiding the subject."

Paul ran ahead of Natalie and Madeleine once they released him from their room, hoping I imagined, that John, Dr. Short and I would be more responsive. He was in high spirits and rattling questions off a mile a minute. What was Stuart doing in the bulrushes? Why did Ibrahim point his cane at the sky when he talked? Is he a teacher like Paul's teachers who point their rods at chalkboards? Would there be any more adventures left on the trip or had we used them all up? All questions that none of us could answer.

"Stuart's back," Dr. Short said, in answer to the question not yet asked.

"He came back already?" Madeleine said. "I was sure that he wanted to stay out there longer."

"He's in my room washing up for dinner. He'll be here in a few minutes."

"Oh, Boy!" Paul said. "I want to know everything that happened."

"Now Paul," Madeleine said, "it's impolite to ask too many questions."

"That's okay Madeleine," Dr. Short said. "It's better to get it out in the open. In the long run it's better for Stuart to talk about whatever he's feeling about the whole affair."

"Stuart does not talk about his feelings," Natalie said.

Dr. Short rejoined, "I know he doesn't, but he would be a happier person if he did."

I can only imagine what Stuart thought when he entered the lobby from the rear hallway and saw a panel of inquisitors standing together, eyes turned on him, faces full of questions. I flashed back to my dissertation defense. Did it meet their expectations? I remembered wondering as I looked about at the questioners. Is it up to their standards? Those questions masked my deeper apprehension. Am I up to their standards? Am I up to my own?

Instead of letting Stuart continue to walk across the lobby with our eyes firmly planted upon him, Dr. Short walked towards him and met him halfway. We followed, and the group of us entered the dining room looking about for a table large enough to accommodate us. We fit nicely at a long table for eight. The waiter came to take our drink orders and directed us to the buffet. My hot chicken stew tasted good after our harrowing morning drive.

Paul broke the ice. "When are you going to tell us what happened?"

Stuart smiled at Paul and said, "Well, they got away."

"How did they do that? How did they get away from you?" Paul asked with all the sincerity of a ten year old who had thought Stuart a superhero.

"I miscalculated."

"You did?" Paul said, his voice growing hesitant, perhaps because superheroes don't miscalculate.

"It never occurred to me that they would try to escape Egypt from the south into Sudan. I thought for sure they would fly back to Cairo and leave from there. So when the planes were grounded, I made the mistake of sleeping on the job, and they got away."

"You're being too harsh on yourself," Dr. Short said. "I would hardly call what you did sleeping on the job. You barely got any sleep the night before. You had to sleep sometime."

"I picked the wrong time."

At that Dr. Short was quiet but not Paul. "Are you gonna follow them there?"

"I can't," Stuart said, "I don't have a visa to get into Sudan, and I doubt they would issue me one."

"Why not?" Natalie inquired.

"Call it politics," Stuart said.

"Well, how did Gabby and Beverly get in then?" she asked.

"Good question. My best guess is that their contact lives there. I thought they were doing business with an Egyptian, but I begin to think otherwise."

"What do you suspect them of doing?" I asked.

"I know they have been smuggling diamonds back to the United States. We intercepted that parcel they mailed from Edfu and found a packet of diamonds hidden among their souvenirs. We suspect now that this has been their method all along. They travel from place to place and mail much of what they buy back to their homes from out of the way post offices. Their husbands probably take care of it from there. That was an important find because it explains why our airport searches of their luggage always failed to turn anything up."

"Don't they inspect all the packages mailed to the United States?" Madeleine asked.

"Unless the inspectors are tipped off, as they were about the packages from Edfu, they only inspect for the purpose of collecting duty. So if the gems are well hidden, as we know now they were, no one would have noticed."

"If you knew they were doing bad things, why didn't you arrest them already?" Paul asked.

"Because we wanted to learn who their contacts are. That was my job."

"You learned something if not the exact names," Dr. Short said. "You learned that the contact or contacts reside in Sudan. That's got to be important."

"It is. I also learned how dangerous these women are."

"What do you mean?" Natalie asked.

"We've had a hard time figuring these two out. We've wondered if their husbands duped them into this, if they were being used. But after what I've seen I think they're really dangerous characters and much smarter than they appear."

"They are smart all right getting away from you," Paul said.

"And pretty vicious I believe," Stuart said.

"Do you think they're the ones who hit Bueller over the head and ransacked his room?" I asked.

"Not only that, I think they knifed him on the cruise, and I think they were responsible for the bullets that nearly struck him in Edfu." Looking at Dr. Short, Stuart said, "You told me Bueller probably engaged in a little artifact smuggling. That was important for me to know. People in that trade keep tabs on each other. I believe Gabby and Beverly learned that Bueller was carrying an extremely valuable item and were hell bent on stealing it. I thought while in Edfu that Bueller was following the women, but now I suspect their accomplice was following him. Had his bullet not missed, they no doubt would have come to Bueller's aid and rifled through his pockets while they were at it. He ducked just in time. To divert suspicion, the ladies feigned that they were the intended targets." Stuart paused. "I even believed them for a while."

"What about the attack on the boat?" Dr. Short said. "They must have known they couldn't rifle through his clothes with all of those people gathered."

"They knew he was going to be in costume for that performance. They must have figured that he wouldn't risk keeping the object on his person in that circumstance, so he would have to leave it in his cabin. I think one of them shut off the lights while the other threw the knife during the performance to direct everybody's attention towards the wounded man. Had I not immediately switched the lights on and ordered everyone not to move, I believe they would have broken into his cabin and stolen the artifact during the confusion they expected would follow."

"And you stopped them!" Paul said, the fullness of his admiration restored.

"Why didn't they just rob his cabin during the performance?" Natalie asked. "The play had diverted everyone's attention, and they wouldn't have had to wound him."

"Their intention was to kill Bueller not wound him. They failed there too. If he were dead, he couldn't come after them. But if they robbed his cabin and he remained alive, he would know who the thieves were and hunt them down."

"How would he know?"

"If you remember, nearly everyone was at the performance except those who had direct responsibility for operating the ship. If they had not been present, that would have been a dead giveaway."

"I see," Natalie said.

"Oh, this gives me the creeps!" I said. "I was in Bueller's cabin right before the performance looking at the very thing they wanted. But if they thought he kept it on his person most of the time, why would they have broken into his hotel room when they thought he was out?"

"They didn't think he was out," Stuart said.

"But the detective said that most hotel robberies occur when the occupants are out of their room and that the robbers were probably surprised to find Bueller there."

"This wasn't like most hotel robberies, although it was meant to look like it. They were pretty sure he had it with him, and they knew it was their last chance to steal it before they left the country. More importantly, they knew none of us would be around and he would be alone and helpless."

"Why didn't they kill him then?" Natalie asked. "Surely he would have seen them and come after them."

"They probably thought they had," Stuart said. "They probably thought it wouldn't take much to knock off that old codger after the injury they had already inflicted on him on the boat. Tell me, how did Bueller look when you found him?"

"Out cold and white as a ghost," John said. "For a few moments I thought...."

"He was dead," Stuart interrupted. "After they couldn't find what they were looking for, they left him for dead. What they didn't know is that the night before your wife had taken the statue into your room."

"Oh god! I put it in the bottom of our dirty laundry bag."

"You did what! I took the laundry down to the hotel lobby to have it washed."

"I had just taken it out right before you did that, while you were in the shower."

"Fate was at work here," Madeleine said. "Those women just were not going to get their hands on that thing. Where is it now?"

"It's in here," I said as I pulled the package out of my handbag.

"Can we see it?" Natalie asked. I carefully unwrapped it and passed it over to her, covering it with my hand. "It's beautiful," she said.

She discreetly passed the statue to her mother through Paul, who looked at it as if to say, what's all the fuss about, but whose curiosity compelled him nonetheless to turn it over in his hands a few times, looking at it from different angles until he acknowledged that a man with the head of a bird is pretty cool.

"I see what you mean," Madeleine said when she held it. "It is charming and charged with symbolism."

Dr. Short took it in his hands. His eyes brightened almost to the intensity of the gold. "It's truly marvelous."

"What do you intend on doing with it?" Stuart asked.

"I'm going to give it back to Dr. Bueller when we return to Aswan, that is if he has regained consciousness. As for the rest of it, well, that's up to him."

Stuart looked at me approvingly. "For now I think you'd better put it back in your bag," he said.

"Yes, we must not tempt fate," Barry said, and handed it back to me.

I wrapped up the beautiful little object and put it back in my bag just before Ahmed approached our table.

"Walter," I didn't see you this afternoon."

"Oh, I was out and about," Stuart said.

Ahmed wagged his finger at him as if to say naughty, naughty and asked him if he would be returning to Aswan with the rest of us tomorrow.

"Yes, if that's okay. Then I need to get back to Cairo."

"Tomorrow? Your friends want to stay in Aswan another night."

"I need to get back to Cairo as soon as possible if that's all right."

"Our plane will be leaving Abu Simbel tomorrow morning at eight. The flight to Cairo leaves at noon. If you like, I could try to get you a seat."

"Yes, if you can."

"The bus will be here early tomorrow morning to take us all to the airport, so please be ready. I don't want to run late again like we did when we left Aswan. And Walter, I will see what I can do for you."

"He apparently doesn't remember that his tardiness was not on our account," Dr. Short said rather indignantly after Ahmed had left.

"It was good of you not to remind him," Madeleine said.

"What are your plans?" Stuart asked.

"We thought we would spend another day in Aswan before returning to Cairo," Madeleine said.

"I want to unload this thing," I said.

"Yes, there's a little unfinished business there," Dr. Short said. "I want to see how old Bueller is doing before I leave, see if he needs anything."

"When will you fly back to the States?" Stuart asked.

"Not right away I hope," Dr. Short said. "I've asked them to stay in Cairo at least a few days."

"Will you be staying at the same hotel as before, the Cairo Kingsley?" Stuart asked.

"If we can get rooms there," John said.

"Oh, you won't have any trouble getting rooms this tourist season," Dr. Short said.

"Then that's where we will be. I liked that hotel."

"I'll be in Cairo for at least a few more weeks. I will give you a call and we'll have dinner," Stuart said looking at Natalie.

Chapter Twenty-Eight

Since I had the window seat on our flight to Abu Simbel, I offered it to John on the flight back. My largesse had an ulterior motive as the aisle seat provided a better view of the rows in front of me. Isabelle's mother was deeply engaged in conversation with Madeleine, who no doubt was as eager as any theatergoer to find out what happened in the last act of the Isabelle and Ahmed drama. I wondered why Natalie was sitting with Paul rather than with Stuart. I considered Stuart's mood last night. I bet he needs to be consoled, I thought, but would rather that consolation come from Barry Short.

The flight was brief and uneventful. We had only to wait a few minutes after we arrived in Aswan for Ahmed to confirm our arrangements going forward. Stuart would leave for Cairo in a few hours, and we would return the next day. Stuart asked Dr. Short to have the hotel send his bags to the airport, and we said our goodbyes. That was that. The seven of us had become six when we hopped into a buggy and returned to our hotel.

"Take me to the shower!" I said when we arrived at the Old Cataract.

As John unlocked the door to our room I looked at the door across the hall and thought of Bueller. And when I looked at our freshly washed and folded clothing stacked neatly in a box next to the laundry bag, it reminded me of the golden statue.

"You go ahead and take your shower first," I said. "I want to check on Bueller and return this burdensome thing."

Bueller's door opened immediately following my knock, but it was the physician, Doctor Shabaka who greeted me. "Welcome," he said, as he opened the door wide for me to enter. "We've been wondering where you were."

"Oh, I'm sorry. We made a sudden and unexpected return to Abu Simbel. I just got back. You will have to excuse my appearance, but I haven't showered or changed my clothes for a few days." I looked over at Bueller who was still lying in his bed. "I wanted to check in on you right away."

"Come in, my dear. Come closer so we can talk."

Bueller looked better than I had ever seen him. He even had roses in his cheeks. "You've done a wonderful job," I said to Doctor Shabaka.

"I am very happy with his progress."

"Doctor Shabaka showed me z'e hieroglyphics you drew and explained z'em to me, but I want to hear what happened from you, everyz'ing."

"Well, when we arrived in Abu Simbel it was still dark. The others went with Ahmed over to the shore of Lake Nasser to view the sunrise. A guide who saw me standing alone offered his services. I asked him to take me inside the temple so I could see the morning light shine in on the statues of Ramses, Amun-Ra and the others. He agreed, but he told me—I guess it would be more accurate to say he ordered me to focus my attention on Amun-Ra. His name is Ibrahim, and there was something very unusual about him. He carried a cane, but he used it mostly to punctuate his remarks." I demonstrated how he would shake it in the air with its curved handle pointing up.

"Osiris!" Dr. Shabaka said looking a bit stunned as I recounted the story in more detail.

"He used it to point to things," I said. "At any rate, I felt like he knew what he was talking about. So when he left me inside the temple in front of the statues, I focused my meditation like he said to do on Amun-Ra. The sun began to rise, and as it did the light entered the temple falling on one statue and then the next, and finally it lit up your statue of Thoth that I had on my lap. And then my hand started to move without my volition. I didn't hear anything. No voice spoke to me. My hand just drew the symbols. I didn't even know what they meant. And then I guess I passed out. John found me later and woke me up. So, that's what happened. I've never had such an experience in my life!"

"Amazing! Z'at is amazing! I had hoped but not for so much."

"But it was such a short message. I drew all of those hieroglyphics, and they say so little."

"No, no, z'ey said everything, everything! It was pride z'at became my people's failing and z'eir curse. And mine too. We z'ought we were z'e chosen. We became z'e damned. Thoth has put me on z'e path of

216

this new wisdom, and I embrace it."

I studied Bueller's face as he spoke. It looked changed. It wasn't just the return of his health that altered his appearance, although that by itself was remarkable. There was a change in his expression; perhaps it was his eyes. They had a look of greater depth. "What will you do now?' I asked.

"I don't know yet. I must z'ink. I have lost so much time. But z'is was not for nothing. I trust z'at my future path will become clear."

"I have a question for you. Did you see who broke into your room and struck you?"

"Why of course, it was z'ose two shopping women from z'e boat."

"Gabby and Beverly?"

"Yes, it was z'em. Z'ey wanted Thoth."

"Well, that's what Stuart thought. We chased them back down to Abu Simbel yesterday, but they got away. They took a ferry to Sudan."

Doctor Shabaka's face broke out into a smile. "Not a good place for two women traveling alone."

"Stuart, who is Stuart?" Bueller asked.

"Walter. Stuart was using the name Walter. He was following those two women because, believe or not, he said they're diamond smugglers."

"I believe it!" the old man said.

I reached into my handbag and pulled out the little package. "I want to give this back to you."

Bueller raised his hand to stop me as I tried to hand it over. "No, please. It has served its purpose. It must go back now."

I stood there completely confused holding the statue that I wanted desperately to be rid of. He could see this in my face.

"Is Barry Short still with you?"

"Yes, I will be seeing him at lunch."

"After you have had your lunch, could you ask him to come with you back to my room, just z'e two of you, and bring Thoth with you."

He shooed me out of the room with a radiance in his smile that I had never before seen in anyone let alone in what hitherto had been such a pasty old face. Doctor Shabaka walked me to the door. "I can't believe how good he looks," I said. "It's a miracle."

He smiled as he opened the door for me. "I am looking forward to your return."

I smiled at him and back at Bueller as I left his room and entered my own. "This room is so beautiful," I said to John as I gazed upon the sunlight streaming through the large window. It danced across the coffee table and chairs, skipped across the carpeted floor and up onto the bed's satin coverlet where John lay like a sunbather on the sun drenched bed reading a book.

"That didn't take long," he said.

"No, it didn't. You should see Bueller. He looks great!"

"Did you hand over the statue?"

"I tried to. He wouldn't take it. He asked me to come back after lunch with Barry. He said something about putting it back. I guess Barry will know what he's talking about. Doctor Shabaka was there."

"Still?"

"Yes, I was surprised too. I think he has taken a special interest in his patient, and I am glad. Bueller needs someone to look after him."

"I wonder what will happen to the old guy?"

"I don't know. He can't continue to be an artifact smuggler now that Stuart found him out. I didn't tell him that part. I don't think he would want to anyway. Oh, and by the way, if you had any doubts, Bueller confirmed Stuart's theory. It was Gabby and Beverly who broke into his room to steal the statue."

"I didn't doubt it."

"Neither did I. Now, where's that shower?"

"The water is good and hot," he said and returned to his book.

"What are you reading?" I asked before I disappeared into the bath.

"A book about the Sphinx. I want to brush up."

"I'm glad we will be spending a few more days in Cairo." I turned on the hot shower, grabbed my scented soap and all conversation ceased, at least for a little while.

The hotel offered a prix fixe luncheon daily, and today was no exception. The menu was roast chicken, green beans and fried potatoes. They called it Bistro fare. For dessert they offered mousse au chocolat.

"Next to crème brulee, my favorite French dessert is chocolate mousse," I told the others.

"I don't know whether I will be able to eat dinner tonight after all of

218

this," Madeleine said.

"Maybe tonight we could just have a nice salad," Dr. Short suggested.

"I thought we weren't supposed to eat salad in Egypt," Natalie said.

"I think we can risk it here," he said.

Remembering the illness I had while in Cairo, I wasn't willing to take that risk, even at this lovely hotel.

"Dr. Bueller looked great when I visited his room earlier," I said. "He confirmed Stuart's suspicions that it was Gabby and Beverly who attempted to rob him."

"It's too bad they got away," Natalie said.

"Doctor Shabaka said that Sudan isn't a safe place for two women traveling alone, so maybe it wasn't so smart of them to use it as an escape route," I said.

"I've heard stories like that," Dr. Short said. "But they had to do with the sex trade, and I doubt those two would be prime candidates for that."

"I shouldn't think so," Madeleine said.

"Bueller asked if you might come up to his room with me after lunch," I said to Dr. Short.

"I'd be happy to. It's nice to know that the old codger wants to see me."

"I think it's about Thoth," I said. "The statue."

"Oh, I see."

"Speaking of statues," John said. "I'm really looking forward to seeing the Sphinx when we go back to Cairo."

"I will be very happy to be your guide. I've been excavating nearby so I see it almost daily, and I still marvel at it."

"How old do you think it is?" John asked.

"It is at least as old as the pyramids. Some say older. Of course, some think the pyramids may be older than is widely believed. These things are hard to pinpoint with any certainty."

"Not to change the subject, I had a long conversation with Isabelle's mother on the plane," Madeleine said.

"I saw you talking to her," I said. "You were sitting across the aisle from her, weren't you?"

"Yes, I was. I talked to Isabelle too. They are very nice people."

"What's up with Isabelle and Ahmed?" I asked.

"They have a very good plan. It seems quite sensible." A long silent pause followed as we waited for Madeleine to explain herself.

"Well, what is it?" John finally asked.

"They've agreed that Ahmed will come and visit Isabelle and her family in America this summer. He will get a chance to see where she lives first hand, and they both will have had some time apart to test their feelings for each other."

"That sounds like a good plan," I said.

"Yes, it seems pretty sensible," Natalie agreed.

"Isabelle's mother is beside herself," Madeleine said. "She told me her daughter was all tears at the hotel in Abu Simbel because those two women threatened Ahmed's job, partly over her. She could barely stand having to stay away from him while they were at the hotel together, but she understood the predicament he was in. Her mother told me that Isabelle threatened to marry Ahmed and stay in Egypt."

"Did he ask her to marry him?" I said.

"She didn't say."

"This is sounding less sensible than I thought," Natalie said.

"Romeo, Romeo," Paul chimed in.

"Well, Ahmed is the sensible one of the two," Madeleine said. "He and Isabelle's mother worked out this plan to persuade Isabelle to calm down and get a grip on herself."

"Do you think he will really go to America?" I asked.

"He said he would. Isabelle's mother believes he will."

"Time will tell," Natalie said.

Dr. Short and I made our excuses and left the others there to speculate on a romance whose outcome we would never know. When we arrived at Bueller's room, Doctor Shabaka opened the door just as we knocked as if he had been standing right beside it in expectation.

"I'm glad you are here. If you don't mind, I will take the opportunity of your presence to have my afternoon meal."

Dr. Short was struck by Bueller's appearance. His eyes were riveted on him as Doctor Shabaka spoke. Pleased with what he saw, he answered, "That's quite all right. You might try the roast chicken."

220

"And chocolate mousse," I said.

"Please, if you will, Doctor Shabaka," continued Dr. Short, "have the hotel bill your lunch to my room."

"That is not necessary."

"No, I would be honored for all that you've done here."

"Very good, and thank you."

"Hans, you look great! I've never seen you look better."

"I feel wonderful too, Barry. I can't remember feeling so good. Doctor Shabaka says tomorrow I can go out. We will begin z'e transition gradually. I can begin eating downstairs and resting outside on z'e veranda."

"Tell me, I'm curious, what kind of treatment have you been given?"

"I feel like a newborn baby. I drink plenty of milk, juices and tea with honey. But I think it is z'e baths and massages z'at make z'e difference. And all of z'is napping. My mind feels clearer z'an it has in years. I feel like I've just woken up. What about you Barry? How long will you be here?"

"We are flying back to Cairo tomorrow."

"I'm sorry to hear z'at. Just as I will be ending my convalescence."

"Well, I'm happy to know you will be in good hands while you're down here. You will be coming back to Cairo soon, won't you?"

"I don't know, Barry. I'm still z'inking about z'at. Z'ere really isn't anything z'ere for me."

"Then perhaps you will return to Austria?"

"No, no I can't do z'at either. I'm not sure. I think I need a change, something new. But never mind about me. I wanted to speak to you about z'e statue, z'e one z'at was in z'e parcel your dear friend Madeleine brought down to Luxor for me."

I took the little package out of my handbag hoping now to transfer it quickly.

"Ja, ja, z'at one dear. Could you unwrap it please?"

I pulled the golden statue out of its wrappings and held it in my hand. Bueller reached for it, and I gladly handed it over.

"I suppose you've already seen z'is Barry."

"Yes, I have. It looks quite valuable. Can you tell me about it?"

"It's valuable beyond its gold. It's so valuable z'at it must be put back from where I borrowed it."

"Borrowed it! Was it in the Cairo Museum?"

"You've never seen it z'ere, have you?"

"No, but I've heard the legends about it."

"And z'at is precisely z'e point. It needs to remain a legend, and z'erefore it must be consigned to obscurity. It must go back to z'e place I found it."

"That's in contradiction to everything archaeology is about, Hans! We bring things to light. Our job is to illuminate the past not to bury it. We can donate it to the museum. They'll never know how you got it."

"But z'ey might figure out from where I got it. I've known you for many years Barry. I've read all of your work, and I believe you will understand. Z'is little statue is too valuable to be in any museum. And knowledge of where it came from would be a disaster. It would result in z'e plundering of Imhotep's tomb."

"You've found it?"

"No, but I could have. Z'is statue marked z'e vicinity of its location. But even I was not tempted to desecrate Imhotep's tomb. Z'at was never my intention. But others would. If z'e location where I found it gets out, it would be inevitable."

"Well, yes, it would be. But isn't the rest of the world as entitled to the knowledge that lies buried there as you? What right have you to hoard it?"

"I never wanted z'at knowledge, not really. I thought I did for my people. But z'ink Barry of what could have happened if z'ey had found it!"

"You're right about that, I grant you. But the Nazis are in the past now, Hans. The world is very different today."

"You only z'ink the world has changed. Some z'ings change and some men change, but other z'ings and most men never do. It would be a tragedy Barry, believe me."

"So you just wanted Thoth's magic?"

"Ja, z'at is what I wanted. Thanks to your dear friend here," Bueller said looking at me, "I've gotten it. I've learned all z'at Thoth had to teach me. It put me on z'e path. Z'e rest is up to me now. Can I trust you? Will you put it back and never tell anyone?"

"That's a heavy burden to ask me to bear. It's hard for a scientist to turn away from knowledge; you know that."

"And z'e fame," Bueller added. "Z'is find could ensure your place in z'e history of Egyptology. But I have to trust someone. I cannot return it. I might be much improved, but I'm not up to z'at. I don't know if I could let go of Thoth," he said as he looked lovingly upon the little golden statue, "if I allow myself to again take possession of him. If z'ere is any Egyptologist z'at I trust z'at can do what I am asking, it is you." He held Thoth out in his hand.

"I will return it," Dr. Short sighed. "And I will keep our secret."

"Dear, could you please leave z'e room? I must tell Barry where to take Thoth, and you are better off not knowing."

I agreed without hesitation for I was now free of the statue, free of the burden Dr. Short had now assumed.

Chapter Twenty-Nine

John, Natalie and Madeleine were entertaining Doctor Shabaka with spirited tales of our trip when I returned to the veranda. John had just finished recounting the story of how Natalie had been taken off into the desert outside of Cairo by a passionate camel driver. She was beet red.

"Oh yes," Doctor Shabaka said smiling broadly, "the collision of cultures can lead to very humorous situations. People have little idea how much custom influences our thinking. They have even less awareness of other people's customs. Indeed, in Egypt we don't always understand each other. Before I went to medical school in Cairo, I was tutored here in Upper Egypt in the medical arts by my father and he by his father. He sent me on to Cairo because he wanted me trained in the most modern medical techniques. As a student I found myself having to teach my northern counterparts the traditional medical arts that I had learned from my father. At first they had no tolerance for these ideas, until finally they had to acknowledge them after I was able to bring about a cure in a few critical cases after nothing else had worked."

"That's very interesting," I said. "I've read that some of the traditional remedies gathered from plants and herbs in the backwoods of America later became the basis for many of today's pharmaceuticals. But Dr. Bueller insists that it's your baths and massages and not pharmaceuticals that brought about his remarkable cure."

"Clean the body, clean the spirit," Doctor Shabaka said. "His obvious wound was one matter and could be easily treated. But I could detect a deeper infection, and the description you gave me of his life suggested I was right. His affliction could be described as psychological or spiritual, depending on the language you are most comfortable with. So the treatment I prescribed was intended to both cleanse and relax his mind to allow him to gain the lucidity necessary for healing insights."

"What treatment is that?" Madeleine asked.

"The first part involves taking in many pure substances to cleanse the body of impurities. I prescribed plenty of milk and freshly squeezed juices, particularly lemons. Honey is very good for healing. I gave him plenty of tea with honey."

"What about the baths and the massages?" she asked.

"Many of the poisons that accumulate in the body are released through the skin. I did not want him to lie in bed bathed in his own poisons as I attempted to flush them out with the drinks I prepared. So I would bathe him in herb baths not only to cleanse his skin but also to stimulate further releases of these poisons. The massages were designed to restore moisture to his skin, and I used specially prepared oils in that endeavor. The massages also had the effect of relaxing him, which is necessary to the restoration of mental clarity."

"You could package those treatments and make millions," I said. "I can't believe how good he looks. I wouldn't have thought it possible."

"In Dr. Bueller's case it is not my treatments alone that are bringing about what I will admit is a rapid and full recovery. I think too it is the message you brought him."

"The hieroglyphics?"

"I do believe they were truly meant for him. I know he thinks so."

"What do you mean?" I said, now every bit as fascinated with Doctor Shabaka's story of the healing arts as Madeleine.

"I told you the hieroglyphics' literal meaning when you asked me to translate them for you. But Dr. Bueller seems to have an insight into their deeper meaning that you or I are lacking. How shall I explain? It is as if they answered questions that were buried inside, perhaps so deep that on a conscious level he was unaware of them. And yet he intuited answers from the hieroglyphics that brought those heretofore unconscious questions to the light, which seems to have led him to an unexpected peace of mind and a mental clarity that I don't believe my treatments alone could have produced."

"What did the hieroglyphics say?" Madeleine asked.

"Embrace charity, let go of pride," I said.

"And the rest?" Doctor Shabaka said.

"You mean the feather and the ankh?"

"Yes, they are very important to understanding the full meaning."

"The message read embrace charity and let go of pride, and then it ended with a kind of signature, a very large feather and ankh, which I"—

I glanced over at Dr. Shabaka—"which we interpreted as having something to do with the heart being light as a feather."

"That's from the 'Egyptian Book of the Dead,' isn't it?" Madeleine said. "The picture that we looked at in the Cairo Museum of the set of scales with a heart in one side and a feather in the other?"

"Yes, that's the one," I said. "It looked like an impossible measure of virtue to me. Your heart could be no heavier than a feather if you are to be deemed worthy to gain admittance into the afterlife."

"Not impossible," Doctor Shabaka said.

"Well, nearly so," Madeleine countered.

Looking intently into Doctor Shabaka's dark eyes, I said, "So you think that's what Bueller has attained?"

"Attained? Maybe not, but he has found the path. That is what is contained in the message you brought to him."

"And everything he has ever done and thought can be changed so late in life?" Madeleine asked.

"He can change, and I think he can be forgiven," Shabaka said. "If the heart is how Osiris measures a man or woman, imagine how great a heart Osiris himself must have to place such value on it."

We all sat silently for a little while contemplating Bueller's story. I broke the silence. "Earlier I thought his recovery seemed like a miracle. Maybe I was right."

"Maybe what you call a miracle is simply the proper application of knowledge. Dr. Bueller's case has given me greater insight into curative knowledge in a case like his, which I will consider further and attempt to replicate. If it were only a miracle that healed Dr. Bueller, then such healing would be only for him. That would be a tragedy."

I thought for a minute about Doctor Shabaka's words, "Only a miracle." I had never before heard of a miracle described in this way. Miracles are the pinnacle of human experience, I had thought, but having listened to Doctor Shabaka's explanation, I could see his point. If it was not a miracle that produced the cure, but something that could be understood and applied repeatedly, that knowledge would far exceed any miracle that had the same outcome. Maybe we should more closely examine experiences we describe as miracles, I thought. Maybe there is knowledge we could derive from them if we only understood them better.

"Now that he is cured, what will become of him?" I asked. "He still is a very old man unless you've found a cure for that too."

"No one has found a cure for old age yet. In the course of talking to him these past few days, I've learned he has nowhere to go; at least nowhere he wants to return to. I have been making inquiries to see if I can find a suitable place for him."

"Suitable, what do you think that would be?" Madeleine asked. "A retirement village?"

"A retirement village. What is a retirement village?" Doctor Shabaka said.

"They are living accommodations for older people, often built on one floor so they won't have to go up and down stairs or sometimes in buildings with elevators. Some have resident nurses," Madeleine explained.

"I don't think such an arrangement would be suitable for Dr. Bueller. I think he needs someplace with a very good library and others to talk to who might share some of his interests, a community of some kind where the housework is shared since he has no one to do it for him. I am looking into a few places now to see if they can offer him accommodation."

"How much would such a place cost?" I asked.

"If he is accepted, it will cost him nothing beyond a certain admission fee. He will be given certain responsibilities, but no more than he could do. Dr. Short is staying in Cairo, isn't he?"

"Yes, at least for now," I said.

"I will ask him for his address so that I can notify him when I've secured Dr. Bueller a place. He can let you know where it is and put your minds at rest."

I thanked Doctor Shabaka, and with that he excused himself so that he might return to his patient.

"What a remarkable man," Madeleine said.

"Yes, and so young to be so remarkable," I agreed.

Dr. Short rejoined us about twenty minutes after Doctor Shabaka's departure.

"Shift over?" I quipped.

"It was the least I could do. A remarkable man."

"That's just what we were saying," Madeleine said.

"I won't feel bad leaving Hans down here knowing who I am leaving him with. Look, we've all fretted quite enough. Let's go out and have some fun. Paul, do you want to ride in another felucca?"

Paul, who had been busying himself tossing sugar cubes over the veranda ledge into the Nile to watch them float, was quick to respond, "Yeah!"

We walked past the guards standing at full alert at the hotel door and found a felucca to take us to Elephantine Island, just across the Nile from our hotel. Dr. Short wanted us to see the Nilometer the Romans had built to measure the level of the river. It looked like a giant crown perched upon a rock. I thought it was probably constructed to look like that, to declare this place as the territory of an empire that is no more. We visited the museum with its artifacts displayed in dusty glass boxes. Dr. Short told us that Elephantine is very ancient, that a city existed here long before Aswan was built and that civilizations had been unearthed here that go back way before the Roman Empire or the first Egyptian Dynasty. I wondered about that time long ago as I looked at the date palms whose arched branches fell gracefully towards the earth. I watched them move in the soft breeze to the melodic songs of the oarsmen and caught sight of the flutter of a green heron gliding across the sky. That ancient time must have looked like this, I thought.

Late in the day we returned to our hotel. The others ate salads to no ill effect while I had some fruit. John and I slid between the sheets of our lovely bed and fell asleep to the scents and breezes that flooded our room through the opened window. That was our last night in this magical place.

Chapter Thirty

Luggage was stacked in the lobby of the Cairo airport nearly blocking our path through the throngs of people who waited to board planes to take them home. We chatted briefly with a British couple who had arrived in Egypt only a few days before the attack near Luxor and had since been ordered to leave by their tour company who did not want to risk further liability. They told us that was probably the situation for most of the others gathered at the airport as tour companies feverishly tried to arrange to have their charges flown out of the country.

"It's too bloody bad!" said the disgruntled man. "That's just what these militants want."

"You don't have to leave if you don't want to," Dr. Short said.

"If we stay, it's on us to make all our own arrangements. That's why we hired a tour company!"

"Oh, I see."

"Just how bad was the attack?" John asked.

"Very bad, I'm afraid."

"Five, ten, twenty, how many tourists were killed?"

"I've heard sixty. Others say as many as seventy-five."

"Oh, my!" Madeleine said.

"They weren't all tourists," his wife interjected. "Egyptians were killed too. The ones who were working there."

"What were the nationalities of the other victims?" Dr. Short asked.

"Swiss, German, Japanese," the woman said.

"So it was random. They weren't targeting any particular nationality."

"They don't care who they kill as long as they cripple the economy," the man said. "That's what this is all about. Men, women, children, tourists, Egyptians, they don't care. Bloody animals!"

Natalie nervously fingered her cartouche.

"Did they catch them, the killers?" a visibly frightened Paul asked.

"The officials say all the attackers were shot, but who knows for sure," the man said.

"And who knows if other attacks aren't in the works," the woman said. "That's why the tour company is sending us home. Prudent, that's what it is."

"What do you think we should do?" John asked us.

"If it's that dangerous here, we ought to leave with everyone else," Madeleine said. "We have Paul to think about."

"But we have no reservations," Natalie said. "Do we really want to hang out here at the airport with no idea when we'll be able to fly?"

"We need to find Yusef and Samia," John said. "They've got to make our flight arrangements for us anyway."

We continued to snake our way through crowds and piles of luggage led by Dr. Short who was far better acquainted with the airport than any of us. The crowds began to thin as we neared the airport entrance.

"I've found them," Dr. Short said when he spied a sign with our name on it. He picked up speed and we followed briskly, luggage and all.

"I couldn't be happier to see you," Madeleine said, pushing ahead to greet Yusef and Samia.

"I'm happy to see all of you too and happy you arrived back safe," Samia said as she glanced at Natalie who stood behind her mother.

Natalie came forward and the two women hugged. Samia stood back and glanced at Natalie's cartouche gleaming in the dull light. She never would have imagined that the real danger the amulet protected Natalie from was her own tender feelings that if left unchecked would have rendered her mute at a time when she needed to speak her heart.

"Well, what do you guys think about all of these people trying to leave?" Natalie asked.

"I think these tour companies are making a mistake," Yusef said. "The government is on full alert. There will be no more attacks for now."

"Even if the threat were greater, these companies could have been far more orderly in their approach," Samia said. "They've brought all of these people here to the airport before they've arranged their transportation."

"When can you get us a flight home?" Madeleine asked. "We have Paul here, and I'm sure his parents are worried sick."

"The soonest we can get you on a flight is the day after tomorrow," Samia said. "You will be very safe at the hotel. Paul can call his parents when you get there. The van is right outside."

Dr. Short turned to Madeleine. "I had hoped you could stay in Cairo longer. There are so many things I want to show you."

"We can't stay here any longer than we have to under these circumstances," Madeleine said. "It's just too risky. If anything should happen! Why don't you get a room at our hotel and we can spend the remaining time together?"

No military presence was evident on the streets of Cairo except for the two guards at our hotel door. Samia and Yusef asked if we had a good time in Upper Egypt. We agreed that we had without mentioning any details of our adventures that we preferred to keep private. They asked us to stay inside the hotel until the day after tomorrow when they would pick us up in the morning at eight and take us to the airport for our flight home.

We said our goodbyes. I looked about the large, modern atrium hotel lobby and immediately missed the veranda at the Old Cataract. I missed the sunlight on my shoulders, the fragrant breezes of the gardens and the hot chocolate. Most of all I missed the soft melodies of the oarsmen who paddled their feluccas along the Nile in Aswan

Natalie told the hotel desk clerk she was expecting a phone call, and if she wasn't in her room when it came, she might be at the juice bar. I objected when Paul wanted to rent a pair of satellite phones, saying they wouldn't be necessary now that we were confined to our hotel. "What's the harm?" Dr. Short said, and rented two phones for himself and gave one to Paul.

"I am amazingly not tired," I said to John as I unpacked my ibis and placed him on the dresser. "You would think after everything I'd collapse."

"I can't even read," John said and closed his book.

Paul was soon at our door. "Aunt Natalie asked me to tell you that we are down in the juice bar if you would like to join us."

"We'll be down in a few minutes," John said.

"Boy, they must be antsier than we are if they're already down there," I said.

231

Twenty minutes later Paul playing elevator operator greeted us. "What floor would you like Madame et Monsieur," he said with a slight bow.

"The juice bar, please," John said in a tone of mock formality.

"Tout de suite," Paul said and pushed the mezzanine button. He hopped off the elevator and led us to Natalie and Madeleine who sat alone at a large table.

"Where's Dr. Short?" John asked.

"He stepped out for a while," Madeleine said. "He wanted to take a look around and see just how dangerous things really are."

"Do you think he'll be all right?" I said.

"He lives here half the year. I'm sure he knows what he's doing."

We ordered our Oranginas and sat around waiting for him and his report.

"It's not Aswan," I said.

"No, it's not," Natalie agreed.

"If it's this hard to adjust to Cairo after having been in Aswan," I said, "what's it going to be like being at home?"

No one answered my question. I suspected they were wondering the same thing except Paul who found ways to entertain himself no matter where he was. He scampered off for several minutes, and then returned to the table. "Can we go to the Japanese restaurant tonight?" he asked. "They've got teriyaki and tempura and sushi!"

"That sounds good," his grandmother said.

"I miss my hot chocolate on the veranda," I lamented.

At first glance Dr. Short looked subdued, troubled in fact when he returned from his outing, but his countenance quickly reverted to its natural vigor as he began to speak. Before he could get his first words out, Paul announced, "We're going to the Japanese restaurant!"

"Fine boy, fine. But tomorrow night we're going to the Blue Nile. On your last day in Egypt you should eat Egyptian. No more of this foreign food."

"We all loved the Blue Nile," Madeleine said. "But is it safe out there?"

"The streets are safe enough."

"Yusef and Samia told us to stay in the hotel," Natalie said.

232

"Stay here if you like, but if you do, you'll be wasting your last day in Cairo. I propose that tomorrow we visit the Sphinx, which I know John wants to see very badly. I've made a reservation for us all tomorrow night at the Blue Nile. But it's entirely up to each of you whether you go or not."

"The Sphinx! That's that big lion," Paul said. "Everybody told me to see the Sphinx."

"I'm with you Paul," John said, relieved at the prospect of being released from the hotel lockup.

"I want to go too," I said. "And I would love to go back to the Blue Nile."

"I'm not sure about the Sphinx, but I'd like to go to the Blue Nile," Natalie said. "Is it all right if I decide tomorrow?"

"I feel the same way," Madeleine said. "I would love to go back to the Blue Nile, but I'm not so sure I need to see the Sphinx."

"Well, if you aren't going, neither am I," Natalie said.

"That's fine if you ladies would like to spend the day here at the hotel," Dr. Short said. "As long as you're not too afraid to go out to dinner."

"I'm not afraid!" Madeleine said. "If you say it's safe, I'm sure that it is. I just don't know if I want to spend another day out on the Giza Plateau after what happened there. It was the worst day of my trip."

Not mine, I thought. The hotel no longer felt imprisoning, and I quit thinking so much about Aswan.

Chapter Thirty-One

My mind was still swimming in ankhs, feathers and scales as I awakened out of a dream. I opened my eyes and saw my ibis looking at me from his perch on the dresser. "If only you could speak," I said.

"What did you say?" John asked from the bathroom.

"I was talking to my bird." I hesitated. "I was talking to myself."

"You were talking to yourself?" John said as he came out of the bathroom wrapped in a towel and drying his hair.

"I was just wondering out loud what this ibis could tell me if it could speak. It's supposed to be a wise bird, you know."

John laughed. "It would probably tell you to hurry up and get ready so you will have time for breakfast before we leave. It could be a long day."

Paul arrived at our room ready to go as I was stepping into the shower. John opened the door of the bath just enough to let me know that they were headed down for breakfast and I should meet them as soon as I could. I took a quick shower and dressed, and when I arrived downstairs John had prepared a nice plate of fruit for me with a tasty looking sweet roll.

"Eat up," he said. "Dr. Short is raring to go."

I obliged, and within minutes I exited the hotel, sweet roll in hand, and hopped into Dr. Short's jeep. It was great fun, especially now that I sat comfortably in the front seat. We tooled through the streets of Cairo, taking advantage of every opportunity to dodge crowds, donkey carts and cars double-parked in this crowded city of twelve million.

"Who taught you to drive?" I asked.

"I taught myself," Dr. Short said. "I thought I wanted to be a stock car racer back then. I used to drag race. Can you believe that?"

"I believe it," I said. "I was always a cautious driver myself. I lacked confidence, I guess. Now, my brother wanted to be a stock car driver too. He wrecked two of my mother's cars when he was a teenager."

"Do you want me to slow down? I didn't mean to frighten you."

"No, that's okay. Actually, I had a lot of confidence in my brother's driving. We used to cruise up to Toronto after my older sister moved up there. Never had an accident on those trips. I missed the legendary trip home, though, when he drove the four hundred and twenty-five miles in five and half hours. My mother was with him that time. She had fallen asleep and didn't know what was going on until she arrived home several hours early."

"I'm not really going that fast. It just seems that way relative to all of this donkey traffic." He slowed down; we nonetheless arrived in Giza in short order. "Do you mind if I drop you off at the Sphinx? I've got a little business to attend to. I'll be back soon."

"No, that's fine," John said.

"He's been reading up on the Sphinx since before we left Aswan," I told Dr. Short.

"I'll be your tour guide today," John told Paul.

"Paul, do you have your satellite phone with you?" Dr. Short asked.

"Sure I do," he said pulling it out of his pocket.

"I've got mine too. So if we need to reach each other, we can. See, it was a good idea to rent these things."

We watched him drive across the desert in the direction of the Great Pyramid and his excavation sites until he disappeared in the cloud of sand his jeep tires kicked up. We hadn't thought to ask him what he was up to or noticed that anything was wrong, although in hindsight we realized we should have known something was not right when he begged off the tour he had promised. But at the time we were too caught up in the moment to think about it.

The three of us stood squarely in front of the massive stone structure. "That's not a lion, that's a man!" Paul said.

"Most Egyptologists believe it is the likeness of Chephren, an Old Kingdom pharaoh, but others have their doubts," John said.

"I thought the Sphinx was a giant lion," Paul objected.

"Look at those paws. Let's walk around and take a look at it from the side," John said and led us around nearly the length of a city block. "See! Doesn't that look like a lion sitting?"

"Yeah, but what about his head?" Paul said.

"Think about the statue of Thoth," I said. "Egyptians joined an animal's head to the human body quite a lot in their art. So it's not surprising they would do the reverse as well."

"It's also possible the original head was a lion's," John said.

"It looks human to me," I said.

"Well, now it does. But some have argued that the head we see before us was carved much later from an earlier head as part of a restoration project. Look at the long muzzle on that guy's profile. Doesn't it look like the muzzle of an animal? And look at the headdress. Couldn't it have been carved from a lion's mane?"

"That's possible," I said, "but why would anyone think that?"

"If you look closely, the head is disproportionally small when compared to the body. A re-carving would explain that," John said.

"It looks shrunken," Paul said and started to laugh. "A shrunken head! Ha, ha!"

Ignoring Paul's joke John went on. "The argument has more to do with disputes about the age of the Sphinx than anything else. Some think it may be twelve thousand or more years old. That's considerably older than if it were contemporary with King Chephren."

"How much older?" I asked.

"Thousands of years older. Chephren was king during the Fourth Dynasty, around 2500 B.C., that's less than half the age of these other estimates. They argue Chephren didn't build the Sphinx at all but repaired it and carving the head anew was part of that repair. Others say the head isn't Chephren's likeness at all."

"It looks a little like a magazine picture I once saw of a face carved out of rock on the surface of Mars."

"I does look like that picture," John agreed. "But that face was only an optical illusion."

"That's what the experts say, but I don't know if I believe them," I said.

"Let's climb down inside," John said.

Although at a distance the Sphinx looks as if it is sitting on the flat desert, it actually sits inside a very large trench. In front of it are the remains of two temples that were constructed from blocks of the same limestone that was cut away to form it. In spite of the threat that had filled the airport with retreating tourists, when we got down there we saw a few remaining groups with their guides touring the Sphinx.

"I want to take a closer look at this limestone," John said. He whispered, "I think I recognize that tour leader from his photo on the back cover of one of the books I've read. If it's him, he's very famous in certain circles. I'm just going to listen for a little while."

The guide methodically compared the erosion on the Sphinx with the erosion on nearby monuments, pointing out that a noted geologist recognized that water had caused the erosion on the Sphinx while wind and sand had caused the erosion on every other monument in the Giza complex.

"This is kind of boring Uncle John," a fidgety Paul said.

"Quiet, listen!" John whispered. "I want to hear this."

"Not only was this erosion caused by water," the guide said, "but specifically by rainwater, not floodwater. This is important to note. Look around you. When was there ever enough rain in this desert to produce this kind of erosion?" After a pause he continued, "We consulted an expert in historical weather patterns for an answer to that question and what we learned is amazing. Twelve thousand years ago what is now the Sahara Desert was full of lakes. Imagine this desert where you now stand green and growing with frequent and heavy rainfalls. That was the weather required to have made the kind of erosion you see today on the Sphinx. According to the historical records, that could have only taken place more than five thousand years before King Chephren lived."

A man dressed in khakis interrupted the lecture. "You speak of the historical records. The archeological record does not support your assertion. According to that record the rise of Pharaonic civilization in its earliest Predynastic stage occurred no sooner than 5500 BC. There simply is no record of any civilization here twelve thousand years ago. There is no evidence whatsoever!"

"What you see here is the evidence!" the tour leader shouted back at the man. "You're looking at it right here. Are you simply going to ignore it because it doesn't fit your preconceived ideas?"

"Where's the cultural context?" the other man said. "Are you asking me to believe that early man crawled out of his cave and built the

Sphinx? Don't be ridiculous. History doesn't work that way. Our Stone Age counterparts didn't build this thing. That's simply impossible. They didn't have the tools."

"History tells us only what we can see in it," the tour leader said. "The scientific dating of the Sphinx, based on geological and climatological science, indicates there was at least one high culture that preexisted history as we know it who must have had the tools."

"Poppycock!" the other man said.

"All you can say is poppycock!" the tour leader shouted in frustration. "Now that's scientific of you! Can't you see the opportunity here for the advancement of our understanding of history? Maybe our models are wrong. Have you thought about that? Here we have evidence that a high culture existed thousands of years before what we believed to be the beginnings of high culture. Doesn't that excite you? Don't you want to learn more?"

John spoke up, "I have a question for the two of you. I have read that the Sphinx and the three pyramids can be seen as an astronomical diagram that parallels the position of the constellation Orion as it was seen in the skies in 10,500 B.C. and that at the spring equinox of that same year, the sun rose in Leo to the east."

"Very good! I see you've read Bauval and Hancock," the tour leader said.

"Oh, my god, another pyramidiot," the man in khaki proclaimed, referring to John who flushed rose.

The tour leader, markedly furious, looked over at the man and said, "Now you resort to name calling, do you!"

"What! Do you expect me to believe in astrology?" the man said.

The tour leader looked at John. "I don't believe you were able to ask your question. Would you continue?"

"Yes, thank you. The Sphinx is looking east, just where Leo rose that year at the very time that Orion crossed the meridian at dawn. And the three stars that make up the constellation of Orion were at the same time in alignment with the three Great Pyramids. That conjunction marked the beginning of the Age of Leo, which the Sphinx in all likelihood represents. I can't believe this is all an accident considering how important Orion is in Egyptian mythology and considering the ancient Egyptian's knowledge of the stars."

"Yes, I quite agree with you. It marks the Zep Tepi," the tour leader said. "It's quite unimaginable that the placement of these great monuments was an accident. And if the Sphinx were built in the year 10,500 B.C., there would have been several thousand years of rain that could have caused the water erosion we now see."

"Next, you will be asking me to believe in Martian visitation," the man in khaki said.

"Nothing of the kind," the tour leader said, addressing both the man and the rest of us. "But I would ask you to take more seriously how the ancient Egyptians understood their past. They speak of Zep Tepi as their beginnings. 'Zep' means 'time,' and 'Tepi' means 'first.' They believed that Zep Tepi marked the time when civilization arrived here in the Nile Valley, long before the pharaohs. And they believed the god Osiris who they identified with the constellation Orion established this civilization. What we call the Paleolithic Age, they called the Golden Age. In their worldview man did not crawl out of caves but instead arose out of a Golden Age that was degraded when Seth slew his brother Osiris. It is no coincidence that the placement and configuration of the three Great Pyramids and the Sphinx mark the date of the Zep Tepi. The question we are left with is how they were able to calculate this date. It has only been since the advent of computer technology that we've been able to reconstruct the ancient skies with such precision." The tour leader turned away from the rest of us and looked directly into the face of the man in khakis. "Isn't that why we are here? Why we tirelessly study ancient Egypt, to learn? If we already knew everything, why go on?"

The khaki clad man turned his back on the tour guide and climbed out of the trench that encircled this great wonder. Paul and I held back as John walked over and talked personally to the guide, the guide that I could tell he now wished had been our guide throughout the trip. I saw John pull a piece of paper from his pocket, and I saw the man write something on it. I later learned that he was in fact the author John had recognized.

"He's not here now," Paul said into his satellite phone. "He's talking to some man. You should have seen the big fight here. It was great! Yes, she's with me." Paul handed me the phone. "He wants to talk to you."

"I've been gone longer than I anticipated," Dr. Short said. "So I thought you might be wondering what happened to me."

"We hardly noticed with all the commotion going on here. John's talking to one of the people involved right now. Apparently, he's very famous."

"I'm on my way back over there," Dr. Short said. "I ran into a problem. I may need to ask for your help if you don't mind."

"With what?" I asked, unable to imagine anything that we might be able to help Dr. Short accomplish in Egypt.

"With Thoth," he said. "You must help me return Thoth."

"Oh," was all that I said while trying to conceal what I was really thinking, which was, Oh No! It had been such a relief to unload that burden. I hated to have to pick it up again. But how could we ever withhold help from Dr. Short who had been such a great help to us.

"I'll be there in a few minutes," he said. "Don't go anywhere."

Chapter Thirty-Two

Paul and I found a flat rock to sit on while we waited for Dr. Short who soon appeared dressed in khakis that looked exactly like those worn by the fellow who had just insulted John. It's a good thing the uniform is a marker of occupation and not personality, I thought. I wondered why khakis are the signature dress of archaeologists.

"I didn't see you coming. Where did you come from?" I said.

"I spotted you two down here in the trench from above," he said. "Consider yourself lucky. This place is usually packed. Where's John?"

"He's over there talking to that tour leader."

"Is that the fellow he had the argument with?"

Paul laughed. "Uncle John didn't have the argument. That man there had a big fight with some other man who left."

"Marched off in a huff, might be a better way to describe it," I said.

"I bet they were arguing about the age of the Sphinx."

"How'd you know?" Paul said, looking at Dr. Short as if he were a seer.

"That's what they all argue about," Dr. Short said, demystifying his foreknowledge for the boy. "That man John is talking to now is one of the most interesting and controversial people in the field."

"John recognized him from the back cover of one of his books."

"He's written many."

"What do you think about this water erosion argument?"

"It's a compelling argument. I think Robert Schoch first made it, and there's yet to be a solid rebuttal. Unless someone can explain the water erosion in another way, well, we're left with the hypothesis that the Sphinx may be more than twelve thousand years old. At least that's what we're left with for now. Like it or not, everything changes in this field. So many mysteries are left unexplained that we are forced from time to time to take another look at what we thought we knew, even Schoch's theory."

"The man who started the argument seemed to think he already has the answers," I said. "He was dressed like you."

"They all think they do, all these archaeologists. It's an occupational hazard. They imagine what they know is the pinnacle of all that can be known. It's hard to give up your theories once established as dogma. Oh, they allow new insights from time to time, as long as they don't disrupt the paradigm that's been embedded in their brains."

"I've seen that too. In legend studies we deal more with belief than knowledge, but I've known many people, smart people, who don't know the difference. They think what they believe is the absolute truth while other people's beliefs are fictions, and that's the truth!"

Dr. Short laughed. "We're a sorry lot, aren't we? It's that way in every field, not just Egyptology. Change comes slowly, but it always comes in spite of the forces that work against it."

"In folklore we use the term 'worldview,' which is very similar to a paradigm since both contain a fixed view of reality. The one is just more culturally learned than academically institutionalized. It's hard, impossible in some cases, to change one's worldview. It's central to our being. It's where our sense of reality comes from."

"Precisely, and even knowing this I bet you have an implicit belief in your own worldview. I know I do," Dr. Short said.

"I guess you're right about that," I admitted.

"You have to," he said. "How else could you navigate through life? Apply this to academics. What would we teach if we didn't feel confident in our knowledge? It would be hard to teach maybe this and maybe that. How could I teach my students that the mission of the archaeologist is to illuminate the past using only those insights that suit him?"

"Or her," I countered.

"Or her. See! I'm still adjusting to change." He sat down and buried his head in his hands.

"You're upset about something, aren't you? It's about what Bueller asked you to do, isn't it?"

"It goes against the grain. I admit, I'm a gravedigger, but I'm not a grave robber. Unfortunately, there are many of them out here, and they make my work tough. They dig for loot; I dig for the knowledge contained in that loot. That's what I do. I dig for knowledge, and he has asked me to bury it, to hide it."

"Bueller really seems to think that statue could be dangerous."

"In the wrong hands, yes, he's right. Unfortunately, that's where this

242

statue would probably end up."

"What happened?" I asked, sensing that there was something more behind Dr. Short's mood.

"Yesterday afternoon when I stopped by my apartment to pick up my jeep, I discovered my rooms had been ransacked. I drove out to my dig site in the hope that the break-in had been a random act of thievery, but it wasn't. My shack had been ransacked too. They're after me, those dogs. If I don't get this thing put back soon, they'll take it and probably take me out too."

"Are you going to put it back now?"

"Yes, now, but I'm going to need your help. Let's talk about it later. Right now I think I have a young boy here who needs some attention."

Paul, who had been entertaining himself climbing around on the nearby temple ruins, approached Dr. Short. "I want to know about the mysteries."

"Okay, follow me," Dr. Short said and led us to the Sphinx's front paws.

"See those stones there, the ones you were just climbing. They were cut away from the massive limestone rock that the Sphinx was carved from. Some estimate that each of those stones weighs two hundred tons."

"Wow!"

"Now, how did the ancient Egyptians move those stones let alone erect a temple out of them?"

"I know! They used slaves."

"Slaves and pulleys and ramps," Dr. Short said. "I bet you've seen pictures of that."

Paul gave an enthusiastic nod.

"Well, those pictures are wrong. Consider how heavy two hundred tons is. How much weight can you lift?"

"I can lift my dog Sandy," Paul bragged. "She weighs fifty pounds."

"Is she heavy?"

"Sure."

"Well, consider that one ton is two thousand pounds. That is forty times heavier than Sandy. And there are two hundred tons in each of these stones. Two hundred tons is four hundred thousand pounds or

243

eight thousand Sandys. You couldn't get enough men around each of those stones to lift it. Today we would need one of our biggest cranes powered by a very large engine to lift one of those stones. So, how those stones were cut, moved and put into place to create the Sphinx Temple is something we still don't know."

"Wow!"

"I have seen those pictures you describe too," I said, "showing many slaves moving massive stones with the assistance of pulleys and wooden ramps. I always thought that was how it was done."

"You thought it because this was the explanation you were provided. And you weren't given any reason to question that explanation."

"But why? Why if it isn't true, are we told…"?

"That it is? I've thought about that for years and concluded we don't like mysteries much. Let me rephrase that. We like mysteries much better when they're solved."

"Like an Agatha Christie novel."

"Good example, like an Agatha Christie novel with a nice tidy ending. But consider that her mystery novels lead us neatly to a resolution because they're fictions, her own creations that she can do with as she wants. But the past is not a fiction, and we can't just fashion a satisfying ending or explanation because it pleases us to do so, or at least we shouldn't be in the business of doing that. But in some cases we are. Sometimes we write history like a novel. And when the history we are trying to describe is as remote as this history, who from the past is going to stand up and correct us? No one. We must correct ourselves. I am encouraged that eventually we do. In spite of our resistance to changing our minds, fabricated explanations stand in place only until real facts are found out. Once they emerge, it's only a matter of time. I'm encouraged that real facts will be uncovered because so many very bright people are seeking them."

"Am I interrupting something?" John said.

"Oh, here you are," I said. "I was beginning to think you'd joined that other tour and we wouldn't see you until who knows when. By the way, I saw you get that guy's autograph."

"Better than an autograph, I got his email address. When I mentioned I wrote a computer program to do archaeoastronomy, he

244

invited me to join his online research group."

"That's great!" I said.

"It could be quite exciting," Dr. Short agreed. "Those people do cutting edge work."

"I know!" John said, obviously very pleased.

"I'm glad you've come back because I'm going to need your help, but first let's have a little lunch. I saw a vendor over by the pyramids who was setting up his grill. He should be making lamb kabobs by now. We can take them over to my shed and eat outside. I've still got some chairs over there. We will be quite comfortable. Shall we?"

"What a big mess!" Paul shouted when he followed Dr. Short inside his shed to retrieve chairs.

John followed Paul inside to correct his manners but was unprepared for what he saw. "What's happened here?"

"I've been ransacked. I haven't had time to clean up."

"It's a good thing you weren't here when it happened."

"Yes," Dr. Short said as he surveyed the place.

"Was it vandals?" John asked.

"I've been working in this area for three years now, and I've never been vandalized. I think perhaps something else is going on. But first let's have our lunch outside where it's pleasant."

The kabobs were small but looked very good. They weren't just meat on a stick but lamb combined with chunks of peppers and onions. Dr. Short, Paul and John brought out camp chairs, paper plates, napkins and individual bottles of water.

"I'm amazed you were able to find this stuff in all that mess," I said.

"The thieves weren't interested in my kitchenware."

"You're really equipped here."

"You have to be. You can't easily run to the grocery. It's a good thing those food vendors are always cooking up something."

"What did they take?" John asked.

"I don't know yet. I haven't had time to look things over closely."

After Paul finished his kabob and wandered off to take a look at the various excavation sites, Dr. Short broached the topic he had only hinted at before. "Can you two keep a secret, a very important secret?"

"That depends," John said. "What kind of secret?"

"The secret that I will ask you to keep is the location where Thoth was hidden. No one will ask you to reveal it because no one will know or even suspect you have such knowledge. It will be between us."

"If no one asks me, I suppose it wouldn't be hard not to say too much," John said. Then his eyes grew distant as he became lost in thought.

"But you could be tempted someday to make public what you know because doing so could bring you celebrity or wealth. I need your solemn promise that you will never tell."

"That kind of celebrity I could do without," I said.

"How about you John?"

"There're too many secrets in Egypt already, too many unknowns. And too many people who ignore the facts even when they're looking right at them," he said thinking of the man who had just ridiculed him for asking a perfectly reasonable question. "Why is it so important to keep this secret?"

"Because the whereabouts of this statue, if it were known, would not only lead to the discovery and plundering of Imhotep's burial place but the whole area of the Giza Plateau including the areas around the Great Sphinx and Pyramids. Look what happened to my shed! They'll dig the whole place up if they think it's anywhere near."

"Would that be such a bad thing? Maybe we could learn something. Maybe it would open a few eyes," John said. "Besides, the Egyptian government could enforce controls. Right now you can't even get inside the Great Pyramid without their permission."

"They would try, but it has never really worked out well. Once they begin to tear things up, Egyptologists would only be one step ahead of the grave robbers. The artifacts they do manage to save would end up sitting in the Cairo Museum like the gold from Tutankhamen's tomb, removed from their rightful place. And so another authentic construction from the ancient past would have been destroyed."

"I hadn't thought about it that way," John conceded. " In order to protect whatever treasure they find, the tomb would be disassembled and the contents taken away."

"Never to be put back as it was," Dr. Short said. "The artifacts' whole context would be lost except what is preserved in photographs.

But it could be even worse, much worse I'm afraid."

"What do you mean?" John asked.

Dr. Short took a deep breath and sighed before he spoke. "I know this will sound fantastic to you. It did to me too when Hans Bueller first told me, but I have every reason to believe that he knows what he's talking about, at least this time. After all, his source was the same that allowed him to locate the statue of Thoth in the first place."

"I have been wondering about that," I said. "How did he know where to look for the statue if its location was such a guarded secret?"

"I asked him that very question. He answered only that it was better that I didn't know. I don't even know if he learned it from a person or from some sort of document he acquired, although I tend to believe it was a document, a very ancient one, the kind he deals with in his business."

"Smuggling?" John asked.

"Well, let's just say he's been in the business of acquiring valuable ancient papyrus scrolls and other treasures and making them available to collectors with money to spend. I reason that Hans must have learned about it from one of these ancient documents, one that had been neglected or not understood by whoever had possessed it. That must be the case. Had another living person known the whereabouts of Thoth, he wouldn't have told old Bueller. No, that person would have taken the statue for himself and earned a hefty sum for his trouble." Dr. Short drifted off in thought for a few moments; perhaps he was struggling against his own temptation.

"Go on, get to the fantastic," John said, letting out the deep breath he had sucked in when Dr. Short broached the topic.

"Hans told me that at the time he learned the location of Thoth, he also learned about a legend associated with the statue and Imhotep's tomb that he has every reason to believe is true. Of course, I've heard such things before but never from an authoritative source. According to Bueller, legend has it that the artifacts buried with Imhotep have magical properties; magic that I don't believe either one of us would want people to have access to. That's why they were closed up with Imhotep."

"I don't doubt those artifacts could be magical," I said. "Not after what I experienced with Thoth on my lap in the temple at Abu Simbel."

"Even if they're not magical," Dr. Short said, "but only thought to be by those ignorant of science, well, given what some think the ancients knew, that knowledge could be extraordinarily dangerous in the wrong hands."

"Why would it be dangerous?" I asked.

"Well, of course I don't know for certain," Dr. Short admitted. "But suppose the tomb contains the records of what Imhotep knew, knowledge that he chose to carry with him to his grave because he didn't trust anyone with it."

"Then we might finally get some answers," John said.

"Yes, but answers not likely to help us better understand this ancient civilization. My instincts tell me what we would uncover would be better left alone. Bueller warned me that we could unleash a power that we might not be able to control, power that in the wrong hands could explode the very planet we live on. My gut tells me he's correct."

"Like being able to manipulate the earth's seismic energy? Being able to manipulate the power of an earthquake or volcano?" John said, as he recalled the more fantastic claims about what the ancient Egyptians knew.

"Something like that. Some believe that the ancient priests had learned to manipulate some kind of gargantuan force that when harnessed allowed them to cut out mammoth stones with perfect precision and move them into place. The great hordes of workers we've all heard so much about were finishers and not, as imagined, a brute labor force capable of assembling stones weighing thousands of pounds. But the knowledge of a force that allowed priestly architects to erect the pyramids had enormous potential to destroy as well as create, which is why they guarded it so closely." Dr. Short paused for a moment, stared off into the distance and shook his downturned head. "Maybe these theories are only legends too. But if they are true, then it probably is also true that Imhotep would have been wise enough to take those records with him to his grave, but not so wise perhaps to have destroyed them altogether. That's a hard thing for a learned man to do." Looking at John intently he continued, "Let me ask you seriously. Would you trust humans with that kind of power?"

"No! Not that kind. I wish I could bury what we already know

248

about nuclear weapons. But maybe Bueller is wrong. What he says could be a legend, that's all," he groaned, torn between opposite longings, the desire to know and the responsibility to protect.

"John," I interrupted, "just because something is a legend doesn't necessarily make it untrue, only unproven. Would you want to be responsible for proving this one?"

"What we might discover in that tomb could be astounding," John said. "The possibilities...."

"I know! I know!" Dr. Short said sadly. "What I'm asking you to do is entirely against my nature too."

Resolute, John turned to Dr. Short. "If the claims are true, what's buried there could be more dangerous than anything we've ever seen, like nuclear weapons set on hair trigger alert. Pow! Just a misunderstanding over a wrong signal and they're off and we would all be done."

"Well then, you understand why this is a secret you can never reveal."

"Yes, I'll keep your secret. You can depend on it."

"Why did you tell us then?" I asked. "Why burden us with such a thing?"

"Because I need your help. I also need Paul's help, but he doesn't have to know what this is about. He's too young. Remember when we were searching for Paul in the Great Pyramid and stumbled on the iron door that was open?"

"The one that went down to the Subterranean Chamber?" John said.

"Yes, that's the one. I was very surprised to find it open. It's always locked to prevent people from climbing down below, which is strictly off limits. When I questioned Paul about the path he took to enter the Great Pyramid, he told me he entered the Subterranean Chamber from one of the tunnels I had unearthed. Fortunately for Paul, the iron door at the top of the stairway was open, which allowed him to climb up and make his way to the King's Chamber where we found him. I remembered something else he said, something rather peculiar that I didn't think much about at the time. He said that once he entered the chamber from below, the hidden door between the chamber and the tunnel mysteriously shut behind him making it impossible for him to return the way he came in. If the iron door above had not been unlocked, we may never have found him because he couldn't have contacted you by satellite phone if he was unable to reach an open air shaft."

Stunned at the thought of Paul trapped in an underground chamber, I said, "Who shut the door?"

"Hans Bueller. I suspect he had stolen the statue of Thoth right before Paul entered the chamber. He concealed himself in an alcove when he heard someone enter through the hidden subterranean door. The sound from the door gave away its existence and location. When the opportunity arose, Bueller quickly exited the pyramid by the same route Paul had entered to avoid the risk of being caught out in the open while climbing the stairs. That's why the upper door was still open. Bueller had managed to get a copy of the key and had entered the Subterranean Chamber from above but was unable to re-lock it as he had planned."

"So why do you need our help to return it?" John asked.

"I used my professional credentials to enter the pyramid as I often do, but to enter the iron door leading to the Subterranean Chamber requires special permission, which I cannot get without answering a lot of questions I would prefer to avoid, particularly since my goal is to draw absolutely no attention to that chamber. In fact, I'm seriously thinking of abandoning my excavation sites altogether now that I know at least one of them provides secret access. Anyway, the officials would probably shut me down if they knew."

"I still don't get why you need our help," John said. "Couldn't you just go into the chamber the way Paul did?"

"That's my intention, but only Paul and Bueller know the route. I could eventually figure it out, but that would take time." Patting his jacket pocket he said with some urgency, "I want to return this statue to its hiding place today."

"I can see why you want to get rid of it. Just look at this place," I said peering inside the door of the ransacked shed.

"You understand my impatience."

"I understand," John said. "But I'm not sure I entirely agree with your solution."

"Maybe I could find someone else," Barry said.

"You don't need to do that. I'll help, and I will keep your secret."

"I knew I could count on the two of you!" Dr. Short put his arms around us both.

"So how are we going to do this without Paul knowing the truth?"

"I will tell him that I am interested in his discovery, which is the truth, I am. And I will ask him if he can retrace his steps and lead us all into the pyramid. When we arrive in the Subterranean Chamber, I thought the two of you could keep him distracted long enough for me to find the shaft and replace the statue without him suspecting anything."

"A shaft! It was in a shaft down there?" John asked.

"Yes, rather ingenious since there are shafts all over the pyramid, most of which go nowhere and therefore no one pays much attention to them, except Gantenbrink. Bueller said that even Gantenbrink wouldn't have seen this one. It's nearly imperceptible if you're not aware of its existence. It's hidden from sight in an alcove that remains dark even when the adjacent main chamber room is lit. And its designers took the precaution of concealing it behind a large removable stone, out of eyeshot, only two feet above the chamber floor. The statue had rested behind a metal door before Bueller took it. Bueller believes the door is fabricated out of the same metal as the door Gantenbrink discovered in the shaft in the Queen's Chamber. It sits back about seven feet, so I've devised this small extension pole to allow me to reach it."

Dr. Short pulled a small tube out of his pocket that he extended out around nine feet. Attached to one end was a magnet.

"A magnet!" John said.

"That's how Bueller was able to open the door. All I need to do is pull the stone out and slide this pole into the shaft until the magnet attaches itself to the door. Then I'll carefully pull the iron door open and out of the shaft, place Thoth inside, then put the door back into the shaft behind it. Using the other end of the pole, I'll push the door and Thoth back into place until I hear a clink, replace the stone and I'm done."

"Sounds like you've rehearsed it," I said.

"Yes, I have, several times" Dr. Short said smiling.

"Okay, it's a go," John said. "We'd better get started. Projects always take longer than you think they will."

Chapter Thirty-Three

Paul was game to lead. He particularly liked the head lanterns Dr. Short pulled out of his equipment box. "Spelunking lights. Cool!"

"I thought you would like these," Dr. Short said. "They free up your hands. I'll bring a lantern too, but we won't light it until we get into the Subterranean Chamber."

Paul was confident he could easily lead us back to the chamber until he set out to do it. He had been looking about at Dr. Short's various excavation sites after lunch, and they all began to look alike.

"Let's see," Dr. Short said. "Hmm, they do look a lot alike, don't they? Well, that's not surprising since I used the same technique to open up each site. We're going to have to retrace your steps, Paul. Let's walk over to where I was taking sound measurements when we first met."

We followed Dr. Short across the desert for about ten minutes or so. He looked about as if he were not altogether sure he had located the right spot.

"Does this look familiar?" he asked.

"I guess so," Paul said.

"It's just flat desert," I said. "It's hard to see anything about it that would distinguish it from any other place out here."

"If we could figure out where we were coming from when we first saw you" John said, as he began to look around. "We came from over there!" He pointed to the far side of a pyramid.

"That's right," I said. "We had to walk all the way around the pyramid, and we came out on that side."

"When we came around we saw the Sphinx and the excavation site where we ate lunch over in that direction," John pointed. "So we would have been coming from over there," John pointed again to the far side of the pyramid, "and walking along there," he said as he marked the path we took across the desert with his finger.

"And we encountered you on the way," I said to Dr. Short who stood with his chin resting in his palm as he surveyed the area.

"Oh, yes, now I remember. I was working right over here," he pointed and led us about twenty yards from where we were standing.

"This looks right," John said.

"Now Paul, where did you go after we first spoke?"

"I think I walked over to where we had lunch because that's where I borrowed the lantern. Wait a minute! I found the hole before I took it. But I think I was walking in that direction anyway."

We marched along the desert together from where we were standing back towards our lunch site.

"I bet I know which excavation you entered," Dr. Short said as he walked ahead of us. "Here, I bet."

Paul skipped ahead and caught up to him. "Yeah, this is it. I found this hole, then I got the lantern and came back and climbed in."

"Now, before we climb in, do you remember the path you took once you got inside?"

"I crawled for a little bit, and then there were two paths. I took one of them, but after a while it got smaller and smaller until I couldn't fit, so I backed out. And then I took the other, and it was small for a while, but then it got bigger and bigger. And then there was a big iron door I had to push open."

"Okay," Dr. Short said, "let's go. Paul will go first. I will follow up in the rear. Wait until it's dark before you turn on your headlamps. I can't guarantee the battery life."

Paul climbed down the ladder and into the tunnel followed by John, then me, then Dr. Short. The tunnel was dark as soon as we entered so we turned on our lights immediately. Even with our lamps we couldn't see much until our eyes adjusted from bright desert sunlight to low beam lamplight in this pitch-black place. Spelunking was an activity I had never participated in, and now in this narrow little tunnel I knew why. It felt absolutely claustrophobic.

"Paul, do you remember how long it took you to get to the door?" I asked after we had been crawling for ten minutes or so.

"Not very long," he called back.

It was already long enough for me. The tunnel was so tight that it rubbed against my hair and hips, and it felt damp.

"How is this possible?" I said to the others. "How could it feel damp and chilly below the Sahara Desert?"

"I can see you've never been spelunking, my dear," Dr. Short said. "If you had, you would know it feels dry down here by comparison to most caves."

"Thank you for warning me. I'll make a point of not taking up the sport. John, is your head all right?"

"What do you mean by that remark?" he asked.

"Nothing really. It's just that I've got my head pretty low, and I still keep rubbing against the top of this tunnel. I just wondered how you're doing since you're about a foot taller."

"I'm fine."

I kept quiet for a good five minutes after I realized the others didn't seem to mind this ordeal half as much as I. I didn't want to sound like I was whining, but after a while I couldn't keep quiet any longer.

"Are we almost there?"

John abruptly stopped before Paul could answer, but I didn't know it until I put the weight of my hands on the back of his heels.

"Ouch!" he cried.

"I'm sorry," I said, "but you stopped so suddenly."

"Paul is trying to remember which path led to the pyramid," John said as he reached back and rubbed the back of his heels.

"Is that all the farther we've come, only to the fork?" I said.

"Don't worry Paul," Dr. Short said. "If you take the wrong one, we will know it soon enough and can back out and take the other one. Just keep moving."

"But try to pick the right one if you can," I said thinking it was bad enough to crawl forward in this low, narrow place and dreading the possibility of having to crawl backward.

"It's this way," Paul said, and he began to move forward again.

We crawled along a good distance. The tunnel did not shrink but seemed gradually to get larger, which was a relief. Paul had picked the right path.

"Halt!" John said.

I halted, and so did Dr. Short behind me.

"What's the problem?" Dr. Short shouted forward.

"Paul's headlamp is flickering," John shouted back. "I think the batteries are about to die. I'm going to give him mine."

"Don't do that!" Dr. Short said. "I'll give him mine. I've got the lantern." He grumbled to himself about how he should have gotten new batteries as he unfastened his headlamp and passed it to me. I passed it to John.

"Hold on while I adjust it to fit Paul," he said.

I turned around in the direction of Dr. Short and saw only eerie darkness.

"Where's the lantern?"

"I thought I would wait until we get to the chamber before I light it. I don't want to waste the kerosene."

"I don't think you should wait. I, for one, need as much light in here as we can get."

I saw the flicker of a match and then the soft, full light of the lantern.

"That's much better," I said and he agreed.

"We're ready," John said and the crawl continued.

In no time we reached a markedly different part of the tunnel. It was still narrow, but it was much higher. I could stand up as long as I kept my head down.

"What a relief," I said.

"Yes, this is much better," Dr. Short agreed. "We must nearly be there."

Minutes later Paul shouted that we had reached the door. I heard him grunt as he tried unsuccessfully to pull it open.

"Here Paul," John said, "let me try. You just squeeze past me."

I heard shuffling as the two changed places. Then I heard John pulling on the door.

"Are you having trouble?" Dr. Short asked.

"It's pretty tight. I need to leverage all my weight as I pull. Paul, could you move back and give me some room?"

I put my hands on the back of Paul's shoulders and pulled him back. He nearly leaped out of his skin. "It's only me," I said. Paul's little frame began to relax. We listened to John continue to grunt and pull in the darkness.

"Here, take this," Dr. Short said and handed me the lantern. "John can use the light."

Paul and I stood together beaming the light on the door as John pulled and pulled.

"How did you get this thing opened?" he asked Paul.

"It wasn't so stuck."

"When the door closed behind you, it must have shut very hard," Dr. Short said. "That's why it's stuck now."

This was the wrong thing to say at that moment. It reminded Paul of how the door had mysteriously closed behind him when he first entered the Subterranean Chamber.

"I don't want it to shut me inside there again!" he cried.

"Don't worry," I said. "If John can get the door open, you and I will stand next to it and make sure it stays open until we leave."

"Do you need some help John?" Dr. Short asked.

"Maybe."

Paul and I pressed against the smooth stone wall to make room for Dr. Short to squeeze past us. Once he was through, we directed the lantern light onto the door.

"Okay," John said, "when I count to three pull. One, two, three pull!"

The iron door swung open, but all we could see was more darkness. We followed Dr. Short through the doorway and entered into a narrow corridor that immediately made a sharp right turn. It led to the slimmest of openings into the Subterranean Chamber, so slim that from the chamber side you could not make it out unless you already knew it was there. Once I had squeezed through the opening and into the chamber, I observed that the corridor wall from this side looked like the rear wall of the room, concealing both the corridor and the tunnel door from view.

"Ingenuous," Dr. Short said. "It's a secret passageway hidden by an optical illusion. I've never seen one like this before. I think I want to have a look around. May I borrow the lantern?"

He took the lantern from Paul and walked off through the center of the chamber while John walked around the edges of the room closely examining the walls with his headlamp. The room looked slightly smaller than the King's Chamber, but like the King's Chamber it had smooth walls constructed of polished stone blocks that were completely unadorned. We saw the stone staircase that led up to the ground floor of the pyramid, but other than that, the room appeared empty. There wasn't even a sarcophagus. Then the room went black.

"Dr. Short!" Paul cried. "Where are you?"

"I'm back here. I'm all right."

John must have turned towards us for at just that moment I could see the dim light emanating from his head lantern. "How did you ever stay in this place alone?" I asked Paul. "It's so spooky."

"Yeah, I went right up the stairs after I heard the door shut."

"But it's spooky up there too."

Paul pulled on my hand. "You said we would guard the door so it won't shut this time."

"Okay. We can't see anything standing here anyway."

"Paul and I are going to guard the door," I called out to the others.

Paul stood like a doorstop, his body propping open the door to prevent it from mysteriously closing. I knew from Dr. Short that it wasn't a mysterious force that had shut the door but Bueller, who having just stolen the statue made his escape just after Paul coincidentally entered the chamber. I couldn't tell Paul though, even to alleviate his fear, because the more he knew the greater the threat to him of real danger now or in the future. It didn't hurt to keep an eye on the door anyway just in case, for who knew what or who might be lurking about. After what seemed an eternity of silent waiting, Paul and I were startled by a loud, low crash. It sounded like metal falling on stone.

"What's that?" Paul said.

"I don't know. You wait here while I find out."

I walked through the corridor back to where Paul and I had stood earlier. The dim light of John's head lantern had disappeared. The room was now entirely dark.

"John! Dr. Short!" I called.

"We're back here," John said.

"I have no idea where here is. It's totally dark. I was just checking to see if everything is all right. Paul and I heard a crash."

"Everything is fine," Dr. Short said. "Just having a little trouble, but we'll be ready to join you in a few more minutes."

As I turned back into the corridor I could see Paul's headlamp begin to flicker. "Paul, your lamp is going out again."

"I want to get out of here now!"

"We're losing another headlamp," I shouted to John and Dr. Short.

"Just another minute," Dr. Short yelled back.

"Here, you can have mine," I said to Paul as I began to unstrap my lamp. But before I could remove my lantern I was startled by another set of sounds that seemed a little more distant and a lot softer than the crashing sound I had just heard. "Wait here," I whispered to Paul as I made my way back through the corridor to the chamber once again.

"Was that you?" I called in a low whisper.

The sounds became more definite, and they seemed to be coming from above the staircase.

"Did you hear that?" I called out.

"I did!" John answered.

I heard Dr. Short's whispered shout, "Get back to the door, turn out your lamps and keep absolutely silent!"

As I ran down the corridor turning my lamp off, I could hear the metal door at the top of the stairs opening. "Shush," I said to Paul.

We stood together absolutely still and in total darkness, hidden by the corridor wall from the men whose footsteps we heard coming down the staircase and whose voices we heard speaking Arabic. After a few moments of absolute silence, the men began to speak again, and we heard the sound of their footsteps as they climbed back up the stone stairway.

"They must be gone," I whispered to Paul. "Wait here while I see."

I walked down the corridor and peered through the sliver-like opening. John's headlamp came darting towards me, followed by Dr. Short whose lantern was still unlit.

"Get into the corridor and be quiet!" Dr. Short whispered with an urgency I had never before heard from him. "And turn off your headlamp! They'll be back. I heard them say they were going for lamps."

Just as John and Dr. Short turned into the concealed corridor, the men returned. We could smell the burning fumes of the oil that fired the torches they brought with them.

"They must have heard us," I whispered. "Let's go!"

Dr. Short said nothing. Instead, he put his fingers over my mouth, then Paul's mouth and finally John's. We waited in total darkness, completely silent and totally frozen, as if our bodies were entombed. Although I could not understand their words, the sounds of their voices indicated their proximity to us. They took their time searching the room with their torches. As they drew near I could see the torch light flicker on the wall near the slivered entrance to the corridor. I prayed they wouldn't come close enough to see the slim opening. We stood silent for fifteen very long minutes. At last we heard their footsteps climb the stone stairway once again, but this time they were followed by a loud clang of the iron door that reverberated throughout the chamber like a bell. If we had had a mirror at that moment, it would have fogged up for all the pent up breath the four of us expelled.

"Apparently they're unaware of this hidden passage," Dr. Short said.

"I guess so!" John said and sighed in relief.

"They probably heard all that noise you were making," Paul said. "What were you doing anyway?"

"You're right Paul," Dr. Short said. "That was clumsy of me. I found a piece of iron and while I was examining it, I dropped it and the sound of the crash amplified. That's why we couldn't attempt a run for it. The slightest sound coming from this metal door here would have echoed throughout this place, just as the piece of iron I dropped did, just as the door upstairs did when they shut it. We couldn't take the risk."

"What do you think would have happened if we'd been caught?" John asked.

"I don't know. I hate to think about it. Maybe only a fine, perhaps jail. It depends on what they suspected us of doing. We couldn't tell them the truth. They never would have believed it. Instead, they would have suspected the opposite. I would lose my archeological license for certain. And I sure would hate to be inside an Egyptian jail."

"The jails are that bad?" John asked.

"They're that bad. Let's get out of here."

I took my headlamp off and strapped it to Paul. Dr. Short took out a match to relight the lantern but the wick wouldn't catch.

"Not enough kerosene in there to get it lit again," he said.

"What will you do without the lamp?" Paul asked.

"I'll be all right. I'll follow right behind you. You can light the way for the two of us."

We exited the chamber and entered the tunnel with only two working lights. Paul led, followed by Dr. Short. I came next, and then John.

"Close the door gently," Dr. Short said. "We don't want to arouse anymore suspicion."

John gently swung the door back into place, and the two of us pressed our weight against it to make sure it was snugly secured.

"Excellent," Dr. Short said. "I'll make first class tomb robbers out of the lot of you." He began to laugh.

The rest of us hesitantly joined him in his merriment for we weren't so sure we liked the joke. Yet we all rejoiced to be out of that chamber. And all of us except Paul, who to this day remains ignorant of the real purpose of our escapade, were celebrating our enormous relief to be rid of that beautiful, golden, some say magical statue of Thoth.

Chapter Thirty-Four

"**W**ow!" I said as I shaded my eyes. "The sun's really bright. How long were we down there?"

Dr. Short looked at his watch. "Longer than you might think. At least three hours. It's almost five."

"Look at us!" I said after my eyes adjusted to the light. "Do I look as bad as you guys?"

"You look like you're wearing a wig," Paul said and began to laugh uproariously.

"A powdered wig," John said, "and white makeup."

I couldn't see myself, but I could see them. John and Paul's hair was matted with light gray dirt and sand. Their faces were smudged with the stuff. Their jeans and shirts were filthy. I tried to brush off the dirt caked on my pants to no avail. It was like glue. The caked, grayish mud seemed all that was holding together the threads of denim that covered my knees. Dr. Short looked almost clean by comparison. He had protected his face and hair with his brimmed hat, and the color of the dirt nearly matched his khaki pants.

"Oh, I get the uniform now," I said.

"What uniform?" Dr. Short said.

"Yours. I can see now why archaeologists all dress alike. It's very practical."

Dr. Short looked down at his clothing. "Well, yes it is, although I wouldn't have described my clothing as a uniform. But in certain respects I guess you're right. I do look a tad better than the rest of you, but it's still going to take a lot of soap and water to get me clean. We'd better get back to the hotel if we're going to make our seven o'clock reservation at the Blue Nile. I wouldn't want to miss that."

We walked briskly to the jeep, elated at having completed a successful mission. Dr. Short raced across the desert until we reached the road, slowing down only because the traffic in Giza made it impossible to do anything else. I wouldn't call his driving reckless; "creative" may be a better word. He knew how to get around anything that got in his way.

"I know who you drive like," I said.

"I thought I drove like your brother."

"You drive in the city like my brother drives on the highway. But as a city driver, I can only compare you to a New York City taxi driver."

"You're right!" John said. "Remember that cab driver that got us from the airport in Newark to our dinner reservation in Soho on time and in the thick of traffic?"

"Oh, I remember. He was a creative driver too. Remember how he dodged all of that traffic lined up at the Holland Tunnel?"

"He knew every shortcut in New York City. Come to think of it he was an Egyptian from Alexandria."

"That's right!" I cried out in delight.

"Yep, come to Egypt to learn how to drive," Dr. Short said as he pulled into the parking garage at the Cairo Kingsley.

"We're here already," Paul said. "You're a great driver!"

We piled out of the jeep wondering how the hotel guests and staff would react to the sight of us. We hardly noticed though because we were confronted by Natalie and Madeleine who had been waiting in the lobby for a good two hours.

"Look at you! What happened?" Madeleine asked.

"We went on an expedition!" Paul said. "And someone tore up Dr. Short's shack!"

Madeleine shot a hard look at all three of us before she led Paul by the hand to the elevator.

"Are you guys going to be ready in time to keep our reservation?" Natalie asked. "Because if you aren't, I need to phone Stu."

"Stuart called?" John said.

"Yes, he's going to meet us at the Blue Nile."

"Well, it's after five now," Dr. Short said looking at his watch. "Can you two be ready in an hour?"

"As long as I get the shower first," I said.

"You go ahead," John said. "I will be up in a few minutes."

I headed straight for the elevator, and when I arrived in the room I peeled off my clothes and left them in a discard pile, hopped into the shower and lathered up from head to foot. I felt like I was undergoing a purification ritual as I watched every bit of the evidence of where we had been pour off of me and flow down into the drain in swirls of muddy water. I lathered up again and watched as the water ran clear. I washed hurriedly, thinking John would arrive at our room any minute with a fresh report from Dr. Short about what we would do next.

"He said he wanted to avoid the topic for now," John said. "Especially at dinner. It's supposed to be a celebration. He said maybe later at the juice bar."

"You can have the shower now," I said in a tone that betrayed my disappointment at not learning anything new.

As if to offer up something, John said from inside the bath, "I could tell he's worried, but we didn't have time to talk much." He dangled his dirty clothes through the opening in the bathroom doorway. "What do you want me to do with these?"

"I'll incinerate them."

The muddied shirts and pants were too dirty to pack, and I doubted I could get them clean anyway. I thought I would toss them in the trash chute I'd seen the staff use at the end of the hall. I threw on some fresh clothes that had been laundered at the Old Cataract, put out some clean clothes for John, braided my wet hair and took my bundle down the hall while John cleaned himself in the hot, surging shower.

Opening the metal flap of the trash chute I stared down into its shaft, a shaft every bit as dark as the underground tunnel I had crawled through earlier. But this one smelled of ash and smoke. No hidden subterranean chamber lay at the other end, no Gantenbrink's concealed door, no Bauval's Orion's Belt.

Tears unexpectedly came to my eyes, as I was about to toss in my load. What was this sadness? For years I had a deep faith in the transformative power of knowledge, imagining that as we grew in knowledge, so might we grow in character. But at this moment my idealism gave way to harsh reality. Humankind hadn't changed much since Imhotep's time. It is as if the same people are born again and again, waging the same battles between those who are driven by greed and those who are inspired by knowledge; those who would bend others to their will and those who want only to live free; those who suffer from delusional hubris and those who are perhaps too humble, the former

263

conceiving grotesque fictions to justify their actions against the latter. Imhotep understood this, I thought, which is why he took to his grave knowledge of power that in the wrong hands might destroy us. In spite of all the changes that have occurred over the last five thousand years, I understood that some things never change.

But then I considered Dr. Bueller. He had been educated by the most ruthless regime in modern history. He had internalized much of that education, believing that the Aryan people were superior and therefore deserving of the ancient knowledge they sought, knowledge that he had pursued his whole, rather long life. I shuddered when I considered what might have happened had the Nazis acquired the secret of harnessing the power of earthquakes and volcanoes, knowledge which some speculate was no secret to the ancient Egyptian priests. And Bueller nearly had it. After more than sixty years of searching he held its golden key in his hands. Yet he placed that key in my hands, trusting I would return it to him. And I did without hesitation. In the end he gave it over to Dr. Short to return to its hiding place, trusting that Dr. Short would. And he did. Had I witnessed a miracle? Was the golden statue of Thoth magical? Why else would Bueller have given it up if it didn't have some strange power over him? And why had Dr. Short resisted the temptation that he warned John of, the allure of great celebrity and wealth the golden statue could have brought him? I began to understand, and my faith was restored. Knowledge can be transformative when coupled with wisdom. It can reshape the heart of a man or a woman, even a man like Dr. Bueller. But certain kinds of knowledge can be deadly if its holder lacks the wisdom to measure its real worth and to know what to do with it.

In a fit of inspiration I held back no longer but tossed the clothing into the dark chute and uttered an evocation. "As this clothing vanishes into fire, let knowledge of the golden statue fade into legend, that his wisdom might prevail." I heard a whoosh as the bundle slid down the chute while I stood gazing into the pitch darkness of the open shaft. Then I heard a familiar voice.

"Are you ready?" John asked.

"Yes, I'm ready."

Chapter Thirty-Five

D r. Short and Natalie stood waiting when John and I got off the elevator, and all four of us awaited the arrival of Madeleine and Paul. Marching music broke the silence. It came from Dr. Short's pocket.

"It's this rental phone," he said a bit embarrassed.

"Who picked the music?" John asked.

"Your nephew," he said before he took the call. "Where are you? Yes, we're all down here waiting for you and your grandmother. The jeep is parked outside and ready to go." He clicked off the phone. "They're coming."

"Mom complained Paul was tough to clean up," Natalie said. "She was having trouble finding something clean for him to wear. He wore his last clean outfit today."

"I'm sorry I got him so dirty," Dr. Short said.

"We all got dirty," John said.

"Our clothes were so dirty I threw them away," I said sympathetically.

The elevator door opened and out popped Paul with his grandmother. He was wearing a brightly colored, oversized novelty T-shirt and a pair of slightly rumpled jeans.

"Where did you get that?" John asked.

"At the hotel gift shop," Madeleine said. "Paul picked it out. He didn't have a clean shirt left. I had to retrieve these pants he's wearing from the dirty laundry."

The T-shirt was royal blue with a large golden depiction of the three pyramids in the background and the Sphinx in the foreground. At the bottom in large yellow embroidered script it read, "Egypt, Land of Mystery."

"You picked it out?" John said.

"Isn't it cool!"

"It certainly is appropriate," I said.

"I like it," Dr. Short said in an admiring tone. "Are we ready?"

Barry departed radically from his usual driving style. He drove slowly. I didn't know if he was trying to confuse me or impress Madeleine but concluded that he was probably trying to impress Madeleine to make up for Paul having gotten so dirty and the rest that she didn't know about.

Three wavy blue lines, stacked horizontally and blinking neon greeted us outside the restaurant's entrance. I recognized the hieroglyph for water, but I understood it much better now after having traveled up the Nile. If you listen carefully as you sail, you hear in the river's soft, ancient waves that ripple gently as the boat cuts through the water, that life endures in spite of the human clamor in towns along its shores. The exception is Aswan, which has its own gentle music. I recalled the perch on the veranda at the Old Cataract with the Nile coursing its way towards Cairo below and the stars shimmering above, and then I looked up. The stars in Giza had just begun to rise, as we were about to enter the Blue Nile.

"You know what I would like to do after dinner," I said. "I would love to go out into the desert and look at the stars. They look brilliant tonight."

"Good idea," Dr. Short said. "I'll drive us all out there in the jeep, and we can have an after dinner walk in the desert."

The waiter greeted Dr. Short and led us back to our table. It was just as I had remembered. Blue floor lights cast their magic making me feel as if I were walking on water while musicians played traditional instruments near the center of the long dining room. The place was exotic. As we neared the table, I could see Stuart already seated. Gone were the preppy clothes he wore while on the cruise ship under the assumed name of Walter. He was dressed just as he was when I first saw him in Cairo, in a black leather jacket and jeans. He looked good, almost cheerful as he stood up and greeted us.

"Good to see you again," Barry said. He put his hand out to Stuart who returned his greeting.

"I'm glad we could get together before you leave," Stuart said and looked over at Natalie.

"It's good that you could find the time," Natalie said.

266

"Would you like me to order?" Dr. Short asked.

The five us agreed to his suggestion immediately. Natalie, more sensitive to Stuart than the rest of us explained, "Dr. Short ordered for all of us when we had dinner here before because the menu is written in Arabic, and it was great!"

"Would you please quit referring to me so formally? My name is Barry."

"I'm sorry if I made you feel uncomfortable," Natalie said.

"You don't make me feel uncomfortable, you make me feel old."

"You are old," Paul said.

"Paul!" Madeleine said, "Mind your manners."

"That's all right Madeleine," Dr. Short said before directing himself to the boy. "A word to the wise young man. Someday you will be my age too, and you won't want to be reminded of it."

"I don't think of you as old," I said. "I think of you as being like one of my professors. I always called them Doctor more as a sign of respect than age. Many of my professors weren't very much older than me."

"But I am not your professor, and you are my friends! Aren't you? All of this formality makes me uncomfortable."

"You should have said something sooner," John said. "I've been calling you Dr. Short for most of the trip."

"Now is the time to stop. Besides, we'll be seeing each other in the future, won't we?"

"Are you coming to Ohio?" Paul asked.

The waiter who came to take our order interrupted our conversation. Dr. Short, or I should say Barry, ordered a feast, much as he had before, and like before ordered San Pellegrino for a toast. Glasses were soon brought to the table and the bubbling water was served.

"To our friendship," he toasted.

"Well, are you coming to Ohio?" John said echoing Paul.

"I'm planning to return home soon."

"Where is home Barry?" Natalie asked. "You've never said."

"I was born in Minnesota, but I haven't lived there in years. I keep an apartment in Chicago near the Institute. It isn't much because I'm so rarely there. But I'm thinking of returning to do some work."

"So you are coming to Ohio!" Paul said.

"I would like to visit. Actually, you are located somewhat close to where I might be working."

"Chicago is only a six hour drive," Madeleine said. "I would love for you to visit."

"Mom has a nice, big house," Natalie said.

"You could go to her Jungian dream analysis meetings in Dayton," John said.

"Or as my mother would have said, if you visit in the summer you could go to the Ohio State Fair," I laughed.

"Oh, I don't know if he would want to do that," Madeleine said.

"I think the fair is pretty cool," Paul said. "They have a butter cow."

"A butter cow!" Barry said.

"They really do," I said. "In the dairy barn. Every year they sculpt a cow out of butter and display it."

"Sounds a lot like Minnesota. Tell you what Paul, if I'm in Ohio during the fair, I will take you."

"Great! You can take my brother Kevin too."

"That's a deal."

The appetizers were placed in the center of our large, round table. Barry filled each of our plates with the delicacies before the conversation continued.

"You said something about working nearby," John said. "What are you going to be doing?"

"I'm not absolutely sure. There's an interesting site located near Pittsburgh that I was invited to work in, oh, about six months ago. I declined at that time because I've been so busy here, but I've reconsidered my plans. I've gone as far as I want to go here, so late today I wrote my colleague to see if the offer is still open."

"What would you be doing?" Madeleine asked.

"They asked if I could help them establish a connection between a very ancient Indian site in Pennsylvania and a site in France, that is if there truly is a connection to be established. Years ago I did quite a bit of work in France at the Solutrean sites. Perhaps you know about them?"

"Wasn't it the Solutreans who did the ancient rock paintings they've found inside caves in France, paintings of horses I believe?" John said.

"Yes, that's them. They lived in France and Spain some twenty thousand years ago and were great hunters and killed many of those horses they painted using flint arrows. They've discovered arrowheads at Meadowcroft Rockshelter near Pittsburgh that look a lot like them. So, that's prompted a great deal of speculation about when the Americas were first settled and by whom."

"I thought the Indians crossed the Bering Straight from Asia when it was frozen over during the Ice Age," John said.

"Yes, that's right. But this site under investigation suggests that settlements appeared much earlier than what we had thought and that some of the earlier settlers may have come from Europe more than nineteen thousand years ago."

"That's fantastic!" John said. "I thought the first Indians arrived four thousand years ago or so."

"Well, that's the established view. But some claim they've found artifacts in Pennsylvania that are twenty thousand years old according to carbon dating tests. Of course, carbon dating is quite controversial."

"Why?" John asked. "I thought it's a well established technique."

"There is quite a bit of coal in the area. Some have argued that the coal contaminated the specimens tested."

"Is that likely?"

"It's possible. It's possible enough to cast doubt on their hypothesis. So they had asked me to join the investigation to see if I could find other links to the Solutreans since I'm knowledgeable in that area. They need more than arrowheads, you see, since their claim, if proven, would dramatically alter our assumptions about the settling of the Americas."

Two waiters appeared carrying trays laden with main dishes that covered our table.

"This looks wonderful," Barry said. He heaped each of our plates with lamb, chicken, fish, rice and fava beans.

"Why would you leave Egypt?" Stuart asked after we were all served.

"Maybe because his dig site was raided," Paul said.

"What!" Stuart said.

"Yesterday I believe. When I went to collect my jeep I found my apartment had been ransacked, so I drove out to my dig site and found that my shed had been ransacked too."

269

"Do you know why?"

"Not exactly," Barry said, but I fear someone thinks I have Bueller's statue."

"The shed looked a lot like Bueller's hotel room when we found him there unconscious," I said. "By the way, have you heard anything more about Gabby and Beverly? It looked like they could have done it."

"I doubt that based on the reports I've read," Stuart said. "But that doesn't mean that someone they're connected to couldn't have done it."

"Yes, that's my concern," Barry said. "I think I would be better off leaving Egypt for the time being. I don't want to end up like poor old Hans Bueller, forced into retirement by a club on the head. Anyway, I'm done with my exploration here on the Giza Plateau, and I don't have anything else lined up. But I really had hoped we would not talk about this at dinner. This is supposed to be a celebration."

"Would you mind taking me out to your camp where it happened?" Stuart asked.

"Well, we could plan to do that in the next few days."

"I mean tonight Barry. If there's anything to this, if Gabby and Beverly could be involved, I need to know. I don't want the evidence to get cold."

"All right, tonight. I had promised an astronomy walk in the desert on their last night here. You and I can go look at my dig site while they're looking at the stars. John knows astronomy better than I anyway."

"Tell us Stuart, what have you heard about Gabby and Beverly?" Natalie asked.

"They were seen getting off the boat they boarded in Abu Simbel at Wadi Halfa, just across the Sudanese border. From there they took a train to Khartoum, the capital. We intercepted some phone calls they made to their husbands from a hotel where they spent the night. Their husbands complained that they were being watched by agents and didn't know why. The women didn't offer much in the way of an explanation, but their husbands' reports would have definitely tipped them off that we are on to them. Of course, their departure route out of Egypt indicated that they probably knew that already. We've gotten reports that while in Khartoum they made a few unsuccessful inquiries for visas at certain countries' embassies. The last report we've gotten said they were seen boarding a small boat traveling from Khartoum up the Blue Nile."

"The Blue Nile! We're at the Blue Nile!" Natalie said.

"It's also a river," Barry pointed out.

"I thought it was a poetic description of the Nile," I said.

"No, it's a real river. The Nile actually flows north into Egypt from where its two major tributaries, the White Nile and the Blue Nile converge in Khartoum in the Sudan. I've never seen the Blue Nile, but I've heard it is very beautiful."

"It isn't a river I'd want to travel on," Stuart said.

"Why not?" Natalie asked.

"It's not navigable."

"Well then, how were they able to get a boat?" she asked.

"It's navigable for short distances. But they will never get to Ethiopia that way if that's what they're trying to do."

"Is that where it goes?"

"That's where it begins," Barry said, "at Lake Tana."

"If they would show up in Addis Ababa," Stuart said, "they will be spotted, but I doubt they will make it out of Sudan."

"Why?"

"To begin with they likely will encounter Sudanese bandits."

"I heard they take slaves there," I said.

"That's possible," Stuart said, and began to laugh. "They could end up scrubbing some sultan's palace floors somewhere. But even if they make it out of Sudan and into Ethiopia, there's the Ethiopian militia, not to mention the crocodiles and hippos."

"Crocodiles and hippos!" Paul said. "I didn't see any crocodiles and hippos."

"You didn't go far enough south."

"Those women seem pretty resourceful," Barry said.

"Well, you are right there," Stuart said. "But they've entered uncharted waters this time."

The waiters came and replaced our now empty plates with dessert bowls filled with a very rich, smooth rice pudding.

"It's too bad you were so busy following those women that you couldn't enjoy the trip," Madeleine said to Stuart.

271

"Oh, I enjoyed myself. But there were many distractions." He looked at Natalie. "I was thinking we could try it again when I'm not so busy." She stared at him, obviously surprised and not fully comprehending the offer. Eyes riveted on her as if no one else was there, he said, "I was thinking that maybe you could come along with me the next time I go to Brazil."

"Brazil!" Natalie said sarcastically, "To buy jewels?"

"I never lied to you about that. I've made some very good connections there, and I really do have a side business."

Natalie looked down at her rice pudding as if she were thinking about what she would say next, but before she could utter a word Madeleine said, "That sounds wonderful. We would all love to go. We have friends there, you know."

Stuart looked puzzled, and then his expression changed from surprise to disappointment. "Yes, we'll have to go sometime."

Chapter Thirty-Six

"I think we have too much weight back here," John said, as we rumbled down the road, the two of us stacked up in Barry's backseat, crammed in with Stuart, Natalie and Paul.

"This vehicle was built for abuse," Barry said from the driver's seat. "Look, I had planned on going out to the Sphinx, but since Stuart wants to look around my shed, let me take you all out there. You can walk out onto the desert where we were earlier."

"As long as it's dark," John said. "That's all I care about."

"It'll be dark. Don't worry about that."

Once we left the town of Giza and started on the road to the pyramids it became immensely dark under a new moon. There simply was no light except the stars, which stood out in the night sky like bright, white lanterns that failed, nonetheless, to cast lamplight upon the stretches of sand we drove through. No sooner had we arrived at Barry's shed than he remembered his lantern was out of kerosene.

"Tell you what I'm going to do. I'm going to turn the jeep towards the door and leave my headlights on to give Stu and me enough light to look around the place. I'll point the rest of you in the direction we walked this afternoon. The lights won't bother you once you've gotten out there a ways."

We wandered further out into the desert by foot, moored only by the jeep's headlamps, a sort of lighthouse in a sea of darkness. After ten minutes or so John thought we were far enough away to get the full effect of a perfectly black desert sky. The effect was actually achieved a yard away from the jeep, but John wanted to be sure the night sky looked just as the ancient Egyptians had seen it, with no artificial light sources whatsoever.

He stood eyes riveted to the sky. "Incredible. They're so bright. You can see the Pleides and Hyades so clearly."

"Where are the Pleides?" Paul asked.

"Up there," John pointed. "That beautiful cluster of stars in Aries, the Seven Sisters."

"I see them. Wow!" Paul said.

John drew a circle in the sky with his finger as he traced the path of the zodiac. "Next to Aries there is Taurus. See that bright red star? That's Aldebaran. Next to that is Gemini, with its twin stars, Castor and Pollux."

"Where's the lion?" Paul asked.

"Over there, rising above the eastern horizon. See Paul, the constellations of the zodiac are lined up in a great circle on the sphere of the heavens. I can trace them with my finger: Aries, Taurus, Gemini, Cancer and there is Leo about thirty degrees above the eastern horizon. Each hour Leo will appear to travel fifteen degrees so at midnight tonight it will be very near the meridian."

"What's the meridian?

"You know where the North Pole and South Poles are, don't you?"

"Yeah, they are at the top and bottom of the world."

"Well, imagine a line passing over the night sky connecting one pole to the other. That's the meridian."

"Oh! So at midnight the lion will move right up there," Paul said, pointing straight up.

"It will appear to have moved, but actually we will have moved because we're standing on the earth, which rotates on its axis. In ancient times people didn't know that the earth rotates. They thought the stars were literally on a sphere that rotated around the earth and that explained why the constellations appeared in different places or weren't visible at all, depending on the day of the year and the time of night. You can see why they thought that."

"Yeah, it looks that way," Paul said.

"After twenty-four hours Leo will have traveled three hundred and sixty degrees because the earth will have fully rotated. So tomorrow night at this time Leo will be where it is now, almost."

"Almost?"

"I hate to make things too complicated."

"It's not too complicated," Paul said.

"Okay, the earth fully rotates every twenty-four hours minus four minutes. Those minutes can begin to add up. Next week, for example, Leo will be just where it is now twenty-eight minutes earlier. After a year's time the constellations return to the same position. So next year on this day Leo will be just as it is now at this very same time."

"I get it."

"But then there is another motion which is very subtle called the precession of the equinoxes that's caused by the slow wobbling of the earth on its axis. It is so slow that it takes about two thousand years to change the position of the constellations by thirty degrees. It's so subtle that it takes very careful observations with well known landmarks to notice the change."

"Landmarks like the lion?"

"Yes, the Sphinx is a good one. Or like Stonehenge in England or the Indian mounds back in Ohio."

"So where was Leo when they built the lion?" Paul asked

"That's the sixty-four thousand dollar question. When did they build the Sphinx? Some scholars believe that the ancient Egyptians built their monuments to reflect the heavens. 'On earth as it is in heaven' so to speak. In that case the Sphinx had to be Leo because the resemblance of the monument to the constellation is too striking to ignore. Now, a good measuring point of where Leo was in the sky might be the vernal equinox since it marks the beginning of spring, which was very important to ancient cultures because for most of them spring marked the beginning of the year."

"Happy New Year!" Paul's laughter was quickly swallowed up by the vast emptiness.

"If we were here on March 21, the vernal equinox, Leo would be rising at six in the evening. But two thousand years ago it would have been thirty degrees lower, rising at eight o'clock. Four thousand years ago it would be below the horizon and wouldn't rise until about two hours later at ten. Six thousand years ago it would rise about midnight, and eight thousand years ago it rose at two in the morning."

"The stars are a big clock," Paul said.

"That's right! If we go back twelve thousand years, Leo would have been rising at six in the morning. This is what's called the heliacal rising.

"What's that?"

"Heliacal just means 'with the sun,' the Greek word for sun being 'helios.' The ancient Egyptians paid attention to the heliacal risings. In fact, the heliacal rising of Sirius was used for their official calendar. This is what makes the geologist's findings that the Sphinx was eroded by rainwater twelve thousand years ago so intriguing."

"Wasn't that what the big argument was about?" Paul asked.

"Yes, it was. Think about it. The Sphinx looks due east. Twelve thousand years ago at the vernal equinox just before sunrise, the Sphinx would have been staring right at Leo. It makes perfect sense that they would have built it to that alignment. But the standard view says that the Sphinx isn't that old; the geological findings may prove otherwise. The Sphinx could be much older than what was thought and so too the culture that arose here on the Giza Plateau."

"Is that Venus?" I said pointing to a very large star.

"It's Jupiter," John said. "Out here it looks bright enough to be Venus."

"The sky is overwhelming," Madeleine said. "It makes you feel so small."

"Look over there" Natalie said as she pointed at a light streaking across the sky.

"It's a meteor," John said.

"Or a UFO!" Paul said.

"I bet if you stand here long enough you would see lots of UFOs," John said and roughed up Paul's hair. "Look over there, that's Orion. Next to it is Sirius."

"Orion," Paul said. "That's heaven."

"That's what ancient Egyptians thought."

"I wonder what they really did think when they looked up at the stars," I said. "The sky is so overpowering, kind of scary."

"I hear something!" Paul said.

"I don't hear anything," John said. "You're spooked because it's so dark."

"I heard talking," Paul insisted.

We all listened for a few moments. Out of the silence we began to detect what sounded like muffled voices.

"I think it's coming from over there. Wait here. I'm going to get closer." John disappeared into the dark and then reappeared in less than a minute. "You've got great hearing Paul." He turned and whispered to the rest of us. "Those voices are coming right out of one of Dr. Short's excavation sites."

"The one we were in earlier today?" I asked.

'Maybe, I can't be sure in this darkness."

"Are they down in there right now?" Madeleine asked.

"Yes, that's why their voices sound muffled. They're very close. Close enough that I think we'd better start walking back before they climb out."

We moved as quietly as we could towards the beacon in the distance.

"Those men will see the headlights when they climb out of there," Natalie said. "The question is will the lights attract them or cause them to flee."

"If they're looking for something connected to Barry, the lights might attract them," John said, picking up the pace of our walk, "particularly if they are the same men who ransacked his shack. If they can't find what the want without his help, they may want to try to force his help."

The light from the headlamps grew brighter, marking our proximity to the shed until we were upon it. John hopped into the jeep and turned out its lights, which caused an immediate stir.

"What the blazes!" Barry shouted as he came out of the shed followed by Stuart.

"Shush!" John said to quiet him. "There are some men out there."

"Out where? What men?" Barry said in an irritated whisper.

"There are some men in one of your holes," Paul said.

"What?"

"Yes, Paul is right. There are some men inside one of your excavation sites," John said. "Their voices were muffled because they were underground. But they definitely came from the opening."

"We were worried that they would see the headlights when they came up so that's why John turned them off right away," Madeleine whispered. "I can't imagine that they will stay down there for long."

"If they're the same men who broke into your shed and ransacked it," John said, "they might come after you if they think you're out here."

"I don't want you to get hurt," Paul cried.

"Well, what do we do?" Barry asked Stuart. "We might have the men who wrecked my shed cornered out there right now."

Turning to John, Stuart asked, "How far from here were you?"

"About ten minutes in that direction. It's pitch dark out there. You can't see much of anything."

"Can you show me?"

"I can try."

"I don't think you should walk back out there," Barry said. "I have a good idea where they are. Let's just take a little ride."

The jeep quickly disappeared into the night. We could hear its tires crunching the desert rock long after we could see it. The four of us huddled together under the stars, which were the only things we could see. I distracted Paul from our situation by pointing back to Orion.

"Imagine what it was like for those ancient people. Night after night out here on the desert with only the stars in view. No electricity. I don't think they even had kerosene lanterns. All they had were these stars. It is no wonder they knew them so well."

"Maybe that's why they had stories about them," Paul said. "I like to hear stories at night. Maybe they did too."

"That's a really good point," I said. "They mixed the science of observation with the art of storytelling and created myths. Remember the story Uncle John told about Osiris?"

Paul looked up at the constellation Orion. "He's in heaven."

"Yes, that's what the ancient Egyptians believed. Orion was the place that Osiris returned to after his death, after he was slain by his brother Seth."

"Why did his brother kill him?"

"Oh, I don't know, probably jealousy."

"Was Seth punished?"

"Eventually. Osiris had a son named Horus who defeated Seth in battle. The gods turned Seth into the voice of thunder, and Horus became the first pharaoh of Egypt. See that really bright star over there that your Uncle John pointed to near Orion, that's Sirius. That's supposed to be Isis' star. She is Horus' mother."

"I see it."

"Just imagine how protected the ancient Egyptians felt at night when they looked up and saw Orion and Sirius. For them these stars were Osiris and Isis, still within their view. And they thought Horus continued to protect them from the murderous Seth because they believed every pharaoh to be Horus, son of Isis and Osiris, reincarnated."

"That sounds very similar to the divine right of kings," Madeleine said.

"What's that?" Paul asked.

"It was a European belief that their kings were from a royal line chosen by God to rule," Madeleine said.

"I don't know why Seth would kill his brother. I love my brother," Paul said.

"It's only a myth, Paul. It didn't really happen. But bad things do happen in life, and these ancient myths acknowledge the human emotions responsible: hate, greed, jealousy and lust for power. That must have helped make these stories seem realistic to the people back then."

Loud firecracker noises disturbed our musings. "What's that?" Paul cried. Stunned and frightened, we looked off in the direction the jeep had gone until we heard the noise of tires crunching desert stone and saw lights emerge out of the darkness. "It's the jeep!" Paul said.

"Your eyes are as sharp as your hearing," I said.

"Get in!" Barry shouted.

There was no time for arranging. Madeleine piled in the back with the rest of us since John occupied the front seat. The jeep tore off. Thankfully, Barry drove at the same speed and with the same skill I had earlier noted. When we left the desert and entered the paved streets of Giza, he slowed down.

"What happened?" Madeleine asked.

"We found them or they found us, who knows," Barry said. "They fired some shots."

"It was eerie," John said. "We just happened upon them. Suddenly there were four men in our lights, standing only yards away. Barry had to swerve. Then they fired at us."

"He should have run right over them," Stuart said.

"What did they look like?" I asked

"They were in the uniform, as you would describe it," Barry said.

"Archaeologists! Shooting at you?"

"No one has ever claimed the profession is free of rascals."

279

"Yes, look at Hans Bueller," Natalie said.

"I would hazard a guess that they're not archaeologists but professional thieves trying to disguise themselves as archaeologists," Stuart retorted.

"Well, I am glad you're leaving here," Madeleine said putting her hand on Barry's shoulder. "I had no idea your work is so dangerous."

"Neither did I. Yes, I will be leaving here very soon," he acknowledged with a greater degree of finality in his tone than when he spoke on the subject earlier at the Blue Nile. "It will only take a few days to close my site."

"How do you do that?" John inquired.

"Why, I just refill the holes I dug leading into the tunnels, that's all. Once they're filled and the wind whips the sand about a little, no one will know where they were."

"Could you tell which site they had been in?" I asked. "Was it the same excavation we were in earlier?"

"No, I don't think so. That one was a lot further out than where you were tonight."

"You were underground today?" Stuart asked looking surprised.

"Yes, we were. I wanted Paul to show me how he got inside the pyramid," Barry said.

"Hmm," was all that Stuart said as if he suspected there was more to the story but had the good judgment not to ask right at that moment.

"I gathered up all my important papers and maps while we were in the shack," Barry said. "Fortunately, the thieves didn't think to take them earlier, but my guess is they will be back for them later. They will find nothing."

"What are they after?" Madeleine asked

Wanting neither to implicate Madeleine or Stuart with the truth nor lie to them, Barry answered quite honestly, "Anything of value they can get their hands on. And they may suspect I have Bueller's statue, which of course I do not."

"Are you going to let them get away?" Paul cried.

"The most important thing is to stop them from getting what they came for," Barry said.

Paul's thoughts were written all over his face. Where was the justice?

Stuart could see this too.

"The cardinal rule of law enforcement, Paul, is to prevent a crime when possible. There are people who do bad things, and we will never catch them all. But if we can foil their efforts, that is our greatest victory."

"I forgot to tell you another part of the myth of Osiris and Isis," I said. "Seth once tried to kill Horus when Horus was only an infant."

"He did! When he was a baby. Why?"

"Probably because he knew Horus would grow up into a very important and powerful man, and Seth wanted everything for himself. But whereas Horus brought peace and prosperity to the ancient Egyptians, Seth would have brought them only war and chaos. But Thoth was able to prevent Horus' death, which stopped Seth from ruining everything. Now, which was more important, capturing Seth or preventing Horus' death?"

"Couldn't he have done both?"

"Many times we can do both," Stuart said, understanding that Paul's question applied more to the current situation than the ancient myth, "but sometimes we can't. And if I have to make a choice, I would rather stop the criminal act because that act could have long term and sometimes deadly consequences."

"Those consequences are really what the myth is about," I said. "Thoth prevented Seth from killing Horus. Horus became king of all Egypt, which saved Egypt from Seth's despotic rule. But Thoth could not do away with Seth altogether because Seth represents all that is bad, and the ancients understood that bad can never be entirely eliminated from life, but it can be lessened by wise and good men and women."

Paul settled down after that explanation, but I'm not sure he took great comfort in what he had heard. The world, he learned, is far more complicated and dangerous than what he had experienced before going on this adventure to Egypt. The path to heaven is a lot more difficult. I suspect that Paul's greatest consolation came from the knowledge that tomorrow he would be flying home.

281

Chapter Thirty-Seven

"It was an unrealistic hope that I should go undetected," Barry said. "As soon as I agreed to Bueller's plan—no, earlier than that. As soon as I was seen associating with him on that cruise ship, I became a marked man. No one would ever believe I was not a party to his intrigue, which of course I became when I agreed to return Thoth. But no one would believe that part of it unless I took them to Thoth's hiding place, which I can never do. Oh, man, I can hardly believe it all myself."

John, Dr. Short and I sat quietly together at the juice bar in the hotel mezzanine. Not long before all seven of us had gathered around two small tables to celebrate our next day's departure and, without uttering the words, to celebrate the fact that we were all alive and unhurt after that evening's brush with gunfire. There was something eerily fitting about that attack coming on our last night, I had thought, as I looked into the faces of those with whom I had shared this remarkable adventure. It came as if it were a warning not to push our luck any further on a trip where we had come perilously close to danger.

Just yesterday, Yusef and Samia had counseled us to stay inside our hotel until they returned to take us to the airport, and once again we disregarded them. They told us before we left for Upper Egypt to stay together and not to separate, advice we ignored as soon as we arrived in Luxor. In fact, they told us when we first arrived in Cairo not to leave the hotel without them, which we did as soon as we got the chance. If we had not gone to the Blue Nile restaurant with Barry Short when we were first in Cairo, we never would have met Dr. Bueller, Madeleine would not have been asked to transport his package to Luxor and nothing that happened as a result would have occurred. In all likelihood Barry would never have become implicated in Bueller's escapade and would not now be compelled to leave Egypt. But then we never would have gotten to know him so intimately had Hans Bueller not entered the picture, which in turn compelled Barry to join our cruise. And Bueller? What actions might he have taken had we not been there? Would he still have received the message that so profoundly changed him? And what of the golden statue? What will become of it and me, I wondered? Had I been changed by the experience?

Madeleine and Paul were the first to retire after she received Barry's solemn promise that he would leave Cairo in a matter of days, that he would call when he arrived in Chicago and that he would most definitely come to visit. Stuart and Natalie followed, needing some time alone together. Before he left, Stuart promised John he would let him know when he arrived back in Washington. He expected it would be in a few weeks.

"So what exactly is your plan?" John asked Barry.

"Well, I know after what happened tonight they're searching the area. The first thing I must do is close my excavation sites since I don't want anyone else to repeat Paul's feat. If a ten-year old boy could find his way into that chamber, they will in no time. Of course, I think Paul has a special talent they lack."

"What talent is that?" I asked, laughing at such an idea.

"I'm not kidding! I'm serious!" he said. "The great people in my field have the knack of knowing. Call it intuition, instinct, I don't know. I had excavated that opening along with five other openings months ago. I had even climbed inside that one, but I took the narrow fork and when it got too tight, I believed the whole tunnel was a dead end, much like those shafts in the pyramid that don't go anywhere. So there I was out in the desert with my scientific equipment trying to discover the location and routes of the tunnels by methodically measuring sound and density inch by inch over the whole blasted area. Paul just marches out there, picks the right hole, climbs in and hits pay dirt."

"It was odd," John said. "What was really strange is that he happened to find his way into the Subterranean Chamber just as Bueller was leaving."

"The whole trip has been odd that way," I said, "filled with unexplainable coincidences."

"Synchronicities, my dear," Barry said. "I'm surprised Madeleine hasn't explained that concept to you by now, she being a devotee of Carl Jung."

"I don't think Mom is exactly a devotee," John said in defense of

Madeleine who prides herself on moderation. "But she is very aware of synchronicities."

"You must be right," I said. "There's too much of a pattern to these events to characterize them as mere coincidence. Even Paul has figured into this strange little drama."

"It's his innocence," Barry said. "His innocence and intelligence. A rare combination."

"A rare combination? I've never heard you sound quite so cynical," I said.

"I'm sorry. I don't think you've ever seen me this upset. I can get this way particularly when my work is ruined by the likes of such men."

"Who do you think they are?" John asked.

"I don't know. There are all manner of people who would be interested in that statue for a variety of reasons. Some would want only the gold, others would be in the business of supplying rare artifacts to those who can pay, but worst of all are those who know the legend of Imhotep's tomb because they would recognize the object's greatest value."

"Any thoughts as to which group the men we saw tonight belong?" John asked.

"Not the last group. They wouldn't risk shooting me. No, they would try to capture me to see what they could get out of me. I don't know which would be worse, being killed or captured. At any rate, neither is desirable."

"I'm not so sure you will be safe out there after what happened tonight," John said.

"Neither is Stu. He thinks he can get a backhoe out there tomorrow. With that kind of equipment we can take care of it in one day. Otherwise, he doesn't want me to leave the hotel until I go to the airport. He says he will have my belongings packed and sent after I leave. Great guy that Stu."

"What if they try to follow you back to the States?" John asked.

"They're not that agile. No, once I'm out of here I'll only be part of the legend."

"What do you mean?" I said intrigued with the idea that Dr. Barry Short would become a part of the local folklore.

"The stories that they tell. They don't expect anything of value to be broadly published. No, everything worth knowing among these types is through word of mouth. My guess is that Gabby and Beverly are hooked into the rumor pipeline, which is why those two women suspected Bueller had something of value. You see, as difficult as it is for the authorities to uncover the activities of these thieves, it is equally as difficult for the thieves and their work to go unnoticed by each other. Rumor and gossip is how I got into this mess, and rumor and gossip is where my name will end up."

"But Bueller didn't book passage until the last minute," I said, "after Gabby and Beverly had already arrived on the ship."

"Bueller wasn't their primary target. He was just an advantageous opportunity. No, they're diamond smugglers all right, but when he appeared they couldn't resist the chance, how should I put it, to diversify. When they couldn't find the golden statue in his room or on his person, I became the prime suspect since word had spread that I had been traveling with him. That was an intelligent conjecture, I have to admit."

"Yes, really," John said.

"After I leave Egypt, rumors will emerge with varying hypotheses as to what I did with Thoth. Over time, the rumors will evolve into legends. I don't care what they say as long as no one knows the truth. And they won't. The truth of the matter is something these types would never think of."

"That's amazing," I said. "You will have made your mark in Egyptology even without a significant find. Oh, let me stand corrected! You and Dr. Bueller made a significant find. You just can't tell anyone. This is funny when you think about it," I mused out loud. "The two of you will be known in legend for a find you actually made but that both of you will publicly deny. The archeological establishment will believe you and dismiss the claim, leaving only those who believe in legend to argue for it. And they will be right!"

Barry visibly brightened. "It's rather amusing put that way," he said. "Maybe my new legendary status will be a greater honor than any published article I might have written."

"What about Bueller?" John asked. "Will he be safe or will they come after him once you've gone?"

"I suspect he'll be fine. I think they know he doesn't have it, and they think I do, which of course was correct. I did. Fortunately they don't know about your involvement although they may know about you in some abstract sense, the group of Americans I kept company with. But these types would no more guess that either Hans or I would have confided in you about such a delicate matter any more than they would believe I returned Thoth to obscurity. They just don't have the imagination."

John looked at me now that he fully comprehended the danger we had been in. "It's a good thing no one saw the statue on your lap when you passed out in Abu Simbel."

"Had anyone seen it, it wouldn't have been on her lap when she awoke," Barry said. Looking at me he continued, "You were very fortunate. A common thief who knew little else would have recognized the gold. You were fortunate indeed."

"We all have been fortunate when you think about it," I said. "Maybe leaving Egypt won't be so bad for you."

"In some respects it could be a good thing. Meeting all of you has been a good thing. I've been too busy most of my life to think about having a family. Both of my parents are gone. I have a brother, but we've never been close. I think he's a pharmaceutical salesman or something like that. He and his family still live in Minnesota. I never see them. We exchange cards at Christmas, that's all."

"Well, consider yourself part of our family," I said. "You've made this trip for us. Without you it would have been interesting enough, but it wouldn't have been an adventure. And that's the sign of a really good trip. Granted, an adventure doesn't have to be quite this harrowing."

"I agree," John said, "it doesn't have to be life threatening, but I'm with you. Something has to happen besides shopping and sightseeing that allows you to understand a place in a deeper sense."

"Do you mean that figuratively or literally John?" Barry said before he broke out laughing.

"You're right," John said. "You took us deep inside of Egypt both figuratively and literally."

"Well, maybe we could do it again, travel together I mean," Barry suggested. "All of us."

That is how we spent the rest of our last night in Egypt, laughing and drinking fruit drinks at the juice bar in the Cairo Kingsley. We toasted our meeting. We toasted new adventures to come. We toasted Barry's project at Meadowcroft Rockshelter. We toasted his anticipated visit to Madeleine's house this summer. We even toasted the butter cow at the Ohio State Fair, until finally we went up to our rooms in high spirits anticipating a good night's sleep.

*****

Morning came with a knock on our door and Paul's cheerful voice delivering the message that it was time to get up and get packing. John hauled our bags out of our room, and I sleepwalked to the hotel lobby where we were met by Yusef and Samia who would take us to the airport. None of us mentioned our dangerous adventure of the night before. The less said, the better we had declared to each other. Natalie thanked Samia for taking her to the jeweler who made her cartouche.

"It will keep you safe," Samia said as we parted. She looked at me and said, "Both of you." She will never know how right she was.

The crowds that had filled the airport only a few days earlier had thinned to the usual number of travelers. It occurred to me as I looked about the lobby that the people looked familiar, not exotic as they had when we had first arrived in Cairo. I knew that meant there was another adjustment to make. And there was.

After an uneventful flight to Kennedy International, and after saying our goodbyes to Natalie who transferred to her flight to D.C., we boarded our plane back to Ohio, where were greeted at Port Columbus by Paul's parents and his brother Kevin, who nearly cried he was so relieved and excited to see Paul. For me their voices sounded like background music. My mind was elsewhere. It had not yet arrived until we exited the airport garage into an Ohio winter.

Gray and black towers of the city loomed in the distance under slate gray skies, and wet freeway ramps lined with dirty snow and ice splattered under the weight of tires. As the van carried us away from the city towards the suburbs, the depth and whiteness of the snow and the bare limbs of trees were a reminder that it would be at least another month or longer before all the whiteness was gone and the pale green of spring would arrive. I felt weary. I wanted color.

287

Where were the donkey carts plodding alongside the fast moving cars? Where were the women draped in black and the turbaned men bustling along crowded sidewalks lined with vendors selling all manner of colorful wares? Where were the beautiful backdrops: the pyramids in Giza, the feluccas in Aswan, the temples in Luxor, the Nile coursing along the full length of Egypt irrigating and fertilizing green fields? Where was the desert that had been so omnipresent? There is no high adventure here, I thought. This will be difficult.

The van pulled up to our home. Shouldn't John have offered his brother baksheesh, I thought for a brief moment, which made me realize just how disoriented I was.

"Are you thinking what I'm thinking?" I said now that John and I were alone.

"This is going to be tough," he said. "I grew to love the place."

"If it is tough for us, imagine what it's going to be like for Barry."

John looked at his watch. "It's one in the morning there. He's asleep. If all went well, he and Stuart closed all the excavation sites and no one will be the wiser."

Suddenly my mind's eye revealed a vision of Thoth glimmering behind the metal door that Barry had opened with magnets, entombed nearly seven feet into an underground shaft hidden behind a stone in an alcove of the Subterranean Chamber of the Great Pyramid. I call it a vision because I had not seen that shaft or the door it concealed. I had stood aside with Paul in the corridor that hid the underground entrance into the chamber while Barry and John returned the statue. But I could see it now as plainly as if it were right before me. The light of Thoth's full golden beauty flooded my imagination, and a revelation made itself clear.

In events such as these there must be a sacrifice. No price was exacted from Dr. Bueller for having removed Thoth. We all had escaped what could have been a violent end. And the statue was returned. "The statue was returned," I repeated out loud. I realized that its return tempered what could have been an exacting punishment. Dr. Bueller was spared. In fact, he was rewarded with a message he had sought after for most of his life, but this message took a very different turn than what he had once expected, opening Bueller to a transformation of the heart that defeated the ideology of his youth. The rest of us had acted our parts well. Had we not, had we been tempted to keep the statue, the fates may not have been so kind. Barry was exiled from Egypt. That was the sacrifice. Had he remained near the golden treasure, eventually he would have succumbed to his own curiosity or the hard avarice of others. Imhotep's tomb and all that it contains would have been revealed. Thoth in his wisdom exacted a small price from our friend to prevent a great tragedy, the corruption of the future.

"It's for the best that Barry leaves," I said to John.

"Yes, I believe you're right."

On the wall just above my computer where I am typing this account is a poster size print of one of our photos. John and I are smiling in our few moments of desert peace atop our camel, and in the background are the three Great Pyramids of Giza. That camel ride cost more than what we had expected, but this photo is a treasure worth far more than the baksheesh we had paid.

Epilogue

Spring has arrived in Ohio. The gray landscape is transformed into intense velvet green as the fields and lawns have sprung to life. The forsythias have burst into golden-bloomed hedges nearly bright enough to cast their own light. The spiky leaves of tulip plants alongside their sister daffodils have emerged out of soil still moist from melted snow. Leaf buds are forming on tall deciduous trees, which will open first into young, yellow green leaves before they acquire their deep summer hue. The ornamental pears are in full flower now, standing in groves like white fairies ushering in springtime. Their flowers will be followed by the white and pink buds of the crabapples, cherries, fragrant viburnum, dogwoods and redbuds. Then the lilacs will bloom. This flowering of spring is the beautiful backdrop of my life here in Ohio, which comes once a year and never stays long enough. I have been observing it in its varying stages through my window as the ibis looks on from his perch on my hearth. I begin to feel renewed.

When we arrived home, John began work on his archaeoastronomy program, refining it so he could be sure of its accuracy. He made email contact with the author he had met at the Sphinx and has begun reading the discussions posted on the research group's blog. John has pulled his homemade telescope out of the garage and into the backyard to observe the stars. The sky has been amazingly clear, he says, for this time of year. Orion's Belt sits near Sirius, just as it did in Egypt. How can it be, I wondered, that we are so far apart and yet share the same stars, the same moon and the same planets? John called me over to look at Saturn's rings through his telescope. "They're so distinct," I said. He has begun a project to measure the sunset as it moves north along the western horizon. He is able to measure the progress of its movement using a row of trees in the distance as his marker. On the vernal equinox he began taking digital photos at sunset and then records the exact time the sunset occurs. He will continue to do so each evening until the summer solstice. He is reading Victor Hugo's *Notre Dame de Paris* for the umpteenth time. I think he wants to go to France.

According to reports we've gotten from Natalie, she and Stuart have been seeing each other occasionally since his return to Washington. As always, she is reluctant to say too much, and we have learned not to press her for news. But we have also learned that those facts she does report are usually an understatement of the actual circumstances in her life, so we surmise that she and Stuart have been seeing quite a lot of each other.

Stuart reports that to his surprise Gabby and Beverly were able to navigate the Blue Nile River without being arrested, shot or eaten by crocodiles. They have taken up residence in a small hotel in Addis Ababa, the capital of Ethiopia, where they are observed daily in its large central marketplace. They are being watched, but no one knows yet exactly what they will end up doing there. They appear to be negotiating the purchase of their own stall and brokering deals with local artisans whose wares they want to sell for a percentage of the profit. It is unclear whether their negotiations will succeed. We think these ladies may have found the perfect occupation for themselves, legal occupation that is. Years of shopping binges in markets such as these should be all the experience they need to work on the other side of the stall. We laugh together as we imagine them in Africa: their loud voices heavily accented in American southern dialect, hawking beads and gaudy apparel to tourists along with T-shirts that say, "I Navigated the Blue Nile."

Stuart doesn't see the humor in the situation. We tell him to lighten up. After all, he shut down their smuggling operation. And they can't go anywhere without running the risk of arrest; in effect, they've made their own prison. Stuart says they will never be able to return to the United States without being arrested. And if they would dare try, he would be there personally with handcuffs. He says their husbands, who still live in Tennessee, claim they had no knowledge that the diamonds their wives asked them to sell were obtained illegally. I don't believe that for a moment, but Stuart does. He feels sorry for the "poor" guys. He thinks their wives tricked them just like they tricked him. According to Stuart the husbands are cooperating fully with the authorities and both have filed for divorce, charging abandonment by their wives.

Barry is still in Chicago resting, negotiating his contract to begin work at the Meadowcroft Rockshelter and writing a report on his most recent pursuits in Egypt. It describes those findings he is willing to make public. He says unfortunately that's not a whole lot, so he is having a great deal of trouble fashioning a report that will justify his time there while not compromising either Thoth or the hidden tunnel leading to the Subterranean Chamber of the Great Pyramid. We asked him if he couldn't at least reveal the tunnel, but he says absolutely not. He doesn't want to even hint at something devious minds may use to guess the location of the statue. We talk to him long distance at least once a week; Madeleine talks to him more often. She plans to visit him while she is in Chicago for a Jungian conference. He says he will drive her back to Ohio in his new jeep. He wants to visit all of us and look at real estate. He says he would like to own a few acres, and Ohio would be a good location since it is nearly halfway between the Institute in Chicago and the Meadowcroft Rockshelter, where he foresees working for quite some time. He says he is looking forward to getting out and doing fieldwork again. He must teach a short summer session on recent finds in Egypt but anticipates that he will be finished in time for the Ohio State Fair, which he says he looks forward to attending with Paul and his brother Kevin. Barry has asked Paul to join him at Meadowcroft for the long Labor Day weekend before school starts. He says he wants Paul to begin developing archeological investigative techniques that he can only acquire in the field, although he is convinced that Paul is a natural. We are looking forward to seeing him soon. He wants us to begin thinking about some other trips we might take together.

Barry sent us a copy of a letter he received just a week ago from Doctor Shabaka, who had promised to keep him posted about Bueller's whereabouts and condition. I've included it here:

My Dear Dr. Short,

Let me again thank you for your help in soliciting the funds necessary to secure a good place for Dr. Bueller. The place of residence I have found for him I think is quite perfect for a man of his temperament and years. He is living here in Egypt in a very old establishment located near the Red Sea. His fellow lodgers share his intellectual interests and some even his years. They have a large library, which I am told he thoroughly enjoys and makes very good use of. All members of his community are assigned tasks and his is to keep the books and shelves dusted. I saw him only a few days ago, and he looks at the peak of health for a man his age. I myself am amazed that my treatments succeeded as well as they have to restore him to full health and vigor. He is keeping himself quite busy writing three books.

The first is a catalog of Egyptian artifacts that have been unknown to scholars or have been lost. Dr. Bueller is fortunate to have photos of many of these objects and is making drawings of those he has no photos of. This work, I believe, will be a hugely valuable contribution to our knowledge of ancient Egypt and no doubt will be praised. His second book details his experience as a child growing up in Germany during the Third Reich. I've read the outline, which is quite gripping. It discloses the false assumptions those Germans made about themselves and analyzes the process by which their intellectual errors transformed sane men into psychopaths who corrupted an entire society. The third book is for children. Dr. Bueller has become very concerned about their education and has even asked that some of his fellow lodgers leave the library for a few hours a day to devote themselves to the education of the children who live nearby. His book, he tells me, will be a picture storybook that will tell the tale of a young boy who learns early the rewards of humility and the perils of pride. Dr. Bueller will do the illustrations as well as the writing. As he described the book to me it reminded me of a fable my father used to tell about a race between a tortoise and a hare. The tortoise won the race in spite of the hare's greater speed because of his steadfastness. His book will be set in Aswan, a perfect setting for a picture book.

All has gone very well, quite better than I could have imagined. I am honored to have been able to assist a nearly miraculous healing.

> *Very Sincerely,*
> *Omar Shabaka*

Barry attached a note of his own:

The old scallywag. He's living in a monastery. Can you believe that! That catalogue of artifacts he smuggled out of Egypt will ensure his place among the leading figures in Egyptology. And his autobiographical analysis of the Third Reich will probably become a best seller. I can't even get this darn report written, thanks in large part to him. The children's book, well, that's another matter. Oh well, I'm glad he is safe and doing well.

> *Yours,*
> *Barry*

About the Author

Linda Oxley Milligan was born in Grandview Heights, in Columbus, Ohio. Her real Columbus home however became The Ohio State University where she earned three degrees culminating in a Ph.D. in English and American Literature with a specialty in folklore. For many years she has taught a variety of composition courses and folklore as an adjunct professor in the English department. Linda is married to John and has a wonderful daughter Stephanie. All three have a passion for travel and the exploration of cultures, which mixed with a love of adventure, serves as the inspiration for her writing.

The Blue Nile Adventure is the first in a series of adventure novels featuring famed archeologist Barry Short. The novel is based on an actual trip Linda and her family took on a packaged tour to Egypt. The trip's inception came about as the book describes. "You long to see the Great Pyramids of Egypt," a Chinese restaurant fortune cookie proclaimed at the very time her husband John was knee deep in books about Ancient Egypt. That was the push, and the longing was there. What they had failed to take into account in their planning was the current situation in the mid-1990s Egypt, in which travelers had become targets for political dissidents.

The settings, the ambiance, the reflections are based on actual travel experience. The plot of the tale, however, layered fiction atop real events.

If you enjoyed the novel, please consider leaving a review on Amazon.com and Goodreads.

Thank you,
Linda

Made in the USA
Columbia, SC
14 April 2021